BEHIND CLOSED DOORS

ELIZABETH HAYNES

sphere

SPHERE

First published in Great Britain in 2015 by Sphere
This paperback edition published by Sphere in 2015

1 3 5 7 9 10 8 6 4 2

A CIP catalogue record for this book
is available from the British Library.

ISBN 978-0-7515-4963-8

Typeset in Times New Roman by M Rules
Printed and bound in Great Britain by
Clays Ltd, St Ives plc

Papers used by Sphere are from well-managed forests
and other responsible sources.

Dedicated to the intelligence analysts,
who make a difference

BEHIND
CLOSED
DOORS

Part One

NOTHING IS REAL
BUT FEAR

SCARLETT – Rhodes, Saturday 23 August 2003, 04:44

To begin with, nothing was certain except her own terror.

Darkness, and stifling heat, so hot that breathing felt like effort, sweat pouring off her so her skin itself became liquid and she thought she would simply melt into a hot puddle of nothing. She tried crying out, screaming, but she could barely hear her own voice above the roar of the engine, the sound of the wheels moving at speed on tarmac. All that did was give her a sore throat. Nobody could hear her.

She tried listening instead, eyes wide with nothing to see. She could hear voices sporadically from somewhere else in the vehicle – two different men – but she didn't recognise them, nor could she understand what they were saying. She assumed they were speaking in Greek, but the harsh rasp of the words sounded different from the voices she'd heard over the past week at the resort. Lots of 'th' sounds, rolled 'r's, words ending in 'a' and 'eh'.

Fear came in cycles. The first endless panicky minutes had been very bad: trawling through vague memories of the past few days, trying to identify the mistake she'd made, because this had to be her fault – *this can't be real, I'm dreaming* – then the shock realisation that this wasn't a nightmare, it was really happening. The worst moment of all.

It had been so quick.

She had arrived a bit early at the place where they'd agreed to meet, and she'd been preparing to wait – he'd said he finished work at two – and a van had pulled up beside her. She hadn't been worried. There were still people around, drunk tourists staggering back up the road towards their hotels. The side door of the van had slid open, and a man got out. He was talking to her, friendly, a smile that showed his teeth. His accent was so strong she couldn't really tell what he was saying.

'No, no,' she'd said. 'English. I don't understand.'

But he'd kept yammering on, standing too close to her. She had begun to feel unnerved by it, and something had made her glance to the right, to the gate which led to the Aktira Studios, and in that split second when she'd seen someone she recognised, made eye contact, she had felt something like relief – and then the man had pushed her, a hard shove that sent her sprawling into the back of the van. He'd climbed in after her, slammed the door shut and the van started moving. The man had held her down, put his hand over her mouth, pressing her head into the metal floor so hard that she'd thought her skull was going to burst.

Seconds. The whole thing had taken seconds.

Now, hours since those terrifying first moments, she had reached a plateau brought on by the monotony of driving, the panic overridden by the pain in her arms and legs and the discomfort of being tied hand and foot and having to lie still on the floor of the van. They'd stopped once, very early on, before she'd had time to get over the shock or formulate any plan of escape; by that time the man in the back with her had already tied her up. He got out, leaving her alone, and the van door shut – and they were moving again.

The noise of the engine was unbearably loud; the van would bump and jolt as it went over potholes. Her head ached as a result, sometimes so badly it made her cry. The fear made her cry. Crying made her headache worse, and then it all became pointless, so she would stop for a while and try to sleep in snatches, because sleeping, at least, gave her a brief respite.

And she would dream of him, remember, and wake with tears on her cheeks, thinking, *This wasn't supposed to happen.* Then the shock and the fear would kick in, and the whole cycle would begin again.

LOU – Briarstone, Thursday 31 October 2013, 14:00

'You look done in,' said Sam, putting a steaming mug of tea on the only part of the desk that wasn't covered by piles of paper.

'Thanks,' Lou replied. 'I feel it. Kind of hoped the make-up was doing a good job of hiding the bags.'

'Anything I can do?'

Lou looked up at Sam and smiled at her. *Such a sweetheart.* 'If there's anything I can hand over, believe me, I'll do it like a shot.'

'Cheers. You know where I am!'

Sam left and Lou went back to answering emails. Yesterday had been so much better. Lou had gone out to a stabbing that the newly renamed North Division were trying to palm off on to Major Crime, but, since the offender was already in custody and happily admitting to his offences in interview, she had been able to hand it back to the Area DI. Elated at such a rare success, she had even managed to slope off before five o'clock, stopping to pick up some food that involved preparation more elaborate than stabbing plastic film with a fork, and had put in a call to a certain dark-haired Canadian senior intelligence analyst.

'Hey,' Jason had said, 'what time are you going to be done?'

'I'm done already,' she'd said smugly.

He was laughing. 'You're winding me up, right?'

'No, I am actually on my way home. What are you doing?'

'Getting my shit together and heading over to yours – right now.'

These opportunities didn't come along very often, and, while both Lou and Jason knew to make the most of them, perfect nights were over far too quickly. Of course, having such diverting company on a 'school night' meant that she ended up getting only four hours' sleep, and, as if the world was exacting its horrible revenge for her daring to leave early, today had already been about as bad as it could get.

A serious assault that had taken place six weeks ago had been somehow linked to the murder a week or so later of a local businessman, which meant the Major Crime department had inherited a half-arsed job from Division and would have to start it all over again, to make sure that nothing had been missed. Both cases had been rumbling on without Lou's involvement and now she was going to have to try to pull the two investigations together, with no real insight into where the local officers had got up to so far. If you didn't have an arrest within a week of an offence, the chances were pretty slim that you would manage to get a good result. And so far there had been no arrests, and no suspects.

A twenty-year-old lad by the name of Ian Palmer had been assaulted after a night out; he'd suffered a serious head injury and had been found in the early hours of the morning lying in a puddle in an alleyway in the town centre. He had not regained consciousness and Major Crime had taken it on because in all probability he never would.

And as for the murder of the businessman – Carl McVey had owned two bars in the town centre and a country pub and restaurant called the Ferryman, beside the river in Baysbury. He was missing for four days before his body was found half-buried in woodland about three miles out of town. He had been badly beaten and his wallet and phone were missing, so the working hypothesis was that it had been a botched robbery.

So far, so good.

There had been no forensic link between the two; nothing obvious connecting the victims, other than that one owned a bar that had possibly been frequented by the other. After this morning's meeting Sam had made contact with the Force Intelligence Bureau to request the latest intel. Meanwhile the DCs were going to re-interview Palmer's mother, his friends – see what they could stir up.

Lou reached for the mug of tea, jolted it with the back of her hand and sent a wave of liquid over the nearest case file. As she swore and rummaged through her bag for a tissue, her phone started ringing. Lou glanced at the caller display. Buchanan – just what she needed. Detective Superintendent Gordon Buchanan, officer in charge of Major Crime and Lou's line manager, was a pain in the backside at the best of times and a dangerous enemy at the worst. The tissue would have to wait.

'Sir?'

'Lou. How are you getting on with McVey and Palmer?'

The tone of his voice was not a good sign. As one of his 'favourites', Lou was used to being on the receiving end of long, chatty phone calls when Buchanan felt bored, out of sorts or in need of a little light flirtation. To start with a question related to the job was unusual.

'Still sorting my way through the paperwork, I'm afraid.' *Only got the jobs this morning*, she thought; *give me a bloody chance*.

She looked at the thin brown card which was wrapped around the witness statements relating to the McVey murder, and the puddle of tea gradually soaking into it. Just as well they weren't the originals.

'Need you to come up and see me. Whenever you're ready.'

That sounded even more ominous. 'I'll come up now. Do I need to bring anything, sir?'

He just answered with an abrupt, 'Thanks,' and hung up.

Lou found a packet of tissues under her hairbrush and wadded two, patting the top of the folder dry. A circle of dark brown stained the lighter brown of the card. Luckily it hadn't seeped through to the statements underneath, which must have used half a tree and taken some poor bugger two hours to photocopy. Even more luckily, most of the tea had remained in the mug and Lou was grateful for it, draining it in several long gulps as she made her way to the office door.

SCARLETT – Greece, Saturday 23 August 2003, 05:25

Footsteps first, then voices, getting closer. She didn't understand what they were saying, but it seemed to be the same two men. The tone of the voices was jovial and one of them laughed. And then the sound of a key scraping in the metal lock and the door of the van opened.

It was dark outside, and two shapes were standing in the doorway. Automatically she closed her eyes, shrank back.

'You want water?' one of the men said. She nodded vigorously and he climbed in beside her. The other one stood at the doorway, his back to them, as though keeping watch.

He was old, in his forties, with dark hair cropped short. He smelled of strong aftershave and cigarettes. He pulled her to a sitting position and put the bottle to her lips; she gulped at it, coughed, choked.

'Please,' she said, her voice sounding hoarse, unlike her own. 'Please . . . '

He answered her by holding the bottle up again, and drinking was more important than talking after all, so she drank. The water was cold and tasted strange, metallic – like blood.

'I won't try to run away,' she said when the bottle was withdrawn again, 'but please, my hands hurt so much . . . '

He looked her in the eyes and to her surprise she saw something like sympathy there, and understanding. Then he reached behind and pulled something from the back of his jeans. He raised it to her face and even in the half-light she saw it was a handgun. She gasped and shrank back from him, and then he laughed.

'You have a little sister – Juliette.'

Scarlett felt her stomach constrict. 'What? What about her?'

'We have people in the town, watching her. You be good, or I call them and they take Juliette too. You understand? We get good money for young girls. Plenty money.'

'Please, I'll be good, I promise I'll be good . . .'

He put the gun back and pulled her by the shoulder, twisting her so that he could access the ligature around her wrists. The relief when the knot gave and her arms were free was intense – the pain, and the relief . . .

'Thank you,' she said, when she was able to stop whimpering. 'Thank you. What's your name?'

He smiled at her. One last drink, and the bottle was empty. 'You stay quiet. You stay still. Yes? I give you more water later.'

'Yes, I promise, I promise.'

He edged his way to the back of the van and she was almost sorry to see him go, but at least now her arms were free.

At the back of the van the conversation between the men resumed, less jovial this time. Urgent, staccato phrases. The man who'd waited at the back door was clearly not happy that she had been left untied.

Then, without a backward glance at her, the door was slammed shut and locked and the darkness surrounded her again, a heavy blanket of heat and the smell of her own body, the smells of the inside of the van.

She woke up and the van wasn't moving. The engine noise was different, somehow; the vibration of the metal floor under her was different. She could feel a rolling, swaying motion. Instantly she felt sick.

As she started to stretch, the pain in her limbs made her cry out. Immediately she heard a sound next to her. A hand went over her mouth. She tried to move but her body felt odd, heavy, as though she was tied up again even though she wasn't.

'You quiet,' a voice said beside her. A man's voice, heavily accented. She thought it was the same one as before, but her ears felt funny, as if she'd been swimming.

It was dark in here but even so it was hard to focus. Something cold and metallic was pushed against her cheek. She smelled oil and garlic on his hands.

'You stay quiet or I will kill you.'

Scarlett was struggling to find focus. The world was rocking, spinning, inside her head. It felt easier just to lie still.

'Where are we?' she whispered, after a few minutes.

He didn't answer, or didn't hear her. She tried to turn her head, to look at him. Whoever he was.

'Please,' she said, a little louder. 'Please, just let me go. I want to go home.'

Movement again, the sounds of shuffling and then his breath on her cheek. 'I said, you quiet. You not understand?'

She didn't say anything else. Closed her eyes and waited.

Buchanan was on the phone. Two of the management secretaries – not Mara, whose services were shared between Buchanan and two other superintendents – were at their desks, both of them typing at a speed that surely was not possible. Through the open door to his office, Buchanan saw her and held up a finger to indicate she should wait. She took one of the visitor's chairs.

Pam and – what *was* the other one called? Lou could never remember her name, began with an S – were tapping their keyboards so fast it almost looked as though they were racing each other. A typing contest. Sue? Sarah? That wasn't right ... Sandra. That sounded more like it. Lou bit her lip.

'He won't be a minute,' Pam said, without looking up.

'Who's he talking to, Pam? Do you know?'

'The chief.'

'Ah. Is something kicking off, then?'

Pam smiled and didn't reply, which meant that it was.

The phone call finished. 'Lou – when you're ready,' he called.

Lou stood up and straightened her skirt. *Here we go*, she thought.

'Sir,' she said as she went into his office and he waved her to a seat. 'Everything all right?'

'What are you working on? I know it's mad down there – just run me through your current priorities.'

'I'm overseeing the case file for the Leuchars murder still. Ali Whitmore is putting that together and Jane Phelps is the exhibits officer. They're pretty self-sufficient, though. I've got that series of armed robberies, and now the two jobs that are being linked. McVey and Palmer – Op Trapeze. Why's that? Something come in?'

He didn't answer. The seriousness of his expression – when Lou was used to him being relaxed enough in her presence to ask what she was planning to do with her evening – made her sit up a little straighter. Had she pissed him off somehow? She started mentally checking through all the jobs she'd worked over the last couple of months – none of them, since the Polly Leuchars murder investigation that had resulted in her DI, Andy Hamilton, being suspended for gross misconduct, had left any cause for concern.

'I had a look through your personnel file, Lou,' he said.

That didn't sound good. What was he doing, rooting through her file?

'One of your first jobs as a DC. Ten years ago. Scarlett Rainsford. That name ring a bell?'

'Of course I remember. Cases like that one stay with you, don't they?'

'Good job they do. Special Branch did a warrant on a brothel in Briarstone this morning as part of Op Pentameter. Guess who they found working there?'

She stared at him. He couldn't mean Scarlett, surely? This must be some kind of cryptic question to which the answer would be one of the many witnesses they'd interviewed all those years ago – one of Scarlett's classmates, perhaps, or her sister?

She cleared her throat, deciding to be brave and suggest the impossible. 'You mean – not Scarlett?'

'The one and only. As you can imagine, when the news leaks all hell's going to break loose. They're working on a media strategy but I don't need to tell you that this has to be kept quiet. I'd like you to get on to DCI Waterhouse at Special Branch. He's expecting your call.'

'Is she all right? What has she said?'

'Not a lot, so far. But she seems okay. Living and breathing, which is more than anyone expected.'

'Where is she now?'

He smiled. 'She's in the Vulnerable Victim Suite for the time being.'

'I thought they'd all been shut down.'

'Technically. But they managed to reopen the Briarstone VVS just for Scarlett. Special treatment and all that. Special Branch don't seem quite sure what to do with her – but if anyone's going to be in on the debrief it should be you.'

'Are they certain it's her?'

'Over the phone Clive Rainsford was muttering something about a DNA test, but it turns out she has a scar on her upper arm that's pretty distinctive.'

Ah, the scar. Lou had forgotten about the scar, despite looking for it on the shoulders of just about every girl of Scarlett's approximate age for years after the abduction.

'What about the family? Has anyone told them?'

'You won't believe it. The mum and dad, sister – remember her? – they're all on holiday. In Spain, this time.'

Intel Reports on Ian Palmer

5x5x5 Intelligence Report

Date: 11 March 2013

Officer: PC 9921 EVANS

Subject: Thomas PALMER DOB 22/04/1990, Ian PALMER
                   DOB 19/04/1993, Ryan COLEMAN DOB
                   12/01/1990, Darren CUNNINGHAM DOB
                   12/11/1976

Grading: B / 2 / 1

Stopcheck outside the Co-op on Turnswood Parade. Darren
CUNNINGHAM sitting in the driver's seat of a stationary
BMW which is registered to his mother Sara CUNNINGHAM
DOB 14/02/1952. CUNNINGHAM was issued with a driving
ban last month but claimed Thomas PALMER has been driving
him around. Despite a strong smell of cannabis around the
vehicle no drugs were found. Vehicle taxed and insured.
Suitable words of advice given. Also in the vehicle were Ian
PALMER and Ryan COLEMAN. A few minutes after the
stopcheck Thomas PALMER and CUNNINGHAM swapped
places in the front seats and Thomas PALMER drove the
vehicle away with all four inside.

5x5x5 Intelligence Report

Date: 23 September 2013

Officer: PC 9921 EVANS

Subject: Ian PALMER DOB 19/04/1993, Ryan COLEMAN
                   DOB 12/01/1990

Grading: B / 4 / 1

Ian PALMER is friends with Ryan COLEMAN. It is believed COLEMAN was at school with PALMER's elder brother Thomas and they have been friends ever since.

(Research shows Thomas PALMER DOB 22/04/1990)

SCARLETT – Saturday 23 August 2003, 18:32

The vehicle had stopped moving, the engine idling. Scarlett, alone again in the back of the van, could hear the sounds of other cars passing at high speed, and she guessed they had pulled into a layby, or a service station. One of the van's doors opened and she waited, holding her breath, expecting the door to open at the side of the van. Footsteps. She could hear the chorus of cicadas outside, then a splashing as one of the men took a piss. A minute later he climbed back into the cab, and then the van moved off again, gaining speed.

She should have shouted, or screamed. Someone might have heard.

Nico had shown her a cicada. A dead one. It had been lying on the sun-baked tiles of the restaurant terrace, presumably having flown into the glass door and stunned itself. He'd put it on the palm of his hand while she shrieked and drew back from him. It was the biggest insect she'd ever seen and had big, ugly bug-eyes and black and grey armour-plating over its body. But when she realised it was definitely dead she got closer, and for a moment she could admire the delicacy of the wings, wonder at how something with a body so big and wings so whisper-thin could ever fly. And then he'd pushed his hand quickly towards her with an angry buzzing sound as though the thing was alive and she'd screamed and jumped back, clutching her chest, and Nico had laughed at her.

'That was mean!' she'd said.

'You're so funny,' he'd replied. 'They don't hurt. They are just loud.' He'd held open Scarlett's shoulder bag, dangling the insect over it by one of its legs. 'We give it to your mother,' he said. 'What you think, she will like it?'

'Nico!'

He'd thrown the bug out on to the street, dusted off his hands. Then he had rested both his arms on her shoulders, head on one side as though he was appraising her. 'You are angry with me?'

How could she be? How could she ever be angry with him?

'No,' she'd said, and smiled.

And he had pinched her cheek between his knuckles and pulled her chin towards him so he could kiss her. The night before, he'd kissed her for the first time and it had been gentle; already their kisses were becoming hungry, hard, possessive. On her part as well as his.

It hurt her, now, to think of him. 'Nico,' she said, whispering into the dirty blanket underneath her that smelled of engine oil and something else, something bad that she could not give a name to.

Nico had not been the first boy who had shown any interest in her.

Mark Braddock had been told to sit next to her one day because she had been talking to Cerys and Mrs Rowden-Knowles had wanted to separate them. She'd used Mark Braddock to hammer home her punishment because he was weird, nobody liked him, and she knew that sitting Scarlett next to anyone else, male or female, would not have done the trick.

As it turned out, Mrs Rowden-Knowles's ploy backfired because, to Scarlett's big surprise, Mark Braddock was all right. Contrary to popular opinion, he didn't smell of BO, he didn't have bad teeth, and behind the glasses he had lovely blue eyes that took everything in. Trouble was, instead of Mark's impeccable behaviour rubbing off on Scarlett, the opposite happened and she ended up corrupting him.

She started it by drawing a cock on his notepad. He blushed and put his hand over it until Mrs Rowden-Knowles's back was turned,

19

but then he lifted the page and turned to a fresh one. And then, the excitement of embarrassing him past, just as she was starting to get bored again, he reached across to her notepad and within a second had drawn a pair of boobs and a big smile underneath.

It made her laugh, stifled because all of a sudden she didn't want to get moved somewhere else, or, worse, sent to see Mr Callaghan.

After that, it progressed to notes. Not about anything dramatic, just a conversation passed back and forth between two people who hadn't realised they had anything in common until precisely that moment.

The next lesson they had together, she chose to sit next to him. She thought she would get some stick for that, especially from Cerys who had a gob on her like you wouldn't believe, but in fact Cerys somehow got the impression that Mrs Rowden-Knowles had put her next to Braddock for the rest of the term, and Scarlett didn't bother to put her straight. Possibly Mark thought the same thing, because his first note to her was an apologetic one saying he was sorry that she'd been put there. And she didn't contradict him, either; she wasn't prepared to admit to anyone, even herself, that she actually *wanted* to sit next to him.

Despite all the notes and the stifled giggles – for to her surprise he was funny, and clever, and very far from boring after all – she must have absorbed a little of his intellect through some kind of psychic osmosis, because she got good marks in the end-of-year exams. Her best results, in fact. Ever.

The last day of term. No lessons with Mark Braddock, but Scarlett had taken to spending time in the library even when all the exams were over and nobody was revising any more, because one day she'd walked past the library at lunchtime and seen Mark in there. Nobody would come looking for her in this of all places. Mark had been surprised to see her, but once he'd recovered his composure he'd sat down next to her and complained via note when she started disturbing him.

So she would sit and watch while he read textbooks that he didn't need to read. She watched the way he pushed his glasses up the bridge of the nose when they slipped down, watched how he moved his hair up out of his eyes with one hand and how it fell down again immediately because it was silky-soft and heavy. He didn't even seem to be aware that she was staring at him, because, unlike her, he could grow completely absorbed in a book and not notice anything that was going on around him.

But if she thought he was ignoring her, she was wrong. On the last day, when the bell went for the afternoon lesson – in her case PE, in his, Biology – he passed her a note that he'd scribbled hastily. It said: *See you in Sept.*

They'd still scarcely spoken to each other directly. Not because they couldn't have done – although the library was supposed to be quiet, people chatted in there all the time. They could have spoken before or after lessons, or in the playground, or anywhere in fact. But it had become a kind of tradition between them, the notes, and Scarlett didn't want to be the one to break it.

Yeah, she wrote back. That was the trouble, she thought. He wrote cool stuff. Her notes to him were always a brief scrawl in response to something; his to her always felt intelligent, challenging, even when it was something straightforward. She was in awe of his brain, how it worked, how he knew the answer to everything without being pushy or loud like Cerys.

When we come back to school I have something to ask you, his next note said.

What? she wrote back, but he was already on his feet, his bag slung over his shoulder, heading for the door.

Dismayed, she said out loud, 'Mark!'

He looked back at her, blushing, surprised. It was the first time she'd spoken to him.

'What do you want to ask me?'

But he'd smiled and turned away. The summer holidays had started and in August she had come to Greece on holiday with her mum and dad and sister Juliette. And then she'd met Nico, and Mark had been forgotten, mentally discarded as if he had meant nothing to her, nothing at all.

Now, in the back of the van, she thought over and over again about Mark and how much she longed to see him right at this moment, how she would have given anything – *anything* – for the chance to ask him again what he wanted, and if it was that he wanted to ask her out she would accept without question, no matter what Cerys had to say about it, no matter that her father had made it very clear that she was too young to go out with boys. Mark Braddock had wanted to ask her out. She believed it now. And at the same time she realised she would never know for sure. She would never see him again.

LOU – Thursday 31 October 2013, 14:27

Lou made the phone call to DCI Waterhouse while walking along the perimeter of the playing field to the rear of HQ. It was the only place she could pretty much guarantee that she would not be disturbed or overheard. She could have just gone back to her office and shut the door, but as she did this so rarely it would have been a general heads-up to everyone that something was going on.

Already she was starting to question why Buchanan had involved her in this. Whatever Lou's previous role, she was Major Crime; Op Pentameter – the UK-wide operation dealing with human trafficking for sexual exploitation – was very much a Special Branch thing. They didn't like to share. The possibility of a media frenzy surrounding Scarlett's reappearance was a likely explanation. A couple of years from retirement as he was, if there was a bit of glory to be obtained, Buchanan would want a chunk of it. Senior officers across the force would be circling the investigation like sharks, all trying to find some tenuous link to the job so that they could get a bite at it.

There was a brisk wind blowing across the grass and not only was it chilly, but she wondered whether Waterhouse would even be able to hear her when the call connected.

Stephen Waterhouse answered with a tone that suggested he was incredibly busy and this-had-better-be-bloody-important. 'Yeah?'

'It's Lou Smith, Major Crime—'

Before she had time even to mention Buchanan's name, Waterhouse interrupted. 'Oh, right, hold on a sec.'

The muffled sound that followed implied he was holding the mobile to his chest while barking instructions at someone else. Then he was back.

'When can you get over here?'

Lou felt her hackles rise, but kept her voice even. 'What exactly do you need from me?'

There was a pause and Lou thought she heard a sigh from the other end. It might have been the wind. 'I don't actually *need* anything. Mr Buchanan suggested you might have some expertise to offer because you dealt with the investigation ten years ago. Personally I can't see what difference that makes, but still . . . '

'She is in the VVS, is that right?'

'At the moment.'

'In that case I'd like to listen in. Presumably you've got a family liaison officer lined up for the family? Mary Nott was the original FLO but she retired three years ago—'

'We're Special Branch; we don't have FLOs. And in any case I don't think she qualifies, since she's not a suspect, nobody's died, and she's not been in an RTC.'

Lou's temper frayed as the line got muffled again – he was clearly carrying on a conversation with someone else. 'Fuck's sake,' she said.

'What?'

'Nothing. When's your next briefing?'

'Four, but—'

'I'll see you then,' she said.

She disconnected the call. What an absolute arse. Four o'clock, and it was half-past two already. She had time for a quick refresher of the main details of the case – the files and notes long since having been archived – and then she would have to head off to

Knapstone. Seaside town, grim in parts, in the centre of it an unattractive concrete block of a building that served as the local police station. In the basement was the headquarters of Eden's Special Branch.

As she walked back the way she'd come, she dialled Jason's mobile. He picked up straight away. 'Don't tell me – you're finishing early again, right?'

She smiled. 'Course not.'

'So I guess our date's off?'

'I have no idea what time I'll be done. I'm sorry.'

'You can still come over. Whatever time it is.'

'Thanks. Don't wait up, though.'

All the way back up to Major Crime, via the canteen for a coffee and the last baguette – cheese, but at least it wasn't tuna – she was thinking about the night before and how she was enjoying every minute she got to spend with Jason Mercer, especially those that happened in bed. Even when she was exhausted, wrung out by the day and the pressure and the constant worry of a job going badly wrong, or by being called out just at the moment when she'd finally allowed herself to relax, being with him made her feel better. Nearly a year together, too. That had gone by fast. They should do something – celebrate, go out for a meal, whatever it was people did. It had been a long time since she'd had a relationship that had lasted all the way to an anniversary. She tried to think when exactly the relationship had started, but there wasn't what you'd call a defining moment. Jason had been the analyst on Operation Nettle last year; with all the stress of heading up a high-profile murder investigation, he had kept her sane by being calm, reliable, getting the job done – and all the time he had been waiting for her to realise that the attraction between them was mutual. There hadn't exactly been a first date.

The trouble was, with such a pressured job, it was hard to make time for Jason. If it wasn't work getting in the way, it was his social life. He was playing hockey and training most weekends, or going to see another team play, or, when it wasn't that, he was out with his brother. She liked that he let her have her own space. But was this how it would continue? True, she didn't have time for a serious relationship, not really, and this was a useful compromise. She wanted someone who was there for her, someone who would escort her to weddings and functions, and thereby allow her to keep the family at bay. Every time she saw or spoke to her parents now, they asked her whether she had 'anyone special', whether she didn't think it was time to 'settle down'.

Lou hadn't phoned them for a couple of weeks. Time to ring them . . . later maybe. The thought was followed immediately afterwards by another: she wouldn't ring; she would find some sort of excuse. She didn't want to lie, but if she admitted that at last she had a boyfriend they would all spin into an excited frenzy. Her mother would tell everybody, from the extended family to her Women's Institute buddies to random strangers at the bus stop. The next phone call would be all about him – *How's Jason? When are we going to meet him?* – which would escalate into requests for them to come and stay, unsubtle hints for him to persuade her to be committed. As if she was somehow less of a person without a ring on her finger. Rootless, feckless, unshackled . . . unhinged.

It wasn't that she thought Jason was not up to this particular task. In fact, they'd fallen into this easy, comfortable relationship so well that it was a bit surprising he hadn't suggested making it official already. But it felt as though he was leaving it up to her, to choose the right time for them both. And it wasn't even as though she had doubts – he was the best relationship she'd had, ever, by far: he wouldn't cheat on her, she knew; wouldn't make unreasonable demands for her attention when she was working on something major.

He had asked about her family. When she had gone to see them, just before Christmas, he had joked about coming with her and surprising them. The look on her face had told him everything. 'Hey, just kidding,' he'd said hastily. After that, he would ask how they were. And that was it. There was no more discussion about visiting.

Her cousin Tracy was getting married in a few weeks, and so far the invitation for 'Louisa plus one' had been left unreplied to, tucked into the flap of her organiser. Lou's mother mentioned this during every conversation, usually either immediately before or after the question about the boyfriend ... the lack of a boyfriend.

'I've requested the day off, and it's been approved. But you know if something comes up I will have to miss it.'

'It's a shame, that's all. If you've got the day off, why can't you just send Tracy an email? Let her know you'll try to be there?'

'I will, Mum.'

'Because even if you can't take someone with you, you know, she needs to know the numbers for the catering ... '

Oh, Jesus, not the catering again. She wasn't invited for the whole day, just the evening, so why was it such an issue? Surely they were only talking about having the right number of sandwiches and chicken drumsticks? She wouldn't eat, if it was such a big deal. She would turn up with some cash in a congratulations card, dance a bit, wish the bride and groom every happiness in their life together, get rat-arsed quickly and completely, and get a taxi home. It was called showing your face.

She didn't need to take Jason with her for that.

27

On the other hand, it would be good to get all of that crap out of the way. It would send a message to the parents that yes, she was seeing someone, a real person – a *man*, no less, since the question of her sexuality had been raised once in public (last Christmas; everyone had been drunk) and at least once in private (an email to her sister Jasmine, which had been accidentally forwarded to her). It would get the whole discussion out of the way and they would leave her in peace for a little while. There would be the inevitable fierce questioning to endure, which would start off benignly enough – *Where did you meet? How long have you been together? Where are you from? Oh, yes, we love Canadians, so polite!* – and would end up being personal and downright intrusive – *What does your father do, Jason? So, it'll be your turn next up the aisle, then, Lou? Your biological clock must be ringing an alarm by now!*

She couldn't inflict that on him. He would run a mile.

Intel Reports on Carl McVey – Op Trapeze

5x5x5 Intelligence Report

Date: 18 March 2013

Officer: PC 9921 EVANS

Subject: Carl McVEY DOB 29/09/1970

Grading: B / 2 / 4

Carl McVEY runs two pubs in Briarstone town centre, the Railway Tavern in Queen Street and the Newarke in Cavendish Lane. He also owns the Ferryman pub and restaurant in Baysbury. It is thought that these businesses are used for laundering the proceeds of various criminal enterprises.

5x5x5 Intelligence Report

Date: 30 July 2013

Officer: PC 9921 EVANS

Subject: Carl McVEY DOB 29/09/1970, Lewis
               McDONNELL DOB 21/10/1953, Harry
               McDONNELL DOB 06/07/1956

Grading: B / 2 / 4

Carl McVEY has been associating with the McDONNELL
brothers recently. They were seen enjoying lunch at the
Ferryman restaurant in Baysbury on Monday 29 July 2013.
Another male was with them who was described as dark-haired
with a large tattoo of a bird on his lower right forearm.

(Research shows this may be Gavin PETRIE DOB
17/03/1975.)

14:56

The office was quiet. Sam Hollands was at her desk, DC Jane Phelps
was on the phone.

'Did I miss anything?' Lou asked Sam.

'I've just been trawling back through the historic intel on McVey.
Nothing too exciting – but there are a couple of reports linking him
to the McDonnells; they had a cosy lunch together back in July. I've
sent Les and Ron out to the Ferryman to see if they've got any
CCTV. I know it's unlikely.'

'Worth a try, though. Let me know if you get a result? I've got to
go to Knapstone.'

'SB?' Sam asked.

'Yes. I'm meeting a DCI called Stephen Waterhouse.'

Sam raised her eyebrows. 'Really? Good luck with that.'

'You know him?'

'He was Jo's line manager for a while, when she was seconded down there. He was still a DI then – can't have been long since he was promoted.'

Lou hesitated, concerned about following any line of thought involving Sam's ex-partner. 'What's he like, then?'

'I don't think I can say without swearing.'

'Oh, God, that bad? Seriously – tell me. I won't tell anyone.'

'Just between us, he was described as "a jumped-up little cock with an attitude problem". No offence. Jo's words, not mine.'

SCARLETT – Saturday 23 August 2003, 19:53

The next time she opened her eyes, it was less bright around the edges of the back door of the van. She had been asleep for some while, then, and it was because she had been untied and could finally move, stretch out her arms and legs and not have that unbearable pain in her shoulders and wrists. It wasn't comfortable now, far from it, and the high-pitched whine of the engine was so loud it should have been impossible to sleep, but she had done just that.

At some point the van must have stopped and they must have opened the door, because next to her was a bottle of water and a paper bag containing a stale-smelling slice of pizza, folded in half to fit in the bag. Stale or not, she ate half of it there and then, and the rest of it less than an hour later. She drank the water, not even caring if they'd drugged it.

Above the noise of the engine she could hear music coming from the radio in the front cab. Some woman wailing a tune with a beat behind it, nothing like the music she was used to. It sounded awful.

The men weren't talking any more. They'd run out of things to say, for now at least. She tried to listen to the music, thinking that she might hear the news or something – hear her name mentioned. But, when the song ended, the voice that introduced the next track was foreign, unintelligible. She could tell it wasn't the news, though. The tone of the voice was the same as any other commercial radio station – unnaturally happy, intoning up and down, shouting almost. There would be a different voice for the news, if indeed they had news on the radio here. Wherever they were.

She found herself thinking about Nico again. Where was he, right now? What was he doing? He would be looking for her, of course. Everyone would be looking for her. Even her father would be out, hunting for her. He would be doing the right thing, and making sure everyone knew it.

Oh, Nico.

Cerys had lost her virginity to Matt Hayward, at the end of the summer term. Scarlett had always thought it would be her first, that she would be the one, but when it came down to it she didn't want any of them, the boys. Being alone with anyone made her feel nervous. She didn't feel safe. And, even though Cerys had wanted to get it out of the way as quickly as she possibly could, Scarlett couldn't help feeling that her friend was making a mistake. But Cerys had curves and an almost unnatural level of self-confidence, and, although Scarlett was the one who got all the attention from the boys, it was still Cerys who did it first.

They had had plenty of discussions about it. How it didn't really hurt. How they'd managed to use a condom the first time but he'd taken it off halfway through the second time because he didn't really like using them but it hadn't mattered because he pulled out just before.

Cerys was suddenly worldly-wise. She was the one with the knowledge, and the balance of power had shifted in their friendship, as if Cerys was the grown-up one and Scarlett was still a child. If only she knew ...

And, despite all the time she'd been spending with Mark, she hadn't really been paying attention. She hadn't thought of him in that way, not really, not until that last day in the library, and not really even then.

She hadn't wanted to come on holiday at all. She'd been dreading it. A whole week with her parents, and her sister? She wouldn't be able to stand it. They'd end up killing each other. Who knew what might happen?

'I'll stay here,' Juliette had said, when they'd been booking the holiday.

'Don't be ridiculous,' her mother had answered. 'We're not leaving you here.'

'I can look after the cat,' she'd volunteered. 'And next door will keep an eye on me.'

Desperate, then, because she was allergic to the cat and avoided it at all costs.

'She can't do that!' Scarlett had shouted, knowing full well that, left with her sister, their pet would go completely untended. And it would just be the three of them on holiday, a fate so hideous that she couldn't bear to think of it.

'Calm down, Scarlett. Juliette, you're coming with us and that's final.'

'I don't want to come!' Juliette wailed. 'I'm scared!'

'Don't be so dramatic. You should be grateful!'

'Don't make me go. Don't make me go.'

Scarlett had seen Annie's cheeks colouring. She had had rows with her mother too, at Juliette's age – but hers had all been about independence and not being a child any more. She wanted to tell Juliette not to bother with the babyish overacting. It was easier just to give in, to let them have their way. *It's better to grow up in private*, she'd thought. *It hurts less if you don't fight all the time.*

The van must have turned off the main road, the long, straight road with the van travelling fast and the whine of the engine underneath her, and there were twists and turns which threw her from one side of the van to the other. It was impossible to sleep. How long had it been? An hour, two? Maybe even longer. In the end she crouched in the corner, bracing her leg against one of the struts that supported the metal side. She felt motion-sick, the pizza and the water churning inside her belly. Despite the sleep she was exhausted; but now the adrenalin had kicked in again.

It was odd, she thought, how quickly the feeling of terror became the norm. The van had become her world. A night and a day and now it was night again, and in the space of that time she had veered along this crazy path between panic and normality.

But now, she was afraid. If they were off the motorway, travelling on smaller roads, then the journey was coming to an end. The van would stop and something would happen. Something was coming, and she would have to deal with it, whatever it was. They weren't going to kill her; if they'd been going to do that they would have done it by now. But it wasn't going to be good, was it? They weren't taking her away from her fucked-up family and her stupid fucked-up life and giving her a better one, were they?

Whatever was coming, it was going to hurt. It was like watching a car heading towards you on the crossroads and knowing it couldn't possibly stop in time. Or lying in bed listening to the sounds of the house and knowing you were better off staying awake.

The van stopped. Scarlett pushed herself, pointlessly, back as far away from the doors as possible. After a few moments, the side door was unlocked and slid open. It was dark outside. There were two of them, and at first she couldn't tell if it was the same two that had taken her. Then she recognised the taller of the two, the one who had given her water. The one who had talked to her out on the street and shoved her into the van.

'You get out now,' he said, his voice low.

Scarlett wondered if it was worth screaming for help. 'No,' she said, before she had even made the decision to say anything. It was automatic. 'No, no no no.'

'You get out, we don't hurt you.'

'Please,' she said, 'just let me call my family. Let me call them. They'll be worried . . .'

They looked at each other, and then the taller one, the one she thought was almost all right, climbed into the back with her. He was going to talk to her, to reason with her. To ask her nicely, or to offer some reassurance, or at worst just pull her out.

So she was off guard when he hit her in the face with his fist.

The shock of it registered before the pain, but when it came it was quick and hard and intense. He pulled her by the hair, dragging her backwards, her feet scrabbling against the floor of the van. There was blood pouring from her nose, blood all down her face. She coughed on it and the screams were coming without her thinking about it then, the pain saw to that.

And now she was struggling, fighting against him, pulling and scratching at his hands to try to get him to release her hair.

The man was saying something in that language, his voice low through gritted teeth, and her voice, crying out with pain, above it.

At the back of the van he released his grip on her hair and she slithered to the ground, curled up into a ball. The ground was rocky, uneven shale. She was sobbing, now, her hand over her nose. It felt as though her face had exploded. She was aware of him crouching beside her, the handgun loose in his hand, casually knocking it against his thigh. 'You look.'

Her eyes cast a glance over him and then she closed her eyes. The pain thrilled her like an electric charge. He grabbed her hair again and lifted her head.

'No, stop, no! It hurts! Let go, let go!'

But she opened her eyes. And the gun was there, held with a kind of easy self-assurance as though it was part of him, as natural a thing for him to be holding as a pen, or a mobile phone.

'You see this? You think you have pain now? You make trouble, I shoot your foot off. Then I go back to Rodos and I shoot Nico, stupid fuck, and then I go find your baby sister and take her because she is worth big money to me, not like you.'

It was the first time there had been any mention of Nico. She sobbed at it and nodded some kind of assent, wiping her face, the blood and mucus and tears sliding across the back of her hand, smearing with the dust and the dirt of the ground beneath her.

'All right now?' he said, his voice almost gentle. 'You stand? I help you, here ...' He put a hand under her armpit and pulled her upright. As though the madness was over, as though it had been someone else, not him, who had smashed her nose and pulled clumps of hair from her scalp.

They were on a road that was no more than a track, and behind them was a structure that looked like some kind of farm shack or out-building – concrete walls, a single window, a bright light like the motion-sensor-activated security light that they had at home on the front of the garage. This one lit up the uneven ground, revealing a rusted pickup truck with no wheels, a kennel.

Somewhere – though not in the kennel – a dog was barking, hadn't stopped since the van doors had opened. It sounded like a big dog, the *ro-ro-ro* of its bark throaty and deep. Above that, the incessant carolling of the crickets and the buzz of the cicadas. She thought of those insects, the great ugly beasts like the one Nico had shown her, all around. Everywhere, out of sight but never out of earshot.

'Where am I?' she said. 'Where is this place?'

'You come with me,' the younger one said. He pulled her by the elbow – not roughly, but then he didn't need to. There was nowhere she could have gone.

'What are you going to do with me?' she asked.

He laughed – a short, high laugh, oddly girlish. 'I do nothing with you. In the morning, you meet your new friends.'

The traffic to Knapstone was bad, unusually. Ferries had once sailed from here to the continent, which meant that the town was accessed by a dual carriageway, straight from the motorway which led back to Briarstone. The ferry company had given up ten years ago, right about the time that a pretty fifteen-year-old named Scarlett Rainsford had disappeared while on a family holiday in Rhodes.

It turned out that a lorry had jack-knifed across both lanes, leading to stationary traffic backed up nearly to the motorway. It was being cleared, apparently.

Lou considered turning on the lights and speeding up the hard shoulder, but only for a moment. Being late for a briefing wasn't technically an emergency, and the traffic was starting to creep forward, suggesting that somewhere up ahead the emergency services had managed to open at least one lane.

Scarlett Rainsford.

She'd always expected to hear that name again one day, but in all honesty she had never for one minute believed the girl was still alive. They had made mistakes with it, undoubtedly, which had been bad for the force at the time; and that was after the initial investigation by the Greeks. The Eden police had come to it late, which was never good. Within forty-eight hours they'd had a team out in Rhodes, but by then they'd all been working on the assumption that Scarlett had been murdered. They were expecting to find a body, because that was what the Greeks were expecting too. By the time they'd established that there was no evidence to support this theory, crucial opportunities had been missed.

Back in the UK, even as a DC new to Major Crime, Lou had been able to smell disaster.

Scarlett's sister and her father had returned to the UK just a week after the holiday had been supposed to end. Her mother stayed out there on her own, but after another two weeks she too returned. The whole family had waited just three weeks for Scarlett. It didn't seem very long. It was as if they, too, believed she was dead. Or maybe, Lou had suspected at the time, they even knew she was.

Well, she thought, as she finally managed to get her car out of first gear, she'd been wrong about that.

Knapstone Police Station had a tiny car park, for which it considered itself lucky. Even so, there were no spaces, and several cars were double-parked. Lou went back out again through the exit barrier, cursing. It was five to four. She hated being late. She drove around the streets nearby, looking for a space that wasn't marked as 'Residents Only', and eventually found half a space, leaving the car with its front tyres sticking out over a double yellow.

She signed in at reception and was directed down the stairs to Special Branch, where she had to knock to be let in. A young woman in jeans eventually answered the door, and when Lou explained why she was here there was a bit of discussion with someone over her shoulder.

'They're upstairs, on the fifth floor. Our briefing room's in use for another job.'

Lou found the lift. She'd been to the fifth-floor briefing room before, because it was the one Major Crime were invariably allocated when something kicked off in Knapstone. That was good: familiar turf.

But of course by the time she got there the briefing had started and she had to creep in. And there weren't many people there either, so everyone turned to look at her and the paunchy man with thinning hair who was speaking at the head of the boardroom table – actually eight scuffed laminate tables pushed together, mismatched chairs around the perimeter – stopped what he was doing.

'You are?' he said.

'DCI Lou Smith,' she said.

'Have a seat,' he said, without introducing himself. He didn't need to. He could only be DCI Stephen Waterhouse, and she hated his guts already.

All the seats around the table were taken, but two guys at the corner nearest to her shuffled their chairs round to make room. She pulled a hard plastic chair from under the window and squeezed between them. As she did so, her mobile buzzed in her bag. She pulled it out, checked the message in case it was urgent – it wasn't – then adjusted the volume to silent. Waterhouse hadn't resumed his speech.

It was stuffy in the room and Lou sensed an atmosphere. She looked around the table: six men, one woman – an older DC with short, greying hair. Nobody was smiling, and now they'd all had a good look at her they were avoiding meeting her eyes.

'Right, for those of you that don't know: DCI Smith was part of the original investigation into Scarlett Rainsford's disappearance – when she was a DC. Mr Buchanan wants her involved.'

Lou chanced a smile but still none of them looked up. SB were not normally this grim. She'd been on nights out with them – not this lot, admittedly, but generally speaking they were a 'work hard, play hard' bunch. People joined SB and didn't leave. It was considered a good place to work.

'So,' Waterhouse said, looking directly at her for the first time, 'what can you tell us?'

He had to be joking, right? She'd barely sat down, and he was wanting her to show her hand first, as if this was some sort of test? She glared at him.

'As you pointed out, I was a DC in Major Crime back then. I interviewed the family.'

'And?'

Lou took a deep breath. She was going to have to put herself on the line, clearly, in order to get into the gang. 'Didn't feel right. I know that's easy to say with hindsight. The family was odd – Scarlett's sister was monosyllabic, hostile at first; the father was polite, helpful as far as it went. When the mother came back she was in a bad state emotionally.'

'What happened with the Greeks?'

'It was pretty chaotic. One minute they wanted our help, the next they didn't. They told us some bits and left out other important things. They thought straight away that she had been killed and disposed of. Somehow the investigators who went out there got the impression they had evidence that she'd been killed, some forensics – but there was nothing like that. So for a couple of days we were looking for a body when we should have been checking the ports.'

'To be honest, we all thought it was the dad.'

Lou looked round in surprise. It was the woman who had spoken. Lou tried to work out who she was, but drew a complete blank. It bugged her – she was normally better at faces than this.

'Go on,' Waterhouse said.

'He was all sorts of weird, wasn't he?' she said, looking at Lou for support.

Lou nodded. Who the hell was she? She couldn't remember –

41

there had been loads of them on the case initially, several women, but none of them fitted. The dark hair, peppered with grey . . . slim figure. Lou stole a look at the woman's ID badge, hanging around her neck on a non-standard issue lanyard. It was a Federation one, she realised. Was she a Federation rep?

'He was helpful,' the woman continued, 'without any of it actually being useful – and then he was keen to go back to the UK with Juliette. She "couldn't miss her schooling". One minute he was out rooting through the undergrowth, organising search parties with all the tourists and ex-pat Brits who were showing an interest, then all of a sudden he'd booked a flight for him and his daughter and he was off. And then, what you said about the forensics, ma'am – there was a suggestion that they'd found blood in the room – the parents' room, not the one the girls were in – but the Greek police didn't secure the scene properly and the place was cleaned. We took a couple of our CSIs out there but we didn't find anything.'

She must have been one of the original lot who went out to Rhodes, Lou thought. She couldn't remember there being a woman on that team.

'So the father wasn't arrested?' Waterhouse was back looking at Lou.

'No. We had nothing to arrest him for,' Lou said. 'When we interviewed him—'

'We've all seen the transcripts,' Waterhouse interrupted.

She glared at him. 'I was going to say this: he came across as personable one minute, aggressive the next. He was getting up out of his seat, fiddling with his glasses. Then he would sit perfectly still, calm. You don't get a sense of that from the transcripts.'

The man sitting immediately to her right – young; fair hair with too much gel on it – straightened in his chair. As if he was expecting the meeting to descend into a physical brawl at any moment and he wanted to leap for the door.

For a moment, Waterhouse stared her out. Then he looked away, his cheeks colouring as though he was hot or dangerously angry. 'Anything else?'

Much as it pained her to provide him with anything other than a single-finger salute, Lou didn't want to give him the satisfaction of shutting her up. 'Yes, actually. I believe there was a crime series going on at the time, with young women going missing from Rhodes and Corfu. From what I understand, Scarlett wasn't included in the series because she didn't fit the criteria. For a start she was so much younger – the others were all in their late teens, early twenties, all on holiday with groups of friends rather than parents. They were multiple nationalities, too; none of the other missing girls were British.'

'How many?'

'There were five, I think,' the other woman said. 'Two went missing from Rhodes, three from Corfu. The Greek police were reluctant to get us involved with that, too.'

Waterhouse considered this. He must have read about it in the file, Lou thought, and he probably knew more about it than any of them. As a DC at the time, Lou had only had access to a tiny part of the investigation. The senior officers at the time – all of whom were now retired – would have had the overview.

'Right then, tasks. Caroline, I want you to direct the debrief interview. You can have Terry and Dave, if you need them. Josh, you're liaising with SOCA or the NCA or whatever the fuck they're calling themselves today, and the UK Border Agency. Once we've done that, we need to bid for a surveillance team on Maitland and another one on Lewis McDonnell – Andy and Tim, you're on that, right?'

Wait, Lou thought. 'Hold on. You said Maitland and McDonnell?'

Waterhouse breathed out heavily through his nose, laid his hand flat on the grey cardboard file on the desk in front of him. 'Yes?'

'I'm assuming you're talking about Nigel Maitland. What's he got to do with it?'

Nigel Maitland – suspect in the murder of Polly Leuchars, the case that had pretty much consumed Lou's every waking moment for the last year. Nothing they'd had had been able to touch him. She'd known SB were looking at him, but even though they'd tried to get some more intelligence, something useful, Major Crime had drawn a complete blank.

Everyone was looking at her again, the way they had when she'd first walked in. Waterhouse clearly wasn't going to share anything that hadn't been prised out of him like a crumbling cork from a bottle. It was Caroline – the one with salt-and-pepper hair, whom Lou suddenly and conclusively recognised as Caro Sumner, then DC with the Metropolitan Police, who had been on attachment to the investigation and had, once, appeared in front of the press with a statement that had gone horribly wrong – who finally spoke and shared the crucial bit of information.

'We think he's the one who trafficked her.'

SCARLETT – Sunday 24 August 2003, 06:57

She had slept. It hadn't been for long, since when she opened her eyes she felt as shattered as when she'd closed them. She had dreamed that she was awake, running, fighting – exhausting dreams about hope and hopelessness, as though her brain was spending the downtime trying to work its way towards a solution, and finding none.

The room she was in held a dirty mattress on which she was lying, and a bucket which she had used last night. She could smell the urine and her own body odour. Her hands were covered in dried blood, crusted around the edges of her fingernails. She rubbed it off her palms and felt her nose carefully, then her eyes. The ache blended seamlessly across her face, and the skin of her nose felt tight and hot. By squinting she could see the bridge of her nose: it was wider than normal, and even in the half-light the colour of it looked wrong. It looked bruised.

She pushed herself to a sitting position and leaned back against the wall, waiting for the pounding, dizzying feeling to subside. She felt as if she was going to be sick, saliva flooding her mouth, and she gulped it back. The door of the room, a rough splintered wood with a space of a couple of inches at the bottom, was closed.

It was worth checking. She stood, gingerly, keeping her head low, her hands on her knees. The nausea swelled and subsided.

It was locked. Even the bottom of the door didn't move against the frame when she gave it a boot. The impact, as feeble as it was, jarred her head.

'Hey!' she called. 'HEY! Let me out, you stupid Greek fuckers!'
Silence. Had they gone, left her behind?

She crossed to the window. It was small, head-height, and the window was pushed open as wide as it would go on a lever. Beyond that, metal bars prevented it opening further. She stood on tiptoe to try to look out, but all she could see was scrubland – uneven ground, dusty-looking trees, and low hills in the distance. No buildings, no vehicles, no people. No sign of life.

Then the hopelessness hit her like a wave and the tears welled up and spilled over her cheeks. She dabbed at them with her sleeve. Her face hurt, her head hurt.

'Mum,' she sobbed. To her own surprise – 'I want my mum . . . '

The tears lasted a while – long enough for it to be properly daylight, and for the heat to start to penetrate into the room – and then her eyes were dry and sore. She sat on the mattress and waited for what would happen next.

10:20

The patch of sunlight had moved from the corner of her room around to the floor.

Scarlett had screamed, given up screaming because nothing happened, no one came; the only result was that it made her head hurt. Eventually she had lain down on the mattress because there was nowhere else to sit.

The dog started barking. It sounded further away, muffled, as though it was in another building some distance from where she was. Again, that throaty bark of a big jowly dog. She had even begun to picture it. Jaws big enough to crush a human skull.

And then she heard voices, from a way off – as though they were approaching the house. A male voice, then a response from another man – a laugh.

And a woman, a girl. High-pitched voice. She couldn't understand what was said but heard the tone of it – she was pleading. Afraid.

The door opened a few moments later and Scarlett got to her feet, thinking they were going to pull her out of the room, but instead two women were shoved into the room with her. The man at the door was not either of the men who had brought her here. The door shut as both women started yelling in a language she didn't understand. The man outside the door shouted something and the tone of his voice – or perhaps they understood him – made them stop; both of them stepped back and away.

The door opened again and he threw in a polythene shrink-wrapped bundle. Bottled water. A pack of six 500ml bottles of water that landed on the floor and bounced once. Then the door closed again.

The two women pounced on the bottles of water, fought over them. The polythene was ripped, the bottles tumbled out over the floor and before she could help herself Scarlett was there with them, grabbing at the bottles before they were gone or busted and spilled.

Somehow despite all the pushing and shoving they managed to end up with two bottles each. Scarlett retreated to the mattress, clutching the bottles to her chest, watching the two newcomers. They were talking to each other in hushed, desperate whispers. Other than fighting over the water they had barely acknowledged her presence, and now they were sitting cross-legged on the floor facing each other as they drank.

The dark-haired one was taller, lankier, her back a long curve; the wrists protruding from her long-sleeved T-shirt were bony, angular.

The other one had bleached hair, dark at the roots, half-tied into a knot to one side of her head, long greasy strands of a fringe that she was growing out either deliberately or for want of a hairdresser falling across her eyes. Both of them looked grimy, in need of a good wash. But then she probably looked the same.

'My name's Scarlett,' she said at last. She felt tears starting again.

The blonde one was talking, and carried on as if she hadn't heard. The dark one turned her head and stared at Scarlett.

'Do you speak English?' Scarlet whimpered. Her voice sounded off-key, thick, as if she was bunged up with a head cold.

'A little,' the dark-haired one said. The blonde one still hadn't so much as cast a glance in her direction. And then she raised a hand, the palm flat in Scarlett's direction. She said something to her companion, the language foreign but the meaning clear from the sharp tone. An instruction: *Don't talk to her. Don't trust her.*

'What's your name?' Scarlett said, gulping back a sob.

'Yelena.'

The blonde girl started yammering, louder now, the flat of her hand striking the top of the other girl's head. *You idiot.* Yelena answered back, shouting, and for a moment there was this top-volume incomprehensible argument going on between them, until the door opened and the man came in, the one who had brought the girls in.

He shouted at them and they shouted back. The blonde one stood, in his face, her head doing the ghetto-style tilt-shake to give him some attitude, and he watched her calmly for a moment, then pulled a gun from his waistband, raised it before any of them could say or do anything, and brought it down with a crack on the side of her head.

She dropped to the floor, face-first. Her head made a loud smack as it hit the floor. Yelena cried out and the man raised his hand to her too. She shut up instantly, hand over her mouth, eyes wide, backing off until she was in the corner of the room.

He said something else, calmly. Pointed the gun at Yelena, then at Scarlett, then at the motionless girl on the floor. *Keep quiet, or it will be worse.*

He went, shut the door behind him. Yelena rushed to the girl, who hadn't moved. Lifted her head, stroked her dirty hair away from her face. There was blood on Yelena's hands; the girl must have cut her head when she fell, or when he had hit her. Yelena was crying now.

Scarlett felt strangely calm, her own tears gone. She opened the second bottle of water and took a few sips, watching.

There was a lot of blood. She thought the girl might be dead.

12:40

After a period of time during which the blonde girl had not moved, Yelena had banged on the door until the man returned. She spoke to him quietly, without anger, but with a desperate pleading sadness that seemed to get through where the yelling and screaming had not.

He said something to her and she sat next to Scarlett on the other end of the mattress, her back to the wall.

Then a second man came in, a giant of a man with a shaven head and a black vest that revealed immense, hairy shoulders. He looked at the blonde girl and the blood and said something to the other one. Then he picked the girl up as though she weighed nothing, under her arms, her head lolling, throwing her over one shoulder. The blood from the wound on her head drip-dripped on to the bare concrete floor. He carried her out, leaving the smaller of the two men standing in the doorway, staring at Scarlett and Yelena. The way he was looking at them made Scarlett feel uncomfortable and then, when he continued to stare and didn't look away, scared. A minute later the giant came back with a bucket of water, which he splashed on to the blood on the floor. Then they both went. The door shut fast.

'I'm sorry,' whispered Scarlett, because she had nothing else to say.

Without looking at her, Yelena turned on to her side and curled up on the mattress, her back to Scarlett, the soles of her dirty trainers and the white skin of her lower back above the tight stonewashed jeans all that she was prepared to share.

For some reason, having someone else in the room with her made Scarlett think of Nico.

The man who had broken her nose had threatened her with hurting Nico. He had mentioned his name. She hadn't thought it at the time but she realised now that Nico must have been in on it all. He had been part of this gang, whatever it was. She thought back over the conversations they'd had, the things he had said to her, trying to make sense of it.

SCARLETT – Monday 18 August 2003, 15:25

She had been out with Juliette when she'd first seen him.

Juliette had not wanted to go. But their mother had been unwell; some food or other she had eaten on the first day of the holiday had disagreed with her, and she had been sick several times. In the late afternoon she was asleep in bed and, although the sisters didn't particularly enjoy spending time together, neither of them wanted to spend time with their father either.

'We could go and have a look at the shops,' Scarlett had said, hopeful.

'What for?' Juliette said, taciturn. Head in a book, of course. Scarlett could never tell if she was actually reading it. The pages turned regularly but she seemed to just stare at it, unmoving, silent. As though it was a diversionary tactic.

Juliette would have preferred to stay in the room, the curtains drawn across the patio doors, the heat in there stifling because their father wouldn't pay for air-conditioning in their room as well as the other room next door, the one he was sharing with their mother.

'You can sit in here,' he had said, when they'd first arrived and had the argument about it, 'if you get too hot.'

They couldn't sit in there with their mother vomiting and moaning, of course.

'I just want to go out somewhere,' Scarlett said. 'Please, Jul, let's go out. For a walk.'

'Leave me alone.'

So she started getting ready, pulling on a loose vest top over her bikini, cut-off denim shorts.

From her bed, Juliette said without looking up, 'He won't let you go on your own, you know.'

'He won't find out unless you tell him.'

'Don't be daft. He knows everything. And he'll see you go.'

The way out of the apartment complex was past the pool, and of course that was where Clive Rainsford was right now, around the other side of the pool on a sun-lounger, as far away from his wife and daughters as he could get while still maintaining control over them. He knew exactly where they were, at every minute of the day. He would not countenance any alternative.

'Come with me, then. Once we're in town we'll find a café or something, you can sit with your book and I'll just have a wander round. It'll be fine, there will be loads of people.'

'Don't be stupid, I can't sit in a café on my own.'

'Why not? What's the difference between that and sitting in here? And you can have a nice cold drink; I'll buy you one.'

In the end, Juliette had relented. They had consulted with their father by the side of the pool. They were given an hour and a half, and then they had to be back.

They had stopped at several cafés on the main road, none of which was suitable. Juliette was incredibly, frustratingly fussy – but she had always been like this. She was quirky at best, downright annoying at worst. But pushing her, goading her, was not the right way to handle things. Even at the age of fifteen Scarlett knew that the best way to bend her sister to her will was to meet her halfway.

They went down a side street and there was a Moroccan-style café, dark red plaster walls, decorative hookahs, low glass tables and dark wooden fretwork screens.

Dark – Juliette's favourite thing. And she could get proper mint tea here, which was what she'd been hankering for.

'You'll be okay in here,' Scarlett said. 'You read your book; I'll be back in an hour. I'll just go along the shops for a bit. I'll look for something for Mum, shall I?'

Juliette had already withdrawn. Scarlett left.

Back up to the main street. It was late afternoon but still searingly hot, the sun glowing off the pavement and reflecting back at her like an oven. She strolled along, browsing through the tourist shops. They all sold exactly the same things. Olive oil soap. Beach toys. Hats, sunglasses, a rack of Hawaiian Tropic sun lotion. Crocheted bags, scarves, ceramic ornaments and fridge magnets. Postcards.

The shops gave way to more cafés and bars. She would have enjoyed coming here at night, but with Cerys rather than her family. That would be fun. When she and Juliette went out to dinner with Mum and Dad they came early in the evening, and when they were done and strolling back to the apartment the bars were just starting to come to life. This time of day they were mostly empty, only the ones with internet terminals temptingly lined up inside the shady interiors showing any signs of life.

She paused outside the Pirate Bay Club and looked. There were three internet PCs on a table, with a sign saying '20 minute = 3 euro'. She thought about Cerys, and what she might be getting up to back at home.

She took a seat at the terminal furthest into the bar, at the back, and pushed three coins into the slot on a metal box next to the grubby monitor. The screensaver – a cartoon pirate bouncing around the edges of a blue screen – remained resolutely active. She moved the mouse, with no success.

She jolted the metal box, in case one of the coins had stuck. Still nothing. There was no 'reject coins' button.

She looked around. Nobody behind the bar. Sitting on the low wall which separated the outdoor seating area from the road was a boy with dark, short hair, a pale blue polo shirt and dark jeans. He was staring at her. When he saw she was looking, he grinned.

'You need something?' he shouted to her. He had an accent, of course, was a local – but she knew that already because he was wearing jeans. How could anyone wear jeans when it was this hot?

Scarlett assumed he worked there, behind the bar. He had a kind of easy casualness about him, as though he owned the place.

'It's not working,' she called back, slapping the top of the metal box with her palm as a final rebuke.

He sauntered over, arms folded. 'You are right,' he said. 'It's not working.'

He laughed, and then she did too.

'Oh, well,' she said. 'It's only three euros.'

'I will ask Vasilis for it.'

She paused, expecting him to go behind the bar and find Vasilis, whoever he was.

'He is not here,' he said. 'The bar is closed.'

It didn't look closed. The TV screen above the bar was showing sports with the subtitles on, and some random Greek pop music radio station was playing through the speakers.

'Are you keeping an eye on it, then?'

He looked puzzled. 'Keeping ... an eye?' He put one hand over his eye, like a pirate's eye-patch, and she laughed again. 'My name is Nico,' he said, holding out his hand for her to shake.

'Scarlett,' she said, taking it.

'Is a beautiful name for a beautiful girl,' he said. He turned her

54

hand over and kissed the back of it. 'You want something to drink?'

'Oh, sure. A Coke?'

Nico went behind the bar and opened one of the glass-fronted fridges, helped himself to two bottles of Coke, which he popped before bringing them back.

'I don't have any more money,' she said.

'Is okay. Vasilis has three euros from you, anyway.'

Scarlett had just over half an hour of mindless chatter with Nico while she drank her Coke – slowly – and then she had to get back. Juliette was all right as long as she had a routine, as long as she knew what to expect, but when the uncertainties crept in she would start to panic. Lots of things seemed to cause that these days. Scarlett had said she would be gone for an hour, and knew better than to be even a minute late. As it was, when she rounded the corner Juliette was waiting outside the café, looking anxiously up and down the road.

Without speaking they fell into step together, walking back up towards the apartment. They had to pass the Pirate Bay and Scarlett looked out for him, the dark-haired boy who'd bought her a Coke – or rather, not bought it but helped himself – but he wasn't there any more.

Tuesday 19 August 2003, 15:19

Scarlett thought about Nico for a whole twenty-four hours and begged Juliette to go for a walk again at the same time next day – using the excuse that they still hadn't managed to get a present for their mother, who was recovering but wan and grouchy.

There was something about the synchronicity of the timing – at the same time of day, Scarlett knew she would stand a better chance of getting Juliette's agreement – that made it easier this time. She took her time choosing what to wear, pinning her hair up in an elaborately messy bun. It was so hot that strands of her freshly washed and dried hair were sticking to the back of her neck with perspiration.

Nico was not sitting where he'd been the day before and Scarlett felt an odd sort of panic. She had convinced herself that he would be there, that he would be waiting for her, and when he wasn't she didn't know what to do. In the end she walked Juliette back down to the same café and then wandered around from shop to shop, as she had the day before.

In one of the tourist shops she bought a bottle of olive oil body lotion for her mum – five euros. She'd seen the same brand, the same bottle in a shop on the main street at seven euros. It was worth shopping around, here; you'd think prices would be fixed for the same product, but the price of everything seemed to vary depending on how close to the main street you were. The most expensive of all were the shops bordering the town square: jewellers and shops selling silk and fur coats. Fur coats! Why would anyone need a fur coat in a place like this? And yet they were everywhere, shops selling furs. She had counted five of them from the window of the coach that had brought them to the resort from the airport, glass-and marble-fronted, expensive-looking, with empty car parks outside.

She had not seen anyone actually wearing a fur coat. Maybe it got cold in the winter? It seemed very unlikely.

Back outside the shop, she slipped the paper bag containing the moisturising lotion into the canvas tote bag she carried over her shoulder, pulled her oversized sunglasses down from her forehead.

After that she went up to the town square and sat on the wall surrounding the fountain, swinging her legs idly, crossed at the ankle. She leaned back, closing her eyes against the glare of the sun.

'Hey, Scarlett.'

She opened her eyes again and looked across the square to one of the cafés, and there was Nico. He walked over to where she sat, weaving between the tourists. He had a handful of leaflets and she watched as he had a half-hearted go at handing some of them out to passers-by. One of them, a woman wearing a gold Lurex top over a leathery décolletage, took a leaflet, glanced at it and then discarded it on the pavement.

He sauntered, giving Scarlett a chance to observe him objectively from behind her huge shades. He must have been seventeen, eighteen maybe, dark hair neatly cut – had he cut it since yesterday? – the same blue shirt and jeans. Dark eyebrows, clear skin, long lovely eyelashes that made him look somehow vulnerable. And then a wide smile showing even white teeth.

He sat down next to her and offered her a flyer. She took it and read it carefully as if he'd offered her a vital document. It was a menu for the pizza restaurant across the way.

'You're a – what do they call it? – promoter, or something?'

'They use other words. Not nice words sometimes.'

'I thought you worked at that Pirate bar.'

He laughed. 'Sometimes there. I work many places.'

And then he reached out and stroked a strand of hair away from her face. She flinched as his hand approached, couldn't help it, but then she relaxed and let him do it.

'You want to come party tonight?'

'I can't,' she said automatically, about to continue that her dad wouldn't let her, but stopping because that sounded childish.

57

'You have a boyfriend?' he asked, pouting with exaggerated disappointment.

She felt herself blushing. He must think she was such a kid, she thought, and she was tempted to lie and say yes.

'Girlfriend?' he asked then, with a cheeky grin.

'No.' Blushing even harder.

'So why don't you come party with me?'

'I have to go out with my family,' she said at last. 'My little sister – I have to look after her.'

'Your sister, what is her name?'

'Juliette.'

'You love her very much? I have a baby sister. She is very sweet, but she is a – how you say it – pain in the butt.'

Scarlett was picturing Juliette and wondering if she could ever be described as sweet. Annoying, definitely.

Nico tried again. 'I have to work tonight until late. But maybe after that we could meet?'

'Where are you working?' she asked, looking down at the flyer he'd given her. 'Is it at this place?'

'Yes. I will be here. Will you come?'

In the end, she gave him her mobile number even though it was switched off most of the time. She was terrified that one of her mates would call from the UK, or text, and would use up all of her Pay As You Go minutes that she had to work so hard to get. At home, she did chores all the time to justify her meagre pocket money, and most of it paid for top-ups.

When they got back she dressed up – a short cotton dress, wedges – and tried to persuade her father to take them down to the town square for pizza. Her mum was still looking very pale and, although she wanted to come with them, or for them not to go at all, her father told her she should stay behind and rest and they'd go on their own. After two days of consuming snacks from the pool bar, he was ready for a decent meal. Scarlett wanted to say something but caught her mother's expression and kept her mouth shut. Then, of course, he had to make it all even worse. 'What more could a man ask?' he said with forced enthusiasm. 'A meal out with my two favourite girls.'

It felt as if there was a row brewing all through the early evening. Their mother withdrew back to the bedroom – claiming a headache, probably dehydration; it would make sense after all that vomiting and diarrhoea. After a while their father followed her and Scarlett and Juliette stayed outside on the patio, trying not to listen to the raised voices. Juliette took her book and went into the girls' room, sliding the glass door shut firmly behind her. Scarlett went off into a fantasy where she lived in Greece all the time, spending her days selling bikinis and sunglasses to tourists on the beach, or handing out flyers in the market square. How old did you have to be, to do that? Nico didn't look very old, but then he was local. Probably the locals were allowed to do what they pleased. And besides, she could speak a bit of French and a tiny bit of Spanish but that was it – these promoter people had to speak lots of languages, didn't they?

At six the three of them walked down the hill into town. Their father wanted to stop at the first place they came to – a basic-looking taverna with uncomfortable wooden chairs outside, set around tables set with red check oilskin tablecloths, unlit tealights in glass jars. He stood outside perusing the menu for several minutes.

'I'd really like pizza,' Scarlett ventured.

'They do pizza here.'

'I mean a proper pizza. Not Greek pizza.'

'What the hell's a "proper pizza"?' he asked, but he moved on, and

Scarlett let out a sigh of relief. Juliette didn't give a stuff where they ate. The chances were she wouldn't eat much anyway.

Walking along, her father draped his arm around Scarlett's shoulder. She was taller now, almost as tall as her mum. He used to hold her hand.

'There are some nice places in the market square,' Scarlett said casually, wanting to push him away because he was her dad and she was too hot to walk along like this.

'Expensive, you mean.'

They carried on walking. Strolling. Clive glanced from side to side at the restaurants and cafés that were starting to line the road, one after the other, but he didn't seem keen on any of them.

'Well,' Scarlett said, risking pushing it even further and wondering whether she was getting close to that scary tipping point when her father's patience would snap, 'at least there's only three of us. If you're going to have a nice meal, tonight would be a good time to do it . . .'

So they ended up at Nico's pizzeria. He was handing out flyers when they approached, and he gave Scarlett a smile as she led the way on to the terrace.

The pizza was good, the meal was good, and thankfully her father had seen the prices on the menu and hadn't complained about them. Hadn't complained about anything much, just for a change – apart from when he'd finished the whole pizza, every crumb including the crust, and mentioned in passing that the Italian sausage had been a little salty. He could not bring himself to eat a meal without spoiling it with a comment.

But for once Scarlett didn't care: the night was becoming wonderful, full of promise. She had chosen a seat facing out towards the market square, which meant that Juliette could sit opposite her, facing into the interior of the restaurant which made her feel safe, enclosed, protected. From this position Scarlett could watch Nico working, stare at his bum and his thighs, the way the denim fabric stretched as he moved.

He wasn't very good at the flyer thing. He chose the wrong tourists – even Scarlett could see that – trying to hand them out to people who clearly wouldn't be interested in pizza. She felt sorry for him, too – what a job to have! Trying to be nice to all these rude sods who ignored him, passed him by without listening or even acknowledging his presence. She resolved to tell him about that later on, to try to make him feel better, because surely doing this night after night would erode his self-confidence, make him miserable.

Later on. She had made that decision, then. The mechanics of it yet to be worked out – how to get out of the apartment without Juliette knowing, sneak off and meet him, risking her life in the process because God knew her father would kill her, would actually genuinely kill her if he knew what she was planning – but the decision had been made.

When they finished their pizzas and stood up to go, she tried to catch Nico's eye – but he had crossed over to the fountain, to try and tempt a young family into the restaurant, and had actually managed to persuade them to stop and talk to him. She looked and looked, hung back a little, even, but his back remained facing her.

'Come on, Scarlett. What are you doing?' her father said, and the tone of his voice made her turn around straight away and follow.

Under her breath, she mouthed the words, 'Later, I'll see you later,' before following them back towards the apartment and her mother.

When the meeting came to an end, Lou phoned Jason from the corridor.

'Hey,' he said when he answered. 'Two calls in one day – you can't tell me you're busy.'

'It's work, though – doesn't count this time.' She kept her voice low, even though the people leaving the briefing room were all talking among themselves, paying her no attention.

'Really? Shame. So what can I do for you?'

'When you were on Op Nettle with me, you were going to do a subject profile for the McDonnells. Do you remember? Did it ever get done?'

He paused before answering. 'It was on the list, but I never did it. Other stuff kept taking priority.'

'That's what I thought. Oh, well.'

She knew him well enough to know that he wouldn't leave it there, and left a hesitation dangling in the conversation between them, waiting for him to fill it. She could almost hear him smiling. Eventually he said, 'You want me to do a profile for you?'

He was in the office with other people listening, of course. Otherwise his response might have been a whole lot cheekier.

'Can you do it on the quiet?'

'Urgently?'

'Doesn't have to be long. Just the latest intel, risks, warnings.

Anything that looks interesting. Check with Sam before you do it; she might have some new stuff.'

'Sure,' he said. 'Leave it with me.'

Waterhouse was an arse. He'd turned his back on her and was walking away without so much as a goodbye. Lou had met officers like him before, but fortunately not many.

'Stephen – wait a minute. I'd like a word.'

When she caught up and stood in front of him so that he could not ignore her, or walk past, she checked to see if anyone was in earshot. The other participants of the meeting were continuing to walk away from them, down the corridor.

'I'm sure you're probably having a very bad day, so maybe we could just start again. I'm here to help, and if there's anything my team can do, let me know. In the meantime, I'd like to speak to Scarlett, and then the family.'

The tone of her voice was firm but calm, and anyone else might have capitulated and agreed with anything she had just said. But, as she'd thought, Waterhouse had been worn down by his years in the Job, and compromise was something that didn't come easily. Nor, it seemed, did apology. Even so, what she got was a lot more than she had expected.

'You're right, it's been a shitty week, let alone day. You can go along with Caroline, if you think it'll help. And by all means, if you want to go and see the family. There's nothing new they can tell us for Op Pentameter, I'm sure. So knock yourself out.'

'Thank you,' Lou said. She'd been on the verge of asking what constituted a shitty week for him, since the moment she'd mentioned it there had been a flicker behind his eyes, as though she'd reminded him of something he'd been trying to forget. But he turned aside quickly and continued on his way – heading down the stairs to the basement, no doubt, instead of taking the lift. Lou wondered if he had a problem with lifts or was just trying to avoid getting stuck in a confined space with her for a moment longer.

Caro Sumner was waiting for her in reception. This time there was eye contact, a warm smile.

'You don't remember me,' she said, 'but I'm not surprised. We only met the once, at the Cold Case review five years ago. You were in the middle of your OSPRE process.'

'I'm sorry,' Lou said. 'You were with the Met, weren't you?'

'That's right. I transferred over, in the end. Have you got time for a coffee?'

Lou looked at her watch. Just past five – there was no point setting off now, anyway. She would just get stuck on the dual carriageway with everyone else.

'I would really like that, thanks. What's happening with her?'

She didn't need to use the name, not here in reception with several people within earshot.

Caro said, 'Don't worry. We've booked her into the Travel Inn tonight. I was going to take her over there later. You can come with me, if you like?'

'Thanks. That would be great. I need to call back into the incident room first, if that's okay?'

'Sure. I was going to go home first anyway. I can meet you there.'

They went into the canteen together. The kitchen was long closed, but there was a whole variety of vending machines at their disposal. Caro went for the coffee machine and came back with something that looked like muddy water. Lou got a can of Coke and a bag of crisps, wondering whether this would end up being dinner.

The canteen was empty, thankfully.

'I'm sorry about the boss,' Caro said, when Lou joined her at a table under the window. It was dark outside, felt like midnight already.

Lou smiled. 'I've met worse, believe me.'

'He's not so bad when you get to know him. Unfortunately Scarlett is a small part of the investigation here – her appearance has just thrown everything up in the air. He's desperate to get some arrests, and he thought Scarlett would just unravel everything neatly for him. Trouble is, she's not talking.'

'She must have been through a lot. Unimaginable things.'

'That's what he doesn't seem to get. Anyway – luckily he's got us, right?'

'You been here long?'

'Six months,' Caro said.

'Enjoying it?'

'Most of the time. Better than where I was before, anyway.'

Lou didn't ask. 'So what's the plan for Scarlett?'

Caro sipped her coffee. 'They've applied to get her the forty-five days' support under the National Referral Mechanism. At least that would mean we could get her some help while she needs it. She'll need to co-operate, though – and there's some discussion about whether it's possible to be trafficked back into your own country.'

'What about her family?'

'Apparently they're on their way back from Spain.'

'Apparently?'

'I'm not convinced. The last we heard this morning, they've managed to get the travel company to subsidise them on a charter flight home tomorrow. I believe they had been planning to stay out there and finish the holiday, though, when it looked as if they were going to have to pay for new tickets to come back early.'

Lou let this information sink in. Their daughter had been missing, presumed by everyone to have been murdered and disposed of. No trace of her for ten years. And now she had been found, and this wasn't important enough to bring them home from holiday?

'Then they must have heard from her,' she said.

'That's what we thought, but Clive denied it over the phone.' There was no way anyone's budget was going to stretch to a flight out to Spain, so all discussions with the family had been conducted by telephone.

'That's insane. Where do they think she's been? You'd think they'd be rushing back.'

'I think it's all to do with the other daughter, Juliette. She's got some sort of mental health problem by all accounts; they take her on holiday every year and she gets upset with routines being disrupted.'

Lou drank her Coke from the can. It was icy cold and made her shiver, but the sugar was beginning to give her a buzz. Thoughts and questions were bombarding her from every angle. Memories of Juliette – she'd been thirteen when Scarlett vanished. Lou had met her, and even then she'd thought her odd. But back then – inexperienced, as much as she hated to admit it – she'd put it down to her being a teenager, and deeply traumatised by her sister's disappearance. 'She did attempt suicide a couple of months after they got back from Greece,' she said, remembering. 'Paracetamol, I think. After that they tried to keep her away from all the drama.'

'The boss is totally focused on the trafficking stuff, you know. He isn't bothered about the family, since they're not to blame for her going missing, for her being trafficked. He's torn between wanting to get shot of her before the press gets involved, and waiting to hear what she's got to say.'

Of course: there had been that mention of Nigel Maitland. To all outward appearances a respectable farm owner, Maitland had apparent connections to organised crime. He'd never been convicted of

66

anything, but his name kept coming up in intelligence reports – and, after a young woman, Polly Leuchars, had been murdered on his property last year, Nigel's business, along with that of his daughter, Flora, had been closely scrutinised. Lou knew as well as any of her colleagues that Nigel Maitland was up to something. The trouble was proving it.

'What's the connection with Maitland and the McDonnells?'

'There's historic intel suggesting that Maitland is the transport man for the McDonnells' trafficking operation.'

'Oh,' Lou said, disappointed. She had seen the same intelligence. And, last year, boxes containing stolen passports had been found in the back of Flora Maitland's car. The lack of forensic evidence, coupled with Flora's steadfast claims that she had merely found the boxes littering the side of the road and had been planning to take them to the nearest police station, meant there was nothing to connect any of it to her father. In turn, there was not enough to pursue a prosecution. Yet.

'Is that it?' Lou asked.

'There was a suggestion that some of the trafficked women had been put to work in Lewis McDonnell's brothel in Carisbrooke Court.'

'And Scarlett was working as a prostitute there?'

Caro shrugged. 'Hard to say. She was on the premises, but the way she was dressed – jeans, T-shirt – looked like she was just doing reception for them, housekeeping maybe. Or it could have been her night off. She's not answered that particular question. There was also a phone call from a number we believe was in use by Maitland to the phone that was seized from Scarlett during the warrant this morning.'

'That's interesting – so she definitely knows him?'

'We asked her about it, but she was vague. Said at first it must have been a wrong number, then she said she used to get calls on her phone for people who might have been in the flat, because they knew she was there most of the time. Wouldn't commit to anything.'

'But you really think the Maitland-McDonnell network trafficked her? I mean – we did consider that she might have run off, didn't we? Why would they kidnap her in Greece, just to transport her all the way back home? And were they even involved in trafficking ten years ago? Maybe she's just worked her way back to Briarstone and she's working for them?'

'Oh, that's what we considered, too. But she won't say a word about them. It's like she's scared – terrified.'

Lou shook her head. Poor Scarlett. As desperate as everyone was to find out where she'd been for the last ten years, they were going to have to take things slowly with her.

'But she's also terrified of meeting her family again.'

Intel Reports on Carl McVey – Op Trapeze

5x5x5 Intelligence Report

Date: 1 October 2013

Officer: PC 9921 EVANS

Subject: Op Trapeze – murder of Carl McVEY DOB
            29/09/1970

Grading: B / 2 / 4

It is believed that Carl McVEY was involved in money laundering for the MAITLAND-McDONNELL Organised Crime Group (ref: OCG 041). He used his businesses in Briarstone town centre including the Railway Tavern in Queen Street and the Newarke in Cavendish Lane in order to do this. He also owned the Ferryman pub and restaurant in Baysbury.

5x5x5 Intelligence Report

Date: 1 October 2013

Officer: PC 9921 EVANS

Subject: Op Trapeze – murder of Carl McVEY DOB
            29/09/1970

Grading: B / 2 / 4

Following the death of Carl McVEY (Op Trapeze), the
McDONNELL brothers are not happy. They believe the murder
was due to McVEY falling out with an associate over a drugs
debt and they are looking for someone to blame.

(Research shows: Lewis McDONNELL DOB 21/10/1953,
Harry McDONNELL DOB 06/07/1956)

5x5x5 Intelligence Report

Date: 1 October 2013

Officer: PC 9921 EVANS

Subject: Op Trapeze – murder of Carl McVEY DOB
            29/09/1970

Grading: B / 2 / 4

Carl McVEY was not thought to be a drug-user himself. He was
very careful to keep the dealers away from his licensed
premises as he wanted to 'keep his nose clean'.

Juliette had taken ages to get to sleep. Scarlett had known that this would be the main problem, as the younger girl usually spent a long time reading before turning her light off, often only doing so after Scarlett had nodded off. She didn't know how long she was going to have to wait. She lay in bed – having changed into her pyjamas early and after suggesting an early night – yawning, going on and on about how tired she was in the hope that some of it would subliminally rub off on to her sister – and waited.

Juliette read.

Lying in the semi-darkness, Scarlett had been worried that she might fall asleep after all, wake up to the bright sunshine and stifling heat of the non-air-conditioned room as she had done every other day; but in fact she felt fizzy with excitement at what she was planning to do.

She lay still with her eyes closed and thought of Nico, thought about kissing him and what it would feel like. She constructed an elaborate fantasy around him asking her to marry him, and how she couldn't tell her father and so she just eloped, pretended to be sixteen or eighteen or whatever the legal age for marriage was here in Greece ... and she moved into Nico's apartment with him. Long hours spent together, lying in bed.

He was going to be her first. She had made that decision the same way she had made the decision to sneak out once Juliette was asleep – quite simply, really. She'd thought about it and thought about it all the way to there being no possible alternative. She wanted him, and she could already tell from the way he had looked at her, the way he'd smiled all the way up to his eyes, the way he'd tucked that strand of hair behind her ear with a hand that might just have been trembling with the force of his feelings for her, that he wanted her just as much.

He was a boy, after all, so probably even more.

She thought a lot about how it would feel and wondered if it would hurt. And whether her parents would be able to tell. She thought about where she was going to get a condom, in case he didn't have one. Of course she couldn't get one herself. He would have one, or she would send him off to a bar or pub and make him get one from the toilets. She wouldn't do it without, of course.

If her father found out – any of this, anything at all – she was dead. And of course, if she ended up pregnant, then he would find out. Her only chance was to not get pregnant.

Nico. His dark eyes, his smile ... she wondered about his family, where they were. If he was working to support them – working to keep them fed because something prevented them working themselves. Or he might be an orphan, someone who had struggled all the time he'd been growing up, living on his wits, taking whatever job came along.

When they were married Scarlett would get a good job, as a translator or something like that – or she would be manager of a fashion shop in the market square, selling silks and furs to the tourists and telling them how fabulous they looked. Or she would write articles about being young and married and living in a foreign country, and sell them to the newspapers and magazines back in the UK. And her parents would read the articles and regret their behaviour towards her – and Cerys would read them and be insanely jealous of her new life with her handsome, gentle, caring husband.

Juliette moved, stretched out an arm, *finally* turned out the bedside light. Scarlett, her back to her in the twin bed, held her breath and waited, listening to Juliette's breathing.

Now it was dark she realised how tired she was. Tired, and yet excited, so excited. It might happen tonight, after all, even though part of her was resolved to go no further than a kiss. Why rush? If he wanted her, if he wanted to be with her, he would wait. That was what she believed to be true: that her virginity was special and precious and not to be given to just anyone.

That was what her dad always said, wasn't it?

Nico wasn't just anyone. He was The One. She'd known him barely two days, talked to him for less than two hours, and yet she was as certain of it as she'd ever been about anything in her whole life. He would be the one to rescue her, to save her from the humiliating restrictions placed on her by her parents. In the darkness, her face turned to the blank white wall, she smiled and hugged herself.

Well, then. She would kiss him. That much was decided. She would see how she felt after that. What if he put his hands on her? The thought of that made her stop for a moment and reconsider. For that was what it was, after all. That was where it started. He would want to touch her. And he would probably want her to touch him. That was the middle ground between a kiss and having sex, the 'sexual contact' made famous by the lie detector tests on *The Jeremy Kyle Show*.

She knew all about that.

Could she do it, with him? Could she actually bring herself to do something like that, through choice?

Wait and see, she thought. *Wait and see how it goes.*

Juliette was breathing deeply. She gave it another five minutes, counting down the snail's pace minutes on the fluorescent minute hand on her wristwatch, and then, slowly, quietly, sat up and turned to look at her sister.

The breathing was regular, deep, the merest hint of a snore catching at the edges of it.

'Juliette?' she whispered.

No response, the breathing the same.

Right, then.

She stood up slowly, making sure the mattress didn't creak beneath her, crept across the room to the bathroom, and shut the door carefully behind her. She had put some clothes into a fabric bag on the hook of the bathroom door, a cover story ready-prepared about it being full of laundry if Juliette asked – which she hadn't. She got dressed in the dark, put her pyjamas into the bag and opened the door with infinite care. From the bed, she could hear Juliette's breathing, unchanged.

The most dangerous part of the enterprise: opening the sliding patio door, and closing it behind her. She had no idea if her parents would still be up – they might be sitting on the patio next door, drinking beer or wine or whatever. The door always made a noise as it opened. If she was caught, she would say she wanted to go for a walk, didn't want to disturb her sister – that it was too hot in the room, and she didn't want to just open the door because if she'd gone back to bed she might have fallen asleep with the door open and they might have been burgled or robbed or murdered in their beds.

Nobody was there. The patio was empty. The bedroom next door was in darkness, the door closed, the air-conditioning unit on the roof humming.

Out here, the noise of the cicadas and the crickets buzzing and drilling was almost deafening. Sandals in hand, she skipped through the shadows to the gate which led to the road and the shops and the market square beyond. When she got out of earshot, she pulled her sandals on and skittered down the road, tugging her skirt a little lower.

It was so busy! She hadn't expected that. So many people, so many drunk people – and the bars all noisy with a constant thud-thud of the Euro-pop beat that was everywhere. People staggering around her, seemingly oblivious – and pushing into her, knocking her off balance. Blokes shouting and swearing at each other, beer bottles being dropped, swung around, girls with their arms around each other for support or sitting in the gutter. One girl puking, on her side, on the ground, and then a distant wail of some kind of emergency vehicle heading towards them.

The darkness was disorientating. It was like a negative image of the town in the daytime, the tourist shops mostly closed and in darkness, the bars and restaurants lit up with neon of every colour, flashing.

She had gone too far, skirted the market square somehow, because suddenly there was the Pirate Bay, transformed into a nightclub, the terrace outside heaving with people drinking and smoking and shouting to make themselves heard above the crashing beat.

How was she going to find him with all these people?

She pushed her way to the bar, conscious of her height and all these people and the fact that she was on her own. How was anyone going to believe she was eighteen? Behind the bar was a big Greek man along with all the other young bar staff who were dashing between customers, serving up beers and mixers and pitchers full of cocktails. He was sitting on a bar stool at the end, smoking a cigarette and with a newspaper spread out over his enormous thighs. This must be Nico's boss – what was his name? Began with a V ... Maybe Nico came on here after the pizza restaurant closed.

'Hey, Vasilis!' someone called out, and when the man looked up and raised his hand in an acknowledging wave Scarlett made a decision and approached him.

'Excuse me,' she said, and then louder when the man did not apparently hear her, 'Excuse me! Vasilis!'

He looked at her with displeasure and then surprise and then amusement.

'Can you tell me where I can find Nico?'

'Who you want?'

'Nico. He works here.'

'I have no Nico work here.'

'Oh. Well – I don't know . . .'

One of the other bar staff shouted something across to him in Greek and laughed, and Vasilis laughed, and said, 'I know who you look for. He is at Leonardo.'

'Leonardo?'

'Is in the centre. He work there on Tuesdays.'

'You mean the pizza place?'

'Yes, yes. Pizza.' He laughed, showing four yellow teeth.

The restaurant must stay open late, then. The Pirate Bay was about a hundred metres from the market square, she realised, navigating through the crowds of people. She was scared. All around her, men and women who were older and taller, and all of them drunk and loud, were pressing against her. A hand went round her middle and grabbed clumsily at her breast, and she shrieked and pulled away and looked round to see nobody in particular. Nobody looking at her, or paying her any attention.

And then suddenly the road opened up and she was in the market square, the fountain in the centre, and hordes of people milling about. There were police officers, she noticed, or at least she assumed that was what they were – uniformed officers standing around the edges of the square, watching everyone.

She made her way to the pizza place where they'd eaten earlier. Chairs were stacked on tables and a young woman was wiping a mop up and down the tiled floor.

'Excuse me,' Scarlett said, and, as she had done with Vasilis, she had to ramp the volume up just to make herself heard. 'Excuse me!'

The young woman stopped mopping and looked up. 'We are closed,' she said.

'I'm looking for Nico,' Scarlett said.

'Who? Who you look for?'

'Nico. The guy who hands out the flyers?'

But the woman just gave an exaggerated shrug and shook her head, and repeated, 'We are closed.'

Scarlett felt her eyes prickle. She walked away, but, turning back to the market square with all the streets leading off it, she couldn't remember which one had brought her here. She walked around the perimeter looking for a landmark she recognised, but all the bars and tourist shops – some of them open, here – looked the same. She wondered about asking one of the uniformed officers for help – but what would they do? They might take her back to the apartment and insist on waking up her father and telling him where they had found her.

The only thing to do was to stand up straight and lift her head and act as if she was eighteen and enjoying herself. Blend in. She was used to that, after all, trying to blend in.

But, as she headed away from the market square down a road that she wasn't sure was right because it was so full of people that she couldn't even see the shops, there were tears pouring down her cheeks.

'Hey, hey!' A man grabbed at her, pulled her round, a strong grip on her upper arm.

'Leave me alone!' She pulled away and started to run, panicking now, pushing people aside and sobbing.

And then – it was so dramatic – he was there, in front of her. 'Hey, Scarlett!'

She collapsed against him, taking deep, gulping, sobbing breaths, unable to speak. His arms went around her back and held her tightly. 'It's okay,' he was saying, and laughing. 'What's the matter?'

But then he pulled her away from the crowds of people, the shouting ones, the drunk ones who were staggering and lurching, into a side street. And he sat her down on a low wall. It was dark here; she could see her feet and didn't want to raise her head. She was still afraid, even with Nico here next to her, his arm heavy across her shoulders. Tucking her head in against his chest, she felt herself trembling. This had been such a mistake, such a stupid idea . . . what had she been thinking?

'Did somebody hurt you? What happened?'

'I need to go back to the apartment,' she said at last, still the odd shuddering sigh taking her over.

'Why go back? You just got here. It's okay. I'm here.'

She raised her head to look at him, wanting to say the words *I'm fifteen, I'm only fifteen* but not quite managing them. And instead of saying anything he bent his head and kissed her. As if he knew.

It felt so different, awkward, even though he was gentle. When his tongue started moving against hers she started to panic again and pulled away.

'Sorry,' she said. 'I'm sorry.'

His fingers stroked her upper arm. 'Beautiful Scarlett,' he said, his voice quiet, the accent so sexy. And then, to her surprise, 'Come. I take you back. Where do you stay? What hotel?'

'It's the Aktira Studios. You know it?'

'I know.'

He stood up and held out his hand. She took it and got to her feet. He kept hold of her hand, tightly. 'I don't want you to be scared.'

'I'm not scared of you,' she said, as they started to walk back the way they had come. He was still holding her hand.

It was a lie. She was afraid of him, or, more specifically, she was afraid of how she felt when he was with her. She was afraid of the feelings deep inside, bubbling to the surface, where everyone could see.

And they walked down another side street, and another, and then they came out the other side of the market square and she realised she was nearly back up at the resort. There was the shop where she'd bought the moisturising lotion for her mum – how had she not recognised it, earlier? And the throngs of drunk people were thinning out, and after another couple of hundred metres it was just the two of them, strolling hand in hand. She could hear the sound of the sea, the waves tumbling and sucking, now that the pounding of the music had died away.

He hadn't spoken since they had left the side street, but there was no tension in his hand. He held her hand gently, casually, as though she might let it slip from his at any moment.

She could see the apartment block on the right hand side, the lights in the pool making a beautiful pale blue glow. Her steps were slowing.

'This is where I'm staying,' she said, quietly. 'Thank you for walking me home.'

He turned towards her. 'You are welcome. You don't be scared any more.'

He took her other hand in his, held both of them as though they were going to start dancing. The thought of this made her smile. The fear had subsided now, and she was feeling stupid. Why had she freaked out like that? Why hadn't she stayed with him, in the town? They could have gone to a bar or something; they could be in a club . . .

She moved closer to him, wondering how to do this. It felt weird, but right. He smiled, a lazy, confident smile. And then put his hand on her cheek, stroked it tenderly, and pulled her close for another kiss. He was good at letting her set the pace. This time he didn't open his mouth, so she did. Invited him in. It was gentle, tender.

'Goodnight,' he said, stepping back, his eyes on her, his hands pulling away.

She watched him go. He was dragging his heels, reluctant. She loved that, loved that he couldn't bear to stop looking. When he turned away, at last, she called after him, 'Wait!' Ran up to him and threw herself against him, into his open arms, and he swung her round and buried his face in her neck. They were both laughing. 'I don't want to go inside yet,' she said.

'It's late,' he said.

'Come to the beach with me,' she said, astounded at her own audacity.

He didn't answer straight away. Then he was pulling her arms gently away from his neck. 'It's late,' he said. 'I will see you again, yes?'

She pouted. 'Nico.'

And a big smile as he left her, walking away. A backward wave, and he blew her a kiss.

Minutes later, sliding the patio door open, Scarlett crept into the room as quietly as she could, sandals clutched in one hand.

She froze when she realised the light was on next to Juliette's bed. Juliette, sitting up in bed, was reading her book again. Bizarrely, Scarlett felt the need to look at her watch – it was almost three in the morning.

There was an odd sort of silence. Juliette didn't look up from her book or even acknowledge Scarlett's return, and for a crazy moment Scarlett wondered if her sister had even noticed that the bed next to hers was empty. Who knew? It was entirely possible. Her sister was peculiar and, although it was the elephant in the room at every family occasion, she was getting more and more strange as the years passed.

Scarlett went into the bathroom and got back into her pyjamas, stuffing her clothes back into the bag hanging on the back of the door. When she came out, the light was still on. Juliette hadn't moved. She got into bed and turned her back on her sister, her heart pounding. Part of her just wanted to go with it, assume that Juliette's silence now indicated her intention to remain silent on this matter in future also.

After a few moments she heard the sound of a page turning. If it was possible for the sound of a page turning to be loaded with unspoken meaning, it was exactly that.

Eventually Scarlett could stand it no longer. She gave a huge sigh and flopped over in bed to face her sister.

'Jul?'

No reaction, no acknowledgement. Another page was turned, slowly.

'Juliette!' The hushed whisper, getting louder.

'What?' came the reply, finally, but without looking up from her book.

'You won't say anything, will you? To Dad, I mean?'

Silence again.

After a few moments, Scarlett turned her face back to the wall and closed her eyes. There was no point pursuing things. When Juliette didn't want to talk, she didn't. If she was reading, she wouldn't talk. Scarlett was lucky to have had that single word out of her. She would try again in the morning.

And although she was tired, her eyes heavy, her heart was buzzing with the kiss. With the taste of him, the feel of his warm, strong arms around her. And tomorrow she would see him again.

LOU – Thursday 31 October 2013, 18:53

Lou had been expecting the Major Incident room to be in darkness, but, when she keyed in the security code and opened the door, all the lights were on.

She headed past empty desks towards the goldfish bowl of an office at the end, and jumped half a mile when she heard a voice behind her. 'Hey.'

'Jesus Christ! You made me jump ...'

Jason put his arms around her waist, lowering his face into her neck and nuzzling her. She put her arms around him and hugged him tightly. 'It's good to see you. I missed you.'

And then she pulled back. She couldn't let that go on, much as she wanted to.

'What are you doing here, anyway?'

'Sam let me in. She only went about ten minutes ago.'

Although Jason was vetted to the appropriate level to work on any of Lou's jobs, it was on a strictly need-to-know basis. He wasn't on any of her jobs currently – and so he was not supposed to be in here.

'I did that profile for you. I figured you wouldn't want me to email it.'

There was something in his tone. She pulled away from him, out of the circle of his arms. 'What did you find?'

'You should read it. It's on your desk. I'll go get you a coffee. Unless you want to go home now?'

He went to get her a coffee from the vending machine outside the canteen. She couldn't take the profile out of the office, and, now that he'd indicated there was something in it that couldn't be emailed, she needed to know what it was.

Subject Profile on the McDonnells

SUBJECT PROFILE: Lewis McDONNELL DOB 21/10/1953

Inference

Lewis McDONNELL is the principal subject of Organised Crime Group 041 (MAITLAND-McDONNELL) and is believed to be involved in the trafficking of vulnerable women and girls from mainland Europe into the UK. The group is also believed to be importing tens of kilos of Class A (cocaine and heroin) which comes into the UK via a fishing vessel berthed in Knapstone harbour. Trafficking is the main criminality of the group, with the drug importation becoming increasingly profitable for them.

Intelligence

Recent intelligence suggests the following key points:

– Lewis McDONNELL had a disagreement with Nigel MAITLAND DOB 17/12/1958 over their trafficking enterprise. MAITLAND, who arranges transport, is thought to want a larger share of the profits, and McDONNELL is considering cutting him out. He is looking for an alternative transport man and believes he has found one. (14/11/12 E/2/1)

– The McDONNELL brothers used Paul 'Reggie' STARK DOB 04/05/1982 to provide security until recently, when he became unreliable. Since then they have been using Gavin

PETRIE DOB 17/03/1975 instead, although the brothers see him as a 'loose cannon'. (21/08/13 E/2/1)

– Nigel MAITLAND and Lewis McDONNELL had an argument at the Newarke pub, Cavendish Lane, Briarstone, on the night of 27 August. Both men were asked to leave by the barman, but only did so when the landlord, Carl McVEY DOB 29/09/1970 (Op Trapeze), intervened.

– Lewis McDONNELL has associates who run brothels in Leeds, Manchester and Liverpool. Some of these brothels are provided with staff who have been trafficked from Europe by OCG 041. It is also believed that Lewis McDONNELL is running a brothel in Briarstone. Intelligence suggests this might be in Carisbrooke Court.

– A shipment of cocaine was due to arrive for Lewis McDONNELL at the end of August destined for his associates in the north, but something went wrong.

Recommendations

– identify the new transport route for OCG 041's trafficking enterprise

– source tasking on Nigel MAITLAND

– identify associates of the McDONNELLs in the north of England

19:03

Ten minutes later Lou was sitting at her desk, Jason across from her in the only other chair, a low visitor's chair that had been purloined from reception when they'd redecorated it last year. The Facilities

Team had a container hidden behind the training school where old furniture went to die, and Lou had gone there herself with Ali Whitmore to try to salvage some desks rather than spend her very snug budget on new ones. The chair had a cushioned seat covered with a hairy sort of grey fabric that might or might not have been its original colour, the corner frayed away to reveal a stained sponge interior.

He was sitting with one leg across the other knee, his hand on his ankle, watching her.

'There's not much,' she said in the end.

'No,' he said. 'Just those few from August, and then, before that, nothing much since last year. There are a couple on Carl McVey that mention the McDonnells, but you've already seen those.'

'Anything else on Maitland specifically?'

'Nothing other than what's there.'

'Thanks,' she said. 'I do appreciate it. I know you've got other stuff to do.'

'You can't tell me what it's about, right?'

'No.'

He shrugged, used to this. 'You don't have an analyst.'

'I can ask Annabel when she gets back from annual leave. Don't worry about it.'

'You saw the stuff about McVey?'

'Yep. Is there any more on him?'

'Nothing recent. One from March with a list of his businesses, and one from July where he was seen with the McDonnells and one of the Petries. The others I think you've seen already.'

Typical, Lou thought. But it was a useful starting point, and, although it wasn't a link between McVey and Ian Palmer, it was a link between McVey and the McDonnells, which meant that being involved with Scarlett Rainsford, found working in Lewis McDonnell's brothel, wasn't going to be a complete waste of time in terms of Op Trapeze. Small relief.

'You look shattered,' Jason said.

The clock on the end of the far wall told her it was past seven. 'I've got to go out in an hour. Got to meet someone from SB – and I've piles to do apart from that.'

'You always have piles to do. You never get to the bottom of the pile.' It sounded like a rebuke, but he was smiling.

'If I don't do it now, it will be a bigger pile in the morning.'

He sighed. 'Okay, here's the deal. I'm going to go away now and get you something to eat. I'll be back in a while.'

He stood and came round to her side of the desk, twisted her chair around and kissed her. It was an I'm-in-charge-here kind of kiss, which didn't allow for argument, and, despite everything she had to work through, for a moment she was tempted. If she touched him, that would be it. She could reach out right now and put her arms around him and then she could pull him closer and—

But he was in charge of the kiss, and therefore it ended. 'Get back to work, Louisa. I'll see you soon.'

Tease, she thought.

19:30

Jason came back half an hour later. He knocked on the door of the main office, pretending that he didn't know the door code, even though it hadn't changed since the job they'd worked on in this room last year.

Lou had been head-down replying to all the admin emails that had stacked up. Leave requests. Case review. Taskings requiring her authorisation.

When she crossed the main office her first thought was *That time went by fast*, and then, when she opened the door, that thought was gone. Not for the first time she was struck by how good-looking he was: the dark hair, the strong jawline, his green eyes. She'd learned to control this, the way she looked at him, not giving anything away. She had to lift her chin, challenging.

It only took a second for this. Then she realised he had a carrier bag that smelled of hot food. Takeaway.

He held it up. 'I brought you a picnic.'

'Oh, my God, I love you.'

She let him in and he followed her back to her little office, and she was glad her back was to him so he couldn't see her cheeks burning. If Sam had brought her food, or Ali, or anyone else on the team, she would have used those exact words – but in this context it had a whole new layer of meaning that was dramatically awkward.

They hadn't used the L word, properly and not jokingly like just now. Not yet.

It had been close a couple of times. A few weeks ago, a rare weekend together, most of Sunday spent in bed with activities that ranged from hard, intense fucking to gentle, tender kisses, from sleep, to sandwiches and a bottle of wine, to long moments face-to-face, just looking. And she'd wanted to say it, longed to say it. But he had to say it first.

He was so relaxed about everything, so easy. It seemed as if the relationship for him was entirely without an agenda. He would not push it forward, would not demand more time with her, suggest moving in, complain about her untidiness, pressure her to meet her family, nothing like that; when she'd commented on this –

positively, as if it was refreshing that he gave her so much space –
he had moved his shoulders in a lazy shrug and said, 'Hey, I'm just
grateful.'

'I am so hungry you would not believe,' she said, unpacking polystyrene containers. A chicken kebab, judging by the smell and the bits
of shredded lettuce hanging out of the side once she'd unwrapped the
paper parcel.

'I would totally believe. What did you eat today?'

'Oh, I don't know. Stuff.' She had a mouthful of it already –
chicken and lettuce and pitta and, yes, oh, brilliant, he'd remembered:
chilli sauce. Lots of it.

The chicken kebab said lots of things. It said, *I am taking care of
you*. It said, *I am going to make you eat healthily* – she knew that,
of all the food choices available to Jason Mercer at this time of the
evening in the town centre, a chicken kebab was the most balanced
meal. She would have chosen Indian, or at a push Chinese, or as a
third option a great big fuck-off pizza with extra garlic bread. And
she could eat all those things and not put on any weight because she
was wired all the time, running from one job to the next, so it wasn't
her weight that was concerning him but his desire to make sure all
the food groups were represented and that she had something with
vegetables in it, even if it was just a bit of shredded iceberg lettuce.
The only possible alternative to a chicken kebab, for Jason, would
have been for him to drive all the way home and cook her something.

Jason was a big guy – built like a hockey player, of course, whatever that meant. He was like a wall, without the sleekness of a
body-builder's muscle-definition. Just strong and solid. And you
didn't get to be as fit and healthy as he was without eating decent
food.

He ate his own kebab watching her, and then from the pocket of his hoodie he brought forth two bottles of water. She wanted a can of Coke to wash it all down and was tempted to run to the vending machine to satisfy the urge for caffeine and sugar, but didn't want to incur his disapproval.

'So,' he said, between mouthfuls, 'are you done?'

'I'm never done, you know that. As I said, I've got to go out again in a minute.'

He rolled his eyes. His phone beeped and he pulled it from the back pocket of his jeans, before unlocking the screen and looking at the message. He laughed, thumbed a short reply. 'Mike says hi.'

'Oh. Say hi back.'

'It would be good to get the two of you together more. He's all right, really, you know?'

'I'm sure he is. It's not that I have anything against him; it's more that you two get together and you suddenly turn twice as Canadian as you were five minutes before.'

He laughed at this. 'What do you mean? I *am* Canadian; how can I get more Canadian?'

'You want to know? The volume gets cranked up, your accent and the idiom gets so strong that I don't have a clue what you're both talking about, but the likelihood is that you're talking about your childhood or some food that we don't have over here, or hockey which I still don't understand, so ... I don't know. I just think you're both having such a great time I might as well not be there.'

'Well, I enjoy being with you and with him, too. I'll be more careful that I don't leave you out.'

'I'm a big girl. I'm not getting all precious about it.'

Lou had finished her kebab and was bundling up the wrapper.

'So who are you meeting?' he asked.

'Caro Sumner from SB. We're going to talk to a witness.'

'And after? You coming over?'

'It might be really late,' she said. 'Best not.'

What she had said must have come across wrong because he stood up abruptly, packing the empty polystyrene and paper into the striped carrier bag. 'Sure,' he said. 'I'll see you tomorrow night?'

She drew a blank for a moment.

'Hockey?'

'Oh, right! Yes, of course. I'll do my best.' He had an important hockey game, and, back when things had been reasonably quiet, she'd promised to go.

'Well, you know, only if you've got the time to spare.'

'Jason, you know I can't promise. But if I can be there, I will,' she repeated. She wanted to point out that he was being too sensitive, that he should know she had other priorities. Other men she'd had relationships with would play this game – get all pissed off on her for no good reason, go off in a sulk. It was hockey, not as though he was collecting a Nobel Prize or something – he wouldn't even notice if she was there or not. And it wasn't as if he didn't have support. Lou remembered the first time she'd gone to a cup match, waiting afterwards in the foyer of the rink outside the players' changing rooms along with a crowd of teenage girls, all wearing Jaguars jerseys, loud and overexcited. When Jason and his teammate Travis had come out they were all over him – asking questions, getting their shirts signed, taking selfies. At the time she'd thought it was hilarious. Later on she'd worked out that she must have looked like one of the girls' mums, standing by the door waiting for all the adulation to finish.

'Thanks for dinner,' she said feebly.

'No problem.'

Without thinking, Lou said, 'Will you come to my cousin's wedding with me?'

That stopped him. He paused for a moment, then sat back down. 'You serious?'

Lou had that feeling of having accidentally opened a massive can of worms. 'Of course. It's on the twenty-third, just in the evening. You've probably got hockey.'

'Nope. Not that weekend.'

'Great,' Lou said. 'I'd like to apologise in advance for anything my mother might say to you.'

He looked at her, studying her face. Lou was trying her best to look excited.

'I'm sure they're not as bad as all that,' he said.

'Tell me again after the twenty-third,' Lou replied.

Jason smiled and nodded. There was something going on behind those eyes, something Lou couldn't quite make out. He certainly didn't look especially happy. *This is a big deal for me*, she wanted to say.

'Okay, then, sure,' he said. 'I'll come with you. At least it might mean I get to spend a bit of time with you, right?'

Ouch. That was it, then? He was getting needy?

He came round the desk and kissed her, despite the kebab breath. 'I'll see you tomorrow night.'

Tempted as she was to carry on working, she was tired and vaguely pissed off, and now she was going to have to go and meet Scarlett Rainsford for the very first time.

SCARLETT – Sunday 24 August 2003, 14:10

Somehow, Yelena had managed to fall asleep. Scarlett watched her, stared at the bumps of her spine showing through the thin, pale skin of her back. If there had been a blanket she would have pulled it over her, despite the stifling heat. There was something about the sight of her bare back, her top ridden up, that made Scarlett want to cover it.

She'd cried, again, trying to keep quiet so as not to wake the other girl, snuffling into her sleeve which was filthy with grime and dried blood. She wished she could sleep too, but the heat and the sunlight and the drilling headache made it impossible. The water was all gone. She had already drained every drop from the bottles that were scattered around the room. *Thirsty, so thirsty. Try not to think about it.*

Eventually she collected all the bottles and moved them into the corner of the room, behind the bucket, which was now stinking badly. There. Now she wouldn't have to look at them.

Yelena stirred, moving over on to her back, one hand thrown casually over her head. Scarlett looked at her and her eyes opened. Almost immediately her face crumpled and she put both hands over her eyes.

'It's okay,' Scarlett said, although it was clearly far from okay. Nothing was okay, never would be again.

23:30

They were in a minibus this time, not the van that had brought Scarlett here; driving back through the winding roads and then, eventually, on to some sort of motorway where the engine whined at the demands that were being placed upon it. The interior of the vehicle was heaped with boxes, suitcases, holdalls, all over the seats at the front. Where they were, at the back, some of the seats had been removed to make a space on the floor. The two windows in the back doors of the minibus were painted over, allowing for a dull light to filter through to their space at the back, but not giving them any way to see out or attract attention from other drivers. In this disorientating space they were sitting facing each other, with their backs against the sides of the bus.

Yelena and Scarlett had been moved quickly, unexpectedly, before they'd had time to prepare or, worse, make use of the bucket.

Right now the bucket was one of the things Scarlett was thinking about a lot. More so because when they'd clambered into the back of the bus there had been another six-pack of water bottles already in there. They had drunk two each, somehow avoiding any spillages as the minibus jolted and swerved, and now they were staring at the remaining two bottles as though they were some sort of talisman.

Once again, the room had become the place she had begun to feel was her space – being taken from it by force had made her feel panicky. Now, her heart had stopped thumping and she was almost relaxed, soothed, by the rhythm of the wheels on the road underneath them.

Yelena was sitting wide-eyed. They'd hardly spoken, even though they had spent the whole afternoon together. Scarlett had so much to say – they should have been plotting escape, planning who was going to leap on the back of the first guy who opened the door and who was going to kick him in the balls. Instead, they were wary of each other. Despite her initial kindness – if that was what you could call it – Scarlett still didn't feel any sort of warmth from the girl. She didn't know what nationality she was, either. Eastern European was her best guess, but she could have been way off there too. And she was older, clearly, than Scarlett. She wanted to feel that Yelena would protect her, would stand up for her because she was still just a kid and vulnerable, but she didn't feel that. She felt as though Yelena would rip her head off if she thought it would do her any good.

She's not the enemy, Scarlett thought. *She's all I've got. And I'm all she's got, too.*

Scarlett longed to stand up and stretch out. She needed the toilet, badly. It had been a mistake to drink those bottles of water so quickly, but she hadn't been able to help herself – so thirsty, so desperate for a drink. She had only used the bucket in the room once, in all the time she was in there – and her urine had been dark and malodorous, telling her all she needed to know about how dehydrated she was. And the next stage after that, she knew having suffered many times before, was a bladder infection, and quite probably, if it wasn't addressed with antibiotics, a kidney infection too.

At least this time nobody could accuse her of inflicting it on herself.

That one time, stressed with schoolwork and Dad and home life and worrying about Juliette and how she didn't seem to talk any more, she'd just forgotten to drink enough and before she knew it she was in agony every time she had to pee. And the inevitable visit to the doctor with her mother, and the shame of it – discussing it over the kitchen table with *him*, in front of Juliette too.

'She's doing it for attention, of course; she always does things like this.'

'This isn't about you, Clive. She hasn't deliberately timed it to coincide with your work project.'

'Every time – *every* time something big is going on at work, Scarlett has to come down with some illness. And this one's because she's not drinking enough water? It's drama, pure and simple. All about the drama.'

She'd sat at the kitchen table between them with tears rolling down her cheeks, not making a sound, not commenting even though she wanted to tell them both where to stick it, and even though she kept her silence this too became a focus for them.

'Oh, do shut up, Scarlett. You're not a baby.'

'See? *See?* It's all about her. All about her and her petty little manipulations . . . '

Leave me alone leave me alone leave me alone leave me alone . . .

She could feel it now, that gnawing ache in her lower back, the dragging feeling in her lower abdomen. Her bladder was full but brewing infection. She wanted to cry but had no tears left – what good would it do? It just gave her a headache to deal with along with everything else.

She had two options: try to talk to Yelena, or retreat into her own head and think of other things. Anything. She tried to remember something that had made her happy, a time when she had felt free and relaxed.

At the leisure centre, with Cerys. Laughing because some of the boys from the college had been mucking around in front of them with some older girls – girlfriends, probably – and then one of them had gone to pull another one into the swimming pool and in revenge had had his shorts pulled down while his arms were occupied in the wrestling. Rough and tumble. All good fun. Lifeguards whistling to draw attention to it even more. And they'd seen his bum and as they'd pushed him over his cock was wobbling around too. And Scarlett had actually recoiled and hidden her eyes behind her hand.

Cerys had laughed at that even more than she'd been laughing at the wrestling match. The group had been asked to leave.

They'd walked home from the bus stop the long way round, because Cerys had bought a pack of ten Marlboro and wanted to smoke on the way home. She'd offered them to Scarlett, who had refused. The thought of them – ugh. No way. They strolled along the pavement, kicking at bits of gravel, sending it skittering ahead of them. Scarlett's All Stars dusty, Cerys scuffing a pair of her eldest sister's kitten-heel boots. She didn't care, although Aimee would most likely kill her when she saw them. That was the price Aimee paid for having small feet.

In the back of the van, the refuge Scarlett had taken in her daydream came to an end.

Perhaps it wouldn't be so bad.

It hadn't been that bad so far, after all, had it? They'd given her water, and yes, they'd kept her prisoner and made her piss in a bucket; they hadn't given her proper food – just the pizza – but apart from that one fist in her face they hadn't hurt her. It could have been worse, far worse, after all. And the fist had been because she had started screaming. Since then, since she'd complied with them and behaved herself, nothing.

So that was it. She would go along with it, see what happened next. She had the choice to fight back, make it difficult for them, try to escape – but equally she had the choice to comply, keep her head down, bide her time.

Nico had betrayed her, of course.

She'd been denying it, but the fact that the men had mentioned him by name meant that they knew him. And they were bad people, so it must mean that Nico was bad, too. Nico had said he had a baby sister, and that made her think about Juliette. How would she be coping, with Scarlett gone? Maybe she hadn't even really noticed; after all, most of the time she was in her own safe little bubble. Scarlett thought it was just the way Juliette was: the real world was less enjoyable to her than the worlds she inhabited while she was reading. Good luck to her, Scarlett thought.

There had been discussions, before the holiday and even more fervently now that she was so obviously not quite right. Scarlett had heard them, sitting out on their patio next door with clinking bottles of beer, while Juliette read her book in bed and Scarlett was sitting by the open patio door, gulping at the fresh, still air, biding her time.

'You're too tough on them sometimes, Clive,' her mum was saying. 'Juliette hardly speaks at all now.'

'She's just being a teenager,' her father replied.

'Scarlett wasn't like that at her age.'

'Scarlett's the other way. Talks too much. Doesn't know when to keep quiet.'

'Even so,' her mother said, 'you should be careful. The school notice things; they'll ask questions.'

'Now you're being hysterical,' her father said.

Scarlett had read about Sigmund Freud at school, about hysteria. She had thought then that her father had been born in the wrong century, that he would be well suited to the Victorian era when women did as they were told and any deviation from the norm, any sign of determination, or even just expressing an opinion, could be diagnosed as part of the female condition. Her father seemed to find it by turns fascinating and repugnant, living in a houseful of women.

Her mum wasn't hysterical at all. She was speaking quietly. 'And you're not taking me seriously.'

'That's *enough*.'

There was quiet for a moment, and then some odd noises – breathing, a chair creaking. A minute later, an abrupt scraping noise of one of the metal chairs being pushed back from the tiled floor, and then the other. The patio door opening, and the whirr of the air-conditioning inside their beautifully cool apartment next door, and then the sound of it sliding shut again.

Scarlett waited, her heart thumping. Just the noise of the insects, the rattling song at a hundred different notes and pitches.

Nico was waiting for her in the doorway where he'd taken her that first night, sitting on the step, his feet splayed. When he saw her approach, he got to his feet and held his arms out for her to run into.

And then, the kiss. She had been longing for it all day. And all the things she had wanted to say to him, the conversations she'd played out in her mind, all evaporated in an instant and she had nothing, nothing but the kiss and the way it made her feel.

And, later, they sat on the beach, talking and kissing. He kept distracting her; kissing her neck, running his tongue along her skin until it made her shiver.

'That tickles!'

'Yes,' he said. 'Good, yes?'

'No, not good.'

He laughed and did it some more.

'Can't we go to your place?' she asked. She had asked this already. Sooner or later, she reasoned, he would give in.

'No,' he said. 'I told you. My family is there.'

Nico lived with his brother, who was called Yannis. He had a big family who lived in Athens but Yannis worked in one of the bars in town. Scarlett had asked to meet Yannis, but Nico had said this was not possible. He was working, working. Nico lived with him here, during the summer. In the winter, they packed up and went back to the mainland. And then, when Scarlett had asked if they could go to the house, for some privacy, Nico had told her about the sister-in-law and the children. Three of them. There wasn't a lot of room in the house, and consequently no privacy at all.

'But I want to be with you,' she protested again now. 'I want to be with you properly.'

He didn't seem to understand what she was getting at. 'We *are* together,' he said. 'Together now.' He stroked his fingers up and down her bare arm. Inside she felt hunger for him.

In the end, she sat astride him, her hands on his chest. 'You don't get it,' she said, desire making her bold. Making her into something she was not. For a moment she thought of Cerys – what would Cerys do? Cerys would not be in this situation, she thought. Cerys would have slept with him on that first night, on the beach, in a doorway, wherever the mood took her.

I am Cerys, she thought. *You want to fuck me, Nico, don't you?*

She could feel him getting hard. The thrill of it: that she was making it happen. 'You want me, don't you?'

'Scarlett, of course I want you.'

'Let's do it, then.'

He laughed, which she hated. He was laughing at her because she was just a kid. She pushed her hands against his chest and climbed off him, sitting with her knees drawn up. It was dark down here but they were not alone – people were walking along the sand by the waves. There were couples, too, sharing the sunbeds. Not close enough to see what they were doing. Some of them had brought towels to hide under, as though that made a difference.

He sat up next to her, stroked her cheek softly. She ignored him.

'Hey,' he said. 'Of course I want you. I said that. You did not hear?'

'Why won't you?'

He put his arm, heavy across her shoulders. His skin was hot, and she could feel the warmth of his body radiating towards her. 'You haven't done this before? It is your first time?'

She thought for a moment about lying to him, about what it would mean. But he was concerned about how she felt, of course. So she nodded.

She saw the gleam in his eye, although he hid it immediately. And she took it to mean that he wanted her even more. They all did, didn't they? All men wanted to be the one to take a girl's virginity.

'Your first time should be special,' he said to her.

'It will be, with you. I want it to be you.'

And he kissed her again, more forcefully this time, his tongue pushing into her mouth immediately, claiming her. She felt breathless with it. He pushed her back on to the sand, his hand stroking the skin of her belly. She felt for his hand, trying to guide it lower. And this time he did it: put his hand inside her shorts and his fingers inside her knickers.

It was rough, though, and she flinched. She had a sudden flash of fear, of panic. He must have felt it because he withdrew. Then he put his hand on hers and led it down to his jeans, to the growing hardness that was straining at the denim. 'You see how much I want you, Scarlett?' he whispered against her mouth. And then, quickly, as though he couldn't wait any longer, he unbuttoned his fly and put her hand inside.

This was safer territory: she knew this, knew how to get him off. It took a while. And her arm ached like hell, even though he kept putting his hand in a vice-like grip over hers, and muttering, 'Faster, oh, yeah. Baby. Faster.'

You wanted this, she was telling herself. *This is what you wanted to happen, isn't it?*

And afterwards, when he pulled up his top so that the semen

pumped over her hand and over the skin of his stomach, he kissed her deeply, roughly.

'You can clean me up,' he said.

'What?'

'Lick me, baby. Lick me clean.'

And she thought about saying no, but of course she didn't; she thought about offering him a tissue from the pocket of her shorts, but in the end she did as he asked because she didn't want him to think of her as a kid, disgusting as it was. Maybe this was a test. Maybe if she passed the test he would make love to her properly next time.

'You are good,' he murmured.

'Am I?'

'Very good, baby, very good. You do this before, with English boys?'

'Not really.'

'You are sad?' His fingers traced over her face, touching the corners of her mouth. 'Don't be sad, baby. I look after you. I make you smile.'

'I wish I could stay with you,' she said. 'I wouldn't be sad with you.'

He propped himself up on one elbow so he could look at her.

'It's my stupid family,' she began. 'My mum thinks I'm still just a kid. She tries to make me wear kids' clothes. She won't let me go anywhere. And my dad – he's – he's ...'

Nico stroked her cheek. He was listening. Nobody had ever listened to her before, properly listened, and now that she had someone she didn't even know how to put it into words. She snaked a hand around his neck and pulled him down into a kiss. Another time, she thought. She would tell him everything. But for tonight she just wanted to enjoy being with him, being kissed, being loved.

He walked her back to the apartment after that, and this time he had his arm around her – not just holding her hand, casually – he actually had his arm around her shoulders. Scarlett felt as though something important had happened, something momentous. She felt brave and adult all of a sudden.

He kept stopping to pull her close for kisses, his mouth smiling against hers. He felt it too, she knew it. And, when the apartments came into view, he asked the question before she had the chance to. 'Tomorrow evening, yes? I see you at the same place?'

Yes, yes! Yes, Nico.

And maybe tomorrow – maybe tomorrow he would make love to her, and he would make her complete.

'Scarlett.'

She didn't hear at first, didn't register that the word referred to her; she was too involved in kissing him. But he heard, and pulled away from her sharply. Right away.

'Scarlett!' This time the voice was urgent, angry, and she recognised it.

'Mum!'

Her mother was standing in the gate that led to the apartment complex, arms crossed over her chest. 'What the hell do you think you're doing?'

She started to say, 'Mum, this is Nico . . . ' but when she looked around he was already walking away, fast, along the dark side of the street. As she watched, he broke into a long, loping run.

'Get inside. Now.'

Scarlett was shivering now, although it wasn't cold. 'Don't tell Dad,' she said, quickly, tears starting. 'Please don't tell Dad, please, please!'

Her mum took hold of Scarlett's elbow and yanked her through the gate. 'Shut up,' she hissed. 'Don't you dare make any noise. You're in enough trouble as it is!'

Scarlett was stumbling, her knees shaking with fear, which made her mother tighten her grip even more. She stopped just inside the gate, gripped Scarlett by her upper arms as if she was about to run.

'Please, Dad'll kill me, I know he will – please, I'll just go to bed, I'll be good, I'll . . .'

'What have you done?' her mother demanded. 'What did you do with that boy?'

'Nothing!'

'You were kissing him!'

'That's all, that's all, I promise, I haven't done anything!'

'You're a child, Scarlett, you're just a child. What the hell you're doing out at this time of the night—'

'I'm not a child!'

Her mother started to say something else but then they both heard a noise. Across the other side of the pool, the glass door slid open and her father stood on the patio, looking across to where they were.

'No, no,' Scarlett whimpered.

'See what you've done now?' her mum hissed, although Scarlett couldn't see that she'd made a sound or alerted him in any way. She took her by the upper arm again and dragged Scarlett around the pool, back to the room. Her father stood aside to let them both in.

Scarlett had seen her father angry before, many times. It was such a regular thing that she should not have been surprised, but his fury now was fierce. He kept clenching and unclenching his fists, as though they were itching for contact.

'Where have you been?' he asked.

'I just went for a walk,' Scarlett said, her teeth chattering. 'I got lost. This boy showed me how to get back. That's all, that's all, I promise.'

'What boy?' he asked, looking at her mother.

'She was with a boy.'

'You don't understand what you've done,' her dad said. 'You filthy child.'

'I haven't done anything,' Scarlett said, quietly. She was looking at him, not with defiance, but with tear-filled eyes, beseeching. She knew that avoiding eye contact was one of the triggers, one of the worst things she could do. So she kept looking at him even though the mere sight of him filled her with terror.

'You'd better not have,' her mum said. She was sitting on the sofa next to Scarlett, which was less a show of support and more about staying between her and the door in case she tried to run for it.

'I haven't. I really haven't. He's lovely, you'd like him, he's—'

'She's lying,' her father said.

'I'm not, I'm not lying, I just—'

'She's slept with him,' her mother said.

'Just because that's what you would have done,' Scarlett said.

'How dare you!'

It had provoked him still further, of course, as she had known it would. Maybe she actually wanted it. Maybe she wanted him to kill her, to get it over with. Or for Nico to come and rescue her. That wasn't going to happen, was it? He had run away. Not even looked back.

'Go next door,' said her father to her mother.

'No, Dad, please,' Scarlett said.

'Why?' her mother asked.

'Go and check on Juliette, Annie.'

'She's asleep, she's fine.'

'I said, go and check on Juliette. I will come and get you in a minute.'

'Clive,' her mother said, 'don't.'

'Go!'

Her mother stood. Scarlett watched her sandalled feet, her thin tanned legs, as they moved. The patio door slid open and slid closed.

In her head, she took herself down to the beach. It would be sunny, the sun would be shining warm on her face, and she looked down to see she was wearing white shorts and a floaty chiffon top over a bikini, and she was tanned and fit and she felt happy, and free. She looked down the beach to see Nico coming towards her, waving. She waved back and she saw that he had a small child with him, a small boy with dark hair like his father's, a big smile that showed white teeth, and he was waving too, as hard as he could. The sand under her feet was hot and she walked to the water's edge, little waves coming in and cooling her toes. She stopped to pick up a shell, split in half, the inside of it a perfect spiral; it was pale and glistening with seawater, shining in the sunlight like a jewel.

It's all right, Scarlett, Nico was saying, although she couldn't get his accent right in her head. She was confused, trying to focus on him, on his face, trying to make him speak.

It's all right, it will be okay.

The Vulnerable Victim Suite that had closed down and reopened was in Kingswood Road, a long avenue that began in the town centre and led all the way out past houses and shops and industrial estates to open countryside. The VVS was in a terraced house that looked like every other one in the row: a plain black door that was in need of a lick of paint, a front yard that was paved over, two wheelie bins parked by the front door. Everything illuminated and made less attractive by orange street-lights.

Lou rang the bell and the door was opened a few moments later by Caro Sumner, wearing a navy blue tracksuit top and jeans.

'Come in,' she said, standing aside. 'All right?'

Lou felt suddenly overdressed in her suit and wished she'd thought to go home and change. She didn't want to be intimidating, didn't want to put anything between herself and Scarlett that would make her feel nervous about talking.

'Good, thanks. How's it going?'

'I was just making coffee and a sandwich. Do you want something?'

'Coffee would be good.'

'Right. I'll make it. You can chat to Scarlett.'

She opened the door to what would have been the living room. A young woman was curled into the battered sofa, knees tucked up in front of her, socked feet, the sleeves of a grey hoodie pulled down over her knuckles. She was sitting on a khaki-coloured coat, as if she'd shrugged her way out of it while already sitting, then twisted into it, making it into some sort of a nest. She had cropped dark hair, big eyes. Wary. If Lou had had to bring up the picture of how she'd expected Scarlett Rainsford to look at the age of twenty-five, this would probably have come close.

'Hey,' Lou said. 'How are you doing?'

Scarlett cleared her throat as though she was going to reply, but didn't.

'My name's Lou Smith,' she said. 'Can I sit with you for a while? Caro is going to make some food.'

Scarlett shrugged and her expression changed from wary to bored. Or resigned? Or something between the two. What – or who – had she been expecting, when the door opened?

Lou sat back in the armchair, feet crossed at the ankle, a relaxed, open posture, in the hope that this would compensate for her formal dress.

'Are you a police officer?' Scarlett asked.

'Yes. I was working on the investigation when you first went missing. I wanted to say how sorry I am that we never managed to find you. It's been one of the biggest regrets of my career.'

The girl was staring at her in surprise. Lou was almost not expecting her to reply at all, but eventually she said, 'Probably wasn't your fault.'

'All the same.'

Caro came in with a tray, a plate of sandwiches and three steaming mugs. The sandwiches were of the Happy Shopper variety, spongy white bread with pre-sliced cheese, made in a big pile and then cut in half with some kind of big knife so the slices were sealed in one big concertinaed lump. Lou took one of the mugs and cradled her cold hands around it. 'Thanks, Caro. You're an angel.'

'What did you say your name was?' Scarlett asked.

108

'Lou. My name's Lou,' she answered, swallowing a mouthful of scalding coffee.

'You're, like, something senior?'

'I'm a detective chief inspector, but don't let that put you off.'

Caro was sitting forward in the other armchair, hands clasped over her knees. She hadn't taken a sandwich, Lou noticed, and neither had Scarlett.

Scarlett lowered her feet to the floor slowly, as though her joints were creaking, and reached for the plate of sandwiches. Never taking her eyes off Lou, she took half of the top one and curled her feet back underneath herself, holding the sandwich up to her mouth with both hands before taking a bite and chewing.

Caro made a sound, a little satisfied sigh, and sat back.

'Were you in charge, ten years ago?'

Lou smiled. 'Far from it. I was a detective constable then.'

'Like you,' Scarlett said, turning her big eyes accusingly towards Caro.

'Yes,' Caro said. 'Like me.'

'You got promoted,' Scarlett added, looking at Lou again. 'You must have done something right.'

'Doesn't really work like that, but thanks for the vote of confidence.'

'What do you mean?'

'We have to do exams, portfolios, interviews if we want promotion. I think it's about finding the job that you're best at.'

'And you're a good DCI?'

Scarlett's use of the abbreviation made Lou stop short.

'She's brilliant,' said Caro.

Scarlett nodded. She reached back to the coffee table and placed the sandwich, one semi-circular bite taken out of it, carefully on the edge of the tray.

'I'll talk to you,' she said. 'But not in front of her.'

Lou and Caro exchanged glances.

'We need to head off to the hotel soon, Scarlett,' Caro said. 'Once you've eaten.'

'Why can't I stay here?'

'This place isn't set up for overnight stays,' Lou said. 'It's just supposed to be somewhere quiet for people to talk.'

'I can sleep on the sofa,' Scarlett said.

'A hotel would be nicer, wouldn't it?' Caro said cheerfully. 'Nice shower in the morning, breakfast? Then we'll come back here, if you like.'

Scarlett shrugged, as if she didn't care much either way. 'I don't have money for a hotel,' she said.

'Well, for a couple of days Eden Police Service is going to foot the bill,' Caro said. 'So you don't need to worry about that.'

Scarlett fixed Caro in a stare until the older woman got up and left the room. Above their heads, the video camera pointed its blank black eye directly, quietly, at Scarlett. It didn't matter if Caro was here or next door; she would witness the entire exchange anyway.

'What's going to happen to me?' Scarlett said, when the door closed behind Caro.

'That depends,' Lou said. 'For the time being the officers are working in partnership with other agencies to determine exactly what help they can offer to you.'

'What sort of help?'

'You should get what they call a "period of rest and recovery". They'll get you housing, access to support, counselling, whatever you need. Just time for you to decide what you want to do with your life now.'

'I don't know what I want.'

'I think your family should be here soon. I heard they're flying home tomorrow morning.'

'Yeah. They told me.'

Lou took note of the flat tone, the lack of interest. Understandable really: it had been ten years and in that time Scarlett had survived, somehow, without her mother and her father and her sister. Meeting up with them again was bound to be very strange.

'Do I have to go with them?'

'No. You don't have to do anything.' Lou looked at Scarlett, watched her eyes, then added, 'You don't even have to see them, if you don't want to.'

Scarlett laughed, hoarse. 'Yeah, right.'

'Do you want to see them? Are you ready for that?'

'Don't give me any of that psycho bullshit; that's all I've had from the rest of them. I want to see my mother. I want to see . . . what she looks like, whether she has changed.'

And she tilted her head, her gaze at Lou direct, challenging, unblinking.

Part Two

DEATH IS NOT THE END

Intel Reports on 4 Carisbrooke Court, Briarstone

5x5x5 Intelligence Report

Date: 12 March 2013

Officer: PC 9921 EVANS

Subject: Paul STARK DOB 04/05/1982, Lewis
             McDONNELL DOB 21/10/1953, Harry
             McDONNELL DOB 06/07/1956

Grading: B / 2 / 1

Paul 'Reggie' STARK is working for the McDONNELL
brothers providing 'security'. He has recently been looking after
the brothel that Lewis McDONNELL controls in Briarstone, as
well as one in Charlmere. Research suggests this may refer to a
property in Carisbrooke Court, Briarstone.

5x5x5 Intelligence Report

Date: 31 October 2013

Officer: PC 10422 DEVINE

Subject: Op Pentameter 2013

Grading: B / 2 / 4

On 31 October 2013 a warrant was carried out under Op
Pentameter 2013 at 4 Carisbrooke Court, Briarstone. Present at
the address were the following:

– Ekaterina IORATOVA DOB 01/12/1996.

– Ella HARTUNEN DOB 22/08/1994.

– Liliana VETTINA DOB 14/05/1997.

– Katie SMITH DOB 11/02/1988.

All the above gave their address as 4 Carisbrooke Court, Briarstone.

Also present were:

– Victor RAMOS DOB 14/01/1971, 91A Queen Street, Briarstone, warnings for violence, weapons and drugs. Intel on RAMOS indicates he is a frequenter of brothels around the county.

– Peter James BRIGHAM DOB 18/04/1957, 151 High Street, Baysbury, no previous intel.

– Edward LITTNER DOB 31/10/1968, The Maltings, Love Lane, Catswood, no previous intel.

5x5x5 Intelligence Report

Date: 31 October 2013

Officer: PC 10422 DEVINE

Subject: Op Pentameter 2013

Grading: B / 2 / 5

On 31 October 2013 a warrant was carried out under Op Pentameter 2013 at 4 Carisbrooke Court, Briarstone. Present at the address was an individual who identified herself as Katie SMITH, DOB 11/02/1988. When she was booked into custody and asked to provide a DNA sample, the woman admitted that her true identity was Scarlett RAINSFORD DOB 11/02/1988 (subject of a missing persons investigation in 2003 under Op Diamond). Due to the likelihood of media attention, SMT were informed.

5x5x5 Intelligence Report

Date: 31 October 2013

Officer: PC 10422 DEVINE

Subject: Op Pentameter 2013

Grading: B / 2 / 4

On 31 October 2013 a warrant was carried out under Op
Pentameter 2013 at 4 Carisbrooke Court, Briarstone. During the
warrant the following mobile phones were seized:

– iPhone 4s containing SIM ending 424 – seized from Victor
RAMOS DOB 14/01/1971.

– black Samsung handset containing SIM ending 191 – seized
from Ella HARTUNEN DOB 22/08/1994.

– black Nokia handset containing SIM ending 891 seized from
Katie SMITH DOB 11/02/1988.

– iPhone 5 containing SIM ending 991 seized from Peter James
BRIGHAM DOB 18/04/1957.

– white Samsung handset containing SIM ending 042 seized
from Edward LITTNER DOB 31/10/1968.

5x5x5 Intelligence Report

Date: 31 October 2013

Officer: PC 10422 DEVINE

Subject: Op Pentameter 2013

Grading: B / 2 / 4

During the execution of the warrant at 4 Carisbrooke Court,
Briarstone, on 31 October 2013, Gavin PETRIE DOB

17/03/1975 was seen outside in a Suzuki Swift vehicle having a conversation on his mobile phone. He was spoken to by officers who asked him to move on, and were told that he was visiting a friend in Roehampton Court, the adjacent block of flats. Despite this he sat in his car outside for at least 30 minutes observing the activity.

5x5x5 Intelligence Report

Date: 31 October 2013

Officer: PC 10422 DEVINE

Subject: Op Pentameter 2013

Grading: B / 2 / 4

Following the warrant carried out at 4 Carisbrooke Court on 31 October, Liliana VETTINA DOB 14/05/1997, who is believed to be of Moldovan nationality, refused to give a statement and when interviewed was claiming to not understand English. However, while waiting in the back of the van to be taken to Briarstone, VETTINA had a lengthy conversation in English with Katie SMITH DOB 11/02/1988.

LOU – Friday 1 November 2013, 09:00

'Right, can we get on with it? Lots to get through.'

The canteen coffee hadn't kicked in yet and Lou felt fuzzy, out of focus. So many late nights on the trot were starting to take their toll; she was looking forward to a lie-in tomorrow and, with a bit of luck, a day off. She perched on the edge of the spare desk and balanced her notebook on her knee. There weren't too many people present: just Jane Phelps, Ron Mitchell, Les Finnegan and Sam Hollands.

'No Ali today?' Lou asked.

'He's got the dentist, ma'am,' Jane said. 'Coming in later.'

'Okay. Jane, you're going to have to fill us in. How are you getting on with the exhibits for Op Nettle?'

'Not too bad. The court date is set for the thirteenth of January. Ali keeps getting calls from Suzanne Martin's sister, though.'

This was new. There was a duty of care to the families of people involved with court cases, but in practice advice and support was a team effort with the solicitors, or Victim Support. It was part of seeing a job through to the end, staying in touch with the families of victims and offenders alike, but this one in particular set off an alarm bell. 'Really? What about?' Lou asked.

'All sorts of things; she's horribly persistent. Have you met her?'

'No. What's she like?'

'Ali quite likes her. She gives me the creeps, though. He keeps explaining that we can't share information with her, telling her to get in touch with the brief, but it doesn't stop her ringing. I have a feeling she's trying to sabotage things somehow. I know Ali's got it all under control but I thought you should know.'

'Thanks, Jane.'

'Apart from that, we're all on track for it.'

'Good to hear. Let's move on to Op Trapeze – Sam, did you see Jason's profile on the McDonnells?' Lou had left it in an envelope on her desk last night, with a big note attached saying 'Read – urgent'.

'I did,' Sam said. 'Interesting that Maitland had a falling-out with them. Wonder what else is behind it.'

'That's what I wondered too. I wish we could get some fresh intel on him.'

'I keep submitting taskings; nothing's coming back.'

Ron murmured something that might have been 'bullet-proof'.

Sam said, 'It's also interesting that the Petries seem to be getting more involved with the McDonnells. They were always Maitland's buddies first and foremost. I wonder if that's got something to do with their disagreement.'

'Nigel's getting isolated,' Ron said. 'That can only be a good thing.'

'Or he's isolating himself,' Lou said. 'Which makes me wonder if he had anything to do with McVey's murder. I would have expected much more intel to float to the surface about that, wouldn't you?'

'There's been next to nothing.'

'Les – what do you think?'

Les Finnegan, a year from retirement and highly skilled at keeping his head down, was keeping his head down. 'About Maitland? Not sure, boss. I can't see him having anything to do with McVey. He's not that hands-on.'

'Nevertheless, it would be good if we could bring him in for something. See if we can stir him up a bit.'

120

Les didn't reply. He was meeting her eyes but not saying anything, rabbit in the headlights. It crossed Lou's mind to mention that SB were trying to get a surveillance team on Maitland, but that wasn't information that needed to be shared, even in this forum.

'What do you think, Les?' Honestly, it was like pulling teeth.

'He won't come in voluntarily.'

Jane interrupted this increasingly tense exchange. 'Ma'am, if it's any help, I need to go up to the farm at some point to return some unused property. I could see if I could get a quiet word then?'

'I think he might be away,' Les said.

'Away? What, on holiday or something?'

'I thought I saw something on intel,' Les said vaguely.

There were times when Les was as sharp as Mr Buchanan's gold-plated tie pin, and others when Lou wondered whether he was just treading water until he got his commutation and his pension.

'Thanks, Jane,' Lou said, 'that would be great. I just want to know what he looks like when he hears McVey's name mentioned.'

'Will do.'

For the next few minutes Lou half-listened as Sam went through the taskings, making sure jobs were covered over the weekend. She was thinking about Nigel Maitland, half-tempted to ask if she could tag along with Jane. If she could just see him, face to face, she would know. Then the task of finding the evidence to nail the bastard could begin. *I will get you*, she thought. *I will find something on you and I will be ready to bring you down.*

SCARLETT – Friday 22 August 2003, 14:18

The next day, the last full day of the holiday, Scarlett tried to stay in bed.

When he had finished, her father had taken her back to the apartment next door and pushed her on to the bed. If she was awake, Juliette had not moved or breathed or given any indication that she was doing anything other than sleeping. Her mum had said nothing. She'd followed her father out of the room.

Once the door had been pulled closed, Scarlett let out a retching, desperate sob, followed by another. She couldn't help it. It had been held inside her for so long that she was going to explode. She tried to keep quiet, to stifle her cries in the pillow, not wanting to wake her sister and have to explain.

Juliette was not asleep. Scarlett could tell by her sister's breathing, once she stopped sobbing, took some deep, shuddering breaths, gulped back the tears. She'd huddled into herself on the bed, trying to think about sleeping, trying not to think about Nico.

Then she heard Juliette moving in bed, shifting awkwardly, and felt a hand on her shoulder. Scarlett froze. But that was it: just a hand on her shoulder, held there for a few moments, and then Juliette turned over in bed and a few minutes later was breathing deeply enough to be asleep.

Until that moment, Scarlett had believed that it had been Juliette who had alerted them to her night-time absences; that she had gone to get them and shown them the empty bed, and that they had waited for her to return based on Juliette's betrayal.

But the next morning, when Scarlett finally opened her eyes and closed them again, not ready to face the day and what it might choose to bring, she realised she had been wrong. Juliette's hand on her shoulder, wordless, had nonetheless communicated plenty.

I hear you. You are not alone. And: *It wasn't me.*

She lay still for a long while after throwing the sheet off. It was stiflingly hot. She could hear splashes, shouts, laughter from the pool outside, which meant that the patio door was probably open. She turned over in bed slowly, her head thumping. Juliette wasn't in the room.

She struggled to sit up and then lay back down again almost immediately. It was like having a hangover, and she knew what that felt like because she'd had one on the Sunday after the sleepover at Cerys's house last summer; they'd made their own cocktails by helping themselves to the booze cabinet. The next day, nauseous and then sick and with a headache like nothing she'd ever experienced, she'd had to spend the day with her family pretending that she was perfectly all right. She had had to eat a roast dinner with enthusiasm, and had vomited it up half an hour later. She'd had to go for a walk with them in the country park, which had temporarily helped, and afterwards she'd gone to her room on the pretext of wanting to check through her homework, even though she had done it all on the Friday night so that she would be allowed to go to Cerys's on the Saturday. And then she had collapsed on her bed.

It felt like that.

Oh, Nico.

Would he even wait for her, tonight, in their usual place? Or would he just melt into the night, go out among the staggering lads and the girls in their tiny dresses and heels, looking for someone new? She couldn't risk going out again. They would be watching her every move, waiting for her to put a foot wrong. Waiting for her to bring disgrace to the family.

It was unfair, so unfair. She hadn't done anything wrong, after all.

And then she remembered that, actually, it had gone further than a kiss. Her bold denials had sunk in so far that she had almost forgotten the thrill of that moment, his loss of self-control, how he had felt in her hand. And everything that it meant. He liked her, he trusted her, he wanted her. He had kissed her afterwards with a new sort of passion, a different level of urgency, as though he knew that she had proved herself.

If she saw him again, he would sleep with her, she knew it. She would go back home to Cerys and be able to tell her that she'd met this guy, how gorgeous he was – she would make sure she got a picture of him – and that she had done it with him.

The only way she was ever going to see Nico again was if she turned her back on the family and didn't go home. Ever.

When things got bad like this, the only thing that ever helped was to retreat into a fantasy world. So she thought about Nico, about somehow slipping away and meeting him. He would be waiting for her, and he would have been waiting all night. He would sweep her into his arms and tell her how worried he'd been, how he had been thinking of her and afraid for her all night. He would tell her he loved her over and over ... he would touch her and soothe her, tell her it was going to be okay, that he would take care of her and nobody would ever hurt her again.

And then he would take her to his house – and the family would all be out somewhere ... he would sneak her in, into his bedroom, and he would take her clothes off one piece at a time, asking her permission at every stage, checking she was all right. He would kiss her, every bit of her skin as it was revealed to him, and then finally the passion would overtake him and he would carry her over to the bed and make love to her. And it might hurt, a little – because that was inevitable, wasn't it, the first time. But it would be fine.

Fantasy, all fantasy, every bit of it. From Nico waiting for her, to Nico taking her virginity. None of it was true. None of it would ever come true, either.

In the early afternoon, Juliette came into the room and went to sit on her bed with the book. The curtains had been drawn across the patio doors to block out as much of the sun's fierce light as possible, and she made sure they were closed behind her. She went to shut the door too, until Scarlett objected.

'There's no air, Jul. Leave the door open a bit.'

Mute as always, Juliette left it open. From outside, the sounds of the pool, splashing, children shouting and shrieking, a happy, discordant tune which was easy to block out.

'What are they doing?'

'Who?' Juliette said. Today, apparently, she felt like talking.

'Mum and Dad. Are they by the pool?'

'They've gone in for a siesta.'

Scarlett sat up on her bed, slowly, as though she was eighty and not fifteen.

'How are you?' Juliette asked. It came out a bit like a statement – flat. But Scarlett appreciated the effort it must have taken for her to say it at all.

'I'm okay,' she said. Managing a smile. 'Thank you, Jul.'

She got to her feet and made her way to the bathroom, washed her face and looked at herself in the mirror. *I hate them*, she thought. *I hate them both*.

Back in the bedroom, she pulled a pair of shorts and a top out of the suitcase that lay on the tiled floor like a felled beast, its guts a tangle of multicoloured fabrics. 'I'm going for a walk,' she said to Juliette. 'I won't be long.'

Juliette was buried in her book already, which meant that this time she went unacknowledged. Her sister was lost in the other world; concentrating on more than one reality at a time was beyond her capability.

'Love you, Jul,' Scarlett said quietly, meaning it. She was the only one.

This, too, was not enough to raise Juliette's head from the book, but there was a hint of a smile playing about her lips, either from the story or from Scarlett's declaration of love, it was impossible to tell.

Scarlett pulled the curtain aside and stepped out into the glaring sunshine. On the clothes-horse on the patio was Scarlett's baseball cap. It was dry now but it had been wet yesterday when she'd jumped into the pool wearing it. It was snug, but at least it shaded the sun from her eyes.

The patio door to the apartment next door was closed, the curtains behind it shut too. The whirr of the air-conditioning told her that they were both inside. She walked down to the gate and thought about what she was about to do, whether it was worth it. Of course it was. Every small measure of freedom she could allow herself felt precious.

She went through the gate and started to walk in the direction of the town. She wasn't going to look for Nico. She wasn't going to do anything more dramatic than stretch her legs, get some fresh air.

She got as far as the market square. The cafés were all busy with tourists enjoying their lunch: pizzas and Greek salads and steaks; chips and beer, even the odd full English, of course, because Brits couldn't do without their bacon and eggs no matter where they were in the world.

There was no sign of him. She walked back past the Pirate Bay bar. The internet terminals were all in use, apparently working. She thought about Cerys and what she might be doing today; wished she could be brave and turn on her mobile phone long enough to call her. Tell her what had happened. Cerys would understand. She would make her laugh.

She was walking away when she heard Nico's voice behind her, calling her name. 'Scarlett! Hey!'

She stopped walking and for a moment considered carrying on, not acknowledging him. Giving him the out he had so clearly wanted last night when he'd run away from her without looking back. She dropped her head, didn't look round, didn't move.

He caught up with her, grabbed her by the waist, lifted her and spun her round, making her gasp.

'Hey! How are you, beautiful girl?'

'Put me down!'

He was laughing and then he stopped. She slid down his body until her feet felt solid ground, pushed him away.

'What is wrong?'

She looked up at him and his face was so beautiful, so full of love and concern and care that she felt tears pricking her eyes again. He put a hand on her arm, tentatively, as though he might not be permitted this contact any more.

She raised both her hands. They felt so heavy. And then he put his arms gently around her and pulled her against him. 'What is wrong?' he asked again. 'Scarlett?'

She sobbed, just once, into his shirt. And then quickly regained her composure. This wouldn't do, wouldn't do at all.

'It's okay. I'm okay. Thank you.'

'You got in trouble yesterday?'

'A bit.'

She chanced a look at him again, falling for him, falling for those dark eyes and that beautiful face all over again. He was so gorgeous, so lovely. And last night . . . she remembered it, remembered the taste of him, and, despite what it had cost her, she wanted that again, and wanted more.

'Maybe they don't understand,' he said. 'Maybe they forget how it feels to be happy with someone.'

'Can we go to the beach?'

They walked side by side to the wooden pallets laid like stepping stones in the hot sand, leading down to the sea. Last night, here, she had lain on the beach next to him and kissed him until he lost control. Now, the beach was crowded with tourists, children playing in the sand. The smell of coconut suntan oil and cigarette smoke.

She wanted to hold his hand but he was keeping his distance from her. *For my sake*, she thought. *He is being careful, for me. He is worried that I'll get in trouble.*

They got down to the water's edge, where the sand was flat and wet and firmer to walk on, and headed up the beach in the direction of the apartments. A few hundred metres away from the town, the beach grew quieter and the shops and bars and tavernas on the promenade gave way to dunes.

'This is no good,' he said, without warning. 'I should say goodbye to you.'

'You're the only person who has ever made me happy,' Scarlett said, her head down.

'You make me happy too,' he said. 'You are a special girl, Scarlett. You are – '

'I love you,' she blurted.

He stopped walking, then, and turned to her. 'This is not a good idea. Your parents? It will be worse for you.'

'I'm fifteen,' she said, unable to stop the words now she had started. 'I'm only fifteen.'

He laughed at her. 'You look younger. I think, maybe, eight, nine . . . '

She pushed him, pretending to be cross. 'How old are you, then?' she asked.

'I am sixteen years old,' he said, smiling at her.

He looked older, Scarlett thought, not having any real concept of how old he should look. She had thought he was around eighteen. Didn't they have a minimum age to be working in bars here in Greece?

She sat down on the sand, sheltered from the breeze by the dunes. Nico sat next to her, his arm draped casually, heavy, over her shoulders. He pulled off her baseball cap, kissed her temple, and she turned her head so he could kiss her properly.

'You want to get away from them?' he asked, after a moment.

Her heart soared at the thought of it, an escape. 'Can I?' she asked, thrilled. 'Can I stay with you?'

'No, no. Not stay with me. But I can help you get away.'

'I don't understand.'

'I have friends, you know – they can find you work.'

'What sort of work?'

He laughed. 'All kinds. Good money. Enough to live.'

Without thinking, she said, 'Yes, yes. Please, yes. I'll do anything, anything. But why can't I stay with you? We could get a house together, we'd be earning money, we could live together . . . '

Laughing again, pushing her back into the sand, shutting her up with a kiss. He wasn't taking her seriously. He thought she was just a kid. *I'll show him*, Scarlett thought. *I'll show him I'm serious about it.*

After a moment he sat up again, looking at the few people sitting on this part of the beach. 'I take you back,' he said. 'You think about what I say to you?'

'It's my last day,' she said. 'We're going home tomorrow.'

Nico frowned. 'That is very sad.'

'I don't want to go; you know I want to stay here.'

He touched her face, stroking his fingers lightly over her cheek. 'I wait for you tonight,' he said. 'You want to get away, you come to me tonight. I wait for you on the road. But now you have to go back. I take you.'

Scarlett was numb with disappointment but she followed him, nonetheless. They walked the remaining three hundred or so metres in silence, up the path through the dunes that led to the road and the apartment complex just past that.

'Best not come any further,' she said.

'Okay.'

He handed her the baseball cap, took a step backwards, away from her. The pleasure she'd had, seeing him again, was being swamped already with the misery of being back here.

'You come tonight, Scarlett?' he asked.

'Yes,' she said. 'Yes. What time?'

'I finish work at two.'

Her mum and dad would be asleep by then. She could do it. It was her last chance, after all: their flight home was at four in the afternoon.

'Where?'

'Here,' he said, nodding towards the apartments. 'I meet you outside, on the road. You wait for me?'

'Yes. I'll wait.'

He hesitated for a moment as if he wanted to kiss her, then he turned and walked away.

Her mum was by the pool, on her own. There was no point avoiding her. 'I went for a walk,' Scarlett said, hoping they were both too hot to argue about it.

'Haven't you learned your lesson?' Annie said, lowering her sunglasses to fix her daughter in a cold stare.

'Where's Dad?'

'Having a lie-down. Luckily for you.'

Scarlett went to the room. Juliette was not there either. She must have been outside with their mother and Scarlett just hadn't noticed.

Right at that moment Scarlett absolutely intended to run away. She spent the next two hours planning it, thinking it through in her head: what she was going to take with her, which clothes, her passport, whatever money she could find. She started to put things into her backpack, ready for the night ahead. She even managed to doze off for a while, in preparation for staying up late again.

When she woke, the room was still empty. The light in the room told her that the sun was setting, but in here it was still stifling. Scarlett opened the door and went outside on to the shaded patio. The pool area was almost deserted, just a couple of older girls in the shallow end, drinking from bottles of beer, which was against the rules, and laughing. There was no sign of her mum. But her dad was there; Juliette too. They were sitting side by side on one of the loungers, under a parasol, their backs to Scarlett. Juliette was hunched over, sitting stiffly, presumably trying to read her book. Their father had his arm around her.

The decision was made in an instant.

She couldn't leave Juliette.

She would meet Nico later, tell him she was sorry, she would have to go back home with her family after all. She couldn't run away. She would kiss him goodbye and it would hurt like hell. But it was the only thing to do.

MG11 WITNESS STATEMENT

Section 1 – Witness details

NAME:	Juliette RAINSFORD		
DOB (if under 18; if over 18 state 'Over 18'):	26/06/1990		
ADDRESS:	14 Russet Avenue Briarstone	**OCCUPATION:**	Full-time education

Section 2 – Investigating Officer

DATE:	2 September 2003
OIC:	DC 9912 Jon BRYAN

Section 3 – Text of Statement

My older sister Scarlett RAINSFORD and I were sharing a studio apartment at the Aktira Studios, Rhodes, during our family holiday, 16 to 23 August 2003. We didn't make any friends while we were on holiday. There were no people our age staying in the apartment block so we stayed together most of the time.

On the evening of Friday 22 August we were supposed to be going out for dinner as usual. Scarlett stayed behind in our apartment. She told Mum that she had a stomach ache. I went with my parents to a restaurant in the town. We had eaten there before. We came back to the apartment later in the evening. Scarlett was lying on her bed asleep. My parents went into their apartment next door and I got ready for bed. I spent about an hour reading my book and then turned the light out. Scarlett did not move or speak to me.

In the morning I woke up early and noticed that Scarlett was not there. I thought she had gone to the pool. I sat and read for a while until my parents got up and Mum came in to the room. She asked where Scarlett was. They both started looking for Scarlett.

Scarlett did not discuss running away. I do not believe now that she ran away.

At the end of the interview DC BRYAN read the statement back to the witness and all present agreed it was an accurate account of information given. Also present was Mr Clive RAINSFORD, acting as appropriate adult for Juliette RAINSFORD.

Section 4 – Signatures

....

WITNESS: (J Rainsford)   OIC: (Jon Bryan DC 9912)
A/A: (C L Rainsford)

They had been in the back of the minibus for hours, hours. Yelena had been fidgeting, grumbling something in her own language. The water had long gone. The grumbling got louder until she was shouting, and when that went ignored she struggled to her feet, pushing some of the bags and luggage out of the way, waving at the front of the vehicle.

Scarlett stayed huddled into the corner, afraid of the other girl's agitation.

From the front of the bus, angry shouts. Eventually Yelena sat back down again, still shouting, thumping with the side of her fist against the back door.

'What?' Scarlett said, trying to make eye contact. 'What's the matter?'

But the girl ignored her; the tirade of unintelligible words continued, and, just at the point when Scarlett thought she couldn't possibly stand another second of the racket and was going to have to kill her, the vehicle swerved off the straight path it had been taking and slowed right down. Moments later it stopped.

Yelena stopped banging and shouting. She sat back against the wall of the bus, breathing hard. The doors at the front opened and shut again, and Scarlett could hear muttered conversation in whatever foreign language it was they were speaking.

Then the back doors were unlocked, and opened. Outside, it was dark, and chilly. Scarlett held her arms folded across her chest.

Yelena started yammering at the men angrily in a language they seemed to understand. One of them did, at least, because he started arguing back.

Then he beckoned Yelena out.

'Where are you going?' Scarlett said, her voice rising in a wail. 'Don't leave me.'

The man wearing the woolly hat had pulled Yelena by the upper arm, out of sight. The second man raised his eyebrows and muttered something, then he beckoned to her. 'Out, you get out.'

She stood on wobbly legs on the tarmac, a dark sky overhead turned orange by lights she could not see. They were in some sort of car park, or more accurately a lorry park. The van was parked between two articulated lorries, sandwiched between them with high canvas walls rising on either side of where she stood.

Scarlett shivered.

The man took hold of her upper arm, slammed the van doors shut with the other hand, and pulled her along in the direction Yelena had taken. When they reached the back of the lorries, the man held her back while he checked left and right.

Then pulled her quickly across a road towards some trees and bushes, dragging her through the undergrowth.

'All right, all right,' she said, 'you don't have to be so bloody rough.'

They had reached a dusty gap in the trees where Yelena was squatting, jeans around her ankles, while the man with the hat watched. It was darker here, but not too dark to see that Yelena was doing a shit.

'I'm okay, thanks,' Scarlett said.

'You do,' her companion said, pushing her roughly next to Yelena.

So she did it. She was desperate to go, in any case, though knowing that it was going to hurt. And it did. The concentrated urine burned, and tears squeezed from the corners of her tightly closed

134

eyes. Her piss splattered noisily into the dust and she could smell her own body – the sweat, the dirt, the discomfort of it.

The men made Yelena and Scarlett wait in the trees, looking carefully at the road. Two strong beams of light swept through the trees. A lorry, or something, was coming. The man ahead of them held up his hand in warning. *Wait*.

They were in some sort of services, Scarlett realised. Across the other side of the car park – maybe three hundred metres or so – Scarlett could see a restaurant. It was well-lit. There were people inside, cleaning.

They could run.

Scarlett looked across at Yelena, tried to catch her eye. The dark-haired girl was staring ahead. They had broken her, she thought. They had killed her friend. They had stood by and watched while she defecated behind a bush. No wonder she looked so done-in.

Eventually she looked across at Scarlett. Scarlett tried to convey her thoughts just in the expression on her face. She looked across to the building, to the various vans and lorries parked, dark and silent, then back to meet Yelena's eyes. They could run. If they both ran in opposite directions, using the lorries for cover, they would have a chance. If they got to the restaurant, they would be safe. There were people there. The men would not risk it, would not risk a scene.

Yelena followed all this unspoken communication, opened her eyes wider and, as the lights from the second lorry swept across their faces, she shook her head, slowly and deliberately.

No.

Just as deliberately, Scarlett nodded, her eyebrows knitted in an insistent frown.

And then the man who was waiting by the road beckoned them forward.

Scarlett saw the chance slipping away. If she ran, Yelena would follow; she would have to. The only chance they had was if both of them ran, to create a diversion. The men would panic. There would be a few seconds of confusion: they would not know which one of them to chase. The old, fat one would not be able to run fast enough in any case. One of them might, then, be able to get away.

The man who was holding Scarlett's upper arm stumbled in the dark undergrowth, released his grip on her as his arms flailed, trying to regain his balance.

That was it.

She ran.

A second later she burst through the trees and she was on the tarmac, running, running. It felt as if she was going so slowly it was almost backwards, like dream-running. She had no energy, her breath already coming in frantic, wheezy gasps, and the air was so cold . . .

Behind her a shout, and Yelena shouting too and then suddenly Yelena was beside her, faster than Scarlett, on longer legs, panicky, wobbly strides.

'Don't follow me!' Scarlett shrieked, darting to her left. Behind them a lorry was coming, they could hear heavy footsteps above the noise of the grinding lorry gears and the lights swept across them as the lorry turned. It must be between them and the men.

They were going to make it. Yelena was ahead of her now, heading for the building, the lights making a halo of her flying hair, and she was screaming, yelling something in that language . . .

Scarlett's legs were giving way. There was still two hundred metres or so between her and safety, and Yelena was a few paces ahead of her.

There was a sudden silence as the lorry parked somewhere and cut

136

its engine. There was no shout, no warning, nothing. There was a fizzing noise as something whistled past Scarlett's ear.

Then the side of Yelena's head exploded and the girl dropped like a stone, the momentum of her running causing her to skid a few feet, face first, on the tarmac in front of Scarlett.

Scarlett stopped instantly. Stood still, waiting for the second shot. She felt as though she was screaming but no sound was coming out of her open mouth. She looked at the body in front of her, the dark puddle spreading out from what was left of Yelena's head.

The man with the hat caught up with her, grabbing her arms, panting and muttering something angry and urgent at her that she didn't understand, and it took a few seconds for her to realise that he was speaking broken English. 'You stupid! You fucking girl!'

Then the minibus was next to them, braking sharply, cutting out the light from the building and separating her from Yelena's body. She was pulled round to the back, the door was opened and she was thrown inside. The door slammed. Seconds later, the bus was moving and she hadn't had time or the thought to hang on to something, so she rolled and tumbled around in the back, fell against the back doors heavily, knocking the last gasping breath out of her body.

And they were back on the road before Scarlett had had time to think.

Oh my god oh my god oh my god no, no no no …

She couldn't stop shaking. Her whole body, shaking, even though she pulled herself into a tight ball, trying to shut everything out. What she had seen. What they had done.

Yelena was dead, lying on the ground in the dark. They had left her. They had just left her where she fell, driven off again.

That could have been me, Scarlett thought. *Should have been me*. She had been the one to run, Yelena had just followed. She hadn't

137

even wanted to do it, had she? She hadn't wanted to. She had been afraid. Yelena had gone along with it because she had no choice. What could she do, let Scarlett run?

They might have shot her anyway.

But why shoot Yelena – why her? Because she was faster, because she'd overtaken Scarlett and they couldn't catch her? Because she was nearly at the restaurant?

Scarlett closed her eyes again. Every time she shut them she could see the same thing, playing over and over again like a video on loop: the side of Yelena's head bursting open, and no sound other than the fizzing of the bullet that went past Scarlett's head.

Tears from between her lashes, sticky on her dirty face. *It's my fault, that was all my fault. She died because I made her run. I made her do it.*

And now she knew something else, too: she couldn't, wouldn't do anything like that again. They would kill her, as quickly as they killed Yelena. And if they did it they would just pick up another girl from somewhere, to drive around in the back of the minibus. Girls, whatever they wanted them for, were expendable, disposable.

Above the sound of the engine and her own sobs, she could hear the two men in the front arguing. One of them was shouting, the other one nasal, placatory. It would stop for a while, as though the discussion had run its inevitable course, and then restart without warning. *Shut up, shut up!* Scarlett wanted to yell. She was afraid of their anger, wanted to silence it. She wanted them to stop, get out somewhere so they could have a reasonable discussion and negotiate whatever it was they wanted in order to let her go. Just leave her, by the side of the motorway in whatever country they were in by now – Eastern Europe somewhere, possibly, given the length of time they'd been driving and the sudden chill in the air. They were heading north.

And then, having thought herself out of the panic, suddenly it was there, again. Yelena was dead. They shot her. They blew the side of her head off. And she had dropped like a stone, not stumbled or tripped, not put her hands forward to stop herself but just BANG and face-down on the tarmac, the momentum of her running feet sending her body skidding and juddering for a second before it fell still.

And Scarlett had stopped.

She should have kept on running. Would they have shot her too? Yes, probably – and what of it? She would be no worse off dead than alive.

I wish it had been me. I wish they'd shot me instead of her.

First things first: Lou gritted her teeth and phoned Waterhouse again. Standing, in case she needed to get assertive with him.

'Waterhouse.'

'Hi, it's Lou Smith.'

To her surprise, he seemed much more cheerful this morning. Maybe he was regretting being such an arse yesterday? 'Oh, hi. How did you get on with our celebrity?'

'All right, I think. With your permission I'd like to get my DS to see her. If anyone can get you a result, Sam can.'

'Fill your boots,' he said chirpily. 'We won't be able to hang on to the VVS for long, Estates are moaning about us using it as it is. I can't see any of my team making progress with her. My guess is that she knows bugger all about the McDonnells, and if she did know something useful, she also knows it's more than her life's worth to share it with us.'

'Something else – you know we were looking at Maitland for a job last year?'

'The stable girl murder, wasn't it?'

Lou bristled at having a young woman with a life, family and people who loved her reduced to such a diminutive. The 'stable girl' – *She was a person, you little shit.*

'Polly Leuchars, her name was. My exhibits officer is going down to the farm at some point to hand back some unused material. Just in case you've got a team on him, I wouldn't want her to get in the way. Do I need to hold her off?'

'I've only got one team so far and we're sticking with Lewis McDonnell. So as long as she goes there in the next day or so, should be okay. I can't see McDonnell going anywhere near the farm, but if he does I'll give you a shout.'

'Thanks,' Lou said.

Her priority for today was going to be making some sort of progress with Op Trapeze: Carl McVey, the murdered bar owner, and Ian Palmer, still unconscious in hospital. Both of them needed her full attention.

Everything she read, though, seemed to be going over old ground. The further back she went, the less relevant it seemed to become. When she found herself reading about a neighbour dispute involving a yew hedge between Carl McVey's house and the property next door, she gave up. Instead, she reached for the Op Diamond file – the historic case notes on Scarlett Rainsford's disappearance. She would sort out the most relevant bits to hand over to Sam.

It was massive, of course, and before going to Special Branch yesterday she had only had the briefest of chances to reacquaint herself with the facts of the case. In reality, it didn't take much to remind her of it, as the memories of her work on this case had stayed fresher than any other. Possibly because it had never been solved; possibly because of the resonance of its being a missing child, the most devastating of all crimes to work with.

But now, flicking through the file, Lou began to realise just what a small part she had played in the investigation. Here, for example, were the initial statements of Clive, Annie and – to her surprise – Juliette Rainsford. By the time Lou had been assigned to the team, a few days after Scarlett's disappearance, all the initial interviews had been conducted under Greek jurisdiction. Everything done very differently.

The last time any of the family had seen Scarlett had been when they had all retired to bed, on the last night of their holiday, which was Friday 22 August 2003. The parents had a studio apartment next to the one shared by Scarlett and her sister, Juliette. They had been out for the evening to a taverna in the main town square, and returned by half-past nine in the evening. They had gone to bed. The next morning, Clive and Annie had gone to the room next door to find Juliette reading, and Scarlett missing. It had been as simple as that.

If she had gone willingly, she had taken nothing with her; her clothes, shoes, passport, even her mobile phone had all been left behind. At first there had been a disagreement about what she had been wearing that night, and whether her pyjamas were missing, or some clothes. Eventually, confused, distressed, Annie had worked out that Scarlett had been wearing shorts and a short-sleeved blouse, with sneakers. Her shortie pyjamas were found in the tangle of clothes that spilled out of the open suitcase on the floor.

They'd asked Annie what she and Clive had done after leaving the girls that evening. They'd sat out on the patio drinking a beer, as they had done most nights. Eventually – Annie wasn't able to give a specific time – they'd gone inside. Had they checked on the girls before retiring? No. There was no need. The light was off in the girls' apartment; they would both have been asleep. They had had no reason to have any concerns.

It wasn't very thorough, Lou decided. They'd asked these open questions but were not getting detailed responses. It would have been better to take Annie through it bit by bit: who said what, how did she seem, what did she do? All of that. It would have been the way the interviews were conducted if Scarlett had disappeared in the UK. As it was, the investigators had limited time, and were working in what they called 'close co-operation' with their colleagues in the Greek police force. There was a strong sense of frustration coming out of the official wording of the notes, what was unsaid telling Lou almost as much as the words that had made it on to the paper.

Could she have run away? they wanted to know.

Annie had answered: *I guess so.*

Lou flicked through the pages until she got to the official witness statements that had been taken after the Rainsfords returned home, and the one she herself had conducted and signed: the first interview with Annie Rainsford, Briarstone Police Station, Interview Room Three.

By that time, they had established that on the night Scarlett went missing the family had eaten out as a threesome – Clive, Annie and Juliette. The taverna owner, who had served the four of them on the Wednesday evening, was certain beyond any doubt that the older girl had not been with them on their second visit. He had asked them about it, and the man had told him that she was not feeling well and they'd left her back at the apartments. The restaurateur had even offered to make up a takeaway parcel for the absent daughter. This had been declined. When questioned further, the taverna owner had found the till receipt indicating that the party had eaten one salad (Juliette), one beef *stifado* (Clive) and one lamb kebab with rice (Annie). One mineral water, and four beers – two each for the adults. That was all.

This had been Lou's objective for the interview – to try to clear up that discrepancy. She remembered Annie well: pale cheeks under her tan; big, liquid blue eyes made even bigger by her habit of keeping a wide, earnest stare going at all times; long straight hair. She was tiny, barely five feet tall, and slightly built. She seemed the sort of person you immediately wanted to look after, and yet she did not invite protection. For the duration of the interview she sat straight in her chair, occasionally sitting on her hands as if they were cold. Other than that, she did not move.

Transcript of Interview in Relation to Op Diamond (Missing Person Enquiry in Relation to Scarlett Rainsford)

Briarstone Police Station, Interview Room Three

Date: 15 September 2003, 09:01

Present: Annie RAINSFORD (AR)

            DC Louisa SMITH (LS)

            DC Sarah JONES (SJ)

LS: Annie, can we go back to the evening Scarlett disappeared? You ate out at the Zeus Taverna, is that right?

AR: Yes.

LS: Can you tell us what you remember, from the time you left the apartments to go out to dinner?

AR: Scarlett wasn't well. We left about . . . seven o'clock. Scarlett was in bed when we went. We walked down towards the town and we got to the taverna about twenty minutes later. We had dinner . . . we were there a couple of hours . . . and then we came back.

LS: What was the matter with Scarlett?

AR: She said she had a tummy ache.

LS: She said? Didn't you believe her?

AR: I never knew what to believe with Scarlett. But we'd all had an upset tummy at some point during the week. It's part of going on holiday, isn't it?

LS: And you were comfortable, leaving her on her own like that?

AR: She knew where we were; we'd eaten there earlier in the week.

LS: When you were interviewed the next day – the Saturday – you told the Greek police that you'd all eaten out together that night. Is that right?

AR: I can't remember what we said. It was all so confusing. I was upset.

LS: You said you all ate together and then went back to the apartments together.

AR: I was confused. I must have been confused.

LS: What time did you get back to the apartments?

AR: I think it was about half-past nine.

LS: And did you see Scarlett then?

AR: We looked in on the girls' apartment and Scarlett was asleep in bed.

LS: In bed, or on the bed?

AR: On the bed.

LS: So she wasn't covered over?

AR: I don't think so. No.

LS: What was she wearing?

AR: Her shorts and blouse.

LS: You didn't think to wake her, to get her changed?

AR: No. She was asleep. She's not a child; she was capable of getting changed herself if she'd wanted to. And she looked comfortable, so we let her sleep.

LS: Did you go right into the apartment, or just look from the door?

AR: We stood in the doorway.

LS: But you were sure she was asleep?

AR: I guess so.

LS: She might have been pretending?

AR: I suppose so; I don't know.

LS: What happened then?

AR: Juliette went into the room. She turned on the bedside light so she could read. We went back to our apartment next door.

LS: Did you close the door behind you?

AR: I think so. Sometimes the girls left the door open to let the breeze in. It was very hot.

LS: So that night, did you close it or leave it open?

AR: I don't remember. I closed it, I think. I don't know if Juliette opened it again.

LS: But it wasn't locked?

AR: No, we never locked it.

LS: So what did you and Clive do then?

AR: We sat on the patio outside drinking the last of the beers we had. Then we did some packing, then went to bed about half-past ten. We were supposed to fly home the next day. The bus was supposed to be picking us up at eleven.

LS: Did you check on the girls before you went to bed?

AR: No.

LS: Did you hear anything from the room next door at all?

AR: No. We woke up at about half-past seven. I got dressed and went next door. Juliette was reading her book. Scarlett wasn't there. I asked Juliette where Scarlett was, and she said she hadn't heard her go out; she assumed she was by the pool.

LS: But she wasn't by the pool?

AR: No. I went to look for her but she wasn't there. We thought she had gone for a walk, so we waited for a while. Clive went down to the beach in case he could see her, then he walked all the way into town and back again. I looked around the apartments. But she wasn't there. She wasn't anywhere. It was like she'd just vanished. We asked some of the people by the pool, and some of them – a British couple, and some girls – they helped us look. One of them said we should call the rep. So we did that. The rep – her name was Jenny – came down with the resort manager, I forget his name. And they called the police for us, and a woman who was acting as an interpreter for us. I can't remember her name either. She was nice. She was kind.

LS: So, just taking things back a step. The last time you saw Scarlett was – say – about 10 pm on the Friday night. And you first reported her absence to the Greek authorities at twenty past twelve on the Saturday?

AR: That sounds about right.

LS: She was missing for over fourteen hours before you reported it?

AR: It wasn't like that. [INDISTINCT]

LS: I'd like you to explain it to me, then. Why were you not more concerned?

AR: Do you have a teenage daughter?

LS: Why were you not more concerned, Annie?

AR: She was a teenager. She went off on her own sometimes, back home. She had sleepovers, she went to the town on her own on the bus, she even went to London with her mates once, on the train. We all thought she'd gone off for a walk somewhere and lost track of time. I thought she would have left me a note. I looked everywhere. I thought there would have been a note.

LS: Did Scarlett have any reason to want to run away?

AR: None at all.

LS: Had there been any arguments, while you were all away?

AR: No. It was fine. We had a good time together – all of us. A great time.

Lou frowned, put the paper down for a moment. Somewhere in the file, someone had mentioned a boy, a Greek boy, whom Scarlett had been seen with. Had it been in Juliette's statement? Lou began to rifle through the pages, looking for it. She got to the end of the file, and went back to the beginning again. And then there it was, a single sheet. Lou started to read without taking it in. There was something else, something in Annie's interview notes that had triggered a feeling of unease. What was it? Something was missing.

It was only twenty minutes and another coffee later that she had it: Annie had answered her questions, but she was not asking questions in return. No, 'Where's my daughter? Why hasn't she been found?' Not even the usual, 'What are you doing asking me questions, when you should be out there looking?'

None of that. Sitting on her hands, gazing at Lou with her eyes wide, Annie had been entirely passive throughout.

Pulling herself back from the distraction, she began leafing through the file again in case there was a second statement from Juliette. Halfway through, she stopped. There it was – it wasn't on Juliette's statement at all. It was on the interpreted statement of Vasilis Kaloudis, aged fifty-three, owner of the Pirate Bay bar.

MG11 WITNESS STATEMENT

Section 1 – Witness details

NAME:	Emma CONSTANTINOPOULOS		
DOB (if under 18; if over 18 state 'Over 18'):	Over 18		
ADDRESS:	Kessler Associates Proofreading & Translation Services	OCCUPATION:	Interpreter/translator

Section 2 – Investigating Officer

DATE:	22 September 2003
OIC:	DC 9912 Jon BRYAN

Section 3 – Text of Statement

My name is Emma CONSTANTINOPOULOS and I work for Kessler Associates as a translator on a freelance basis. On 22 September 2003 at 09:30 I was present when the witness statement of Vasilis KALOUDIS was taken and I translated this from Greek to English. The English translation of the witness statement I now exhibit as reference EC/1.

Section 4 – Signatures

....

....

WITNESS: (E Constantinopoulos)

OIC: (Jon Bryan DC 9912)

MG11 WITNESS STATEMENT

Section 1 – Witness details

NAME:	Vasilis KALOUDIS		
DOB (if under 18; if over 18 state 'Over 18'):		Over 18	
ADDRESS:	(withheld by Greek police)	OCCUPATION:	Bar owner

Section 2 – Investigating Officer

DATE:	22 September 2003
OIC:	DC 9912 Jon BRYAN

Section 3 – Text of Statement

My name is Vasilis KALOUDIS and I am the owner of the Pirate Bay Club in a resort in Rhodes. I have owned the bar for more than ten years.

I heard of the English girl Scarlett RAINSFORD who has been reported missing and I saw a picture of her on a poster. I recognised this girl. She came into the bar a few weeks ago, I am not sure of the date. She was looking for a local boy called Nico. She believed he worked in the bar, but this was not the case. I believe this to be a boy I once employed casually to look after the bar. I do not know his last name or his address. He is known in the area as he is always trying to find work with the local traders, but he is unreliable.

I told the girl I did not know where he was, but she should try the market square. She left. I did not see her again.

Section 4 – Signatures

....
WITNESS: (V Kaloudis)

....
OIC: (Jon Bryan DC 9912)

A local boy who was unreliable.

That was it.

Lou looked in case she'd missed a second page of the statement, but at the top it said clearly 'page 1 of 1'. From the date of the statement onwards Lou worked through the file trying to find further mention of Nico. Then she logged on to HOLMES to cross-reference the name.

The only 'Nico' in the system was in connection to this statement; nowhere else was the name mentioned. Lou searched under other spellings, other possible permutations, but they all drew a blank.

They'd never bothered to follow it up, she thought. Despite the line of enquiry that they'd all hurtled down for so long: that Scarlett had run away. If she'd run away, with no clothes or food or money or passport, she had done it with help. But then there was that crime series, the one that had been discounted at the time – foreign girls going missing from Rhodes and Corfu. Even if they were much older, it felt as though that lead had been dismissed far too easily.

Lou put in a call to Caro's mobile number, but it went unanswered. She left her a message, asking if she knew any more about Nico and why this wasn't followed up at the time. Said that Caro could ring her back on the mobile whenever.

On the top of Scarlett's file was Juliette's statement. The short sentences gave a sense of the girl who'd given it, as much as of the DC who'd interpreted what she'd said and written it up. There was a suggestion of something behind it, some deep, unspoken trauma.

Scarlett did not discuss running away. I do not believe now that she ran away.

Lou hadn't interviewed Juliette. It had been obvious early on that Juliette was in a fragile, vulnerable state. They'd used their best ABE-trained interviewers, who had submitted the transcript as evidence. The statement was made separately. A few weeks after Scarlett's disappearance, Juliette had attempted suicide and ended up in hospital. There had been an investigation by the IPCC, but luckily they'd all followed policy to the letter and eventually it had been dropped. There had been no further interviews with Scarlett's sister.

What did she mean, *now*? Had she believed at some point, then, that Scarlett had run away?

There was a knock at Lou's open door and she looked up to see Caro.

'Hi,' she said, 'that was quick.'

'I was just heading to the car park; I didn't hear it ring. Sorry.'

'No problem – come and have a seat. Are you in a hurry?'

'To get back on the motorway? Not likely. How can I help?'

'It's this statement from Scarlett's sister.'

'Have you seen something interesting?'

'Juliette said that she doesn't believe *now* that Scarlett ran away. As if she'd changed her mind about it.'

Caro thought about this. 'Scarlett was fifteen; I think we were all hoping that she'd run away and not been abducted. Maybe Juliette was hoping the same thing, but by the time she gave her statement she had resigned herself because we hadn't heard anything or found her?'

'Had she run away before?'

'No. She'd been getting into a bit of trouble at school, though. By the sound of it she was just a typical teenager, testing her boundaries.'

Lou slotted the statement back into the case file. 'I'm in danger of losing sight of the real aim here – getting some useful intel that SB can use in Op Pentameter. It's easy to get lost in the file, wondering where it all went wrong, what we missed.'

Caro nodded. 'I understand. All we want to know is where exactly she's been for the last ten years, and it all starts with that night she disappeared.'

'That reminds me: did you get my message about that boy – Nico? Do you know if that was followed up?'

'Yes, they looked, but we never got anything more on him. The resort has a transient population of kids that come and work in the holiday season, and then disappear back to the mainland once the tourists leave. There's not much of a system for monitoring casual employees. They work on a day-by-day basis, some of them. The Greek police seemed to give up on that line of enquiry pretty quickly.'

'Even though she might have run away with him?'

'We only had that bar owner's statement. The girl who came in might not even have been Scarlett. The family denied all knowledge of a connection with a local boy. Even Juliette.'

Lou pulled out the statement again. 'She was asked about him, specifically?'

'I'd need to check the transcripts,' Caro said, 'but from the statement – doesn't it say something about friends? She had no friends in Greece?'

Lou read aloud from the statement: '*We didn't make any friends while we were on holiday. There were no people our age staying in the apartment block so we stayed together most of the time.*' Again, even that sounded loaded – nobody their age? At all?

'If they'd mentioned a boy she'd met, we would have made more of that connection. As it was, you remember, it was all about putting a watch on the ports . . .'

'I remember that,' Lou said. And spending days poring over maps of Greece, looking for possible routes away from Rhodes. 'Where's Scarlett now?'

'Back in the VVS, for the time being. I collected her from the hotel this morning and took her back there. We've connected her with Social Services and one of their officers has been trying to find her some emergency accommodation. And, in between that, I've been trying to talk to her. She won't say anything about her life, about what's happened. She just shuts up.'

'I've had a bit of an idea about that. I've got someone who might be able to help.'

SAM – Friday 1 November 2013, 11:30

Scarlett Rainsford. Sam couldn't quite believe it.

They were sitting in Lou's office, the door shut behind them. Sam was enjoying the warm, slightly uncomfortable feeling of having been proved right. She had sensed yesterday that something big was kicking off, not least because of the boss's unexpected trip to Knapstone, and this must have been it. Scarlett Rainsford.

'Where's she been?' was the first thing Sam thought to ask.

'She hasn't told anyone yet,' Lou said. 'Which is why I want you to talk to her.'

'Me?'

'If you've got nothing more urgent on. I'll give you a couple of hours to get up to speed with it – I've got the file here, you can have a look – and then I'll take you to meet her after lunch.'

'Right,' Sam said.

'It's supposed to be informal – intel-gathering for SB, that's the

155

focus. And from my point of view, if we can persuade her to access the National Referral Mechanism, so much the better. SB haven't had any luck there. Have you met Caro Sumner?'

'No, is she SB?'

'She used to be Met. I wondered if you'd met her when you were there.'

'No, doesn't ring any bells.'

'Waterhouse has got her acting as Scarlett's personal minder for the time being. I think she could use a hand.'

'How is she?' Sam asked. 'Scarlett, I mean?'

Lou looked her straight in the eye, and Sam was struck by how exhausted she looked.

'She looks and acts perfectly in control. I doubt that's really the case.'

SCARLETT – Monday 25 August 2003, 11:16

The back of the minibus was full of people. That was what it felt like, anyway.

Towards dawn Scarlett had woken up to find the bus jolting, slowing down. Instantly she was alert, wondering if this was it: they were going to finish her off, bury her in the woods. When the vehicle stopped, she pulled herself back into the piles of luggage, trying to hide. Outside she could hear a conversation, voices she did not recognise, and then some women in the background, laughing. The sound of the language was different.

The back doors opened. Scarlett shrank back, tucking herself into a tight ball, expecting at any moment to be hauled out. But instead something else happened – someone got in. Then another person. Just as she lifted her head to see, the doors shut again. In the small space at the back of the bus were two new girls. One of them was barely conscious, her head lolling against the shoulder of the other. Both dark-haired.

Then the side door of the minibus slid open and the vehicle swayed as people climbed in. She counted – one, two ... three ... four ... and then lost count. Women, by the sounds of the voices, all of them talking and laughing in a language Scarlett could not understand. More luggage was piled in up to the roof, effectively sealing the three of them inside a tight, airless cave. Through a small gap at floor level Scarlett could feel a cold draught from the open door. She wriggled until her cheek was against the dirty floor, saw through the gap pairs of feet, dusty shoes, long skirts, bags and boxes.

Did they know?

Scarlett thought of calling out, trying to attract their attention. In the end, her dry throat giving out a croak, she shouted, just once, 'Hey! Can you hear me?'

The voices grew louder, all talking at once.

A moment later the back doors opened. Scarlett gasped and rolled into a ball.

'You,' said a man's voice. Something hard jabbed her in the back.

'Please help me,' she whispered. 'Please don't kill me. I want my mum. I want to go home ... '

'You be quiet,' the man's voice said. 'You make a sound, I kill these first and then you. Understand? Yes?'

Without turning, without looking, she nodded. Tears were pouring down her cheeks all over again. Just when she'd thought she couldn't cry any more.

Lou clearly didn't recognise the older woman who opened the door to her. 'DCI Smith,' she said, showing her warrant card. 'And DS Sam Hollands. We're hoping to see Scarlett.'

'Oh, come in. I'll let her know. You can wait in the kitchen.'

'You're Social Services?' Lou asked, when the woman didn't identify herself.

'That's right. My name's Orla. Have a seat.'

She shut the door behind her. Sam and Lou remained standing. There was a monitor on the work surface in the kitchen which was turned off. It was early afternoon and the sun was casting a golden light over the sorry-looking laminate units, the microwave which had been overlooked by the Cleaning Fairy, the mugs piled in the sink.

The door opened and another woman came in – short, greying hair, a smile that was kind. Sam had a vague feeling that she recognised her.

'Sam,' Lou said, 'this is Caro Sumner. Caro, this is DS Sam Hollands.'

'Nice to meet you,' Caro said. 'Lou told me you were coming. All help appreciated, and all that.'

'Hope I can be of use,' Sam said. 'Where's she going to go, after this?'

'No idea at the moment. It all depends on whether she's willing to access the National Referral Mechanism. At the moment she's refusing.'

'Why would she refuse?'

The door opened and Orla came back in. 'She's half-asleep, but she agreed to see you. I'm going to leave you to it for an hour or so, if that's okay. I need to get back to the office.'

'Thank you,' Lou said.

'I'll let you two go in,' Caro said. 'It'd be a bit crowded in there with all of us.'

They went into the living room.

Scarlett Rainsford was curled on the sofa, the hood of her sweat-shirt up, concealing much of her face. Her khaki coat was covering her like a blanket, just a pair of thick socks with grubby soles poking out. The television was tuned to one of the music channels, the sound down.

'Hi again, Scarlett. Remember me from last night? My name's Lou Smith.'

Scarlett remained where she was.

'This is my colleague, Detective Sergeant Sam Hollands.'

'Hello,' Sam said, sitting down on the armchair opposite Scarlett's sofa.

Scarlett raised her head, briefly. 'I'm sick of being asked questions.'

'I bet,' Sam said. 'Hard to sort things out without them, though.'

'Nobody's asking the right questions, either,' Scarlett said, rolling her eyes.

'It's not easy to know what the right questions are. This isn't the sort of thing that happens every day. Certainly not in Briarstone.'

Scarlett smirked at this, and Sam breathed out.

'I just want to get out of here,' Scarlett said. At last she sat up, pulling the coat over her knees, hugging them.

'Where will you go?' Sam asked.

'Anywhere. I have got friends I can stay with. Or I can find some-where.'

'We need to be sure you'll be safe,' Lou said.

'I can look after myself. I'm only here because you lot keep giving me free food and hotels and I'm too fucking tired to get up and walk out. Sooner or later you're going to get bored with me in any case.'

'We can get you access to housing, anything else you need for a fresh start, through a system that looks after victims of trafficking,' Sam said. 'But, in order to get that, you have to talk to us about what happened to you, about where you've been.'

'I don't need housing. I told you, I can look after myself.'

'I'm sure you can,' Sam said. 'You're an adult, and a UK citizen. All I'm saying is, there's help for you – so why not take it?'

Scarlett's right foot was dancing an impatient little beat. 'Because there's nothing I can tell you that will help. It's a trade-off, right? I tell you stuff and you help me. If there's nothing to tell, there's noth-ing to give. It's bloody extortion just like everything else.'

The three women sat in silence for several seconds.

At last Sam said, 'You spoke to Caro, didn't you? When they first found you?'

Scarlett answered this with a shrug.

'You mentioned you'd been brought here in a lorry – ' she con-sulted her notes ' – and that someone in Briarstone was responsible for bringing you here.'

'You want me to give you names,' Scarlett said, 'and I'm not going to do that. It wouldn't help you anyway. I don't know who you think I am. I'm a nobody. I cook them oven chips and beans and wash their sheets. I don't know anything about anything.' The sweatshirt had ridden up her arms, revealing pale skin, scratches.

Sam and Lou exchanged glances. These things took time, there was no doubt about it, but time wasn't something they had in abundance. If Waterhouse didn't get what he wanted out of Scarlett, then it wouldn't be long before the press found her. Tempting as it was to threaten her with this potential scenario, in all probability it would make her leave the house and disappear. Free pizza – or whatever it was keeping her here – was good only as long as it did the trick.

Lou had one more question to ask. 'Scarlett, can you tell us about Nico?'

The reaction was immediate. The hooded head snapped up and the eyes that fixed on Lou were cold. 'Who?'

Lou risked continuing. 'A couple of days before you disappeared, you were looking for a boy called Nico. I just wondered who he was.'

Scarlett smiled, then hid her mouth behind the sleeve of her sweatshirt. She chewed the cuff. Still watching. 'He was just a lad I met in Greece. I thought he was all right but he turned out to be an arsehole. Like all men.'

'How was he an arsehole?' Sam asked.

But, to this, Scarlett shrugged and shook her head. 'What time's my mother turning up?'

Lou said, 'I think the flight was this morning.'

'Some of your lot are bringing her from the airport, apparently,' Scarlett said. 'I'd like something to drink.'

'What? Tea? Coffee?' Lou asked.

'I can make it,' Sam said.

'No, don't worry, I'll go.'

'Tea,' said Scarlett.

The living room door shut behind Lou. Scarlett's eye contact was unwavering. 'You gay?' she asked, out of nowhere.

162

Sam had been asked this in interviews before; often it was a diversionary tactic, reasonably easily squashed, worth doing to establish who was in charge of the interview. This was different. She thought for a moment how to respond.

But Scarlett wasn't waiting. 'In a relationship? Got a girlfriend?'

'Not currently.'

There was a pause. Sam defused the rising tension in the room as best she could, maintaining her own relaxed posture, keeping her breathing steady. 'How about you?' she asked.

'Don't do relationships,' Scarlett said. 'I don't think I ever will. Why are you here? What's your name again?'

'My name's Sam.'

'Are you, like, the last resort or something?'

'You're wasting everyone's time, Scarlett. I think you're desperate to get out of this whole situation but you don't know how to do it because you don't trust anyone. I can't tell you to trust me, or Lou, or anyone else. You have to decide that for yourself.'

'You have no idea. You have absolutely no idea.'

'So tell me.'

There was another silence. Sam watched Scarlett's chest rise and fall, her breathing quickening.

'You ever had a boyfriend? No, you're not going to answer, are you? You ever been fucked by a bloke, Sam, or have you always liked girls?'

Another pause. 'Tell me,' Sam said, gently. 'I'm listening.'

'My first time,' Scarlett said, 'was on a damp mattress, in a room in the back of a flat in Prague. There were three of them, three men. Later on I found out they all paid top rates because they knew I was a virgin. Two and a half hours, it took, with them taking it in turns. They held me down and when I kept fighting and struggling they punched me in the face until I was out of it, until I was too hurt to fight back any more. Once they'd finished I got to have a shower and wash the blood off, even though I could barely stand up. They gave me something to eat and drink, and then the bastard who was minding me had a go, too. He was grinning the whole time while I was crying with pain, because the woman who'd taken me to the flat was filming it for him on his mobile phone. I was fifteen years old. Before that night I'd only ever kissed one boy. A Greek boy called Nico.'

Outside, a car door slammed, then another. Voices, and then, moments later, the doorbell went.

'I'm guessing that's your mother,' Sam said.

Caro went to answer the door. Lou strained to hear the conversation on the doorstep.

Annie Rainsford had arrived in the back of an unmarked Škoda Octavia, collected from the airport at significant cost to the taxpayer by Terry Cartwright and Dave Porter. Police officers were used to travelling in twos, but even so it seemed a bit of an unnecessary extravagance to Lou, to have two Special Branch detectives providing a taxi service all the way from Gatwick. Clive was driving Juliette home separately. The family car had been in one of the long-stay car parks.

A few moments later Caro brought Annie into the kitchen. Lou had a brief moment to size her up. Ten years had passed since the last time they'd seen each other, but Lou would have recognised her in an instant. Dark, straight hair, big blue eyes rimmed with silky, wet-looking lashes. The tiny lines around her eyes were the only indication of the time that had passed. She was fifty-two, but she looked much, much younger. From a distance you might have thought she was a teenager herself: she was small and slight, with a girlish physique almost, an illusion completed by the tanned feet in plastic flip-flops, bitten fingernails, chipped bubblegum-pink nail polish. During the investigation, Lou remembered thinking that she and Clive made an unlikely couple: she was attractive, bright, pretty in fact – and Clive was much older, pale, clever but without any accompanying humour or wit. And yet they were married, and still married and holidaying together ten years down the line, despite everything their family had endured.

There was a flicker of recognition in Annie's eyes, a look that said, *I know you from somewhere.*

'Lou Smith,' she said, holding out her hand with a warm smile. 'It's been a long time, I know. I was a DC on the investigation when Scarlett went missing.'

'Oh! That's right. I remember. How are you?'

All very polite and friendly, despite the peculiar circumstances. But how did she expect her to be? Lou thought. There was no frame of reference for how you were supposed to behave after ten years without your daughter. Losing her as a child, finding her again as an adult.

And then Annie said something that took Lou's breath away.

'I told you she didn't run away. You didn't believe me, did you?'

Lou knocked on the door of the sitting room. Sam opened it; Scarlett didn't even look up, concentrating on the wet sleeve of the hoodie.

'Scarlett,' Lou said gently, 'your mum's here.'

'I'll be next door,' Sam said. 'Just call if you need anything.'

Lou had time to register Annie's face, the shock on it, something else there, too – fear? Confusion? – before she withdrew.

And as the door was closing, she heard something – Scarlett's hushed, urgent whisper, 'I haven't forgotten, you know. I saw you. *I saw you.*'

14:45

The conversation between the two women in the front room had been punctuated by long periods of silence. More than once Caro had got

166

to her feet, ready to go in there and see if they needed a break from each other, ask if they wanted tea or food or some other sustenance, and then, before she had made it to the door, one or other of them had started speaking again.

Annie had been by turns cold, dry-eyed and then sobbing like a child, hands over her face. Scarlett had remained on the sofa with her knees drawn up, seemingly immune to the emotional charge in the room.

Once they'd been left alone together, and the door had closed, Annie had taken a step towards Scarlett, her arms spread ready for an embrace. Scarlett had flinched, shrunk back into the sofa away from her, and then the strange thing Scarlett said: *I saw you*.

Annie had not reacted to that at all. She'd lowered herself gently down on to one of the armchairs, her gaze fixed on her daughter.

From the kitchen, Lou, Sam and Caro had watched the scene play out on the monitor with all the greedy fascination of fans watching the final of a Sunday night drama serial, but, from that opening, things quickly drew to an uncomfortable halt.

'Where have you been?' Annie asked at last.

Scarlett had shrugged in reply. 'All over the place.'

'How long have you been here? In Briarstone?'

There was silence in reply, and as they were both sitting motionless staring at each other Lou actually wondered if the camera had stopped working and had frozen on the last image.

And then, minutes later, Scarlett stretched out an arm, scratched the back of her wrist, and answered the question with another. 'When did you stop looking for me?'

And then it was Annie's turn to be silent.

'Did you even start?'

Annie responded, 'Sometimes you make mistakes. And if you

don't own up to them, sooner or later they turn into bigger mistakes and bigger ones, and then you can't admit to them at all, ever.'

They could see her face, just about, but the features looked impassive. What on earth was that about? Lou thought. Why didn't she grab Scarlett in a crushing hug, swear that they'd never stopped looking, never given up hope, not for a moment . . . say how her life had been crippled by losing her and how overjoyed she was to see her here, alive and breathing . . .

There was no accounting for people. That was one thing Lou had learned over the years – that people behaved in entirely unexpected ways. And that it didn't necessarily make them criminals, or guilty of anything – it just meant they were individuals. Who knew how you were supposed to react to a situation such as this one? It was unprecedented. Yesterday Annie had been relaxing by the pool; today she was back in the English drizzle, suffering another emotional turmoil and dealing with it as best she could.

'Your father and Juliette would like to see you,' Annie said then. She hadn't moved.

Your father, Lou noticed. Not *Dad* or *Daddy*.

'She's missed you,' Annie ventured. 'Don't you want to know how she is?'

Silence, in reply, and this time it went on for much longer. Ten minutes together and they had already run out of things to say.

'Awkward,' said Lou eventually.

'Something tells me it's going to be a long day,' Caro replied.

Lou looked at her watch. Early afternoon already, and that hockey game to go to tonight. She would have to go home first, because there was no way she was going to spend a couple of hours sitting rinkside without some serious winter clothing to keep her warm.

She wasn't looking forward to it. Most of the other hockey games she'd been to (hockey, not ice hockey, because in Canada the distinction made was the reverse of the traditional one in the UK – in other words, 'hockey' was played on the ice, and 'field hockey' was what Lou had been tortured with at school) had been with Jason by her side as a fellow spectator. When he had been playing, she'd usually taken the opportunity to be elsewhere.

This time he'd insisted – something about it being a crucial league match and how he really wanted her there. And, since they both had the day off the next day, they could spend some time together.

She had asked in reply if she couldn't just meet up with him after the match, maybe even cook dinner for him and have it ready for when he came back, but his response to that had been clear. 'Yeah, right.'

'What's that supposed to mean?'

He'd raised an eyebrow. 'You know what's going to happen, Lou. You're going to work late and you won't make it to the match, you'll make it just in time for something to eat from the takeaway if I'm lucky, or maybe not even make it at all. So what's the point?'

He was right, of course. The chances were high that she would stay here listening to Annie and Scarlett, and would miss the match entirely.

In the living room, Annie and Scarlett stared each other out. Lou looked at her watch again.

15:40

Annie Rainsford emerged from the living room of the VVS after an hour and a half of stilted conversation with Scarlett.

She headed for the kitchen, but Lou got up from the monitor quickly and intercepted her in the hallway. Her eyes were red and puffy from crying, but her complexion was clear. She brushed her hair away from her face and it fell in a glossy wave. Freshly washed this morning, before leaving for the airport.

'I need to get back home,' she said. 'Get some washing on, check that Juliette is okay.'

'How did you get on?' Sam asked.

Annie wiped her eye with the back of her index finger, as though to prevent her eye make-up from running down her cheek, even though it didn't look as if she was wearing any. 'Not good,' she said.

Lou thought about it for a second, glancing back towards the kitchen door where Caro was waiting. 'I'll run you home, shall I?'

'That would be great. Thank you. I have no idea where this place even is.'

'Mind if I stay for a bit?' Sam asked.

'Sure,' Lou said. 'Ring me later?'

It had started to rain properly, great heavy drops that splashed up from the pavement and soaked through Lou's suit jacket within minutes. Lou led the way to her car, Annie dashing behind her. They were both drenched. Doors slammed, *clunk-clunk*, and almost immediately the car started to steam up. Lou started the engine and turned up the fan.

'Bit of a change from Spain,' she said.

'Yes,' Annie said. And actually laughed. 'It was hot when I left this morning.'

'It must have come as a huge shock,' Lou said. 'After all this time.'

Annie clicked her seatbelt into place. 'Yes and no. I knew I would get a call sooner or later.'

170

Lou let this hang in the air between them for a few moments while the windscreen cleared. Her mind raced through the interviews, the transcripts, all the information and intelligence she had handled ten years ago and whether Annie and Clive had seemed to give any idea, at all, that Scarlett's disappearance had been somehow expected, or her whereabouts known. She'd been fifteen. That had been the only thing. She'd been fifteen, and if Clive and Annie had known about Nico – the Greek boy that Scarlett had met in Rhodes – they had not shared that information with the police.

'What makes you say that?' Lou asked, pulling out of the parking space.

'I just knew,' Annie said. She had her face turned away, towards the rain-spattered window, so Lou could not see her expression. 'Are you a mum?'

'No,' Lou said.

'Well. A mother knows these things. I always knew she was alive.'

It felt as if Annie was backtracking now, that she realised she'd said something out of place and was playing the old 'mother's instinct' card, the one non-mothers had no right to argue with.

Lou changed the subject. 'I'm glad you managed to get a flight back.'

Annie didn't answer immediately. Her light summer skirt was wet from the rain, clinging to her legs. Lou noticed she was shivering, so she turned up the heater.

'They were going to charge us for a full-price ticket to come back, you know. We couldn't really do that for all three of us – you wouldn't believe how much it cost. Clive got on to the management and then they caved in. Still charged us an admin fee to change the tickets, though. Juliette's struggling with everything. She can't deal with changes to her routine.'

'What's the issue with Juliette?' It was like tugging at a fraying cloth, trying to get Annie to unravel.

'She has behavioural problems. We still can't get a firm diagnosis. She falls through all the cracks.'

'I'm sorry. That must be incredibly difficult.' *Behavioural problems?* Lou thought. *She must be twenty-three by now ...*

Annie nodded. 'She's fine most of the time. I mean, we all have our quirks, don't we? But it takes so long to get her used to an idea ... so to change things around without notice is, um, catastrophic.'

'Did you tell her that Scarlett has come back?'

'No. Not yet. Maybe tonight, when she's had a chance to settle.'

'Has she ever talked about Scarlett?'

Another long pause, so long that Lou wondered if Annie had even heard. She was on the verge of repeating the question when Annie came back with an answer. Wistful, as though the thought of it had taken her back across the years to the time when they had all, possibly, been in a happier place. 'All the time.'

'She must have found it very, very difficult to deal with.'

'She wasn't quite so bad then. I mean, she was ... unusual. But it's like Scarlett's disappearance set her off. When we came back ... ' She trailed off. Something on the road had distracted her. They were at the traffic lights by the bridge, waiting to join the interminable queues around the one-way system. 'I didn't realise they'd closed down.'

'Sorry?'

'The pub on the corner. I used to drink in there when I was a student.'

'Oh,' Lou said. 'Yes. It closed about a month ago. You were saying? About Juliette?'

'Mm? Oh ... ' Annie seemed lost in thought again. 'Yes. When we came back – she kept talking about Scarlett as though she wasn't missing at all. As though she'd gone to visit someone. She kept asking when she was coming back. I mean, she was thirteen, not a baby. She just didn't seem to understand.'

'What about the school?'

'She didn't go back for months. She was self-harming, tried suicide – you probably know about that. She got counselling, but it didn't seem to help. She just wouldn't talk, not to us, not to anyone.'

'But she talks about Scarlett now?'

Annie gave a short laugh, and turned to look at Lou for the first time since they'd left the VVS. 'It's the only thing she does talk about. The only thing. Every day. "When's Scarlett coming home?" It drives everyone mad. She doesn't acknowledge us at all any more. That's why we think she's going to find it hard to deal with her actual return. She's not the same Scarlett that Juliette remembers, is she?'

They got stuck in traffic, of course. It was only a couple of miles across town but a bin lorry appeared to have broken down in the middle of a pedestrian crossing and there was gridlock either side of it.

'Are you going to try to talk to Clive?' Annie said. 'I can't say he'll be pleased to see you again. You were the one who was always hanging around the house.'

'Yes,' Lou said, trying to make light of the less-than-favourable description.

'He was in a bad place back then. You can't blame him.'

'No, I don't. I can't imagine what it must have been like for both of you, coming home from Greece without your daughter. But Clive just didn't want to be interviewed, did he?'

'He saw it as wasting time. He thought you should all have been out there looking for her, not asking stupid questions. You all kept asking us the same questions, over and over. It was like nobody was listening to the answers.'

I was listening, Lou thought. *I listened to everything. None of it made sense.*

The traffic ahead cleared and a few minutes later Lou pulled up outside the house. It had stopped raining, thank goodness. Annie was staring up at the hedge as though she'd been away for months. Somewhere nearby, someone was digging up the road or drilling; the noise reverberated around the neighbourhood, then mercifully stopped.

'It's a nice house,' Lou said, her voice suddenly loud.

'Yes. And nice to get home after a holiday, isn't it?'

Lou watched her face, trying to read the unreadable. 'Here's my card,' she said. 'You can ring me any time, if there's anything you want to talk about. I'll give you a call in a day or so, maybe to talk to Clive and Juliette. Would that be okay?'

Annie nodded, distracted. She was still looking up at the house. 'Has she been here?'

'Has who been here?'

'Scarlett. Did she sleep here last night?'

Of all the questions, Lou thought. How would they have got inside? Break in, just so Scarlett could sleep in her old room without anyone else there?

'No. She hasn't been here since . . . ' *Since you all left for Greece*, she thought. And left the sentence hanging.

She tried again. 'Is there anything else you need, Annie? Anything you'd like to ask?'

That seemed to do the trick. Annie looked away at last, opened the door and got out. 'No – no. Thank you for the lift. It's very kind of you.'

Lou waited, watching Annie who was standing by the gate, rooting around in her oversized shoulder bag, presumably for her keys. A green Volvo was on the driveway; Clive and Juliette must have got back from the airport too.

The drilling started up again, and Lou drove away.

What was Annie so afraid of? And was it even that – was it fear? After so many years in 'the Job', so many interviews and meetings and discussions with all manner of individuals, Lou believed she was good at reading people, good at interpreting emotional states and even better at exploiting them to get the best possible resolution. No, 'exploiting' was the wrong word. Turning situations to an advantage, perhaps. You couldn't rely on someone to behave in a particular way just because you yourself would act like that in a given situation. But, even so, there were certain things you could expect: a missing child would cause grief, panic, hysteria, numbness . . . and any number of other reactions. But what Annie had displayed instead had been quite different.

The family's strange behaviour had given the original investigation team cause for concern, and for a long time one of the main lines of enquiry had been that Clive – and Annie – had been responsible for Scarlett's death and the disposal of her body. They'd been so weird, it had made everyone think they were hiding something. Lou had worked through her allocated investigative tasks, all the time thinking through the options and considering why they might be behaving as they were. She'd thought about Annie being afraid of Clive, but that didn't seem to fit. Clive wasn't afraid of Annie, either. They interacted with each other as a perfectly normal family, but with any outsiders they were – well, odd.

She couldn't read Annie. She hadn't been able to read her all those years ago, and even less so now.

SAM – Friday 1 November 2013, 17:30

Caro had gone out to get food when the Social Services woman came back. She had brought a bag of clothes for Scarlett, which were glanced at and discarded at the other end of the sofa.

'I've got my own sodding clothes,' she said. 'I don't need any cast-off shit.'

'I'll see if I can sort out a visit to the house where you were living, so you can collect some stuff,' Sam said. 'Won't be till tomorrow, though.'

Scarlett shrugged. 'I don't care. I do want my phone back, though. Bastards took it. It's got all my numbers in it.' She fixed Sam with an accusing stare.

'I'll ask tomorrow,' Sam said. Not lying, exactly. She could still ask, even if she knew already what the answer was going to be. 'You were telling me about Nico.'

'I wasn't. Your boss mentioned him, not me.'

'You met him on holiday,' Sam prompted. 'It's just that nobody else – the family I mean – talked about him. Did you keep him a secret?'

Scarlett glanced out of the window, as if Annie might be there, listening in. 'No. They all knew.'

'Why do you think they didn't tell us you'd met someone?'

She picked at a thumbnail, studying it closely, before answering. 'No idea. You'll have to ask them. Did your lot interview him? Nico, I mean.'

'No. They never located him.'

176

Scarlett gave a short, humourless laugh. 'Not surprised.'

The front door opened and closed, and Sam heard Caro talking to Orla in the kitchen. Moments later Caro came in with fish and chips, three packets of it, cans of Pepsi, a big tub of table salt and a bottle of ketchup. The smell of the chips made Sam realise how hungry she was.

'They have chips with mayo in Holland,' Scarlett said, unwrapping and chewing. 'I thought I liked it at the time. They never asked if I wanted ketchup – it always just came with mayo.'

'Nothing like red sauce with chips,' Caro said cheerfully.

'I guess it's good to have a choice,' said Sam.

Scarlett stopped chewing. After a moment she put the open packet of food down on to the coffee table, cracked open a can and drank. Belched.

'Talking of choice . . . you do need to have a think about what's next, Scarlett,' Caro said. 'Where you're going to go. Think about your options, decide what you want to do.'

Scarlett was motionless, staring at Caro. There was a fiery ball of emotion there, being held back, and Sam recognised that the energy Scarlett was expending just holding herself together was fuelling it. She was going to explode, and there was something about the last part of the conversation that had just lit the fuse.

She got to her feet. 'I need to go,' she said.

'What?' Caro asked. 'Go where?'

But Scarlett was already out of the door, flinging it open so hard that the door handle cracked the plaster on the wall, running, running from the room to the hallway, flinging that door open as well. By the time Sam had reacted and followed her, Scarlett was halfway down the street, running down the middle of the road.

She was fast – God, she was fast. Sam was struggling to catch

177

up, realising that she was losing ground. *How's she so fit?* The air was cold enough to make Sam's lungs burn with it.

'Wait!' Sam shouted, trying to get her to slow down at least, or stop.

'Fuck off!' Scarlett screamed, without looking back. 'Leave me alone!'

At the end of the road Scarlett turned abruptly left into an alleyway. Sam followed, running as hard as she could to catch up. She didn't know this part of town well, but when she turned the corner Sam realised the alleyway led directly into Memorial Park. Darkness, trees, a playground, a boating lake, a café, which would be closed, of course – where the hell was she going?

By the time Sam got through the metal gate that was supposed to be locked but regularly got broken open, Scarlett had disappeared. Beyond was blackness, nothing but a few feet of path in front of her, street-lights ahead in the distance. Sam stopped, panting hard, coughing, hands on her knees. 'Scarlett!'

Sam listened. A dog was barking somewhere in the blackness. And then she heard something else. A cry, rising in the chilly air, turning into something unearthly. A wail, a scream.

'Scarlett!' Sam followed the path ahead, trying a light jog.

'I said piss off!' The voice came from up ahead, high-pitched, ending on a sob. 'Leave me alone!'

As Sam's eyes grew accustomed to the darkness she could make out shapes: trees, bushes, the edge of the grass. A bench, with a dark shape hunched at one end of it. Sam made for the bench, sat at the other end. She could hear Scarlett's breath, coming in jerky spasms.

'She has no idea,' Scarlett said. 'Choice! What choice have I got? What choice have I ever had? It's a fucking joke . . . '

Sam said nothing. She waited, while Scarlett cried and cried. After several minutes the breathing began to even out again and the sobs subsided. Sam found a tissue in the pocket of her jeans, passed it down to the other end of the bench.

'Why are you even still here?' Scarlett said, snatching the tissue.

'I'm not sure,' Sam said cautiously.

'What sort of an answer's that?'

'I don't want to presume I know what's best for you, Scarlett. But in the meantime I'm just going to hang around in case there's anything you need that I can provide. Like, you know, a tissue.'

'What I need is my bloody phone back. I have got mates, you know. I could be at Reg's house, watching Sky Movies and entertaining his kid, instead of being holed up in a grotty police house with a bunch of jobsworths.'

'We may be jobsworths but at least we're giving you free food, and a hotel room.'

Scarlett made a noise that might have been a laugh. 'Don't make me laugh. It's the Travel Inn. It's hardly the bloody Ritz, is it?' There was a pause. 'Fucking freezing out here. I left my coat behind.'

'Shall we head back?'

'In a minute.'

She was taking deep breaths. Steeling herself to go back.

'I can't imagine how difficult that must have been, seeing your mother again.'

In the dim light Sam could see Scarlett's head turn to face her. 'I bet nobody else sees it like that: *difficult*. Everyone seems to expect me to be bloody overjoyed.'

'If you'd wanted to see her, you would have done it before now, wouldn't you?'

'Exactly. The only person I want to see is Juliette, and the trouble is I can't see her without seeing them first.'

'Haven't you tried to contact Juliette, since you've been back?'

There was a long pause. 'You don't know them. They would have found out.'

'So you haven't contacted anyone at all?'

'Nobody.'

'Were they keeping you prisoner, Scarlett?' It was not meant as an accusation. As soon as she'd uttered the words Sam regretted them, thinking it too much of a challenge. But Scarlett didn't take it that way.

'No. They were all right to me most of the time. I don't think you lot understand what it's like, being dead for ten years. It's actually quite liberating. It's suddenly being alive again that's hard work.'

Abruptly Scarlett stood up.

'I'm ready to go back now.'

She started walking towards the gate, Sam beside her. When they were out on the road again, under the street-lights, Sam saw her hugging her arms across her chest. She was small – tiny, really. Like her mother. Sam's heart lurched. She wanted to give her a big hug, tell her it was okay, that things would get better.

'Why does your mother dress like a teenager?' Sam asked.

Scarlett didn't look up. 'She's just weird.'

As they approached the house, Scarlett's steps slowed.

'Okay?' Sam asked.

Scarlett shook her head vigorously.

'Come on,' Sam coaxed. 'It'll be all right. I'll sit with you for a bit, shall I?'

'Can you make her go away?' Scarlett asked, her voice just a whisper.

'Who? Caro?'

Scarlett nodded. 'She doesn't understand. She doesn't get it.'

'You should try and explain it to her, then. Or to me.'

'Maybe.'

At the doorway, Sam paused. 'You go on in,' she said. 'I'll follow you in a sec.'

Back in her car, Sam rooted through her glovebox for the cheap Pay As You Go handset she'd bought from the supermarket two months ago. She kept it in the car, charged and turned off, just in case she ended up stranded somewhere without a phone, because on more than one occasion she had left her mobile at home or in the office and been lost without it. Of course, since she'd bought this emergency replacement, she'd managed to keep her own phone on her at all times. Right at the back, under a pile of CDs and some windscreen wipes, she found the charger for it, with the wire tie still wrapped round the cord.

Walking back up towards the house, Sam turned on the phone, relieved to see it was fully charged, and dialled her own number. She let it ring in her pocket for a moment before she disconnected.

When she went back inside and into the living room, Scarlett had finished eating and packed away all the cartons and greasy chip paper into the carrier bag. She was watching the news with the sound turned down.

'Here,' Sam said, handing Scarlett the phone and the charger.

'What's this?'

'It's my spare phone. It's got a tenner's worth of credit on it.'

'You're giving me a phone?'

'I'm lending you a phone. I just rang mine, so the last number dialled is my number. Keep it safe, right?'

She took the bag of rubbish back to the kitchen. Caro and Orla were in there discussing the shortage of emergency accommodation and whether the magnanimity of the chief constable would stretch to a few more nights in the Travel Inn.

'How is she?' Caro asked.

'She's okay. Just a bit of a meltdown.'

'Was it something I said?'

'I think it was us trying to get her to make decisions. But it was only the trigger, don't beat yourself up about it.'

'I need to get off home now,' Caro said. 'Are you staying?'

'I'll sit with her for an hour or so,' said Sam. 'Then I need to go too.'

She went back through to the living room. Scarlett was playing with the phone. 'Wish I could remember people's numbers. Not much use having a phone without them.'

'I'll have it back, then, if you don't want it,' Sam said. 'Orla made you a tea.'

She put it down on the coffee table firmly, slopping a little on to the stained formica.

'Thanks.'

'And Caro's gone, for now. She'll be back tomorrow.'

Scarlett tucked the little phone into the pocket of her hoodie, leaned her head back against the cushion. 'I'm so tired but I don't want to sleep. I have nightmares. Every single night. It's exhausting.'

'What sort of nightmares?'

Scarlett didn't answer straight away. Her eyes closed and Sam was beginning to think she was falling asleep. Then she said, quietly, 'I saw a girl get her head blown off once. They did things like that. If you didn't do what they wanted, they just – *bang* – you know. It was so easy for them. I see her all the time – her face. She

182

didn't know it was going to happen. Sometimes I dream it's happening to me, it's *my* head being blown apart and I can't feel it; it doesn't hurt or anything. But I can just see it happening.'

'Does anything make it better?'

'When I get so shattered that I'm too tired to dream. So I stay up as late as I can. Doesn't always work. What is it you want? What is it you all want me to do?'

Hearing it put so baldly, Sam was taken aback for a moment.

'I mean, you're all on at me to decide what to do next. You must want something. What is it?'

'We're trying to find out what happened to you, Scarlett. So we can stop it happening to other people. We need you to give us a statement.'

'About Greece?'

'About everything.'

'And then you'll leave me alone?'

Sam thought about her response. 'You're an adult, Scarlett. Far as I know, you haven't done anything wrong. You're free to walk out any time, if you want to.'

Scarlett nodded, slowly. 'I can't think straight right now. Maybe I'll feel better tomorrow.'

'I hope so. Scarlett, when your mum arrived, I overheard you say quite a strange thing. You said, "I saw you." Can you tell me what you meant?'

Sam had chosen her moment deliberately, trying to catch Scarlett off guard. And there was a flicker, a swift look, a moment, and then she composed herself again.

'Oh. I saw her on the telly. Giving an interview about me.'

It was a lie.

'Really? When?'

183

'Not long after I got taken. I was in a flat somewhere. I saw her being interviewed on the news but the sound was off and the subtitles were in Polish or whatever, so I couldn't understand what she was saying.'

In the months following Scarlett's abduction, her parents had been interviewed several times, made appeals, even been on *Crimewatch*. Annie had never been interviewed without Clive, and as far as Sam could remember Annie had never said more than two or three words.

Back then, Clive had done all the talking.

SCARLETT – Amsterdam, Wednesday 12 September 2012, 13:49

Scarlett watched the man for a long time from the window, waiting for him to approach.

Some of them stared at her; she was used to that. They'd stand back a bit, sometimes with their mates, two or three of them, pointing, smiling, egging each other on. Other people walked past without even acknowledging her, without looking, avoiding eye contact as though she was a mannequin, modelling clothes.

Modelling her own skin.

Sometimes they stood right in front of her, window-shoppers, on their own, staring at her full on, challenging. It wasn't a comfortable feeling. She coped with it by smiling, beckoning to them, trying to get them out of the way at least – sometimes they sent people like this to test her, make sure she was performing properly. Once she'd given a guy the finger and she'd taken a beating for it.

This one was unnerving her, though. He was standing in the alleyway opposite, leaning against the wall. In another place and time he might have been waiting for a bus, or a friend, or just passing the time by people-watching. But his eyes were on her window, and he hadn't looked away. Not once. He might have been checking up on her. He might have been police. He might just have been nervous, afraid, never been with a girl before. Whatever, she had to behave in exactly the same way. Look beguiling. Tempt him. Make money from the poor bastard.

If nothing else, it passed the time.

So far she had given him a smile and nothing else. He'd not responded, other than to maintain his stare. The trouble was, it was quiet out there. Not even many shoppers passing by; certainly not many tourists on a rainy Wednesday. She had made less than two hundred euros so far and it was already early afternoon. If she didn't make some more money before the runner came at six, she would be in trouble. She got to her feet and moved to the glass, pressing her hands high and spreading her legs, arching her back. She tried another smile.

He was young, but that didn't necessarily mean anything. They sent out police officers who looked young, thinking they wouldn't be suspected, thinking the runners wouldn't notice them. And she definitely hadn't seen him before.

When she had first arrived in Amsterdam she would not have noticed if the same man had visited her two days running, but these days she paid more attention. Part of it was self-preservation – knowing the ones who would get a kick out of smacking her one – and then there was the other extreme: the easy ones who just wanted to talk or cry or be held, and paid you the same and sometimes more. It helped to know what you were likely to have to deal with. The other girls dealt with it by getting off their faces on smack. Scarlett dealt with it by trying to stay in control.

The man moved.

Scarlett watched him approach, saw the way he looked left and right up the street, as if he wanted to make sure nobody was checking him out. When he got closer his mouth twitched in a smile. It made him look mean. She closed the curtains and went to let him in.

'Hi,' she said. 'How are you? What is it you'd like?'

'You're English?' he said. His accent was Dutch. He was still by the door.

'Yes,' she said, nervous now, determined not to show it. Chin up. 'What do you want?'

'Just to talk,' he said.

Shit, shit. He was police, she knew it. And he was putting his hand in his pocket and pulling out his ID.

'You still have to pay,' she said. 'Hundred an hour.'

'Sure.'

The wallet came out and he counted five twenty-euro notes, put them on the bed. No ID card. Not yet. She smiled, tried to relax. Maybe he wasn't police after all; maybe he was going to tell her about how his girlfriend didn't understand his needs, how his mother hadn't listened to him, how his father had laughed at him. She counted the notes, stuffed them through the letterbox in the back wall.

'What do you want to talk about?' she asked, trying not to sound suspicious. She sat down on the edge of the bed, patted the grubby coverlet invitingly. 'You want me to talk dirty?'

'No, no. I am interested that you are English,' he said, sitting down. He took off his jacket, laid it carefully over the hard wooden chair that stood next to the bed.

'If you want to improve your language skills, I am sure there are people who charge less than me.'

He laughed. 'So how is it that you are working here?'

Scarlett stared at him for a moment. 'That's none of your business,' she said. She'd heard this question many times before, and it never ceased to amaze her, the crazy things people thought. Did they genuinely think she was here through choice? That she would choose to sit in a window in her underwear, on display, waiting for the next ugly, filthy, sexually inadequate bastard to come and use her body? Why did none of them ever stop to *think* about it, about the hideousness of it all, of what they were doing? How could this ever, ever be right?

'I know, I know. I'm sorry. I am just – interested.'

She knew he was more than likely police, then. She fantasised about this all the time, dreamed about someone coming to take her away from this nightmare to a place where she'd be safe. She'd gone over in her head what she would say, how she would react, knowing as she did so that there was only one way to handle this. The voice in her head was screaming for help.

'I came here because I always wanted to do this,' she recited, trying to keep her voice light, knowing it sounded flat. 'I always wanted to make people happy. You see, I have an insanely high sex drive. I need to fuck guys all the time or else I feel sad. So this is the perfect job for me.'

She had used this answer so many times that it got trotted out without any stumbling or hesitation. And none of them even considered that it might not be true! They believed it, because the truth was too awful to contemplate. Stupid fuckers, all of them.

'Don't you have family? People who are missing you?'

'No,' Scarlett said. 'My parents don't miss me at all.' The first thing she'd said that had been honest.

Before he could ask her another question, she tried to divert him. 'What about you?' she asked. 'Do your family know you come looking for girls in the red light district on a Wednesday afternoon?'

He laughed, and his skin coloured. He had kind eyes. 'No, no. This is our secret. What's your name?'

'Stella.'

'Is that your real name?'

'No, but it's the only name I use now. What's yours?'

'Stefan. Have you been working here a long time?'

I've been here years, Scarlett thought. *Before this I was in Poland, and the Czech Republic.* The thought of it made her think about Cerys's sister Aimee, how she'd gone travelling with her friends, backpacking round Europe. Seeing the sights. Had come home with a memory stick full of photos of old buildings, and boys.

'A little while,' she said eventually.

He was pushing it, really pushing it, Scarlett thought. It meant one of two things. Either he was with the police, trying to get information out of her, because he wanted to rescue her and protect her. Or he had been sent by them, to test her out. See how likely it was that she would try to run. If he was with the police, then there was no way they could guarantee her safety. She was already in danger if any of the runners had seen him come in – any minute now the enforcers would burst in, haul him out and beat her for good measure. If he was one of them, then she needed to be more forceful with this, or else she would get a beating when he reported back to them.

'Look, Stefan,' she said, 'this isn't how I usually entertain my clients. I know you're trying to be kind, but I really don't need your help, okay? I just want to get on with my job. Now – ' she checked the clock next to the bed ' – you've had ten minutes already; is this really what you want from me, or would you like me to give you the best blowjob of your life?'

And after that he relented. Twenty minutes later, he left her alone to return to the window and wait for the next one. She watched him walk away, the saunter in his step. When he'd come, he'd actually cried out. She hadn't expected that. The cops sometimes took advantage, so she was still none the wiser.

LOU – Friday 1 November 2013, 18:40

Instead of going straight home after leaving Annie, Lou went back to the office. She wanted to write up the details of what had happened with Scarlett and Annie before the conversations went out of her head.

That task completed, she got distracted reading more of the original Op Diamond file: the details of the searches that had been conducted around the resort in Rhodes. Initially the searches had been haphazard, including all manner of people who had turned up and shown an interest, including tourists, locals, and Clive Rainsford himself. Later, the same areas were combed by police with dogs. Nothing useful had been found.

Further down, the search reports and witness statements gave way to letters from concerned members of the public: British tourists who had been in the resort at the time and had opinions about Scarlett and what might have happened to her, and people who knew the Rainsfords in Briarstone and felt the need to share what they thought. It seemed everyone had a theory about where Scarlett had gone.

And none of them had got it right.

Lou checked her watch. If she was going to make it to Jason's hockey game she was already cutting it fine. She looked back at the file, the stack of papers that were still sitting, unread. Somewhere in that stack might just be something useful, something Sam could use to persuade Scarlett to open up.

She picked up her phone and sent Jason a text.

Really sorry, held up at work. Hope game goes well.
Maybe see you later? Xxx

SCARLETT – Saturday 15 September 2012, 16:42

There was a pattern to the days.

She spent the afternoon, evening and most of the night in the room, seeing men who came in off the street. Some days were busier, and she almost liked that because the time passed quickly. Over the course of the evening, the runners would pay her regular visits in between clients, to collect the money that had accumulated in the back room, replenish her supply of condoms and check that she was still alive, still behaving. If the money wasn't enough, she would get pushed around a bit, threatened. One particularly slow day they'd spent nearly an hour slapping her and kicking her, pulling her hair, telling her that if she didn't get some customers in they would sell her to the Lithuanians.

This particular threat had not meant much, until she'd plucked up the courage to ask one of the other girls what was so bad about the Lithuanians.

'They don't feed you,' she had said. 'They work you until you can't work any more, then they dispose of you. It's the end. Going to them is like the end. And they film it.'

She did get food, at least. Once or twice during the evening they would bring her something – a burger, a Coke, chips smothered with mayonnaise. It was a brief respite – the chance to eat while they collected the money, checked her over; then they would take what she hadn't had a chance to cram in her mouth away with them.

They brought drugs, too. They tried hard to get her to take them. The other girls relied on them totally. At the beginning, something had stopped her, maybe some urge to rebel; and now she knew it

191

was a good thing. The other girls were all dependent on the stuff, utterly reliant on their supply. They used it to keep going, to block out the misery of their existence, not realising that it was also reinforcing the bars of their prison. What was the point in worrying about your life coming to an end, when inside you were already half-dead?

Sometimes, along with the food, they still brought her crack. Usually when she was having a bad day. When they tried to get her to take it, she put on the fake smile and told them that she was better to them alive and awake, that she loved her job and that taking drugs would make her less appealing to the customers. As long as she didn't try anything, as long as she worked for them and did as she was told and brought the money in, they let her have this one small rebellion. At some point she had realised that she must be making good money, and because she wasn't off her face all the time she didn't attract unwanted attention, didn't generate complaints – maybe this was why they didn't force her to do the drugs. So she would decline, and they would shrug and take the crack to the next girl, who paid for it out of the wages she was theoretically earning but never saw. Scarlett was paid the same amount whether she took the drugs or not. This was not a point she felt able to argue. After all, what could she spend the money on, if it even existed?

Although she was saving them money and making them money, she was still a risk to them. Scarlett was awake and alert and that made her unpredictable. They watched her more closely than the others. They checked her more often. In the early hours of the morning, when she was so dead tired she could hardly keep her eyes open, they would come to fetch her. Sometimes, if it had been busy, they'd bring another girl in to replace her in the room; sometimes they locked up behind them. She always knew when she was done for the night because there would be two of them, maybe three: so that she was never without a hand on her arm, never without someone watching her with the open door.

Even back at the flat, which was a dingy four-roomed apartment over a pharmacy near the docks, she was never alone. She slept in a room with other girls; the erratic shifts they all worked, coupled with the inevitable exhaustion whenever they were brought together, meant that it was almost impossible to form friendships. Talking was discouraged, and not just by the men who brought them in; once in the room, all anyone ever wanted to do was sleep. Sleep was their only escape, their brief snatch at peace. Besides, any sort of discussion was dangerous. They all knew that.

So she slept, on dirty sheets, between two girls she might or might not recognise; and, when they came to wake her up, sometimes she was allowed a shower. Sometimes she got clean clothes, too; they were never hers. Sometimes there was food in the kitchen; usually there was coffee, strong and black. Towards noon she would be taken with other girls back to the strip, where they were delivered like packages to the various rooms, ready for action, and left alone.

But she wasn't really alone, ever. Even when she was in the window, tapping on the glass to try to attract attention, she was being watched. They were never far away.

SAM – Friday 1 November 2013, 22:30

When she finally got back to her car, Sam took some slow, deep breaths before dialling Lou's mobile number. Her chest hurt – probably from all that running earlier, not a good sign – and she couldn't stop coughing.

'Hi, Sam,' Lou said, when she picked up the call. 'How are you getting on?'

'Okay. I'm heading home now.'

'How's Scarlett?'

'Apart from a bit of a meltdown earlier, surprisingly good, I think. She's more or less agreed to give me a statement tomorrow. I'm meeting Ali first, though; I promised to go and see Ian Palmer's mum with him. I'll do that, go to the office and then go and see Scarlett late morning, if that's okay with you? You've got a rest day tomorrow, haven't you?'

'Yes, but you can ring me. Let me know how you get on.'

'Thanks,' Sam replied. 'Sorry to call so late. Hope I didn't interrupt anything.'

'No, I'm at home, don't worry. I was supposed to go and watch Jason play hockey but I ended up reading through the case file.'

'You work too hard, boss.'

Lou laughed. 'Maybe. I think it's more a case of not wanting to freeze my bum off watching grown men crash around on an ice rink.'

'Poor Jason.'

'Oh, don't worry, he's probably quite happy in the pub getting ratarsed with his brother. And meanwhile I'm going to get into my pyjamas and have an early night.'

SCARLETT – Tuesday 18 September 2012, 22:18

For the first few months in Amsterdam Scarlett had thought constantly about how she was going to escape. Thought about it every day. When there were men with her she was sizing up whether she could trust them, ask them for help; when she was alone she was fantasising about just opening the door and running away. It gave her focus. Gave her something to do.

She was never quite sure what stopped her – fear of the punishment, perhaps. Or maybe they just hadn't pushed her far enough yet. Everyone had their limit, the tipping point when tolerating the abuse was just not possible any more.

One summer's night the sounds of the rowdy crowds outside had been drowned out by an ear-splitting shriek. Scarlett was in her window, between customers, and saw the girl, half-naked, blouse unbuttoned showing her small breasts, running headlong down the cobbled street. She was small, chestnut hair in messy curls falling across her face, pale skin, eyes and mouth wide, desperate. Her arm had a bruise, a big one, yellowing. Scarlett had been struck by the thought that there would be other bruises, other injuries; there always were. Even if you couldn't see them. Watching through the window was like being slightly removed from reality, like watching a drama being played out on the television screen. Nothing but glass between her and the girl, and yet she was a world away: grabbing at passersby, crying and begging for help. Scarlett could hear her. 'Help, help me, please help me, *hilfe, bitte* . . . '

But she'd kept running. Nobody was following her or doing anything but staring.

At the corner a police car had pulled over. She got in the back and they took her away.

Scarlett had felt relief for her. It had been quite easy, hadn't it? The police had got to her quickly. Maybe that was the solution. You just had to be brave, go and find the police, you'd be okay.

But the next night Scarlett had overheard a whispered

conversation between two of the others, as they all tried to sleep in the flat. The girl's name was never spoken; probably nobody knew who she was anyway, and if they'd known her name it would not have been her real one. She'd been interviewed, then she'd left the police station because she needed to score. They'd offered her help, but couldn't provide it quickly enough for her needs. Of course her minder had found her – tipped off by someone in the police station, or someone watching it for him – and she was gone. 'Gone' meant she was probably dead. That was what they did that to girls who became a liability. They didn't just kill them quickly, of course. They used them first – filmed it. High prices could be obtained for those sorts of films.

One day, that will happen to me, Scarlett had thought. *One day, it will be my turn.*

As much as they didn't like the girls talking, this sort of conversation was rarely interrupted. It kept the girls quiet, well-behaved. What other option was there?

For days afterwards Scarlett had obsessed over the girl who had run down the street, wishing she had known her, wishing she had been able to talk to her, comfort her, tell her to just hold on. If only she had known the girl's name, it might have helped. They were all nameless here and that made it worse: the very last level of losing your dignity was to lose your own name; to have your identity, your very existence scrubbed out. *We are not human any more. We don't even exist.*

Whenever she thought of it, it reminded Scarlett of Yelena, running across the car park at that service station, freedom and safety just metres away . . . and the way her head had burst open, blood and bone and thought and hope and desire spraying in a wide arc in the night sky. How in that moment, that one split

196

second, the nightmare had ended for her. Ended before it had even begun.

It ended for all of them, sooner or later. *Where's my ending?* Scarlett thought, in the darkness of the bedroom. The other girls had fallen silent. She pulled the sheet over her shoulders, turned her face to the wall. *When is this going to end for me?*

LOU – Friday 1 November 2013, 23:45

Nothing less attractive than trying to sleep next to a man who's so drunk you've put a bucket beside the bed, just in case.

So romantic.

There had been no reply to Lou's text apologising for not making it to the hockey game, so it had been something of a surprise when Jason had turned up at her house hours later, drunk enough to require him to keep one hand leaning on the doorframe as he waved goodbye to the taxi that was idling outside.

'I got two assists,' he said.

'That's great,' she said, 'well done. You've been celebrating, then?'

'Yeah. I'm sorry, I had lots of beers.'

'Really?'

Lou had done the dutiful girlfriend bit: helped him to bed, half-listened to mumbled apologies that didn't make much sense, relieved at least that he was here and not passed out in an alleyway or even at home alone with nobody to listen out for him potentially choking, later on. She left the hall light on, in case he had trouble finding the bucket.

And of course she had just dropped off to sleep, finally, after what felt like hours of listening to him snore and then randomly stop breathing for long moments, when he turned over in bed and snaked his arm around her middle, pulling her against him and burying kisses in her hair. He smelled of alcohol but that wasn't the end of the world. Being woken up when you'd just fallen asleep was a little harder to forgive.

'Hey, beautiful girl,' he murmured into her ear. 'What are you sleeping for?'

'You're not going to throw up on me, are you?' she asked in reply.

'Would I do that to the woman I love, eh?'

Lou turned over to face him, and as she did so his hands pushed up inside her pyjama top and then his mouth followed, planting kisses on her bare stomach. She ran her fingers through his hair, encouraging him lower. 'You're just saying that because you're drunk.'

He was busy, or pretending that he couldn't hear. And then she became distracted at what he was doing, pleasantly surprised that he was even more skilled at it after all that alcohol. After a few minutes she didn't even mind having been woken up; she had a rest day booked, so there was a lie-in to look forward to.

'Relax,' he said, muffled. 'You need to let go.'

Several minutes later, full of endorphins and sleepy, Jason's arms around her, Louisa was heading back off to sleep when he said it again. 'You still awake? I love you. Just, you know. Thought I should tell you that.'

She lifted her head to look at him. He smiled at her and pushed her hair out of her eyes.

'You mean it? Really?'

'Yeah. Absolutely mean it.'

She kissed him, a long, slow kiss that went on for a while and almost, but not quite, developed into Round Two. But Lou could barely keep her eyes open. She rested her head back on to his chest and fell asleep, still smiling.

Part Three

IF YOU DON'T QUESTION IT, IT ISN'T REAL

Detective Constable Alastair Whitmore, known to everybody as Ali, was waiting for Sam in the foyer of Briarstone General Hospital.

'Couldn't find a space,' she said, out of breath, when he raised his eyebrows at her.

'Been here hours,' he complained, giving her a wink.

'Are we sure they're here?' Sam asked as they made their way up the corridor towards the High Dependency Unit.

'Mrs Palmer normally comes in first thing, when she's finished work. She's an office cleaner, gets here by eight most days. Saturdays she gets a bit of a lie-in but she said she'd be here.'

Ian Palmer had been moved to the HDU from the Intensive Care ward a few days ago. It seemed to indicate progress of a sort, although he had not regained consciousness.

'I'm sure this bloody corridor gets longer every time I come here,' Sam said.

'Hello,' said Ali under his breath. 'Look who it is.'

Coming out of the door to the HDU was a dark-haired lad with a well-developed beer gut, wearing a beige jacket and jeans. Dark hair that had once been razor-cut in an elaborate tribal pattern into the side of a shaven head, growing out now at all sorts of different lengths so that it looked as though he'd attacked himself with a pair of scissors.

'Hello, Reggie,' Ali said cheerfully.

He'd been keeping his head down, trying to walk past without acknowledging Ali until he stood right in front of him, blocking his path.

'All right,' came the reply.

Sam had no idea who the young man was, but from Ali's approach she knew to let him get on with it.

'Fancy seeing you here,' Ali went on, in a relaxed manner, clearly seeing what he could get. 'What you up to, then? Visiting?'

'Um, yeah. Visiting a friend.'

'Funny, that – same as us. Who you visiting, then?'

'Just a friend ... look, I got to get away, me bus is due, if I miss it there in't another one till twelve.'

'All right, mate,' Ali said. 'Mind how you go.'

They stood together by the door to the HDU and watched him scoot off down the corridor as fast as he could without actually breaking into a run.

'He seems nice,' Sam said.

'Paul Stark, commonly known as Reggie,' Ali said. 'First nicked him when he was thirteen; he was trying to sell stolen catalytic converters to the scrap merchants. Lovely lad. Such potential.'

Valerie Palmer was sitting in a comfy chair next to her son's bed, poring over a copy of *Take a Break* with a pen in her hand. Not for the first time, Sam thought how she must have had Ian at an alarmingly young age because she scarcely looked more than thirty, dark hair cut in a smooth bob, a long fringe over her eyes. Slender legs in skin-tight jeans, high-heeled suede boots up to the knee.

'Mrs Palmer,' Sam said. 'How's Ian today?'

'Same,' she said in reply, tossing the magazine and the pen on to the table next to her.

Ian Palmer was lying inert, tubes and wires all over the place. Sam had only ever seen him like this; she wondered what he was like walking and talking. Wondered if he was kind to his mum, or if he was a mouthy git with an attitude. It wasn't the sort of question you could ask.

'Has he had many visitors?' Ali asked.

'A couple. His girlfriend's stopped coming, that didn't last long.'

'We saw Reggie outside,' Ali volunteered.

'Yeah, he's been good as gold, bless his heart.'

'I didn't realise they were such good mates.'

Valerie looked guarded, all of a sudden. 'He's all right, Paul is. I know he's been in trouble with you lot before, but that was his brother's fault. Don't you go getting any ideas about my Ian, just because he's got friends.'

'Course not,' Sam said, 'don't worry. It's just that he might know something, you know, but not feel he can come and talk to us.'

Without warning Valerie Palmer crumpled, her face in her hands. Sam sat on one of the hard plastic chairs opposite her, put a hand gently on her shoulder. 'I'm so sorry,' she said. 'It doesn't get any easier.'

'I just wish he could come home!' Valerie wailed. 'I haven't seen the other kids for more than five minutes a day. I haven't slept properly since it happened. I'm so tired. I just want him back the way he was.'

She recovered herself, taking some deep breaths. Whipping a tissue from the box on the table with one decisive move, she dabbed under her eyes. 'I'm okay, sorry. Just lost it for a minute there.'

'Is there anything you need?' Sam asked.

'No, no. I'll be all right. It's a waiting game, right?'

'I'm afraid so.'

'Look,' she said, 'I'll ask Paul to talk to you, shall I?'

A few minutes later, rubbing alcohol gel into their hands, Ali and Sam headed back towards the car park.

'I feel so sorry for her,' Sam said. 'Such a shame.'

'Yes,' Ali said. 'Although she knew full well what he was up to, for all this "my Ian" business. She knew he was mixing with the wrong type of person; she used to be the same herself, back in the day.'

'You think?'

'Her sister Chloe – not that she talks to her any more, mind you – but her little sister Chloe used to be shacked up with Darren Cunningham. Come to that, Ian's brother Tom was supposed to be working as Cunningham's driver a while back. They're up to their necks in it.'

'You're kidding – really?'

'You can bet your life that Ian Palmer's current condition is all down to him being somewhere he shouldn't have been, or ripping someone off, or basically just being a mouthy idiot. Unfortunately, until one of his mates decides to tell us what he was up to, we're not going to be any the wiser.'

Darren Cunningham was the principal subject of another of Eden's organised crime groups, the most active group of several which focused on drug distribution. They were like businesses, Sam often thought: some specialised in stealing cars, some did armed robberies, others, like the McDonnell-Maitland OCG, earned money by trafficking people into the country through the ports. Cunningham didn't bother with any of that. He was earning quite enough by distributing drugs. Most of the drugs that were served up and consumed in Briarstone had allegedly passed through his network. Sam knew quite a bit about Cunningham himself – he featured on the morning briefing almost every day – but his associations, his history . . . all that was a bit woolly. This was the problem with transferring from another force, Sam thought, driving back towards HQ. Much as it had been an advantage to learn policing in the Met, where anything could and did happen, once you moved to another force you lost all those years of knowledge about the local criminals. Reading the information on the force's crime database only got you so far. Ali, Les and Jane had watched these lads grow up, knew them so well they could tell you what Ian Palmer had tattooed on his backside and what Paul Stark's preferred way to break into a Fiesta was. And yes, even Sam could tell that Valerie Palmer, hard-working mum of four, had a bit of a past – but that didn't stop her feeling a lurch of pity for Valerie now. Ian had been her baby, her gorgeous baby son. Hulking great teenager now, pretty much a grown man, but he was still her little boy – and, whatever the moment of stupidity that had brought him to the HDU, there was a strong possibility that he would never recover.

Back in the car, Sam checked her phone and saw she had a missed call from Caro Sumner. She called back straight away.

'Hi, it's Sam – you called?'

'Oh, thanks for ringing me back. I've got a couple of jobs to do this morning before I go and collect our mutual friend from the Travel Inn. I wondered if you'd like to come with me, if you're free? Might be something of interest for you.'

SCARLETT – Thursday 20 September 2012, 22:00

There was something odd about the man. They were all odd, of course they were – what sort of normal man paid for sex anyway? – but Scarlett had grown to recognise the types, the ones that wanted something weird, before they even opened their mouths.

This one wanted to taste her blood. He came straight out with it, told her he was a vampire and he needed blood – not much of it, just a little bit to keep him going. He wasn't going to hurt her, he said, pulling a thin metal object from his pocket that turned out to be a scalpel, complete with clear plastic guard over the blade.

'I pay you double,' he said.

'No,' she said. 'You need to leave right now.'

'It won't show,' he said. 'Just a little blood, I just need a taste, and I make sure I use antiseptic.'

He was standing between her and the door, sweating in his thick winter coat. His hair, dark and streaked with grey, was sticking to his forehead. He smiled encouragingly, as though she was on the verge of saying yes.

There had been a time she'd thought they were bugging the room, and she had always been careful what she said, in case they listened in. But one day a customer had beat her badly and despite her screams they'd taken nearly ten minutes to get to her. Since then, she'd assumed they just watched from the street outside, and even then not all the time. It wasn't worth the risk to try to escape, to try to find someone who would help her, but she had been thinking of that man who called himself Stefan, wondering if he had, after all, been a good man. She thought that, if he came back, she might just try and talk to him properly.

'I said no,' she said.

'Three times,' he said.

Scarlett was considering her options. A little blood? That was what he wanted? And he was willing to pay her treble the usual rate . . .

'What I do is this,' he said, pulling his collar away from his neck. 'A little tiny cut, just on your shoulder. Not near any big vessel. Then I suck out a little blood – just a little; it will be like I am kissing your shoulder – and then I clean with a wipe – ' he pulled a sachet from his pocket and tossed it on to the bed ' – and put on a dressing and then I leave you in peace, nothing else. I pay you. It take just a minute.'

'You're mad,' she said.

'No,' he said. 'I just need blood.'

He didn't look like a vampire. He looked like a sad, desperate, middle-aged freak, and for a fraction of a second she felt sorry for him.

'Money up front,' she said.

He threw a handful of notes on the bed and she picked them up and counted. It was actually more than treble her rate – five hundred euros.

'That's all I have,' he said.

She could tell by the expression on his face that he was telling the truth, just as he could probably tell from hers that she had already made up her mind. It didn't feel dangerous, after all, this transaction: they both had a need. In a way, it was like meeting on neutral ground. That wasn't something she felt very often. They dominated her, they bullied her, or sometimes the reverse was true and people came to her wanting to be abused. Sometimes she felt she could take advantage of them – the scared ones, the first-timers, the ones who were embarrassed and ashamed of their bodies – but she didn't want to give them cause to complain. And they were the easy ones – they might even come back to her, might even turn into regulars. But this one was different. There was a risk on both sides.

Scarlett didn't answer him, but sat on the edge of the bed, her back to him, drawing her hair over one shoulder, exposing the other. She could hear his breathing quicken, then she felt his weight on the bed. He was kneeling over her, and for the first time she could smell him. A hint of deodorant, but above it the smell of sweat, excitement, and fear.

'It might sting a little,' he said, his voice a whisper. 'I'll be quick.'

It was a sharp stab of pain that made her wince. She felt a warm dribble of blood trickling over her shoulder-blade, and then the rasp of his tongue as he caught it. She closed her eyes and tried not to shudder as his mouth closed over the wound he'd made. She felt his hand on her upper arm, gripping her firmly, in case she decided to move away. From the corner of her tightly closed eyes, tears began to leak. She gritted her teeth and breathed through her nose. The sucking did sting. She heard him swallow deeply, breathing through his nose, fast against the skin of her shoulder.

After another moment she couldn't stand it. 'That's enough!'

He stopped immediately and released her, gasping. Scarlett heard him make a sound, almost a groan. She opened her eyes as she heard him tearing open the antiseptic wipe, and then felt the cold bite of the alcohol against her skin as he rubbed it vigorously.

'There, there,' he said, as if she was a child who'd fallen and scraped her knee. 'All better now.'

A plaster was applied.

'It might bleed for a moment or two,' he said. 'Can I come back tomorrow?'

'No!' she said. More sharply than she'd intended. 'Maybe – maybe next week.'

'Of course,' he said. 'Thank you.'

Scarlett stood on shaky legs that had nothing to do with blood loss and everything to do with the sudden awareness of her own fragility, and turned to face him. He was just a man, a weedy, desperate man who was no more weird than any of them. And he had paid her. She gave him a tentative smile.

'What's your name?' she asked.

He gave a high-pitched sort of a laugh. 'Nosferatu,' he said.

'Of course it is,' she said, and saw him out of the door. Before she went back in the window she counted the money again, and posted her going rate through the hole into the back room. The rest of it she hid in the hollow heel of her shoe. Sometimes they checked. But she was going to risk it.

211

LOU – Saturday 2 November 2013, 10:25

'Hey. Open your eyes.'

'What time is it?'

'I don't know. Your phone's been bleeping.'

Lou sat up, sleep-crumpled and still dazed, wondering how come it was broad daylight. *Oh – rest day.* She fell back against the pillow.

'Oh, no, you don't,' Jason said, kissing her neck. 'Come on. Rise and shine.'

Lou groaned. 'How come you're so bloody perky? Haven't you even got the decency to have a hangover?'

'I never get hangovers, you know that.'

'Wait till you get to my age,' Lou said, thinking how unfair it was that she always suffered the next day, even when she'd drunk hardly anything.

'Here we go with the age thing. You want me to make you coffee, Grandma?'

Jason went downstairs and for a moment Lou lay still with her eyes closed. But then her phone bleeped again, and it was too late to pretend the day hadn't started. She checked the phone and saw the missed calls from her mother, one new voicemail and two emails. It could all wait ten more minutes. She went to the bathroom and had a shower, washing her tangled hair under the warm spray and thinking about what Jason had said last night. It had been a long, long time since anyone had told her they loved her. It felt good.

By the time she emerged, wrapped in a towel, hair hanging in damp strands around her shoulders, there was a mug of black coffee next to the bed and the landline was ringing.

'Hi, Mum,' she said.

'How did you know it was me?' her mother asked.

Caller display, thought Lou. 'You're the only person who rings me this early on my day off. How are you?'

'I'm fine, darling. I tried your mobile earlier; I left you a message. Just wondered if you'd had a chance to talk to Tracy.'

'Not yet. I was going to call her later.'

'Oh?'

'Well, I might as well tell you. I've managed to find someone to bring to the wedding. His name is Jason. Go easy on him, all right?'

There was an audible breath on the other end of the phone. 'Really? Oh, how lovely! What do you mean, go easy on him? What do you think we're going to do?'

Scare him off?

'It's nothing serious, Mum, don't get your hopes up.'

At that moment Jason himself appeared, standing in the doorway. Mug in hand, wearing jeans and nothing else. He looked gorgeous. Louisa smiled at him.

'Oh. Who is he? Not someone from work, is it?'

Louisa gritted her teeth at that. Where else was she supposed to meet people? And besides, what was wrong with dating a fellow officer? It wasn't as if she was selecting her future life partner from the cells, was it? 'Look, you'll get to meet him soon, all right? Unless something comes up and I can't make it.'

'Oh, Louisa.'

Jason put his mug down on the chest of drawers and carried on

213

getting dressed. He sat on the end of the bed, pulling his socks on.

'How are you, anyway? How's Dad?'

'Oh, he's okay, do you want to speak to him?'

'Not especially ...'

But her mother had already put down the phone and was wandering through the house calling, 'Roger? Roger! Louisa wants to talk to you!'

Lou stretched out a hand and placed it on Jason's back. He didn't move for a minute, then he got up, retrieved his mug and took it downstairs.

'I don't know where he's buggered off to,' Lou's mother said eventually, coming back to the phone. 'Typical.'

'It doesn't matter – just give him my love, okay?'

A few minutes later Lou was dressed and downstairs. Jason was in the living room, putting on his trainers. 'Hey,' she said. 'Are you going somewhere?'

He didn't answer at first, just finished what he was doing and stood up.

'What is it?' Lou asked. 'What's wrong?'

He looked so lost, so sad, that for a moment Lou thought something terrible had happened. Then he shook his head, smiled at her and kissed her cheek, his hand on her upper arm.

'I've got stuff to do today,' he said. 'I might catch up with you later.'

'Jason?'

But he was already retrieving his wallet and his phone from the table, and then he was gone.

*

```
Email

Date:   2 November 2013

To:     DCI Lou SMITH

From:   DC Jane PHELPS

Re:     Nigel MAITLAND DOB 17/12/1958

Ma'am,

As discussed, I visited Hermitage Farm
yesterday afternoon to return some unused
property to the MAITLANDs. The only person at
the premises was Connor PETRIE, who informed me
that Nigel and Felicity MAITLAND have gone
away. He did not seem to know where they had
gone, or when they would be back. He said he
had been left in charge. When I got back to the
office I put in a call to Flora MAITLAND. She
said her parents had gone on a last-minute
holiday to Madeira. She thinks they will be
back on the 15th.
```

SAM – Saturday 2 November 2013, 10:45

Caro had already retrieved a job car when Sam found her in the car park behind Headquarters. Caro's rear end was reversing out of the back seat.

'Oh, morning,' Caro said cheerfully. 'Just clearing up a bit. Want me to drive?'

'You know where we're going.'

Caro deposited a supermarket carrier bag full of rubbish from the back of the car into one of the skips and they both got in. Despite the clean-up there was a lingering smell in the car, something between damp trainers, cherry air-freshener and fried food. Sam opened her window a crack as Caro swiped her security pass at the exit barrier.

'The McDonnells live out near Catswood,' Caro began. 'Lewis and his girlfriend, I mean. They have offices in the town but I'm guessing they won't be there on a Saturday, so catching them at home is the best idea.'

'I've never met either of the McDonnell brothers,' Sam said. 'What are they like?'

'Perfectly pleasant, unless you've got something on them.'

'You've dealt with them a lot?'

'Only since I moved here. They're among Special Branch's favourite targets, thanks to the trafficking.'

'And our plan for today?'

'Well,' Caro said, turning on to the main road out of town, 'at our briefing this morning it turns out that Lewis McDonnell's company, or one of them at least, owns Carisbrooke Court. We've been trying to nail that link ever since the warrant. Needless to say, the businesses involved have been tricky to unravel. The short version is that the building used to be owned by KJK Enterprises, which is a management lettings company that also owns a beauty salon in King Street managed by Kimberly Kerber, none other than Lewis McDonnell's girlfriend. But quite recently – a couple of months ago – ownership transferred to GEMA Holdings, which has offices in Spain and Leeds. And that business has got links to Golden Eagle Associates Ltd, which is McDonnell's property management company, based right here in Briarstone. Follow all that?'

'I thought we already knew he had links to the location?'

'Just the intel. And that was pretty sketchy.'

The car sped through the narrow lanes towards Catswood, passing farms and hamlets grouped around a church or a pub. It had rained earlier but now the sun was shining, making the wet road ahead gleam so brightly it was hard to look at. A few minutes later Caro pulled off the main road into a driveway, flanked by curved brick walls that ended abruptly in an imposing wooden gate. Caro got out to press the button on the intercom. From the top of the wall, a security camera watched their every move.

To Sam's surprise, the wooden gates started to swing soundlessly open. Caro got back in the car and drove through.

'Apparently Lewis isn't home,' she said. 'But Kim said she'd be more than happy to welcome us into her charming country kitchen.'

They parked in front of a modern brick-built house that was made vastly more attractive by the sunshine and the two oversized stone lions that guarded the front door. As soon as they got out of the car, the door opened and three small dogs skittered out, yapping and jumping up.

'Get in here! I said get in!' a dark-haired woman was yelling.

Sam was hopeful she was talking to the dogs, which completely ignored her until she stopped yelling, and then sauntered back inside one by one.

'Kim,' Caro said. 'Thanks for seeing us. I'm DC Caro Sumner; this is my colleague, DS Sam Hollands.'

'You can come in if you like. I told you, though, he ain't here.'

Sam and Caro followed Kim into a large hallway with a polished slate floor. Sam glanced through a wide arch to a sitting room with cream carpets – *great idea, with dogs*, she thought – to plate-glass windows at the back. A little glimpse of garden, bordered by a thick hedge, and what looked like some serious building work going on out there. Mini-diggers abandoned, piles of bricks on pallets, big rolls of plastic sheeting.

They continued through to a vast modern kitchen that looked as if it rarely got used for anything more elaborate than toast and corn-flakes, both of which were in evidence on the breakfast bar. Kim Kerber was wearing a biscuit-coloured tracksuit with some motif on the chest that Sam thought was probably something designer. She had long, dark hair extensions, eyelash extensions and a shiny French manicure. They'd obviously caught her just as she was about to begin her morning make-up routine, as what looked like a chrome toolbox was scissored open on the large stripped-pine table, spewing its brightly coloured contents.

'Having some work done?' Sam asked.

'Eh?'

'Outside. Looks like you're getting an extension built or something. Must be a pain.'

'Oh, that. No, we're having a pool put in. Takes ages, digging. Have a seat,' she said, waving vaguely at the chairs.

'Thanks,' Caro said. 'So where did you say Lewis has gone?'

'I didn't say,' Kim murmured, fingering a tube of something that looked like oil paint. 'He's probs at the office.'

'On a Saturday?'

'My day off, innit. It's either the office or golf. What you want him for, anyway?'

'We wanted to ask about a property in Carisbrooke Court. It used to be owned by KJK, which is your business, isn't it?'

Kim looked wary all of a sudden, then laughed. 'My business? You're having a laugh.'

218

'You're the registered owner.'

'Yeah, right. He puts stuff in my name all the time. Anyway, you said it *used* to be owned by KJK. So it isn't any more, right? Not my problem.'

'I understood that you and Lewis are partners, Kim. You do help out with the property management side of it, don't you?'

On the table, Kim's smartphone buzzed. She looked at it, smiled, and began to reply to the text with the pads of her fingers. Sam thought she wasn't going to bother answering their question, but a moment later she dropped the phone again, looked Caro in the eye and said, 'I do the interior design. I sort out the decorators and go to Asda and IKEA to buy all the furniture, cushions and shit. I tart the places up before he gets tenants in, or before he sells them on. That's it.'

'You don't help with the tenants? Take calls from them, stuff like that?'

'Do I bollocks.'

'So who looks after the properties once the tenants are inside?' Sam asked.

'I don't fucking know, honestly. Go and speak to the organ grinder. You want to know something about foils or straighteners, I can help. The rest of it, you need to see Lewis.'

Back in the car, Sam took a deep breath in. 'That went well.'

'Better than I expected,' Caro said cheerfully. 'She usually doesn't let us in when he's not there. You saw all the stuff out in the back garden?'

'What, the building work?'

'They bury stuff. That's what the digger's for. They've been "having a pool put in" for the last four years.'

'Bury stuff? You mean drugs?'

219

Caro gave Sam a cheerful grin. 'Drugs, guns, people. Whatever they want to hide. Rumour has it Mr McDonnell has two or three whole shipping containers somewhere in the back garden that he uses to teach people how to keep their mouths shut. That's how he does it. Dig a nice big hole and pretend it's going to be a swimming pool.'

SCARLETT – Tuesday 25 September 2012, 21:19

Despite the alcohol wipe, the wound on Scarlett's shoulder became infected. Eating crap food and barely sleeping meant she was susceptible to infections in any case, but this one hit her particularly badly. She was running a fever and on the verge of hallucinating when they pulled her out of the room early – replacing her with a girl she'd never seen before, or maybe she had, it was impossible to tell – and two of them took her to the clinic.

It wasn't a clinic by any normal definition of the word, but Scarlett knew she was lucky to be taken there. It consisted of two rooms – a waiting room and a treatment room – behind a fast food shop in Bijlmer, twenty minutes out of the city. The doctor was a Russian, who spoke Dutch and no more than a few words of English, and she had seen him before, once, when she'd needed stitches after a customer had cut her head open with his signet ring. They didn't always take the women for medical treatment. It had to be bad, and you had to be worth the money to be taken there. And there was a cost involved, because of course this wasn't an official clinic; although she had heard that the Dutch helpfully provided medical assistance and treatment to prostitutes, they couldn't have her interacting with anyone official.

So they paid the Russian on her behalf, and the money came out of her fictitious wages, added to the debt she owed them for her board and lodging, clothing, condoms, protection, the drugs she didn't use . . . the debt that got larger every day.

221

She waited in the first room with one of them. The other one waited outside in the car, partly because there wasn't room for two thugs in the tiny, stifling room, partly to protect the car and watch the door in case Scarlett decided to run for it.

She felt too wretched to run, in any case.

The doctor, who was dressed in jeans that were slung low on his hips under a belly, and a shirt with yellow stains under the armpits, did not touch her. She was glad. He gave the antibiotics to her companion and muttered a few words in Russian.

'You keep clean,' he said to her, by way of a translation.

Scarlett nodded.

As they walked back through the waiting room, Scarlett saw the next woman waiting for attention with her minder. She was a girl, young, with bruises colouring her left eye and nose. She was visibly shaking, and Scarlett wondered what was wrong with her. She raised her head and Scarlett met her eyes. There was a brief connection between them. Nothing was said. Scarlett smiled at her, trying to give her some encouragement.

It will be okay. This isn't the worst thing you're going to have to face. It will get better.

Two lies, sandwiching a truth.

SAM – Saturday 2 November 2013, 11:25

Lewis McDonnell's business premises were on the ground floor of a former printworks in the town centre. Other offices surrounded a courtyard that doubled as a haphazard car park, full of signs promising imminent clamping and towing at vast expense to the unwary.

All the way across town, Sam had been thinking of the digging equipment in the back garden of McDonnell's house, and what it was for. She had worked on a job once, years ago when she'd been with the Met. A piece of land behind an industrial complex was being redeveloped; the excavators had hit something metal, uncovered the doors of what looked like a whole shipping container buried at an almost vertical angle. The doors, at ground level, were covered over with rubble, rubbish and overgrown with brambles. The construction workers had managed to force open the door and then had shut it again quickly and called the police. Sam had been right there when they'd opened it all up again. Three bodies at the bottom of the container, badly decomposed. When the pathologist had finally worked through the remains she had reported that the three individuals – two adult men, and a young woman – had been left in there at separate times, probably years apart. The woman had been the last. It was impossible to tell if any of them had been alive when they'd gone in, but marks on the steep inside slope of the container suggested that at least one of them had made several attempts to climb their way out.

At the point when Sam had moved to Eden the case had remained unsolved, the bodies unidentified.

McDonnell himself welcomed them in, offering them a seat and a coffee to go with it. He was shorter than Sam and stocky, with gelled, silver hair cut short on a square head, intelligent blue eyes, and a smile which showed his teeth.

'Kim told me you might stop by,' he called from the small kitchen. The sound of a kettle could be heard, rumbling to a boil. 'You were lucky to catch me.'

'Do you usually work weekends?' Sam asked.

'You can't keep regular hours when you own your own business,' McDonnell said. 'You know how it is.'

Aside from the kitchen, the office was open-plan – two big desks covered in piles of paper, boxes and computer equipment, and a little coffee table with three easy chairs under the window.

'Now,' he said, bringing through a tray with three small mugs and some sachets of sugar on it, 'what can I do for you?'

'Sorry to hear about Carl McVey,' Sam said. 'Friend of yours, wasn't he?'

McDonnell looked uncomfortable for a second, ran his thumb over his eyebrow. 'Well, not a friend exactly. But yeah, bad news. You lot found who killed him?'

'We're working on a number of leads,' Sam said. 'Is there anything you can tell us that might help?'

'I heard it was a robbery? Could've been anyone.'

'That's one possible motive. Do you know of anyone who might have argued with him recently?'

He barked a laugh. 'Come on, officer. I don't do gossip. Now, is that it? You just came to offer your condolences because someone I met a few times got himself killed?'

'Carisbrooke Court,' Caro said, leaning forward. 'You own some flats there. It's number four we're interested in, on the ground floor.'

Legs casually crossed at the knee, one canvas deck shoe shaking out a rhythm, Lewis McDonnell looked upwards as if searching for the memory. 'Can't say I know off the top of my head. The company has lots of properties, as I'm sure you're aware.'

'This might help: four Carisbrooke Court was being used as a brothel until last week. Nobody in it right now. So it'll be the one without any tenants – ringing bells?'

The blue gaze became sharper. 'Can't say for sure it's one of ours. You'll have to talk to Rich or Dan; they do the day-to-day management for me.'

'You'd think they would have told you, wouldn't you?' Sam said.

'I've been busy. But you know I trust them to get on with things. I'm sure they've got it all in hand.'

'When we executed the warrant at the address, Gavin Petrie was outside watching what was going on. Another of your associates, I believe?'

'I know him. And?'

'Didn't he let you know about your property being searched? I'd have thought he would have had the courtesy to tell you.'

McDonnell shrugged. 'Haven't seen him in months.'

Caro looked at the desk, the computers. 'I'm sure you have all the information we need, Mr McDonnell. Can you tell us who the tenants were at that property?'

He maintained eye contact for a long moment, a muscle working in his jaw. Then abruptly he stood up, hands on his knees, and went to one of the desks. Hammering on the keyboard of the computer with both of his thick index fingers. 'Carisbrooke Court?'

'That's right. Number four.'

More hammering. One finger at a time.

'Here we go. It's not showing an income. Yeah, right, I remember now. Katie Smith.'

'Katie Smith is the tenant?' Sam asked. She had read the intelligence reports relating to the Op Pentameter raid – Katie Smith, alias Scarlett Rainsford.

McDonnell got up from the desk and came back to where they were sitting, drank from his mug of coffee before sitting down again. 'Not a tenant exactly. More of a squatter.'

Sam said, 'I can't imagine your company having a problem with squatters, Mr McDonnell. Don't you have a system for organising evictions when you need them?'

He laughed out loud. 'You must be mistaking me for some kind of thug. I'm far from it, I can assure you. In fact, I have more of a generous nature than anyone gives me credit for. Poor girl had fallen on hard times, so I was letting her live there rent-free. Been there a while, mind you, probably should have asked her to move on by now, but there you go. And she was on the game? Goes to show, don't it? I had no idea.'

Caro raised an eyebrow slightly. Even her sunny nature was finding it hard to believe that McDonnell was that altruistic. 'So what can you tell us about Katie Smith?'

Once again, McDonnell paused and considered, as if racking his brains for the memory. 'She was introduced to me by a friend of a friend. Said she'd been having some trouble and needed somewhere to stay for a bit. That flat had just come available, and I was waiting for my renovations guys to finish a big project over in Charlmere, so I couldn't let it. I said she could stay until she found her feet.'

'That's very generous of you,' Sam said. 'When was this?'

'God, a while ago. Months.'

'What sort of trouble was she in?'

'I didn't ask. Look, she reminded me of my daughter, all right? Felt sorry for the poor cow.'

'I didn't know you had a daughter,' Caro said brightly.

'Yeah, don't see her much. Lives in Spain. Her mother's a bitch.'

Sam cleared her throat. She'd drunk most of the coffee, which was quite good.

'It's a three-bedroomed flat,' Caro said. 'Big old place, to let a youngster live in all on her own. You didn't have anyone else living there?'

'Look,' McDonnell said, 'far as the books are concerned, the place is empty still. We didn't put her on a tenancy agreement or any of that shit. It was only supposed to be a couple of weeks until I could get the place decorated and re-let.'

'And this person who introduced you. Friend of a friend, you said. Who's that?'

McDonnell stared. 'Can't remember.'

'Really?'

He looked at his watch. 'Is there anything else I can help you with, officers? Only I've got things to do.'

Sam and Caro got to their feet. McDonnell showed them out, following them down the narrow corridor. Sam felt him close behind her. He wasn't someone she was comfortable turning her back on. He had to squeeze past both women to open the door, which was deadlocked. The thought of having been locked in with him all this time was alarming.

He held the door open and watched them as Caro unlocked the car door. 'One other thing,' he said.

'What's that?' Caro said.

'You can tell your boys I'm teeing off at twelve. You know, just in case they can't find me again. Tell your Mr Waterhouse they're a bunch of idiots, need better training.'

SCARLETT – Wednesday 26 September 2012, 10:47

They let her have the rest of the night off.

The next morning, whether the antibiotics were kicking in or a good night's sleep had helped, Scarlett was feeling better. She was feeling focused. Good things had happened, which she was taking as a sign. Firstly, they hadn't found that extra money that the vampire had given her. It was still in her shoe. When they had asked her how she got the wound on her shoulder, she'd told them it was a customer, and they hadn't pressed it further than that. The vampire – Nosferatu or whatever the bastard's name was – might have given her an infection, but if he came back again Scarlett had already decided to let him do it again. This time she would clean the wound herself afterwards, keep swabbing it until it healed. It had only been a small cut, less than a half-inch long, but it was deep and the strap of her bra kept opening it up again. She would tell him exactly where to cut, too.

If she was going to get away, ever, she would need money. Maybe then she could find someone to bribe, someone she could trust just enough to help her get away. And once she'd done that she'd need money to get a cab to a safe place. Enough for a room for a few nights, enough to travel far away from this shithole. She hadn't decided where the safe place was, nor how she was ever going to escape since surely she could never trust anyone to help her – they were all bastards, and watching her all the time – but one thing was certain: if she didn't do something soon, she would die here.

The room was cold when she got into it, so for a while she could see her own breath in the window as she watched the shoppers and the tourists – the few that there were – passing by. Four Japanese men stopped by her window and stood staring for a while, talking and laughing among themselves. She smiled at them and beckoned them with her finger, sat astride her chair and tried to look appealing. Then one of them made the mistake of trying to take her picture with the camera around his neck. She turned her face away in time, but in any case a few seconds later one of her minders had come across to have a word with the offending photographer. 'Having a word' meant removing the memory card and stamping on it. There was a brief argument – the guy was a foot taller and twice as wide – but really the tourist didn't have any grounds for complaint. Everyone should know that taking pictures wasn't allowed. It was in all the guide books – in every language.

The man watching out for her didn't so much as glance in Scarlett's direction as the tourists walked off, arguing among themselves and gesticulating. Such a commotion wasn't a good thing. Scarlett rubbed the chill out of her upper arms and, because no one was looking, blew into her cupped hands.

The smashed pieces of the little memory card lay on the cobbles in front of the window. All those pictures, hundreds no doubt, of the glorious sights of the city that Scarlett had lived in all this time and scarcely knew – holiday snaps destroyed in a moment. The tourist would have to get copies from his friends. Scarlett thought about the picture the man had taken of her, framed by her window – a girl in nylon underwear, turning her face away. No matter. No one would ever see that picture now.

LOU – Saturday 2 November 2013, 12:10

So much for a day off. So much for spending the day with the man of your dreams. Lou got dressed and went into work.

Sam Hollands was the only one in the office, and she was on the phone. When Lou walked in, Sam looked up at her questioningly. Lou mouthed the word, 'Coffee?' by way of a reply, and when Sam nodded Lou postponed the inevitable questions by going on ahead to the canteen with her purse. The servery was closed at weekends, but the vending machines still permitted refreshments of a sort, and it was mercifully quiet.

Sam joined her within moments and found them a table. 'So, you were supposed to be having today off,' she said before Lou had even sat down.

'Yeah, I know, I know.'

'And?'

Oh, Sam, Lou thought. She just had a knack of spotting trouble. 'Got bored.'

Lou had bought a bag of crisps, a KitKat and a Snickers from the vending machine. All of a sudden she was ravenously hungry. That always happened when she was miserable. Never mind: if she didn't get too distracted she would stop by at the gym on the way home – for the first time in about four months. She always carried her gym kit in the back of the car just in case the urge took her. It didn't very often. She kept thinking it would be a good idea to cancel her membership, it was such a massive waste of money, but somehow merely having gym membership made her feel that she wasn't a complete lard-arse.

There was nothing like a dose of sugar and carbs at a time of crisis, Lou thought, feeling much better already.

'What have I missed?' she said, between mouthfuls.

'Ian is still no change,' Sam said. 'I went with Ali to the hospital first thing. His mum has barely left his side. I really feel for her, you know. Whatever happens to him, his life has pretty much gone forever. Even if he regains consciousness, which seems pretty unlikely, he'll end up needing round-the-clock care.'

'What about McVey?'

Sam shook her head, finished her mouthful before replying. 'Still nothing. We've explored the connection with Nigel Maitland as far

230

as we possibly can. Until they get some new sources on it, that one's drawing a complete blank. Frustrating. Anyway, after the hospital I went with Caro Sumner to see Lewis McDonnell.'

'Oh, really? And?'

'His company definitely owns the flat at Carisbrooke Court. He had one Katie Smith down as the tenant, although he claims she wasn't paying rent. Says he was doing her a favour because she was down on her luck. Claims to know nothing about what was going on there.'

'You're going to see Scarlett later?'

'Yes,' Sam said. 'Just want to check through her file again and then I'll head over there. Caro's gone to collect her from the hotel.'

'I had an email from Mr Buchanan this morning, came in on my mobile. There's some pressure to get her out of the VVS. He'd copied in SB, so unless you can get something useful out of her I can see Waterhouse is going to be itching to pass her over to Social Services today. I can't see her going home to Annie and Clive somehow, can you?'

'I think they've been trying to find her some emergency accommodation. Want me to talk to Orla, if she's there?'

'Yes, please.'

'Another thing about McDonnell. He thinks there's a team on him – told us to let them know they weren't doing a very good job. I don't know if he was just winding us up – power trip thing, you know. I expect Caro has passed it on to Mr Waterhouse by now but I thought you should know too.'

The canteen door swung open then, taking them by surprise. A uniformed sergeant came in, had a look round, and left.

'So . . . anything else you feel like talking about?' Sam asked, leaning across the table.

Lou managed a smile. 'I have no idea what you mean.'

Sam nodded. 'Hm, okay, then.'

'I think I had a row with Jason.'

'You think? What about?'

'I'm not even sure. Last night he told me he loved me – when he was drunk, mind you – and then this morning he was all frosty, gone off in a huff.'

'What did you say?'

'Nothing significant. I was on the phone to Mum; next thing I knew he was out the door. I've got a horrible feeling it's because I've invited him to come to my cousin's wedding with me, because I was telling Mum about it. I think he's got cold feet about meeting them all, and I can't say I blame him—'

'I meant, what did you say when he used the L word?'

'Oh! I can't remember. I don't think I said anything in particular. Kissed him.'

'You didn't say it back?'

'No . . .'

'Do you love him?'

Lou was about to open her mouth to say *Yes, of course I do*, but something stopped her.

Sam put her hand over Lou's, on the table, gave it a squeeze.

'Don't,' she said. 'Don't be kind to me, Sam, you'll start me off. I know you all think I'm some sort of cougar. Probably for the best if it is all over with.'

'Nobody thinks you're a cougar, for heaven's sake. You're only – what – five years older than him? What difference does that make?'

'I know if it was the other way round nobody would give a shit.'

'Nobody gives a shit anyway! It's not as if you look like his mum or anything.'

That made Lou smile. She had seen pictures of his parents: his mum was a right-on radical, white hair cropped short, neat glasses with funky red frames, university lecturer. His dad was a retired police officer. She'd even spoken to them on the phone once or twice, a little awkwardly.

Sam said, 'I think the only person who's even noticed there's an age gap is you.'

'My mother will notice, believe me. It'll be the first thing she comments on.'

'And if she does? You don't see them that much; does it really bother you what they think, as long as you and Jason are happy with each other? What is it you're so scared of?'

Lou thought about this for a long time, and unbidden a small voice inside said, *I'm scared that he'll wake up one day and think I'm old.*

'Right,' she said, getting to her feet. 'Enough moping. I've got a good feeling about today. Scarlett's going to tell you everything she knows.'

'That'd be nice.'

The crisps and chocolate had disappeared as if by magic. Lou found herself wondering what sort of takeaway to pick up later. Likely to be an Indian, since the Akash Tandoori was next door to the off licence, which would be her first stop. Outside the canteen they went their separate ways, Sam towards the car park, Lou back to the office.

Her mobile started to ring as she got inside the door – not a number she recognised.

'Louisa Smith.'

'Oh – hello. Hi. It's Annie here. Annie Rainsford.'

Lou tried not to let her surprise register in her voice. 'Hi, what can I do for you?'

'You said I could call. You gave me your card.'

'That's right,' Lou said. 'Is everything okay?'

A long pause. Lou could hear her breathing, otherwise she might have thought Annie had hung up.

'Annie? What is it?'

'Look, could we meet? Somewhere – I don't know – a pub, maybe?'

'Of course. Where?'

'Somewhere out of town ... the Coach and Horses, on the Charlmere Road. Do you know it?'

'I know it. Do you want me to pick you up?'

'No, no. I can get there. Can you be there at about half-past two?'

SAM – Saturday 2 November 2013, 13:55

'I don't know where to start,' Scarlett said. 'This isn't official, is it?'

'It should be,' Sam said. 'But, if you just want to talk for now, that's fine too. It's up to you. You might not want to say all this a second time.'

'Or even a first time.'

'I'd like to take notes, if you don't mind?'

Scarlett didn't answer, but she didn't object either. They were alone in the kitchen in the VVS. Caro had gone straight back to work after dropping Scarlett off, and Orla had gone to the office to make some calls about emergency accommodation.

'You and that Lou Smith asked me about Nico,' she said.

'That's right. You called him an arsehole.'

234

Scarlett laughed, briefly. 'I think he had something to do with it,' she said.

'What – your abduction?'

'Yes. I was so innocent – you wouldn't believe it now, would you? He was older than me. He said he was sixteen but he could have been any age. I was just so miserable; he cheered me up and I fell for him. He told me he could help me escape, from my family. I would have done it, too. He said I should meet him on the last night of the holi-day. I was going to go, but that day I realised I couldn't leave Juliette behind. She was – well, you know. She was finding things tough. I needed to watch out for her, and I couldn't go and leave her. And she wouldn't have come with me. So I went to meet him ... Nico. I was going to tell him I couldn't go with him after all. Then a van came along the road and stopped next to where I was waiting. This man got out and he started talking to me in Greek; I didn't understand what he was saying. He just kept yammering at me, and then he pushed me into the back of the van. One of them got in with me, and when I started screaming and kicking this man in the back put his hand over my mouth ...'

Scarlett stopped, then, reached for her tea mug. Sam noticed her hand was unsteady.

'I'm sorry,' Scarlett said. 'It was so long ago but at the same time, you know, it's like it just happened.'

'Take your time,' Sam said.

'I thought it was Nico, at first. I thought it was part of his plan. That's why I didn't scream harder, or fight more. I thought they were taking me to him. When I realised they weren't, I was a long way away. They took me on this fucking endless road trip north, in the back of this van. There were other girls too. The other two were older than me. They didn't speak English.'

235

'Did you ever find out their names?'

'Krystyna and Ysabella. I think. Before them, there were two other ones but they both died.'

'They died?'

'One of them hit her head, and the other one – Yelena – she got shot in a car park. I saw it happen. She's the one I dream about, like I told you yesterday.'

There was silence for a moment. Sam was watching Scarlett's face, wondering if this was true or something that the fifteen-year-old Scarlett had imagined, or exaggerated.

'I used to make up stories about Yelena. We never really got to talk, even though we were together for hours. It felt like we were, I don't know, in it together. And then she died and it was my fault – we were trying to run. I never knew anything about her, where she was from, how old she was. So I tried to keep her alive in my head by making up this history for her. I invented her family, her school, her friends. I imagined her a boyfriend and then her getting married and having children and being happy.'

A single tear slipped from Scarlett's eye. She wiped it away. 'She never got any of that, of course.'

'What happened to her?' Sam asked. 'After she got shot?'

Scarlett shrugged. 'They drove off and left her.'

Sam made a note. There would be records; surely there would be records. It wouldn't be impossible to find out. Europe was much more open than it had been, even ten years ago. It felt like an important thing to check.

'We ended up in Poland and we were there for weeks, months. I lost track. It was September when we arrived and when we left it was snowing. The other two girls got taken out of the flat every day; they left me behind. Sometimes with this woman, this old fat woman. She was really nasty. Sometimes there were men there, too. They had drugs, a lot of drugs, in the flat. They used to cut the drugs up on the dining room table, bag them up. I didn't understand what they wanted with me. I thought I was there as a maid or something, so I used to clean the flat when I got bored. The old woman was supposed to do it but she was lazy. The men didn't use the drugs – not when I was there, anyway – but they smoked skunk the whole time. Tried to get me on it too. I kept refusing. They used to laugh at me, said I'd start taking it soon enough. Said I'd need it.'

Scarlett chewed on a thumbnail, inspected it, chewed it again.

'Where did they take the other girls?' Sam asked. 'You said the other girls went out every day.'

'They were making them work. When they got back it was the early hours. I didn't really twig at the time, but I guess they were putting them in a room somewhere. Within a few weeks they were both smacked up, anyway.'

'So you were there – in this flat – until the winter. What happened then?'

'One day, without warning, these two men came for me. They put me in another van for a day and a night. There was a week I was in a flat with five other girls. I have no idea where that was. I was ill; I spent most of the time asleep. Then they took me somewhere else – only a few hours away. Then I was in Prague. I was there for years.'

Sam took a drink of cold tea. 'Can you remember any names?' she asked. 'Any of the people who transported you from place to place?'

'No. I only ever found out the girls' names, some of them. If they were even their real names ... In any case they were all talking in foreign languages – fast, you know? Half the time I was out of it. I think

237

they put sleeping tablets in the bottles of water. Kept us quiet when we were going across borders.'

'I know it was a long time ago,' Sam said, 'but do you think you would recognise any of them? I might be able to get some pictures for you to look at.'

Scarlett stared at Sam, unblinking. 'They all looked the same. Fucking big men with jackets. And you know what? After a while I stopped trying to look them in the face, because they all scared the shit out of me.'

It was understandable, Sam thought. They had more chance of identifying the people who had brought Scarlett into the UK, and for their purposes that would be more useful anyway. Who knew where all those people were right now? Some of them might even be dead.

'Wait,' Scarlett said. 'The old fat woman was called Irene. Something like that – Irina maybe. But that's not much good, is it? I don't even know where in Poland that was. And since it was her that told me I was in Poland, I can't even be certain that it was. Could have been bloody anywhere cold.'

Sam paused, aware of Scarlett's eyes on her.

'It's okay,' Sam said, softly. 'You know you're doing really well.'

There was a tension in Scarlett's shoulders. 'It was when we got to Prague that they made me have sex with men for money. I told you what happened the first time. They'd been trying to sell me all that time. I don't think the men in Poland were that bothered about virgins, or else they didn't have the money.'

A pause. Sam said, 'I remember. You said there was a man who was minding you, and a woman who filmed him. Do you remember their names?'

Sam saw instantly that the question had heightened Scarlett's anxiety. She looked away, to the left, looking for the memories.

'Not the man. The woman was supposed to be training us; she said her name was Tina. Who knows if that was her real name or not. She wasn't English but she could speak it quite well. Had a funny accent.'

'What do you mean, she was there to "train" you?'

Scarlett said, 'She told us that we were going to work in the city's red light district. She told us how the system worked: that we had a debt to pay off, and that if we were good and did as we were told we would earn money to pay off the debt quickly and then have a nice life. She said once we had paid off the debt we could do as we pleased, but that we would be earning such good money that we would probably carry on with it. She said that was what she was doing. She said she had been an estate agent but that this job earned her three times as much money and it was the best job she'd ever had. But after we'd had that nice little chat she took me to another apartment somewhere else in the city for that first time. I thought she was there to make sure they didn't hurt me. Afterwards, when she was driving me back, she made me sit on a carrier bag. Bitch.'

There was a pause. Sam gave her a moment. 'Can you describe what she looked like?'

'Bleached blonde hair, shoulder-length. Wore clothes that were too tight for her. It was years ago; you really think that'll help?'

'What about the other girls? What do you remember about them?'

Scarlett looked down at her thumbnail. 'They were young too. One of them looked like a child. Her name was Suzy, I think. She was from Eastern Europe somewhere but her mother was from Scotland so she spoke a bit of English. The other one was older, had some kind of mental problem.'

'What about this Tina?' Sam said. 'Would you recognise her again?'

'No,' Sam said. 'Anyway, she was only there for that week and then we never saw her again.'

'So how long were you in Prague?' Sam asked.

'I lost track. Years. Then one day they moved me without warning. I got put back in a van and shipped to Amsterdam. I was there for years too.'

'Do you know the address where you were living? Or where you were moved to?'

'No. It was an apartment in the city. I can tell you it was the third buzzer down out of ten. They never left me alone, not for a second. The whole time I was there I was shipped between the apartment and the rooms where I worked. I never went anywhere else – oh, apart from to the doctor once or twice. And then they took me there. I was never alone.'

'The doctor?' Sam said hopefully. 'Did you know his name?'

Scarlett shook her head. 'I'm not being deliberately obstructive, you know. He wasn't a real doctor in any case. He was some Russian medical student who gave us antibiotics for an extortionate fee and didn't bother to ask if we were allergic to anything. And, before you ask, his office was behind a shop in Bijlmer. I could possibly find it if you drove me there, but it would be a struggle. The last time I saw him was over a year ago. And I only ever went there at night-time.'

'How long have you been back in the UK, Scarlett?' Sam asked. She felt as though Scarlett was relaxed enough with their discussion for her to start talking about more recent events.

Scarlett shrugged. 'I don't know. Months. It was before Christmas that I came back. What month are we in now? November? Well, then. Nearly a year.'

'And you've been here in Briarstone the whole time?'

240

'More or less,' she said. 'I've been keeping my head down.'

Sam's hand was aching. She flexed her wrist, turning over to the next page.

'Can we stop for a bit?' Scarlett asked.

While Scarlett went to use the bathroom, Sam stood at the kitchen window and stretched. The weather was closing in, almost dark outside already, the afternoon fading into evening before the world was ready for it. The garden was a tangled mess of waist-high weeds, a plastic slide half-hidden in the undergrowth, a tree at the bottom with the remainder of a rope swing hanging forlornly from a branch. Grim, this place, however much they'd tried to make it feel like a place of sanctuary. No wonder they were going to get rid of it. Of course, they weren't replacing it with something better — thcy weren't replacing it at all. Vulnerable victims were going to be dealt with at regular police stations like everyone else. They'd redecorated two of the interview rooms at Briarstone nick, but, whatever the management thought, a nice pot plant and a box of tissues weren't going to help people feel comfortable enough to talk.

The front door opened and Orla came in, bringing with her a gust of wind.

'In here,' Sam called.

'Hi. Where's Scarlett?'

'Gone to the loo. How did you get on?'

'Not ideal, but I've got a place at a hostel in Charlmere.'

'Gosh, that's a trek. Nowhere closer?'

'Everything's full to bursting. I'll take her over there this evening.'

'Take me where?' Scarlett said, from the doorway.

LOU – Saturday 2 November 2013, 14:30

The Coach and Horses was what Lou would have called an old man's pub. A bar with a tiled floor, rough plaster walls and waist-height dark wood panelling, sticky wooden tables, mismatched chairs and a fireplace that might well have cheered things up had the fire in it been lit. The place was empty. Next door, the snug was not much better, but at least it had a carpet. There were three blokes sitting around a table in the corner upon which sat three half-drunk pints of bitter and three empties. Lou caught the words 'overhead cam' and 'four-wheel drive', followed by something that sounded like 'but it's all about the gravy. You get the gravy right, everything's right'. Sky Sports was on the TV bolted to the wall above the bar, the sound mercifully turned down.

The woman behind the bar looked ridiculously pleased to see a fresh customer approaching. 'Yes, love! What can I get you?'

Lou looked at the optics and the fridges, wondering what she could get away with. Decided it wasn't worth it. 'Just a Diet Coke, please.'

'Can't tempt you to a late lunch?' the woman said, pointing with a heavily manicured finger at the 'Specials' board. 'Got some beef curry left.'

'No, thanks,' Lou said, thinking of the crisps and chocolate she'd already consumed and wishing she'd waited.

She sat down where she could see the door, got out her mobile and ran through her messages. There was no signal this far out in the sticks, but even pretending to read old messages was preferable to staring into space or making eye contact with any of the other occupants.

The door opened and Annie came in, bringing with her a blast of cold air. 'Thank you for meeting me,' she said. 'Can I get you something?'

'I've just got one, thanks.'

Annie went to the bar. She was wearing skinny jeans, trainers, a hooded top under a black wool coat, a thick scarf wound around her neck several times, her hair tucked inside. While she waited for her drink, she tucked one trainered foot behind the other.

'Can I tempt you to a late lunch?' the woman behind the bar offered, and Annie shook her head.

A moment later she came back with a large glass of red wine. She sat down next to Lou. Her eyes were wide, tears brimming. 'I didn't know who else to call,' Annie said. 'You gave me your card. You said I should ring.'

'That's right,' Lou said. 'Has something happened?'

Annie was breathing fast. 'It's Clive – it's just all starting to go wrong again. Everything was ... normal ... and now it's not normal any more.'

'What do you mean? What's going wrong?'

'Clive,' Annie said with desperation in her voice. 'He keeps trying to tell me I'm going mad. He says I'm neurotic. He doesn't understand how hard all this is for me.'

She pulled a tattered tissue from the pocket of her coat and wiped her eyes with it. Her hands were shaking. Lou noticed the brown spots on them, the deep grooves of tendons running along the back. Annie might dress like a teenager, but her hands gave away her real age.

'I'm guessing he doesn't know you're here?'

'No. He doesn't. You won't tell him, will you? Please?'

Annie stretched out a hand and took Louisa's, unexpectedly, making her want to recoil. Her hand was cold, the fingernails sharp. Lou patted the hand and released it in a way she hoped was reassuring.

'Of course. This is between us.'

'He doesn't think I should tell you what happened in Spain. He says you'll prosecute us for wasting police time. Is that true?'

'It depends,' Lou said, suddenly on high alert. 'It sounds as if this is something we should talk about properly, Annie. If you want to make another statement, it would be a better idea to—'

'No, I don't want to – I mean – I don't have to make a statement, do I? I just want to explain. It wasn't how you think. It wasn't because I was hiding things, I was just confused at the time, and then when Scarlett didn't come back it didn't really seem to matter that much. But now – well, Clive thinks Scarlett is going to try and make things look bad for us. And we had nothing to do with her going, nothing at all.'

'Annie,' Lou said, 'if you don't want to make a statement then at least let me record our conversation. Just for me to refer to later. Whatever you tell me, I am going to need to write it up.'

For a moment Lou thought Annie was going to refuse, or was about to get up and walk out again – in which case she would have given in and just listened. But to her surprise Annie nodded. Lou found the sound recording app on her phone and started it, hoping to God it picked up the conversation well enough.

'Go on,' Lou said. 'You tell me what happened. I'm listening.'

'Well,' Annie said, keeping one eye on the phone, lying on the table next to her wine glass, 'I saw her go. That's the second thing. I suppose the first thing was that boy she was with . . .'

'The boy?'

'She had somehow met a Greek boy while we were on holiday. It didn't much seem to matter. But you see, I thought she might have run away with him.'

'But you didn't tell the police this at the time? Why ever not?'

'Clive didn't want to. He didn't believe she had run away. He thought if the police knew she'd met a boy, then they wouldn't bother to look for her properly.'

Lou kept her face neutral, although at times like this it was a struggle. Had they not considered that the boy might have had something to do with Scarlett going missing against her will? That finding the boy might have meant finding Scarlett? It was difficult, too, not to feel the sinister undertones in what Annie was saying. Deliberately withholding information during a live investigation into the kidnapping of a child? How could they possibly have thought that was the right thing to do?

'So what happened with the boy?' Lou said. 'Who was he?'

'I don't know,' Annie said, shaking her head. 'I never spoke to him. I saw her kissing him, out on the road, the night before she disappeared. He ran off when Scarlett saw me.'

'Did you discuss it with her?'

Annie smiled. 'Yes. Her father wasn't very happy, put it like that.'

'You asked her about him?'

'She said he was just a boy she'd met. She denied anything had happened, just kissing.'

'But Clive was angry?'

Annie paused before answering. 'Yes.'

'Did he hurt her? Punish her?'

'Oh, no! Not – not really. I mean, he was angry, he might have shouted a bit, but then she was being deliberately disobedient. She knew what our expectations of her were. She was only fifteen! Still a child! Clive has this thing—'

Annie broke off suddenly, and Lou caught the thread of something important that she had almost let slip. She hid it by taking a sip of wine, almost putting the glass back on the table and picking it up and sipping again, giving herself time to think.

'What were you going to say?' Lou asked.

'Nothing. Clive just – he doesn't want our daughters to grow up too fast. These days, girls are sexualised at a younger and younger age, aren't they? We didn't want that for our girls. They both knew that. They knew the difference between right and wrong; we'd told them often enough.'

'So what happened after you discussed the boy with Scarlett? Did she see him again?'

'She stayed indoors, sulking. She said she didn't feel well, and I guess she might have had that tummy bug we'd all had, so she didn't come out to dinner with us the night after. That was the night she went.'

Annie lifted her glass again and drank the last of the wine in two noisy gulps.

'You said earlier that you saw her go,' Lou said. 'What did you mean?'

Annie looked at her hands, rubbed the fingers of her right hand over the back of the left. Lou could see a tear hanging on the bottom lashes of her eye.

'Annie?'

But she shook her head, causing two tears to fall in wet splashes on to the table. 'I can't, I can't.'

'It will be much better if you tell me,' Lou offered, 'it really will.

It sounds as if you've been carrying this around with you all these years.'

'You don't understand,' she said, taking a shuddering breath in. 'If Clive knew I was telling you this . . . '

'What would he do, Annie?'

'Nothing, nothing! But he'd be so upset. He thinks you don't understand us, how it is between us and Juliette – with both of the girls, before . . . We're happy together. We make each other happy. Nobody seems to understand that.'

'Tell me what happened,' Lou said softly. 'Take your time.'

'I . . . I heard the patio door go. It was the middle of the night – well, the early hours of the morning, really. I thought I'd dreamed it, but then I couldn't get to sleep. I got up and went next door a few minutes later. Scarlett's bed was empty. I went looking for her.'

'And – you found her?'

'She was on the road outside the resort where we were staying. I was standing just by the gate. I was about to shout out for her, and then I saw her getting into a van.'

'Getting into a van?' Lou echoed.

'A white van – like, I don't know, a Transit, something like that, with a door at the side. It pulled up next to her. I saw her talking to someone, and then she moved closer to the van – it was blocking my view. And a few seconds later it drove off and she was gone.'

Lou couldn't say anything for a moment. She waited for Annie to continue, but the woman was staring at her wine glass as if hoping it would magically fill up again. Lou wanted to shake her.

'I know I should have said something.'

'Yes,' Lou said. Left it there.

'But it didn't cross my mind that she'd been taken. I thought she was meeting that boy. I thought he'd just picked her up. What could

I do? I couldn't chase after a van at two in the morning. I thought she'd be back in a couple of hours, back in her bed pretending nothing had happened.'

'So what did you do?'

'I went back to the room. Clive woke up when I came in. I told him what I'd seen. He was cross, of course he was. We sat up for a bit hoping she'd come back, then after an hour or so we went back to bed.'

'And the next morning, when she still wasn't back?'

'We went out to look for her. I was getting worried. I hadn't thought for a minute that she wouldn't come back. I thought she might have run away, but that she'd think better of it and come back of her own accord before the bus came to collect us for the airport. Or we thought – we thought she might have slept with him, this boy, and that she'd fallen asleep and hadn't realised that it was morning. Then we thought maybe she was too scared to come back, in case we were angry.'

Lou breathed in. 'But you still didn't think to tell the police all this?'

'When we called the police, we agreed that something must have happened to stop her coming back. So the best way to deal with it was to say we assumed someone had taken her against her will. And that was true, wasn't it?' She looked at Lou defiantly.

'But the police could have been looking for a white van. Did you not think about that?'

'Clive said she would probably have been moved into a building by then, or into a different vehicle. There was no point.'

'What did *you* think?'

Annie looked baffled. 'Me?'

Clive was clearly something of an expert in missing person

enquiries, Lou thought. Annie didn't seem capable of an independent thought. As much as she was struggling with the gravity of what Annie was choosing to share with her, the fact remained that ten years had passed.

'What made you decide to tell me this now, Annie?'

'Oh, lots of reasons. I've wanted to tell someone for a long time. Since it happened. I didn't want to keep it quiet, not really. It was Clive. And I do want you to try to understand: we didn't keep it to ourselves for any bad reason, it was for a good reason – to keep everyone looking for our daughter until she was found. Not that it worked, did it? And we're not going to get into trouble now, are we? Please say we won't be prosecuted, or anything like that. After all, she's back safe and sound, isn't she?'

'But why now?'

'Oh! Clive's got me worried about what she's going to say. Because she saw me, you see. Scarlett saw me waiting at the gate, just before she got into the van.'

The vampire never returned. Scarlett wondered if she'd not given him enough of her blood, or if she'd been too dismissive of him. There were girls who would let their customers do anything, especially if they paid over the odds and left them with some spare money. Scarlett doubted that any of the others were saving for a possible future, though. If they were saving, it would be for an extra fix.

He had probably found another willing vein to suck.

She was gazing out of the window, wondering idly if the blood of a crack addict tasted different, or if it would be possible to get addicted to drugs yourself by doing that. It was sleeting outside, unseasonably early, the light fading already although it was only just past three. The cold had put the tourists off. Inside, they'd turned the heating on – for a change – and, as there was no real ventilation unless she opened the front door, it was stiflingly hot in here. She had seen one of her regulars, and a couple of Eastern European lorry drivers who'd taken it in turns, one waiting outside while the other one had his fun. Their accent had unnerved her; she'd wondered if they were the Lithuanians, sent to check her out. But they weren't the type – big lads, but several days' growth of stubble, the smell of coffee and burgers on their clothes. Laughing and joking on the doorstep outside as they discussed her fees and which one of them would get to go first.

Sooner or later they would turn up and demand to know why takings were so low today, no matter what the weather. For the time being, though, she was enjoying the thought that they were probably tucked up in a nice warm café somewhere playing cards, not watching her from the street outside.

In the past month, the wound on her shoulder now healed, Scarlett had begun to slide into a depression. It happened fairly regularly, prompted sometimes by an act of violence or cruelty – however common they were, she was not unaffected – or it might be something as simple as a change in the weather. This time, the black cloud came down over her because of the vampire. She'd seen that extra money as a door opening out of the blackness of her nightmare, but what she had was barely enough for a night in a hotel and a taxi to get her there, much less a set of reasonable clothes and transport out of the city. Or even a bribe – not that there was anyone she could trust to help her. And now she faced another winter here, long dark nights after long dark days, with bad weather and cold and not enough customers to keep her minders from beating her, not enough customers to take her mind off the passing hours, the grinding despair.

Scarlett stood to stretch her legs, sauntering to the window and leaning her arms against the cold glass. That was when she saw him, standing in the doorway of the bar on the corner, looking across to her window. That man again. The one that had called himself Stefan, and was probably a rival pimp.

Scarlett had that feeling that sometimes came over her, an almost uncontrollable urge to scream, to hammer on the glass, to run for the door and rush out into the street, to run and run, screaming her head off, attracting attention from the tourists and the members of the public – who knew, maybe there were actually police around who weren't taking back-handers from the pimps too.

The guy who called himself Stefan was at her window now,

looking at her. She turned her head. He must know the minders, she thought. He must know they weren't watching right now. Unless he'd been sent by them.

A few minutes later, he crossed the road and she opened the door to let him in. He followed her into her room, taking off his jacket as he did so. 'Christ, it is so warm in here!'

'It's cosy,' she said. 'How are your studies coming along?'

'Good, thank you. I have been practising as much as I can.'

Good on him for remembering his cover story, she thought. She stroked her hand up his arm, across to his shoulder, trying to get him to respond, to play the game, fuck her or whatever it was he wanted to do today and then get out.

'No,' he said. 'Stella, I'm not here for that.'

Her hand dropped to her side. 'You should go, then,' she said. 'I'm not making enough money today as it is. I'll be in big trouble.'

He pulled money out of his pocket and dropped it on to the bed. 'I'll pay you for your time,' he said. 'I just want to talk.'

She took the money anyway, posted it – all of it, making sure he was watching – straight through the hole in the wall. 'Look,' she said, 'you're wasting your time, whatever it is you want to talk about. Practising English? Your English is already fine. You want me to leave here and work for you? It isn't going to happen.'

'I'm not a pimp,' he said. 'I get people out.'

Scarlett caught her breath but tried hard, so hard, not to show the effect his words were having on her. 'Who are you?' she said.

His demeanour had changed, almost instantly. He was businesslike now, authoritative. 'My name is Stefan Lassen. I work with a team that looks for trafficking victims and gets them to safety. We can provide a safe house, transport, access to medical care; drug rehab, if you need it.'

252

'Medical care? You mean the fucking Russian in that back-room clinic?'

'No,' Stefan said, not rising to her challenging tone. 'There are doctors and specialist nurses who work with our team. If you need it, they can refer you to hospital.'

Scarlett felt tears pricking the corners of her eyes. That in itself took her by surprise – nothing made her cry these days. Wasted tears, wasted days – what was the point? Crying changed nothing. But this – this scent of rebellion, a glimpse of freedom ...

It could happen, she thought. *It could be true.*

'I don't understand what you mean,' she said, but making direct eye contact while she did so. There was still a chance that this was a set-up. Still a chance that the room was bugged, that they'd sent their stooge to test her out on a slow day, for their own amusement as much as anything else.

'This is how it works,' he said. 'You give me your real name, date of birth, relatives in your own country who can confirm who you are. I can arrange to get you a new passport. When you're ready, when everything's in place, I'll come here and take you straight away to a safe house. Your minders are getting lax – they must trust you. I've been watching you, and them. They're only visiting you twice a day. That's a good sign.'

'They're always keeping an eye on me,' she said softly. 'I never know when they're out there.'

'I've been watching them,' he said again.

'There are lots of different ones.' She was testing him.

'I know that. I'm telling you that right now they are in a private bar in a hotel around the corner, drinking schnapps and watching football on a big screen. I know this because my colleague is there with them, making sure they don't come to check on you until we're done with our conversation.' He pulled a mobile phone from his pocket and held it up. 'He will text me the minute they move.'

She thought about it – thought about the dark cloud and how desperate she had been to see a man who wanted to suck blood out of her shoulder, and how perhaps this might actually be another way to escape; thought about the girl with the bruises in the clinic, the desperation on her face; the girl who'd run screaming from her room and ended up with her final, awful moments of life being filmed for sick men to get off watching. Thought about what this might mean for her. A life-or-death decision, right here, right now.

She took a deep breath.

'Why can't we go now?' she asked.

'Because it has to be done properly. We have to prepare for you, set things up. It can be done quickly, though. Three or four days, at most. All you have to do to start things off is tell me your name.'

'I don't want my family to know.'

'You don't?'

'They don't need to know, do they? You can get me out without telling them?'

'If you want it that way.'

Scarlett paused. The words, when they came, sounded unfamiliar, strange.

'My name's Scarlett Rainsford,' she said. 'I'm from a town called Briarstone, in England. I was on holiday with my family when they took me, nine years ago . . . '

LOU – Saturday 2 November 2013, 15:40

Lou's journey back to the office was one of those slightly scary affairs where you would reach your destination and realise that you could remember no details at all about the drive. She parked close to the Major Crime department at the back of HQ and swiped her card to get in, hurrying to get back to her computer before everything that had taken place started to go out of her head. Thank God Annie had let her record it.

Nobody was in the office, for which Lou was grateful. While she waited for the workstation to log on to the system, she retrieved the recording from her phone and, holding her breath, pressed 'play'.

Go on, said Lou's voice, sounding alarmingly nasal. *You tell me what happened. I'm listening . . .*

Lou spent the next hour and a half typing, putting as much detail into her report as she possibly could. If she was submitting it to Special Branch to be used as intelligence for their investigation, it needed to be accurate. If they ever conducted a review into Scarlett's abduction and the way it had been handled, or if Annie and Clive were ever cautioned for failing to provide information when questioned, then what she had on her phone was potentially evidence. For now, her report would suffice.

Once she had finished, she tried Waterhouse. The mobile number went directly to voicemail, with instructions to call a Special Branch inspector she had met once, briefly, at a retirement do, in the event of something requiring urgent attention. She dialled Caro Sumner instead.

'Ma'am,' Caro said, clearly recognising the number. 'How are you?'

'Good – good, thanks. Are you free to talk?'

'Sure, I'm just in the office.'

'HQ?'

'No, I'm down at Knapstone. Do you need me?'

Lou shuffled the pages of her report together and explained what Annie had told her. Caro's response was, 'What? You're kidding?'

'I'm afraid not. I've been trying to get hold of Mr Waterhouse to let him know, but his phone's off. I'm emailing the report to you and to him, and I've printed a copy for Mr Buchanan. I don't think there's much we can do, but it might make a difference to how we look at the Rainsfords. Are you going to be seeing Sam again at all today?'

'I was going to call her before booking off – I wanted to see if she wants to visit Clive Rainsford with me tomorrow morning. So we can discuss it once we've read your report.'

'Good plan. Get Sam to call me if she needs to?'

When she ended the call, Lou sat for a few moments in the silence of the office. She had done everything she needed to do. She logged off the system and, because she couldn't quite bring herself to go home just yet, she went to the kitchen area that served this end of the building and washed up all the mugs that were sitting in the sink. Autopilot. Thinking about Annie, those huge eyes brimming with tears. The desperation in her clutching hand.

SCARLETT – Wednesday 24 October 2012, 03:35

He came for her in the early hours of the morning.

She was already bone-tired and the streets outside were dead; even

256

the hardened clubgoers had headed home for the night. Just the street cleaners – it was even too cold for rough sleepers to be out. Nobody to see what was about to happen.

Scarlett had begun to think her minders had forgotten her. She'd even lain down on the bed, curled up into a ball, half-dozing, when she heard a knock at the door. She went to open it, wondering why they didn't let themselves in, but it was Stefan, with a big woollen coat which he held out for her.

'Come now,' he said. 'Be quick.'

She didn't argue or hesitate, half-asleep to wide awake in a moment. As she pulled the coat around her she glanced up and down the street to check if anyone had seen.

'Don't worry,' he said. 'My colleague is watching them. They are in a bar.'

One arm around her waist, protective and also hurrying her along, he indicated a silver Audi estate parked at the end of the street. He opened the passenger door for her and she slipped inside. He got into the driver's seat a moment later. Only then did he pause, look at her and smile.

'Where are we going?' Scarlett asked, as the car's engine fired into life.

He turned up the fan heater as they drove down the narrow cobbled street towards the main road. 'We are going to a safe house for tonight where you can rest and get something to eat, and some clothes. Don't worry about anything. You are safe now.'

Scarlett's heart was beating so fast she thought it was going to explode. She had to put a hand over her mouth to stifle the scream of excitement and terror, drumming her stilettoed feet on the worn mats in the footwell.

'Hey,' he laughed, 'it is okay. You are okay.'

257

It felt like forever until they got to the motorway heading out of the city.

'What's going to happen?' Scarlett asked. 'Have you managed to get me a passport?'

'Don't worry,' he repeated, 'everything is fine.'

'You haven't told my parents?'

'No, you said I should not do that.'

'Thank God. I can't believe this, I can't! Thank you,' she said, 'thank you so much.'

'Try to relax, okay? We have a little way to go yet. Here.'

He reached behind the seat and brought out a carrier bag, which he handed to Scarlett. Inside was a bottle of whisky.

'To celebrate,' he said, smiling.

She unscrewed the cap and took a gulp of it, choked a little, feeling the burn travelling down her throat.

'Cheers,' he said, with a laugh.

Scarlett took another gulp. It felt good. She offered the bottle to him.

'No, no,' he said. 'I have some later when I do not need to drive any more.'

'Okay,' she said, and screwed the lid back on.

'You had enough already?'

'What's going to happen next?' she asked again. 'When do I go back to England?'

'Please,' he said. 'It is important that you stay calm, if you can. You need some time to recover.'

And he turned on the radio, turned it up loud to drown out her excitement and her chatter. Scarlett didn't mind. She looked out of the window at the lights of the city rushing past, the bottle of whisky cold between her knees. This time of night there were not many cars, a few lorries, as the Audi moved between them. To Scarlett, the speed of the car felt exhilarating and terrifying, like being on a fairground ride.

'Is it far?' she shouted.

But Stefan pretended not to hear, his eyes on the road.

LOU – Saturday 2 November 2013, 18:30

Heading back to her car, Lou answered her mobile without checking who it was. Immediately she wished she hadn't.

'Hi, Louisa!' said a bright, chirpy female voice. 'Hope you don't mind me ringing.'

'Course not, Tracy. I'm really sorry I haven't had a chance to do my RSVP yet . . . '

'Oh, no, don't worry! I know you must be really busy! It's just that the hotel keep pestering me for final numbers for the evening, you know what they're like . . . '

Lou didn't know what they were like, and didn't particularly care either. There was something unremittingly grim about being forced to think happy thoughts about a wedding when your boyfriend had gone off in a strop. For a moment she thought of crying off altogether, pleading some likely clash with work, but it would get back to her mother in a matter of moments and she couldn't, she just couldn't take another conversation with her mother right now.

'Well – I guess – you know there's always a chance I won't be able to make it at the last minute . . . '

'Aw, I understand,' Tracy said. Her tone was nauseatingly sympathetic. 'But I really want to include you, even if you have to let us down. Please say you'll come. And your mum said that you were going to bring – ' a moment's pause ' – someone called Jason?'

'Hopefully,' Lou said, thinking how sad it was that Tracy's whole existence at the moment was revolving around one day in a white dress. 'Thanks, Tracy. We'll be there.'

'That's great to hear. I'll put you both on the table plan.'

'Sure,' Lou said. 'How's all the planning going?'

'Oh, it's nearly there. I've got the final dress-fitting tomorrow, I hope I still fit in it although I've been doing really well on the diet ...'

Lou had stopped listening. She had had a sudden awful realisation that, as much as she felt sorry for Tracy, who seemed so happy to commit the rest of her life to someone at the age of twenty-one, Tracy at the same time sounded as if she was sorry for Lou – who was apparently struggling to find a bloke to come with her to a wedding, at the grand old age of thirty-three.

When Tracy finally finished talking and rang off, the mobile buzzed again. She had a premonition that it was going to be her mother, but the caller display told her it was Sam.

'Sorry to ruin your evening,' Sam said. 'It's Scarlett. She's taken off.'

22:45

Lou stopped on the way home and got a takeaway curry from her second-favourite curry place, because her favourite was down the street from Jason's house, and she didn't want to go anywhere near it.

Lou was keeping an eye on her mobile phone, which was on the arm of the chair, waiting for Sam to call with news. They'd been

260

about to drive Scarlett to Charlmere to put her in a hostel when they'd realised she wasn't in the front room after all. There wasn't a lot they could do. Scarlett wasn't wanted for anything, she wasn't necessarily at risk – unless she ran into the McDonnells, and even then nobody could really do anything about it until something happened. Frustrating, though. And, much as Lou wouldn't tell Sam not to spend her evening looking for her, she knew that was exactly what her friend would be doing anyway.

Lou had just finished eating, and was more than three-quarters of the way down a bottle of Rioja that was actually far too nice to be wasted on one person determined to get fuck-off drunk – or *hammered*, as the Canadians so quaintly put it – when her mobile phone bleeped with a text message.

It was from Jason. She looked at the message and then at her watch – quarter to eleven. Bit late for a social call, wasn't it?

How you doing?

She thought about ignoring it, which would have been the sensible thing to do. In the cold light of day she would have left it, but she was now close to finishing a very nice bottle of wine and she hadn't communicated with anyone since Omar at the Star of India had wished her a pleasant evening to go with her complimentary poppadom.

And wine always made her garrulous.

Oh, but what to say? So many things . . . and in the end she settled on:

Fine thanks. Nothing a bottle of good wine won't cure.
How are you?

Regretted it immediately, of course. Too flippant. And it made it sound as though she was in some way consoling herself with alcohol.

Good, just checking u are ok.

Lou reached for the bottle and her glass; the last of it filled only a quarter of the way to the brim. And even that only lasted a few sips. While she waited for his reply, she contemplated what to do. Open another bottle? The trouble with the Rioja was that it was too good; anything she picked out of her sadly depleted wine cellar – a metal rack that sat under the work surface and didn't hold nearly enough bottles when full – would taste like vinegar in comparison.

She went over to the kitchen a little unsteadily and reviewed the selection. A merlot, plus a pinot grigio and a bottle of sauvignon blanc in the fridge. None of them was ideal.

She went back to the phone. No reply as yet. Before she had a chance to regret it, think about it or be sensible, she sent him a text.

If you bring another bottle of Rioja, I might actually open the door.

There was no reply to that one. Calling his bluff was the best thing she could have done – though in the cold light of day she would probably realise that, of course, it wasn't. She opened the merlot and took it back to the living room. She had been thinking about what Sam had said this morning, knowing in her heart that she had a point. The age gap didn't matter, not really. It wasn't as if she saw her parents often; what did it matter if they thought she had a toyboy? Once they met Jason, they would love him just as she did. She wished she'd said it back when she had had the chance. If she told him now, it would look desperate.

She tried to watch a film but couldn't concentrate. Maybe it would be best to talk it through, to tell him the truth. *This is how I feel, Jason. I do love you. I really do. I'm just rubbish at expressing it . . .*

Lou tried out several different versions in her head and gave up. If she could see him face to face, it would be easier. She reached for the phone and dialled his number.

He answered straight away. 'Hey,' he said.

'It's me.'

'Yep, I know.'

The best way to approach this was probably to get straight to the point. 'You want to come over?'

'It's kind of late.'

Lou peered at the clock. 'Well, you sent me a text. I thought you were probably still up.'

'You just sitting there getting drunk on your own?'

'Don't say it like that – makes me sound like a right case. You were so wasted last night I had to leave you next to a bucket, don't forget. I've just had a glass of wine to chill out, that's all.'

'Sure.'

'Are you still cross because I didn't come to hockey?'

'Nope. I'm pissed because of what you said to your mom.'

At first Lou thought she hadn't heard him properly. 'What?'

'So, last night? I tell you how I feel. The truth – and yes, I do love you – and this morning I hear you talking to your mom and you make it sound to her like I'm some guy you just picked up off the street to take with you to this wedding.'

'I didn't, at all!'

263

'Yeah. You said "it's nothing serious" and – what was the other thing? Oh, yeah. You "managed to find someone to bring" to the wedding. And that your mom would get to meet me soon "unless something comes up", in which case you won't bother to go. I think those are exactly the words you used, since I've had them going round and round in my brain pretty much the whole day.'

Lou had felt her mouth drop open somewhere in the middle of his speech.

'This is all wrong,' she said. 'You've got it all wrong.'

'I don't think so.'

'I don't want to rush things with you because I don't want to mess things up. I want this to work. I don't want to show you off to my family, only for you to get scared off by them and run a mile.'

'You seriously think I'd do that?'

You might, Lou thought. This was daft, having an argument on the phone. 'Look, why don't you come over so we can talk about it properly? Please?'

There was a pause as if he was thinking about it, and although it didn't sound like much of an offer she was hoping he would give in, because it just felt wrong to not be together when they had the chance.

'I don't think so. I just don't want to play this game any more. It feels like you can't switch off from work properly unless you've had a bottle of wine first. And I want a relationship that's based on more than getting drunk on the few occasions we get to spend time with each other.'

Ouch.

'Louisa,' he said, his voice softening, 'I'm sorry, that came out badly. But it's how I feel. The whole thing just feels like you're not ready.'

264

'Ready for what?'

'A relationship. A serious relationship.'

'What you mean is, I'm not ready for a nine-to-five and coming home to a nice tofu stir-fry, with my kind boyfriend able to track where I am from one moment to the next.'

Now she was just trying to hurt him back – not a good idea. Not very mature.

'What?'

'You seem to have this really fixed idea about what this relationship should look like. Actually I quite liked it how it was. It was fun. And you never gave me any indication that you weren't happy.'

'Every time I tried to talk to you about it, you had a call or a meeting or something urgent to do, or you were too tired. And you have this weird thing with your family, like you're embarrassed about going out with me, or something. Like you're not committed enough to introduce me to them.'

She bit her lip. Were they really doing this? 'I asked you to the wedding!'

'Yes, you did, but I'm guessing if it hadn't been for this event coming up it would have been years before I got to meet them, if ever. Am I right?'

'But that's because they're so bloody obsessed with my ageing ovaries, not because I'm embarrassed about *you*, for crying out loud.'

Silence. Then she heard him laugh. 'Sorry. I have a mental picture of a couple of wrinkly ovaries right now. Like walnuts.'

'Fuck off,' she said. And laughed in spite of herself.

'If you still want me to,' he said, 'I'll come with you to the wedding and they can say whatever the hell they want to me and I won't mind. Okay?'

Lou sighed. What the hell – it solved a load of problems.

'Whatever. Thanks. If you don't fancy it nearer the time I can say something came up. It's what they're expecting me to do anyway.'

'Whatever you think, I would like to meet them. I'm kind of hoping we can get past this.'

'Me too,' Lou said, and she meant it.

'It's late,' he said. 'I need to get some sleep. I'll see you at work, okay?'

'Sure.'

There was still two-thirds of the merlot left but it didn't look quite so appealing any more. Lou pushed the cork back in and left it in the kitchen. Then she collected all the takeaway containers and stuffed them into the kitchen bin, which was full. The whole house seemed to smell of curry and no doubt it would be worse in the morning, so she took the bin bag outside. The cold air was refreshing, and although it was late she was feeling clear-headed, alert. She ran a bath upstairs and by the time she came out it felt as if she was relaxed and tired enough to sleep. Much as it had hurt to hear it put quite so baldly, Jason had a point. Unless she was on call, or driving somewhere, she couldn't remember the last evening she'd had without at least one glass of wine.

Before getting into bed Lou checked her phone, as she always did. There was one message, from Jason.

Always love you Louisa, sleep well x

SCARLETT – Amsterdam outskirts, Wednesday 24 October 2012, 04:09

The car stopped. Scarlett had been dozing a little, lulled by the motion of the car and by the whisky she'd drunk on an empty stomach.

'Where are we?' she said.

'We are here,' he said. 'You can get out.'

She clicked her seatbelt free and opened the door, stepping out into the cold. They were in some kind of industrial estate, behind a warehouse. There was no car park as such, just an expanse of concrete through which weeds sprouted in tufts, litter pressed against a chain-link fence by an icy wind, lit from overhead by street-lights that gave everything a sickly greenish glow. Another car was parked next to them, a grubby Opel, half-rusted, and a Transit van that looked newer. From behind the corrugated iron wall of the unit, a crane rose high above her head. She looked up. The top of it was half-hidden in low, misty cloud. The chill in the air and the metallic, salty smell made her wonder if they were near the docks.

'Is this the safe house?' she asked. 'It doesn't look like much of a house.'

'Come,' Stefan said, taking her by the arm. 'It's okay.'

She was shivering against the cold as he pulled her along towards the building. A door opened inwards, through what must once have been an office of some kind. Abandoned, by the look of it, although the fluorescent lights overhead were on, showing a bare room with a desk, a filing cabinet, waste paper on the floor. A bad smell was coming from somewhere and Scarlett recognised it – raw meat, gone off. Blood. Something soiled. Fear.

That was when she panicked.

At the same moment that she pulled back, away from him, he gripped her tight enough to bruise and called out something in Dutch. Immediately two men appeared from inside the warehouse, big guys with shaven heads, and Scarlett screamed.

SAM – Sunday 3 November 2013, 00:13

Scarlett wasn't answering her phone – or, more specifically, Sam's spare phone – which was annoying. It would have been so easy for her to have just answered it, said, 'Yeah, thanks, I'm staying with friends,' and then Sam could have gone home, put her feet up and relaxed. Instead, of course, she was out driving around hunting for Scarlett – just in case she'd got herself into trouble, just in case she had nowhere else to go.

Past midnight, there weren't many public places offering shelter from the rain, and Sam had almost given up when she finally struck lucky.

Scarlett was in the bus station, the grey hood of her sweatshirt pulled up over her head, buried inside her brown coat. She was sitting on a bench with her knees drawn up, while around her the drunks waited for sleep on their own benches, and the clubbers waited for buses that at this time of night were sporadic at best.

Sam sat down on the bench. Scarlett looked in her direction, alarmed, ready to run.

'Oh, it's you,' she said.

'Yeah, it's me.'

'You know, when you ring someone six times and they don't answer, it usually means they don't want to talk to you.'

'I'm not so good at taking hints, sorry.'

Scarlett chewed at her cuff. 'You can't make me go to bloody Charlmere,' she said. 'Fucking hostel with homeless alkies and smackheads. No, thanks.'

'I know. Just wanted to check you were okay, that's all.'

'I'm fine. And you can piss off now, too.'

But Sam stayed where she was, not moving. She half-expected Scarlett to get up and walk off, and, if she had, Sam would have had to let her go, but for the time being they sat like bookends at either end of the bench and waited. Sam wondered if Scarlett realised that detective sergeants didn't routinely go looking for missing persons – not that she fitted into that particular category. She was an adult, and, after what she'd probably been through in the last few years, a streetwise adult at that. So Sam had, realistically, nothing to offer her.

'Why are you still here?' Scarlett said at last, clearly irritated.

Sam took a deep breath. 'Look, I'm not going to follow you around. I just wanted to check you were okay. I've done that; now I'm going to leave you alone. If you need a friend, someone to talk to, or if you need help, you can ring me.'

'You can't help me. Nobody can.'

Sam got to her feet. Scarlett looked up at her. In the grim orange light of the concrete bus station she looked so young, Sam could easily have believed she was still fifteen. For a moment she looked lost, and then she offered Sam a smile. When she smiled, she looked totally different: beautiful.

Sam looked away immediately.

'Thanks,' Scarlett said. 'And thanks for lending me the phone. I will give it back.'

'Whenever,' said Sam, keeping her eyes down.

'No, I will. You're not like the rest of them.'

Sam chanced a look back at the girl on the bench. Whatever she'd seen there – that moment when something had wrenched inside her – it had passed.

'Take care, Scarlett,' she said, and walked away up the slope towards the bowling alley which had closed down, conveniently leaving three parking spaces outside.

Back in the car, the doors locked, Sam sent a text to Lou.

Found her. She's OK, won't come back though. She's got my number etc. Sorry x

It wasn't a good result. In all probability they might never see Scarlett again, and Sam had lost her emergency phone.

SCARLETT – Wednesday 24 October 2012, 04:16

Inside the main warehouse it was dark. Scarlett was being half-dragged, half-carried across the concrete floor and she could make out several large, corrugated rectangular shapes – shipping containers, and one larger unit with a pair of metal doors that stood open. A dull light was coming from inside. She could hear voices, laughter from somewhere, and another voice that sounded muffled. They passed the open doors to the unit. Inside Scarlett could see that the walls were lined with ridged foam, as though the whole thing was a giant, room-sized packing crate for some expensive electronic equipment.

The smell was worse.

I am going to die in here.

A man came out from the soundproofed room, resting his hands on the metal doors as if to pull them shut behind him. He saw Scarlett and stopped, watching. The light was behind him. She couldn't see his face. She saw him move, take hold of something and drag it, scraping along the floor, to the doors of the room. When the light illuminated it, she saw it was a spotlight on a tripod-like stand, an electric cable coiled around the height adjuster.

'Help me,' she said, but not loudly, whimpering. 'Help me. Please.'

They pulled her to one of the smaller shipping crates and opened it, shoving her inside. The door boomed shut behind her and she heard the metal bang of the locks being pulled across.

It was pitch black. Not a glimmer of light. 'No, no!' Scarlett shouted. 'Don't leave me here!'

She pummelled with her fists on the cold metal of the door, then listened. The echo of their retreating footsteps on the poured-concrete floor outside.

And then a different sound to replace it.

Breathing.

Someone – something – was in here with her.

'Hello?' she whispered.

There was a movement behind her. '*Engels?*' came a whispered reply.

'*Ja, Engels. Ik ben Engels.* I'm English.'

No response.

271

'Let me out!' Scarlett screamed, pounding with her fists.

Abruptly she heard the footsteps coming back and the sound of metal scraping against metal. She expected the door to open, but it didn't. She could hear voices close by, a foreign language she didn't recognise or understand. And then, without warning, a woman's voice rising quickly to a panicked wail – '*Nee! Nee, alsjeblieft!*' No. Please.

A second female voice, moaning. Footsteps.

'What are they doing?' Scarlett asked.

In her crate, silence other than the breathing.

Outside in the warehouse, the voices of two women lifted in screams, and then another metallic door closing. The women were in the soundproofed box.

And then, without warning, muffled but still audible, a bang.

Silence for a second, other than the pounding of Scarlett's heart in her chest. She pressed her cheek to the metal, straining to hear what was going on.

Seconds passed. Another bang.

Silence.

Scarlett choked back a sob.

From the back wall of her crate, she heard her companion.

'Next time is us.'

Part Four

DEAD INSIDE

LOU – Sunday 3 November 2013, 09:25

There was no more opportunity to worry about Scarlett Rainsford.

Area had arrested a nineteen-year-old called Aaron Sutcliffe, who had been mouthing off in one of the pubs formerly owned by Carl McVey. He'd had a go at breaking a glass and threatening a member of the door staff with it, then he'd run off. They'd identified him from the CCTV outside the pub and found him vomiting his way out of a hangover in the back bedroom at his mum's house.

Lou had seen his name before. He had been at school with Ian Palmer; they'd interviewed him early on, more than once, since he had a record for GBH and assault as well as criminal damage and theft. But he'd had nothing useful to tell them, at the time. On the night Palmer was assaulted Aaron had been in hospital himself – attending the birth of his first daughter.

The custody photo of Aaron Sutcliffe showed he had acquired another tattoo on his neck since his last visit – 'Ella-Mae' – just scabbing over nicely, an elaborate, swirly font. Being a father clearly hadn't endowed him with a renewed sense of personal responsibility, however. He was sneering at the camera, one eye twitching in a wink just as the image was taken. For that to have got through to the main database, Lou knew, the detention officer would no doubt have taken several pictures and finally given up.

Lou had sent Les Finnegan down to Briarstone nick to meet with the Division CID and collaborate with the interview. It was worth a shot, and from other witness statements taken in the Railway Tavern

Aaron's argument with the doorman seemed to have something to do with what had happened to Ian six weeks ago.

While she waited for Les to report back, Lou received a phone call from Caro.

'I heard Sam Hollands found Scarlett last night,' she said.

'Yes. Couldn't get her back, unfortunately. She was at the bus station. Let's hope it was just the safest place she could find to sleep, and not the first step in her moving somewhere far away.'

'I don't think she has, yet. Have you seen this morning's CAD about the burglary?'

Lou sat up straight, moving her mouse and clicking over to the Computer Aided Dispatch program that logged all the calls to police as they were received. 'No – have you got the number?'

Caro recited the eight-digit identifier and Lou repeated it as she typed it in.

'Shit,' Lou said, when the details of the call came up on her screen. 'A car key burglary?'

'Last night. They were all asleep, apparently. I found out about it when I rang Clive Rainsford this morning to ask for a meeting. He won't leave the house at the moment; they're all waiting for CID and Forensics. And they can't actually go anywhere, so I'm going to go down and speak to my captive audience. Do you want to come with me? I said I'd be there at eleven.'

Lou pulled a face. 'I can't, really – can I send Sam instead?'

Sam was on her way into the office. Lou asked her to meet Caro in the CID office at Briarstone at a quarter to eleven, and then went back to her computer and read through the CAD again, slowly.

She knew better than to jump to conclusions, but even the scant information on the CAD had set alarm bells ringing. There were usually at least two or three criminal gangs involved in car key burglaries at any one time – breaking into properties in order to steal the keys of the expensive-looking car on the driveway, and then the car itself. This particular offence was unusual. The method of entry was odd, but not unheard of. Often thieves would take any-thing of value that they came across while looking for the car keys, so easily portable items like cash, cards, laptops and mobile phones were frequently added to the property list. In this case, though, the car had been an eight-year-old Volvo. Again, they had seen car key burglaries for lower-value vehicles before, but those cases often involved large-scale theft from the property, where the car had been taken as a means to transport heavier items like TVs, computers, even the odd safe. Sometimes the lower-value car was taken along-side the higher-value vehicle parked next to it – possibly to be used in other crimes, rather than being sold on. But neither was a factor here.

She sent Sam a text.

Update me asap? Have you seen the CAD? Think it might be linked to our job?

A few moments later, Sam sent a reply.

I thought that too – does she even drive, though? I'll let you know when I'm done.

Lou went back to the CAD, read through the list of items that had been stolen. The items of jewellery suggested a thorough search – that the burglar had had time to look. And yet the occupants had been asleep upstairs.

Lou sent another text.

277

Odd that no laptop, no mobile. Didn't he work for electronics firm? Let me know how you get on with him.

Crime Report

CRIME NUMBER	PZ/015567/13
CRIME TYPE	Burglary Dwelling
CRIME SUBTYPE	Car Key
REPORTED DATE	03/11/2013 08:25
COMMITTED DATE	02/11/2013 22:30 – 03/11/2013 08:15
OIC	DC 10898 SIMON ADEJO
CRIME VENUE	14 RUSSET AVENUE BRIARSTONE
TELEPHONE	BRIARSTONE 411924
BEAT CODE	PZ023
VICTIM	
Name	Clive RAINSFORD
DOB	21/10/1943
Address	14 Russet Avenue, Briarstone

PROPERTY

Property Type £	Description	Value
Cards	Nationwide debit card	1.00
	Nationwide VISA card	1.00
	Burtons storecard	1.00

	M&S storecard	1.00
	RAC membership card	1.00
Documents	Driving licence photocard	1.00
Cash	Bank notes	275.00
	Coins	25.00
Jewellery	Rolex Air-King 14010	2,000.00
	Diamond and emerald ring	1,900.00
	18ct gold chain	500.00
	18ct gold bracelet	300.00
	Diamond and pearl bracelet	650.00
	Diamond earrings	850.00
Clothing	Grey woollen hat	10.00
Food	Loaf of bread	1.00
	Bag of Gala apples	1.00
Keys	Car keys	1.00
	House keys	1.00

VEHICLES

Type	_Description_	_Value_
Volvo S40 1.6S	Green 4dr 2005 reg	2,000.00

MO

Entry location	Window
Entry method	Levered
Exit location	Front door
Exit method	Unsecure

CRIME ENQUIRIES

Family went to bed at approximately 22:30hrs leaving the downstairs of the property secure.

At 08:15hrs Mrs RAINSFORD found the front door ajar and noticed the car missing from the driveway.

The window of the utility room at the rear of the house had been levered and items had been moved from the work surface under the window to the floor.

Burglar alarm had not been set.

Items taken from the downstairs living room. Car keys were kept in a wooden bowl on a table in the hallway. Jewellery and cash was taken from an unsecured safe in the study. Food items were on the dining table.

Nothing suspicious heard or seen.

No suspects.

FORENSICS/SHOE MARKS

Type	*Location*	*Result*
Tool marks	*Rear window*	*No match*
Glove mark	*Glass / kitchen*	*No match*

SAM – Sunday 3 November 2013, 11:45

It was rare for Sam to take an instant dislike to someone, but she had to admit she hadn't been keen on Clive Rainsford from the moment she'd met him. Armed with the details of Lou's report about her meeting with Annie, she didn't trust him as far as she could throw him.

He had been perfectly polite, inviting her and Caro into the kitchen. He didn't look to the outside world like the sort of man anyone would have cause to fear. But Sam, who had cheerfully conversed with some of the nastiest individuals society had produced, knew better than to judge on appearances. Clive had celebrated his seventieth birthday the week before the family had flown to Spain. Sam wondered if it had been a birthday treat, the holiday, and, if it was, how he felt having had it interrupted. He looked fit and well, his hair thinning but still fair enough for the grey not to show too much. He didn't look seventy.

'Your forensics people have been,' he said, 'so apparently we can make ourselves at home again. We're just waiting for the locksmith now. Have a seat. Coffee?'

Sam sat next to Caro at the large, stripped-pine kitchen table. 'Thanks, that would be great. I'm sorry to hear about the burglary. It looks like you lost quite a few valuable things.'

'Yes,' he said. 'All insured, of course, but a pain. Annie is finding it very difficult to cope – the thought of those people in the house while we were asleep. Dreadful.'

'Do you have a laptop? Mobile phones?'

'My phone was upstairs, by the bed. The laptop – well, I cracked the screen just before we went away. I left it with a former colleague; he was going to try and fix it. Lucky really, since I imagine that would have been stolen too. I was going to take the girls out for a meal tonight, take their mind off things. Do you think that would be okay? Leaving the house, I mean . . . they're not going to come back, are they?'

'I think it's very unlikely,' Sam said, 'but it's your decision.'

He filled mugs from an ancient-looking filter machine on the counter and passed them across, then leaned back, arms folded, one leg crossed casually over the other. Relaxed, but closed. Sam wondered what his reaction had been to the news about Scarlett. She would have paid to see it. She could picture him in a pair of unfortunate Speedos on a sun-lounger by a pool, being approached by the rep and the hotel manager: *There's a call for you, sir, I think it's urgent . . .*

'Annie and Juliette have gone out,' Clive said. 'Juliette's not having a good day. Any upheaval throws her off balance, you know.'

'I'd really like to meet her,' Sam said. 'What time will they be back?'

Clive frowned. 'I couldn't say,' he said, 'sorry.'

'Oh, well,' Caro began cheerfully, 'at least we've got you, Clive. Shall we get comfy?'

She fixed him in a pointed stare until he finally took the hint and sat down opposite them. The interview, it seemed, had begun.

'Has Scarlett been in touch?' Caro asked. She had called them after Scarlett had walked out of the VVS, last night.

Clive thought about this for a moment before answering. Sam wondered if this was going to be one of *those* discussions, the ones that took forever and achieved no real result. She was itching to intervene already, but Caro had her own plan – and this job was hers more than Sam's. So far, at least.

'No,' he said, at last.

He didn't ask if there was any more news. He didn't ask if Scarlett had contacted the police.

'I wonder why you didn't make contact with her when she was in our accommodation,' Caro said. Her tone had changed.

Clive stared at her for a moment, as if he was thinking up a suitable response. 'I thought you were here to discuss the burglary,' he said.

'Clive, I'm working on an investigation into trafficking operations here in the UK. Do you understand what trafficking is?'

'Yes, of course,' he said.

'In many cases,' Caro continued, as if he hadn't answered, 'young women and girls – some of them not even teenagers – are taken from their families against their will and forced to work as prostitutes in countries across Europe – including Britain. They are abused, physically as well as sexually, and have little or no prospect of escape or rescue unless people like us can find them, get them to a place of safety, and then see their captors convicted. You can't imagine how difficult this problem is to tackle. So, as I'm sure you appreciate, every bit of intelligence we can gather is vital.'

He couldn't seem to maintain eye contact with her for more than a few seconds. Eventually he said, 'The fact that Scarlett is in this country at all is no thanks to you lot. So I think it's unfair to ask her – or us – for help, when you had none to give her ten years ago.'

Sam heard Caro take a sharp breath in.

'Clive,' Sam said, 'I'm sure you appreciate that it was thanks to a police investigation into trafficking that Scarlett was found at all. Otherwise your daughter would still be missing.'

283

'It might have escaped your attention, sergeant, but she *is* still missing. It has been as if we have lost her all over again.'

There was an emotion behind his words that Sam found strange: as though he was holding back a vast tide of something, unable or unwilling to express it.

'I can appreciate this must be an incredibly difficult time for the whole family,' Sam said. 'Nevertheless, anything Scarlett can tell us that could help us find other victims of trafficking, and bring some of these offenders to justice, would be invaluable.'

Clive spread his hands on the table top, breathing deeply. For the first time, he managed a small smile. 'I'm sure it would. And there are quite a few things I'd like to talk to her about myself. However, the fact remains, she has disappeared. Again.'

Caro cast a glance at Sam, the look that said *anything else?*

'I'd like to see Scarlett's room,' Sam said. 'Would you mind?'

He looked taken aback by her request. 'Sure,' he said. 'Follow me.'

The walls of the hallway and the staircase were lined with framed family pictures. A large canvas showing Annie and Clive's wedding was opposite the front door: classic Seventies styling with Annie's dead straight hair, and Clive's wide lapels, flares and mullet. It wasn't a flattering picture by any means; the parents flanking them both sides, two adult bridesmaids in mint green, and a laughing best man who looked drunk. Tiny Annie, looking impossibly young, Clive next to her, at least a foot and a half taller. The picture dominated the view when you entered the house.

And then there were pictures of Scarlett and Juliette as children; school photos, matching uniforms and gap-toothed smiles, alongside cheesy family studio shots, all white shirts and nylon-socked feet. And there were more of Annie and Clive, just the two of them. It was almost unnaturally narcissistic; this image of the perfect family on display.

There was another picture of Scarlett, aged about three, with a baby Juliette on her knee. Juliette with a quiff of black hair, Scarlett not so much smiling as baring her teeth. Sam caught sight of one final picture of Juliette at the top of the stairs – a smaller picture of an older teenager, on her own, a smile that didn't seem genuine: clearly forced into a portrait-sitting that she was having to endure. Dark top, hair down, glasses, awkward in the shoulders, the expression in her eyes levelled at the photographer one of loathing.

'Here you go,' Clive said, opening a door at the top of the stairs.

'Oh,' said Sam.

She'd been expecting something of Scarlett to remain, but the room had nothing of the girl inside it. Magnolia walls, beige curtains across the window, and a single bed, a wardrobe, a chest of drawers with a mirror on it, an iron, a radio and a vase containing dusty fabric roses, all of which screamed 'spare room'. The mattress was bare and on top of it was a pile of laundry. Propped against the wall was an ironing board. Sam walked over to the window, looked out at the back garden. The grass was overgrown, tussocky, but the garden was landscaped with a variety of shrubs and trees. At the end was a greenhouse and a vegetable patch. Next to it, a bare patch where some bush had obviously been removed and shredded, wood chippings in a wide, pale circle providing a sharp contrast with the dark earth. A wheelbarrow sat abandoned, full of dead leaves, a rake balanced across it.

'You're a keen gardener?'

'I'm retired,' Clive said, as if this answered the question.

Sam thought carefully for a polite way to phrase what she was thinking. After a moment she came up with, 'How long has the room been like this?'

'After a while it didn't seem likely that she'd be coming back.'

'What did you do with all her things?'

'Annie dealt with all of that. Most of it went in the bin, I think . . . you know what teenage girls are like. It was a mess, no matter how many times we told her to clean it up.'

Sam nodded, as though she had teenagers herself and could empathise. Trying to keep her tone light, she asked, 'Did you keep anything?'

Clive turned to go back downstairs. 'As I said, you'll have to ask Annie.'

'When will she be back?' Sam asked again.

Through an open door Sam caught a glimpse of the master bedroom, the neatly made bed with a satin quilt over it, suitcases open on the floor next to the bed, piles of clothes. All the other doors on the landing were firmly shut. Clive had stopped at the top of the stairs, frozen, one hand on the banister and the other on the wall as if to stop himself pitching forward. He made a small, strange sound.

'Clive?'

Without answering her, he turned and walked past into the bedroom, lowered himself on to the edge of the bed slowly. Dropped his head into his hands. Then he took a deep breath in and sat up straight again, offered her a brief, tight smile through the open door.

'Sorry,' he said. 'I just needed . . . a moment.'

'What is it?' Sam asked.

He shook his head slowly. 'I . . . I can't. I'm finding all this a bit . . . difficult . . . '

'Difficult? You mean – the burglary?'

'All of it. Annie is – she can't cope with it very well. I'm worried about her all the time, with Scarlett being missing and then suddenly reappearing. She is very fragile. I think she's – I don't know. It feels as if she is . . . falling apart.'

On the last two words his voice cracked and broke and he lowered his head into his hands again.

'Why don't you come back downstairs?' Sam asked. 'Let's have another coffee and talk it through, shall we?'

Downstairs, Caro was in the hallway with her coat on, examining the wedding portrait of Scarlett's parents with a smile on her face, as though she was a family friend. When Sam came down she directed a raised eyebrow at Caro, and a quick nod to the kitchen, and they all filed in without another word.

'Sit down,' Sam said to Clive gently.

While Sam pulled up the chair next to Clive's, Caro set about filling the kettle and rinsing out the mugs.

'Annie needs counselling,' Clive said, his voice an octave higher, 'but she won't go. She says nobody understands but I don't see why she won't even try. She's been on so many different tablets from the doctor, I can't keep track of them all. I don't think they do any good. She wakes up crying every day. She doesn't sleep. She comes downstairs in the middle of the night and sits here waiting for Scarlett to come home.'

He paused for breath, mouth open a little. Sam looked at the protruding lip, a pout like a little boy being told off.

'You mean recently?'

Clive shook his head. 'Every night. She hasn't slept a whole night since Scarlett went, even with tablets. And she makes Juliette worse. They wind each other up. Juliette gets fretful and then Annie panics that something's going to happen to Juliette. She hasn't wanted to let Juliette out of her sight since she tried to take her own life, and that was – well, it was ten years ago. Ten years of this . . . hell. And now

287

Scarlett's back, and neither of them is able to cope with it! I don't know what we're going to do.'

'It sounds as if you're going through a lot, Clive,' Caro said. The kettle was boiling and she had found teabags.

'I'm so tired,' he said, his voice trailing away. 'So tired of it all.'

'You're the one that has to hold everything together, aren't you,' Caro was saying. 'It's a lot for one person to take on for all this time.'

That wasn't what Sam thought at all, and quite probably it wasn't what Caro was thinking either. What Sam actually thought amounted to something along the lines of *you selfish bastard, your daughter has been through ten years of hell and you're feeling sad and sorry for yourself because you had to carry on with your life?*

'I worry that she's going to do something,' Clive said then.

'Do something? You mean – harm herself?'

'I don't know. She just seems so unpredictable, so unstable. I don't know which one of them's worse.'

'I'm sorry, Clive,' Caro said, 'you've lost me. Are you talking about Annie? Or Juliette?'

He gave a short grunt. 'Both of them. They're both as bad as each other. I'm walking on eggshells the whole time. Every single day.'

'Sorry, but what did you mean, you worry that she's going to do something? What sort of thing?'

'Annie has panic attacks, spends most of the day crying. Juliette sometimes harms herself. Usually we don't go out and leave her, not now.'

Sam looked at Caro, who pulled a face over Clive's shoulder.

'I just wish things had been different,' Clive was saying. 'I wish Scarlett had just listened to me, behaved herself. She was only fifteen. Just a girl.'

Just a girl.

288

SCARLETT – Wednesday 24 October 2012, 06:23

'We can run.'

Saying it into the darkness made it suddenly real. It brought back a memory, of standing in some trees in the early hours of a cold night, trying to make eye contact with a scared girl, trying to get her to summon up a bit of spirit and fight back. It hadn't done Yelena any good, back then. It had cost her her life... and possibly saved Scarlett's.

The same thing might happen again. Or, this time, it might be Scarlett's turn to get the bullet through the head.

In the darkness there was a soft, sarcastic grunt. 'You crazy.'

'If we both run, when they open the door ... they won't expect it. It will take them seconds to react.'

'Where we run to?'

Scarlett kept quiet. There was no answer to that, and besides, they had to run in different directions – that was the whole point. Outside, she could hear footsteps again, voices. They'd already been in this hell-hole for what felt like hours, it must be nearly morning, and it sounded as if the men were going to come for them any minute now. Whether the girl was in agreement or not – and it didn't sound as if she was – there was no point discussing it further. Careful not to make a sound, Scarlett slipped off the stupid high-heeled shoes. The metal of the container was freezing against her bare feet. She stuck her nail under the rubber heel and twisted it off, feeling inside for the roll of notes. Her fingers were numb, trembling.

They were coming closer, she could hear them. She had seconds, maybe.

She tugged the money free, tearing it a little but not caring now. Then she had it. Shoved the notes into her bra, pushed the heel back together.

The men were outside now, laughing and joking with each other as if they were about to go out for a drink with a mate. Not watch two girls die, while they filmed it. Scarlett was shaking from head to foot. She wouldn't be able to keep to her feet, never mind run.

The metal door scraped open and as the crate flooded with light – it was still dark outside but compared to the inside of the container it was broad daylight – Scarlett half-closed her eyes, screaming like a banshee and launching herself forward, stilettos in one hand, gripped and held overhead like a weapon.

The man grabbed at the sleeve of the woollen coat. Scarlett spun and slipped out of it, leaving him clutching the coat and not her.

She ran.

There was shouting from behind her. The concrete floor slipped under her feet and she ran into the dark warehouse, skidding behind containers. She heard the metal door clanging shut again, and then screaming from somewhere else, another woman – the girl who had been with her? Was she running too? It was so dark that Scarlett could just make out the metal walls of containers either side. Her bare feet made no noise as she ran, checking around each corner before moving on. She could hear their footsteps – how many? – two, three of them?

Scarlett crouched against a container, breathing. She had lost the advantage. She should be out of here by now. Without the distraction of the other girl they only had her to focus on. She peered round the end of the container. It was a blank wall, breeze blocks: the back of the warehouse. It was a dead end.

Concentrate.

She held back a sob, hugging her knees to stop the shaking, the stilettos still clutched in her hand. Her feet were icy and it was so cold she was shivering. A breeze lifted the hair from her cheeks, a cold blast from somewhere. Footsteps again, urgent whispers. They were on the move again. The sounds echoed around the walls, making it impossible to tell where they were coming from. Scarlett's eyes had grown accustomed to the lighting now and she could see more than just shapes – the corrugated metal ceiling, far overhead, all the way to the other end of the warehouse, just visible in the narrow space between two of the crates. And in that split second she saw a figure cross the gap. She gasped and shrank back.

This was no good. They would keep looking until they found her, and then she would die. She had to get out.

She headed for the back wall: there might be a fire escape or something. The breeze chilled her flushed cheeks. There *had* to be a door.

The crate next to her was much larger than the others; the wall seemed to go on and on. And then she realised it was the sound-proofed room they were using as a film studio. If they'd bothered to soundproof it, that must mean that they were bothered about people hearing what was going on. Which meant that there must be people nearby! Probably they did their business overnight, when the other units in the industrial estate were empty, but, even so, they didn't like noise.

On the wall next to her Scarlett saw a big red button in a box. It was a fire alarm. Would it work? Would it distract them? She took hold of her stiletto and smacked the glass as hard as she could.

Almost instantly the warehouse seemed to come alive with sound, a shrieking, wailing clamour that rang in her ears and echoed from wall to metal wall.

She ran.

A wall rose in front of her – the corner of the warehouse, a thin gap – not big enough to squeeze through – behind the soundproofed room and the far wall. Another dead end. She turned sharply and ran back the way she had come, sobbing now because over the din nobody could have heard her anyway. It had been a stupid thing to do because now she couldn't hear footsteps, couldn't hear their shouts, never mind whispers.

Then she saw it – the grey outline of light, the shape of a door. When she reached it she realised there was a bar across it. A fire exit – thank God! She shoved, expecting it to be chained shut or rusted or painted closed. The door stayed shut. She shoved again, pushed harder, and this time it gave, slightly.

From behind her came a bang and a spark of bright light next to her face as a bullet hit the metal door. They had her now.

She shoved the door one last time with all her strength and it flew open, propelling her out into the darkness, over the tufts of rough grass that had grown up around the door outside and had held it closed.

And now, the cold, fresh air giving her a new blast of energy, Scarlett ran.

LOU – Sunday 3 November 2013, 12:30

With no further news about Scarlett's whereabouts, Lou tried Stephen Waterhouse again, who managed to answer this time. He seemed to have regained his former belligerence.

'How are you getting on with McDonnell?' Lou asked.

'Why do you ask?' he said, his tone anything but friendly.

'Just that when my sergeant saw him yesterday he indicated that he was aware of the surveillance—'

'He always tries that one. It's a bluff. Unless someone's tipped him off, that is.'

Lou hesitated. 'Nobody on my team knows about our discussion in the SB briefing, if that's what you're suggesting.'

'Well, I heard you've got a leak.'

Lou paused again, trying to gauge the tone of his voice; eventually she decided he was trying to wind her up, get her properly angry so she'd say something unprofessional. What was wrong with him?

'I trust my team, but I still don't discuss things that aren't relevant to the jobs we've got. Unless you've got some evidence to back up that accusation, I suggest you wind your bloody neck in.'

Waterhouse gave a throaty laugh, which reassured her that it had been a bad joke. 'Just don't expect me to keep you updated with what my teams are doing.'

Time to change the subject. 'Did you see my report about my meeting with Annie Rainsford?' Lou asked.

'Yes, all very interesting, but what they failed to tell you ten years ago isn't actually that much use to us right now, is it? That Greek boy, whoever he is or was, could be anywhere on the planet now. Probably running his own little crime empire. Or running for parliament. And since we can't even ask Scarlett to confirm her mother's account . . . '

'As you know,' Lou said evenly, 'she's twenty-five. She hasn't committed any crime, as far as we're aware, so we don't have a reason to arrest her or hold her against her will.'

'I was counting on you to *persuade* her to engage with us,' Waterhouse said.

'You didn't *actually* want me to have anything to do with it,' Lou said, 'in case you'd forgotten.'

He hung up on her.

Well, let's hope I never have to ask a favour of SB, she thought. *Bastard shitting tosser.*

There were thirty-four emails – on a Sunday, for crying out loud, it never stopped – and yet Lou was still distracted by the crime report of the burglary at 14 Russet Avenue. It would be interesting to know if the unusual features of this offence weren't unusual after all. It was easy to lose touch with what was going on in the area and it was possible that someone out there was actively targeting older cars, or even Volvos. Russet Avenue might just be part of a crime series and therefore it might be nothing more than a coincidence that the Rainsford property had been targeted. Yet this wasn't the sort of thing she could look into without drawing attention to the Rainsfords and her interest in them.

One possible solution presented itself – someone she knew she could trust.

Email

Date: 3 November 2013

To: PSE Jason MERCER

From: DCI Lou SMITH

Re: Crime series

Hi, Jason,

Could you let me know if there are any current
crime series in Briarstone involving car key
burglaries? If so, what the series criteria
are?

Thanks,

Lou

SCARLETT – Wednesday 24 October 2012, 07:09

Scarlett ran without stopping, ran and ran until she was out of the industrial area and on a wide main road, with shops on one side and apartment buildings on the other. The traffic was building as dawn started to break. She slowed to a walk when she realised nobody was behind her, and, because the soles of her feet were stinging, she stopped and put the stupid shoes back on. She kept to the shadows of the buildings, realising that cars were slowing down as they passed her.

I need clothes, she thought, pulling her thin blouse tighter across her chest, folding her arms over it. *I need food. I need somewhere to hide, to think.*

She was vulnerable here, on the main road. If they followed her in the car, they would spot her. She turned into a passageway to the right, a stairwell, and through the other side was a sort of open space, a courtyard shared by the flats; across the middle, a washing line was strung between four concrete posts in a wide Z. There was a wall running at head height, and beyond it a row of dumpster bins. She rounded the corner and saw another passageway leading back to the road. A low wall separated the ground-floor apartment from the passageway, bikes chained together behind it.

She sank down slowly, catching her breath.

What to do next? Maybe if she waited an hour or two, till it was light and busy, they would have given up looking for her, if they were even bothering at all. In any case, it couldn't hurt to wait here; she was out of the wind. Scarlett kept thinking of the overheard conversations, late at night; the other girls talking about the men who were sent to test them out, and what happened to them afterwards. None of them knew that someone else might come to take you away too – a man who pretended to be your rescuer. Presumably most of the girls who had gone with Stefan had died. And if any of them, like her, had managed to get away ... who would ever risk going back?

She thought about ways in which she might be able to get a message back to the other girls, at the same time knowing that she never would. Even if she could summon up the courage, she didn't know where the apartment was. She didn't even know any of their real names.

A while later Scarlett heard a sound and looked up. A woman was in the courtyard, hanging washing on the line, her back to Scarlett. She looked young, Scarlett's age or maybe a little older, and she was dressed in blue jeans and a pastel-pink sweater that looked as though it would be soft to touch. Too tired to move, rooted to her doorstep with a mixture of exhaustion and fear, Scarlett could not tear her gaze away from the woman. The washing she was hanging up was a mixture of baby clothes – brightly coloured dresses and tights and onesies – and adult gear: a man's boiler suit, three blue shirts with some sort of logo on them. A ray of golden dawn sunlight burst unexpectedly through the space between the apartment blocks, illuminating the scrubby patch of grass. The woman's hair, brown and wavy and loose down her back, almost to her waist, shone. Scarlett couldn't take her eyes off her: the shape of her, the normal clothes, the sheer ordinariness of a life that involved hanging out washing early on a weekday morning.

Scarlett closed her eyes and let the sunlight fall on to her face. She couldn't remember the last time she'd felt the sun on her skin.

'*Hee, is alles goed met je? Kan ik helpen?*' The woman had turned and seen her. Are you okay? Can I help you?

'*Ben okay*,' Scarlett stammered. Stood up quickly – too quickly, had to lean on the wall for support.

'*Wacht even*.' Wait a minute.

The woman put the washing basket down, looked as if she was coming over. Scarlett started walking back down the passageway, speeding up. She rounded the corner on to the main road, tottering on her stupid heels and feet that hurt, wondering where she could go next, where she could hide. The sun had gone in and it was cold, shiveringly cold.

'Hey!'

Behind her, the woman was running to catch up. Scarlett looked around. She wanted to run, but where would she go?

'*Hier.*'

The woman handed her something. It was a coat, a khaki-brown-coloured parka. Scarlett stared at it, looked up at the woman. '*Nee, nee, dank je . . .*'

'*Neem maar, het is goed zo.*'

She handed over the coat and pressed something into Scarlett's hand, then smiled, and walked back towards the passageway, back towards her washing and her normal life.

'*Dank je*,' Scarlett said, her voice rising in a sob.

'*T'is gewoon karma*,' the woman called cheerfully.

In Scarlett's hand was a twenty-euro note.

She wrapped the coat around herself gratefully. It was warm and smelled of the woman's scent and, faintly, of pizza or something like that. It was too big but that didn't matter, it was warm and soft and cottony, quilted and lined with fleece. The relief of the warmth of it, the protection of it, made Scarlett suddenly feel invincible.

The kindness of strangers, she thought. *I never believed in it until now*.

SAM – Sunday 3 November 2013, 12:45

They left Clive Rainsford in his kitchen, waiting for his wife and daughter to return home. Sam had spent some time taking a statement from him, and his demeanour had changed again, from desolate to taciturn. He clearly didn't feel that recording his emotional response to his family's problems was a worthwhile activity. Nevertheless Sam had persisted, and they had their statement.

Sam walked Caro back to her car, which was parked in the next street.

'However dysfunctional they are,' Caro was saying, 'it doesn't make them necessarily guilty of anything.'

'What do you think all that was about?' Sam said. 'You think he's genuinely having a wobble about it all?'

'Who knows? Looked real enough.'

'I was looking at that wedding picture,' Sam said. 'Annie looked very young.'

'Oh, yes. She was only just sixteen.'

'My God,' Sam said. 'Seriously?'

Caro nodded. 'Clive was friends with Annie's parents. He was a schoolteacher, and Annie's father was the headmaster at the school where he worked. They married as soon as Annie turned sixteen, with the consent of her parents. They didn't have the girls straight away, though. I think they were married ten or eleven years before Scarlett came along.'

Sam fell silent, considering.

'And before you ask,' Caro continued, 'yes, we did look at Clive's relationship with his daughters. But Juliette wasn't saying anything much, and there were no concerns at Scarlett's school. Social Services had had no contact with the family, either.'

Sam said, 'I didn't realise he was a teacher.'

'He wasn't when Scarlett went missing. He gave up teaching when they got married, worked as a manager in an electronics business. Retired from that a few years ago.'

When Sam got back to her own car a few minutes later, a wave of something so despairing came over her suddenly that she had to sit still, taking deep breaths, unable to drive until it passed. There were some houses you went in as a police officer that made you want to go straight home and get in the shower, put your clothes in the wash and scrub your shoes. The Rainsford house hadn't been like that, it was clean and tidy, but there was something so hideous about it that Sam felt overwhelmed.

Driving through the town centre, she took a detour past the bus station, and then up to the railway station for good measure, looking at all the kids wearing hoodies, looking for a khaki coat, looking for Scarlett's shape and posture, but there was no sign.

MG11 WITNESS STATEMENT

Section 1 – Witness details			
NAME:	Aaron George Anthony SUTCLIFFE		
DOB (if under 18; if over 18 state 'Over 18'):	Over 18		
ADDRESS:	14a Midland Street Briarstone	**OCCUPATION:**	Unemployed

Section 2 – Investigating Officer	
DATE:	3 November 2013
OIC:	DC 8244 Les FINNEGAN

Section 3 – Text of Statement

My name is Aaron SUTCLIFFE. I have been friends with Ian PALMER since we were at school together. I know Ian had been having some bother in some of the pubs in town. This is because he had been dealing for someone, I am not sure who. The pubs he went in didn't like him dealing and so he was warned off. On the night he was beaten up Ian had been in lots of pubs but one of them was probably the Railway Tavern in Queen Street because he liked it in there and he had previously told me that he was going there on Thursday night. I wasn't with him that night because I was in the hospital where my girlfriend was giving birth.

Section 4 – Signatures

....

WITNESS: (A Sutcliffe)   OIC: (Les Finnegan DC 8244)

LOU – Sunday 3 November 2013, 14:20

Les Finnegan was loitering in the doorway to Lou's office. Tempting as it was to tell him to sit down, he'd just been outside for a fag and it was a small room. Lou had been out to the supermarket to find some lunch and the carrier bag was calling her from below the desk.

'So tell me about Sutcliffe.'

'He ended up not being charged for the assault, so I got him to agree to be interviewed about Palmer before he disappeared. He was basically just mouthing off, half a ton of crap with a little diamond or two buried in there if you know what you're looking for. Apparently Palmer had been dealing in the Railway Tavern a while back.'

'McVey liked to keep drugs out of his establishments,' Lou said. 'Made him feel like a fine upstanding citizen, or something.'

'Sutcliffe seems to think Palmer might have been dealing for Darren Cunningham. Or Mitchell Roberts. Or he actually doesn't know and is trying to pretend he's smarter than he is.'

'That's not in his statement,' Lou said, reading it on the screen.

'No, well, when I was taking his statement, funnily enough, he was a bit less keen to sign his name to that bit.'

While Les was talking, Lou could see over his shoulder into the main office where Sam had just come in.

'I think the dealing link is the way forward,' she said. 'Can we try to narrow it down? Maybe Palmer tried to short-change one of them. Didn't I read something about one of Cunningham's shipments going wrong? Perhaps Palmer decided to keep some of the stash. We

302

don't have much at the moment; we might as well work through possible motives.'

Sam appeared behind Les. 'Afternoon, ma'am, sorry to interrupt . . . '

'That's okay, Sam. I need you, in any case. Les, can you see what you can find on the intel?'

Les nodded and went back in the main office, squeezing unnecessarily close to Sam on the way past.

'Shut the door,' Lou said, 'and have a seat. How's your morning been? How was Clive Rainsford?'

'I can't tell you how much that house gave me the creeps,' Sam said.

Now that Les was gone, Lou began to dig into her egg salad. It was so cold from the supermarket's chiller cabinet, it made her teeth ache. There hadn't been much left to choose from.

'I haven't had a chance to look at the updates,' said Sam. 'What else has come in on that burglary?'

'They've got the property list,' Lou said. 'Interesting mix of small, portable things and then the car. And food, too – specifically bread and a bag of apples, both of which were in a carrier on the kitchen table. You're thinking it was Scarlett?'

'I don't know. It's just worth considering, I guess.'

Lou was crunching on grated carrot. 'Just too many slightly odd things,' she said. 'But, as you said, we don't know if she can drive, do we?'

Sam shook her head. 'I feel awful about the whole thing. I wish we could have got her somewhere decent to stay. She just deserves a chance, and it feels like I let her down.'

'Sam, you did your best. And she's not fifteen any more – she's an adult. But I agree it's a bloody nightmare.'

'I'm not surprised she doesn't want to go home, having met Clive.'

'From my conversation with Annie yesterday, it feels to me as if she's not allowed to have her own opinions about anything. Clive's completely in control.'

'He was giving a good old show of losing it this morning,' Sam said.

'But you didn't buy it?'

Sam shrugged.

Lou threw the plastic container containing the last few watery bits of salad into the bin. Her stomach was still rumbling but that would have to do – and she had so much else to catch up on, it was quite possible she'd have to miss dinner too. Coffee and KitKats would keep her going till then.

'So,' Lou said, 'this afternoon. Anything you're already committed to?'

'I need to write things up, then I was going to go have a look for Scarlett.'

'Can you do something else for me? Les had a chat with Aaron Sutcliffe this morning – he's a friend of Ian Palmer's. Seemed to think Palmer might have been dealing for Darren Cunningham. It's not much of a link, but we don't have anything else. Les is looking it up now to see if there's something to go on, but can you task him or someone else to follow it up?'

SCARLETT – Wednesday 24 October 2012, 09:15

It was only when Scarlett was sitting at the back of a McDonald's, with a coffee and a breakfast muffin, that she remembered the money she had hidden inside her bra. The woman had given her money and she hadn't needed it. Scarlett felt a pang of guilt at this, and resolved to pass on the karma somehow. It wasn't her money to keep. She should give it to someone else who needed it more than she did.

The coat was warm, like a duvet around her. She loved it fervently, passionately already, because she had been given it by someone who cared. And it was hers; it was her lovely warm coat. It was the only thing she owned.

More than that, it had afforded her an unexpected level of protection: turned her from a half-dressed, shivering, terrified-looking girl into someone respectable and therefore invisible. She could do with a pair of jeans and some proper shoes, too – but the coat was a great start.

She had one eye on the door, in case the men should come in, looking for her. But there was something comforting about the bright, cold daylight outside, the sudden bursts of sunshine; the strangeness of being around people in a public place without someone watching her; the fact that, once she'd sat down, she had become suddenly, unexpectedly normal, which meant nobody seemed to be paying her any attention at all.

This was what real life looked like. There were families in here, kids, teenagers chatting and laughing. All sorts of people walking past outside, going about their business as if nothing was wrong.

Yet, a few miles away, a warehouse in a desolate industrial estate was being used to film young women being tortured, being shot. Women who had been through unimaginable hell already; women who had been bought and sold like a commodity and, having reached the end of their usefulness, were being given one last job to do before they were discarded. The coldness of the whole process and the fact that she had escaped from this fate made Scarlett feel detached. She wanted to go up to people, shake them, say, *Do you not know what's going on, right under your noses?* But who would listen? Who would believe her?

She needed to form some sort of plan, something to focus on. She couldn't sit here all day; she would start to attract attention. She needed to keep moving, and in order to do that safely she needed a plan. The coffee was helping, the daylight was helping, but inside her the adrenalin was starting to metabolise out of her system and the exhaustion of having been awake for more than twenty-four hours was beginning to overwhelm her.

Focus, Scarlett.

She needed to get far away from here, that much was certain. She didn't want go to the police. There was nobody she trusted – she was on her own – but this wasn't entirely a bad thing. On her own she had survived so far, and she had escaped. There was a triumph in that, at least.

She needed to get away from here, then. Once she was out of the town she would find somewhere safe to sleep tonight. This would mean spending some of the money she had, and it would not last long. How could she get more, without drawing attention to herself?

In the pocket of her new coat was a handful of coins. Across the road, in the shelter of an office block, Scarlett could see two green public telephones. They were fixed to the wall of the building, under a concrete overhang which provided shelter for the smokers and the coatless.

She had been away for years. Would Juliette even remember her? Would they even still be living in the same place? What if *he* answered the phone?

Scarlett got out of her seat and left the restaurant, staying close to the building, looking up and down the street in case she saw someone she recognised. Then she crossed the road quickly, to the payphones. One of them just accepted cards, but the one on the right had a slot for coins. The instructions were in English and Dutch. The first time she tried, she forgot to add the international dialling code. The second time, there was a pause, and then the sound of the phone ringing on the other end.

JANE – Sunday 3 November 2013, 15:50

Les Finnegan and Jane Phelps eventually found Darren Cunningham enjoying a smoke outside his office: one of them, anyway, since he had several. The establishment he was frequenting today was also known as YouBet, or David Henderson Bookmakers and Turf Accountants Limited, one of Briarstone's few independent bookies and Cunningham's particular favourite.

Les parked the job Peugeot in a space outside the chip shop, two doors down from the betting shop in Turnswood Parade. 'There he is,' he said, nodding towards a little group of individuals who were hanging around outside.

There were two lads straddling BMXs, a bloke sitting on the bench and a lad sitting on the railing separating the pedestrian walkway from the car park, which was a good four feet lower, swinging his legs. It would be worth it to watch in case he fell off. All four of them were wearing Sports Direct's autumn/winter collection, a mishmash of nylon and sweat fabric, greys and navy-blues and blacks, baseball caps worn the wrong way round.

Both officers paused before getting out. It was just possible – you never knew – that some deal was about to go down, which would give them a couple of arrests and a nice little bit of disruption to cheer everyone up. Cunningham didn't deal on the streets, though; he was way beyond that now, even if he did still live at home with his mum.

The two lads on bikes were moving on. There were some elaborate handshakes, and, by the time Les and Jane approached, the bikes were weaving alarmingly between the pensioners making their way from the bus stop to Iceland. One of the lads passed, turned back and shouted, 'Daz!' over his shoulder, alerting Cunningham to the approaching officers of the law. Oh, well. It wasn't as if they were going for stealth.

The lad on the railing, a long, thin streak of drool with skinny white ankles sticking out of his trainers – no socks; there was something deeply offensive about the lack of socks, in November – jumped to his feet when he clocked them.

'Don't want to interrupt,' Jane said cheerfully.

'I'm just off,' said the thin lad. Dark hair, full of gel or grease or something.

'Stay where you are, mate,' Cunningham told him.

Obligingly he clambered back up to the railing, snagging the back of his nylon trackie bottoms on the metal and treating Jane to the sight of a hairy white crack above the words 'Calvin Klein'.

'Mr Cunningham,' Les said, leaning casually against the railing. 'DC Les Finnegan; this is my colleague, DC Jane Phelps.'

'I know,' Cunningham said.

Jane remained standing next to the bench. It wasn't often she had a height advantage and she wasn't about to waste it by sitting down. To the charmer on the railing she said, 'I don't think we've had the pleasure. What's your name?'

308

The lad looked to Cunningham as if asking permission to speak. 'Jonny.'

'Jonny . . . ?'

'Parkinson.'

'Look,' Cunningham said, 'we're not doing nothing. What's the problem?'

Les turned his attention back to Cunningham. 'No problem, Darren. Just wanted to have a little chat, see how you are.'

Cunningham snorted. 'Yeah, right.'

'Sorry to hear about what happened to Ian,' Jane said.

'Who?'

'Ian Palmer. One of your mates, isn't he?'

'No,' Cunningham said. 'Don't ring a bell. You know him, Jonny?'

'No.'

'Oh? We heard he was working for you – doing the odd bit here and there. And there's no point pretending you don't know him, Darren; you've been stopchecked in his company before.'

'What happened to him, then?' Cunningham asked. He scratched his half-arsed beard with bitten grubby nails.

Jane couldn't help thinking that he didn't look like Eden's current drug overlord, but then she caught sight of the shiny watch, heavy, under his hoodie sleeve. And when your mum did your washing and cooked you pizza and potato waffles for your tea, what were you going to spend your money on? She was willing to bet his bedroom looked as if he'd won *The Gadget Show*'s tech giveaway. He was older than he looked, too – late thirties, but not exactly a magnet for the ladies, despite the wealth. These days his mum was driving around in a 2013-reg BMW, Darren himself not actually able to get behind the wheel thanks to a twelve-month ban. If he had that much

309

money kicking about, no wonder he was spending his afternoons laundering it in YouBet.

'He got his head kicked in,' Les continued. 'Still in hospital. We thought you might have paid him a visit, poor lad.'

'Look, we ain't mates. Just 'cause I've been seen with him once or twice.'

'He knows you, all right,' said Les. 'Knows you very well. And all about your business.'

Well, that did the trick. Cunningham's eyes narrowed and he sat up a little straighter.

'What's that supposed to mean?'

Jane said, 'We just wanted to ask if you'd got anything to share with us about what happened to him. His poor mum's beside herself, you know. And I'm sure it would help you out to get whoever assaulted him put away, wouldn't it?'

Jonny Parkinson wobbled slightly on his perch.

Cunningham scuffed at the dirty tarmac with the toe of his trainer. 'Got nothing to tell you.'

Jane gave Les a look.

'If you change your mind,' Les said, offering a card, 'give us a call, right?'

Darren Cunningham glanced at the proffered card, looked pointedly away.

Les pocketed it again. 'You can always get hold of us, anyway. Dial 101. Might be trickier to get through that way, but I'm sure you can remember the number, can't you? Just a word to the wise, Mr Cunningham. Be careful who you trust – know what I'm saying? Gets a bit difficult to tell your enemies from your friends, after a while, especially in your line of work, where allegiances change all the time.'

They walked back to the car in silence. Jane waited until Les was in the driver's seat with his seatbelt done up.

'What was that all about?' she asked.

'All what?' Les answered, performing a neat turn in the crowded car park using the flat of his hand on the steering wheel.

'You were on the verge of threatening him. All that stuff about Palmer knowing his business, enemies and friends? What are you trying to do: get Palmer finished off?'

'Don't be daft. In any case, who says I was talking about Palmer?'

'Who were you talking about, then?'

Les actually tapped the side of his long, skinny nose. 'Might've been speaking in general. Sometimes you only have to give them a little nudge and watch what happens next. I've known whole crime enterprises crumble into the dust because of a tiny little suggestion, made at just the right time.'

SAM – Sunday 3 November 2013, 23:58

Sam had spent the evening worrying about Scarlett, wishing fruitlessly that she knew she was safe. Several times she thought of going out in the car, just to see if she was still in the bus station, which was ludicrous. She would be on a mate's sofa somewhere. She would be safe and warm and dry, and getting on with her life, of course she would. Sam distracted herself with the television, watching but not taking anything in, until she started watching a film about zombies and finally got absorbed in it.

When she next looked at the clock it was nearly midnight. Definitely time for bed.

Turning out the lights, she heard a sound outside, and, as she was on her way to investigate, the doorbell sounded.

She turned on the outside light before opening the door, and there, on her doorstep, was Scarlett Rainsford, drowned in that brown coat that was several sizes too big for her, and now hidden even more under a woollen beanie hat. Beside her was another woman, someone Sam had never met.

'Hi, Scarlett,' Sam said. 'Good to see you.'

'Are you Sam Hollands?' the woman asked. She looked tired.

'Yes.' Torn between the inherent dangers of being a lone, off-duty police officer admitting a stranger and a relative stranger into your house, and wanting whatever drama was going to follow to not happen out on the street, Sam gave up and said, 'Do you want to come in?'

The two followed Sam into the hallway and she went ahead, turning the lights back on.

In the living room, Scarlett took off her shoes and tucked her feet under her on the sofa. The woman was still standing. 'I won't be staying,' she said. 'Scarlett said you told her she could come here, if she needed help.'

'I said she could ring me, but never mind,' Sam said. She felt herself coming over all official. 'And you are . . . ?'

'My name is Samantha Rowden-Knowles. I'm – I used to be one of Scarlett's teachers. I heard all about what happened. I'd like to stay in touch, I'd like to help, but Scarlett can't stay with me. She's got my number, though. I told her she can call me any time.'

Sam looked at Scarlett, who had rested her head on the arm of the sofa and looked as though she was about to fall asleep.

'Come into the kitchen,' she said to the teacher. 'Let me make a note of your details.'

'So it's all right for her to stay with you?'

Sam shut the door behind them. 'No, but I can find somewhere for her where she'll be safe. Where did you find her?'

'She came to me,' Mrs Rowden-Knowles said. 'She turned up at my house, out of the blue. I was shocked when she told me who she was. I didn't recognise her. We all thought she was dead.'

'The press haven't got hold of it yet,' Sam said, 'but I'm sure it won't be long. Are you okay?'

There were tears in the woman's eyes and Sam realised she was shaking. Then she took a deep breath in and stood up straight. 'I'm fine. Really, I am. She told me a bit about what has happened to her, where she's been. I've told her she has to tell you. She seems to find it very difficult to trust people. I told her she should trust you. That's right, isn't it, Sergeant Hollands? You won't let her down, will you?'

'No,' Sam said. 'Of course not.'

Sam wrote down the address and telephone number in her notebook and promised to call the teacher tomorrow. They would need to talk more. Back in the living room, Scarlett was fast asleep on Sam's couch, her mouth open.

'I'll leave you to it,' said Mrs Rowden-Knowles.

Sam showed her out, and then went back through to the living room.

For a moment she looked at Scarlett and thought about just leaving her there, but the sight had triggered a memory of coming home from work, two years ago almost to the day, and finding a dark-haired boy who didn't speak any English sitting exactly where Scarlett was now. In the kitchen, Sam's partner Jo – already off work with stress – was working up to an anxiety attack, terrified that Sam would send the boy away again. Jo had had a habit of collecting

313

waifs and strays, an inbuilt need to rescue and protect. She had been a civilian detention officer, responsible for looking after those who found themselves in police custody, including teenage asylum-seekers left to cross continents on their own. Even Sam knew how hard it was to remain detached when confronted with someone young and vulnerable, especially when the system that was supposed to protect them failed. But Jo had taken matters into her own hands, and, however good her motives, the rules were there to protect everyone concerned, and Jo had broken them.

The day after her disciplinary hearing, at which she had been sacked, Sam had come home to find Jo gone.

Jo would love this one, Sam thought, looking at the sleeping girl and allowing herself a brief smile at the thought. Perhaps it was just as well that Sam was on her own. Whether she wanted to help was irrelevant – letting the girl stay was a bad idea for all sorts of reasons. The danger of repeating Jo's mistakes was one of them. Her own personal safety was another.

'Scarlett,' Sam said, in a voice guaranteed to wake her up.

The girl's eyes opened. 'I didn't want to come here,' she said. 'But she wouldn't let me stay. She insisted on bringing me.'

'How did you know where I live?'

Scarlett smiled. 'I followed you home from work earlier. Sorry. I didn't have anything else to do.'

'On foot?'

'Sure. I saw you in your car, turning into the street. You're really close to the town centre. You're not going to send me away too, are you?'

Sam had not sat down. Her mobile phone was still in her hand. 'You can't stay here, Scarlett. But I can find you somewhere to stay for a few nights, somewhere you'll be safe. Okay?'

'It's really latc,' Scarlett said. 'You won't find anywhere, and I'm bloody well not going to that hostel in Charlmere, so don't even ask. Look, I might as well just go.'

Despite her words, Scarlett stayed glued to the sofa.

'You can make a cup of tea,' Sam said. 'I'll start phoning around.'

Part Five

THE RETURN

SCARLETT – Amsterdam outskirts, Thursday 25 October 2012, 08:50

Scarlett had been watching for a long time, from the shelter of a bench outside the motorway services building. Her bench faced the lorry parking, and was tucked into an alcove next to one of the fire escapes. She made an effort to pretend she was waiting for someone, and she looked casual enough, but she had seen two police cars already and knew she could not sit here much longer.

A day had passed since she had phoned home.

In that time she had gained a measure of confidence, and in a way she was glad that she had done it, because she had replaced the receiver and known with a sudden startling clarity exactly what she had to do. And yes, she had spent some of her precious money, yesterday. She had bought a pair of jeans, socks, a hoodie and a pair of sneakers from C&A. After that she had managed to get on board a hotel shuttle bus at the same time as a family with a teenage son. Sitting behind them, with another older couple and three Asian men wearing suits, she seemed to pass without notice. The bus drove to the airport and Scarlett got off with the rest of them, loitering near the family until the driver departed again. She had managed a few hours' sleep in the airport, along with a whole load of other people who were clearly delayed.

As dawn broke and the airport started to get busier, Scarlett had noticed two police officers standing outside one of the coffee shops in the terminal. Two big guys with bomber jackets, *'Politie'* on the

319

back. They were watching people, talking among themselves, laughing. Scarlett had thought about going up to them and asking them for help. It would be so easy – to let someone else take over. And here she was safe, wasn't she? With all these people?

What would they do, though?

They would – eventually – send her home. The authorities would ring Clive and Annie. And they would be forced to help her, forced to take her back. The thought of it made her stomach twist.

A third officer had joined the first two, his back to Scarlett. There was something about his shape that was familiar, something about the closely shaven hair under his cap. Scarlett had felt queasy about it. When he'd turned to face her, she'd thought she recognised him. He looked like one of her regulars, a guy who showed up once every three months or so, never told her his name, liked to grip her by the hair when she was giving him a blowjob. Shouted at her if she winced or choked. Smacked her around the head, once, hard enough to bruise.

It might not be him, of course – after all, she tried not to look at them too hard, tried to forget as soon as they were out of the door – but the thought of it was enough. She had got up from her seat and hurried out of the airport, across the road and down the ramp towards the motorway.

At the bottom a set of steps led down to a cycle path which ran below the motorway, parallel to it, stretching into the distance. A *fietspad*, they were called. They were everywhere, a network of little roads and paths. Scarlett had walked for miles with the intention of walking until she got to the ports. It was going to be a long way but she could do it. And then she'd seen that the *fietspad* intersected up ahead with a road which was leading up to some motorway services, and she'd decided to stop and use the toilets and maybe spend a bit of her money on a burger.

The services were good. She'd even managed to have a shower, although she'd had to do without a towel, wiping herself off with her hands and standing there shivering until she was dry enough to get dressed, and then blasting her hair under the hand-dryer. But she felt much better for it.

She had seen a number of lorries with British numberplates come and go from the services, had watched the men – and one woman – who emerged from them and headed for the services building. They'd all been quite young. None of them felt right to her, until she saw the Charlmere Logistics lorry with its distinctive blue and yellow livery parking at the back. From her position in the sheltered alcove, she saw the phone numbers on the side of the van – a Charlmere number, a Briarstone number. The driver that climbed down from the cab a few minutes later lumbered over towards her, his gait showing the discomfort of many hours sitting. He was a short, wide man with a half-growth of beard and hair that was too long at the back and too thin on top, wearing a grubby polo shirt that would once have been a smart royal blue. On his chest was an embroidered 'CL'.

Scarlett got up and followed him in. He was going to the Gents, of course he was. She waited in the arcade, watching a machine closely as if she was considering playing it, one eye on the entrance to the toilets. There he was, lumbering out. To her immense relief she watched him heading for the food court and she followed, joining him in the queue.

This was it. One chance at this, only one.

'Oh!' she said brightly. 'You work for Charlmere. My uncle worked for them.'

The man turned in surprise. To her relief he was smiling, revealing a set of half-absent teeth. 'Oh, yeah? What's 'is name?'

'Jeff. Jeff Smith. You know him?'

He shook his head, slowly. 'Nah. Mind you, there's lots of us drivers. People come and go all the time.'

Scarlett nodded. 'He used to say that, too. He's working for DHL
now. You heading back, are you?'

'Yeah, 'sright. Been over on a run to the north of Holland.'

There was a strange sort of smell about him, something she
couldn't quite put her finger on, a stench lingering on his clothes. Not
quite body odour.

'Jeff used to do Eastern Europe,' she chanced, hoping he wasn't
going to say Charlmere Logistics never went out that way. When he just
nodded and smiled, she added, 'He used to take me out sometimes,
half-terms, you know, on his shorter runs. Keep me out of mischief.
Wasn't allowed, of course, but he let me come along anyway.'

They had reached the tills. He was getting a breakfast sandwich
and a coffee. At the adjacent till, she collected a Sprite and a bag of
crisps.

'Mind if I join you?' she asked, following him to a seat.

'Nah,' he said, 'go ahead. Free country, innit.'

He was looking at her a little warily now, Scarlett thought. She
would have to be careful.

'I've been travelling,' she said. 'I was with some mates but they
wanted to go round Germany and I've had enough now. I want to get
back.'

'Oh, yeah?'

'Miss my mum's cooking.'

'Ha, yes. I know.'

'I'm hitching to the docks – going to get the ferry, I think.'

'Don't get many people hitching these days. You wanna be careful.'

'Yeah. Don't tell my dad. Or my uncle Jeff.'

He was chewing on his sandwich, grubby fingernails and fingers shiny with grease. She sipped at her straw, not making eye contact, aware that his eyes were on her. Sizing her up. Despite the shower, she must look rough as anything.

'Nice to meet someone who speaks proper English,' she said.

'You from Charlmere, then?' he asked.

'Briarstone,' she said.

There was a long, painful pause.

Another mouthful of bread and meat was chewed and swallowed. He slurped at his drink, several noisy gulps followed by a repressed, airy belch.

'Well,' he said, 'I suppose you could get a lift with me. I'm going to Briarstone depot once I've dropped off a load in Morden.'

'Thanks,' she said, trying not to look too grateful, too relieved. 'My name's Katie. What's yours?'

'Barry,' he said, offering her a meaty, greasy shovel of a hand to shake. 'You know it's against company rules to give lifts.'

'I won't tell anyone,' she said. 'Promise.'

'Nah,' he said. 'You better bloody not.'

Twenty minutes later they were walking across the car park back towards the blue and yellow lorry. It was clean – looked new. As they got closer Scarlett caught a whiff of the smell that had been on Barry's clothes, getting stronger and stronger. When he opened up the cab and stood aside for her to clamber up, Scarlett had to breathe through her mouth. It was as though something had died and got caught under the wheels of the trailer.

'What's that smell?' she said.

'Chicken shit,' he said. 'One-tonne bags. They use it as fertiliser. You get used to it after a while; an hour or so and you won't even smell it any more.'

Belgium, 11:30

It was nice, riding up so high in the cab. You could see for miles. And Barry had been right: after a while the smell of chicken poo faded and all that remained was the sunshine, the vast blue skies of southern Holland, the long road stretching ahead.

Barry seemed quite happy to have someone to talk to.

'Yeah, I do this run regular. Bring over a high-value load – nothing exciting, it's just watermarked paper, but even so I have to take a security guard with me. I drop the load off in Haarlem, then I take the security guard to the airport. Then it's a few hours to the north of Holland, right up near the border, place called Drenthe – know it? No, why would you, no bugger ever goes there, although I think it's all right. Anyway, I pick up the load to come back with; normally I get down to Belgium before the overnight stop, 'cept I got stuck in traffic yesterday so I stopped up near the airport again. I like those services, anyway; some of 'em are a bit rough, you know?'

'Where's the chicken poo going?' Scarlett asked.

'This lot's going to the depot but I'm dropping one bag off at a farm on the way. Kind of a favour for a mate, like.'

The crossing into Belgium had been no more complicated than the colour of the motorway sign changing. Scarlett had worried about whether they would be stopped, but there wasn't even a barrier. They didn't even have to slow down.

That didn't last long, however, as the traffic ground to a halt when they were skirting a city. 'Always bad round here,' Barry told her. 'See, thing is, Belgium is so small that people don't ever move house. You live in Bruges and you get a job in Antwerp, you just drive there. Not far enough to warrant moving house. So people end up crisscrossing the whole bloody country every day. Crazy, I call it.'

Eventually the traffic eased again and they were on a long, straight motorway, bordered by fields and the occasional wind turbine, the shadows of the blades slicing across the tarmac in front of them.

'I go via Dunkirk, short a crossing as possible without bloody going into France. I went via Hook of Holland a couple of times but not when it's bad weather. Costs more too. I'd rather drive further and just have two hours across the Channel.'

If they were nearing the ports already, Scarlett didn't have much time left. She waited for a suitable gap in the conversation, which took a while.

'Barry,' she said, 'I need to tell you something.'

'What is it?'

There was no way round this bit. Despite the happy bond that seemed to have developed over the past couple of hours, all that bonhomie could disappear if she got this bit wrong.

'Fact is, I haven't got a passport. I got my bag nicked from a youth hostel in Amsterdam.'

'Yeah? Did you call the police?'

'I did, and I went to the embassy, but they were just useless. It's going to take forever to sort it out – and most of my money got nicked as well, so I can't pay for a new one. I thought it would just be easier to see if I could get home my own way.'

'What about your folks, can't they send you some money?'

'My dad'll kill me. He didn't want me to go travelling in the first place.'

'You can't get through without a passport.'

'It's okay, Barry, I understand. I don't want to get you in any bother. If you can drop me off outside somewhere, I'll sort myself out.'

There was an awkward silence, broken only by the lumbering lorry engine.

'I have got some cash, though. I mean, I've got about fifty euros left.'

Silence.

'I was wondering if I could, maybe, hide in the back of the cab. If they found me, you can deny all knowledge and I'll back you up. I'll say I sneaked in when you stopped at the service station. I mean, it's not like I'm an illegal. I went to Briarstone Grammar.'

Barry said nothing, his eyes fixed on the road.

'I'm sorry, I should have said earlier. I don't want to make it awkward.'

The lorry indicated and turned off the motorway a few moments later. It wasn't the ports. It was another service station. He was going to leave her here, and her best chance of getting across the Channel and back to Briarstone was flying out of the window.

'Where are we?' she asked.

'Jabbeke,' Barry said. 'This is the last truck stop before the ports that doesn't have a dedicated police presence. After this they're watching all the activity around the trucks. So this is the only chance to hide you. If that's what you really want.'

Scarlett's face broke into a wide smile of relief. 'Thank you. Seriously, that's really kind of you.'

But Barry hadn't finished. As the truck shuddered to a halt, he turned to her and added, 'No need to spin me all that crap about your passport. You don't look to me like the sort of girl who's been off round Europe with her mates. You're a worker, am I right?'

'What?' Scarlett asked, although it was too late.

'Thing is, Katie or whatever your name is, it's a lonely old life on the road. And it's a big risk taking you through without a passport or a ticket. Could get caught, then I'd lose my job, get a fine. Fifty euros ain't going to cover it.'

She watched as he undid his fly, looked away quickly.

'I ain't going to force you. But that's the price. 'Sup to you.'

11:55

Afterwards they went into the services so Scarlett could go to the Ladies and Barry could get himself a coffee and a snack. Once he'd stowed her away in the cab she would not be able to get out again until they were well past Customs on the other side.

'They watch the trucks, all the laybys all the way up the A2 for five or ten miles,' he said. 'I won't stop till I get to Morden. So it's going to be three, maybe four hours, what with the crossing and waiting to board.'

In the back of the cab were bunks, two of them, one above the other. The bottom bunk held a sleeping bag, and a duvet in a faded navy blue duvet cover. The top bunk was strapped up at a forty-five-degree angle. When he unclipped it, it flipped out to show a couple of holdalls, a laptop case and a Sainsbury's bag containing a lunch-box and a flask. There was a reasonable space between the bunk and the back wall of the cab.

'You can hide in there,' he said. 'I'll have to fasten the bunk back up. You won't have a lot of room, but it's the only place you'd be all right. As long as you keep quiet.'

'Will they stop the truck?' Scarlett said.

'They don't often,' he said. 'Nice tidy truck, no problems with it,

327

you usually get a green light. Sometimes they stop it just for a once-over, but once they get a whiff of the chicken shit they usually let me go through.'

Barry pulled the holdalls and the carrier bag down on to the lower bunk, moved the duvet up to the top so she had something reasonably comfortable to lie on. Then she climbed up and tucked herself into the space at the back. Barry lifted up the bunk and fastened the straps holding it in place. It was dark and, although there was a little light around the edges, it felt airless and stuffy almost immediately.

'All right up there?' he asked.

'Yes,' she said, swallowing the sudden wave of fear.

The truck started up again and moments later swung back on to the motorway. She stayed quiet, listening to the radio and Barry singing along to it.

Once they had driven on board the ferry, Barry locked up the cab without another word and left her alone. It was claustrophobic and Scarlett had to concentrate on breathing slowly and deeply to stop herself panicking. It smelled bad – not the fertiliser smell but like food that had gone off. Three or four hours, he'd said.

The vehicle deck of the ferry was a noisy place, and, once the ship had passed the protection of the harbour wall, the swell of the sea rocked the boat, and the lorries parked inside it, and Scarlett, pinned into the secret space behind the bunk. She could still taste him, even though she'd rinsed out her mouth in the sink in the Ladies at the services. She'd washed her hands with soap, too, but she could still smell him; or maybe it was the duvet.

He had given her the option to walk away. He hadn't forced himself on her. It had been her decision, whether to do this and get across the Channel, or get out of the cab and take her chances on the other drivers at Jabbeke. She'd made the decision freely, but at the same moment she had decided something else: it would be the last time. The last time, ever.

Near Morden, 15:00

When Barry had got back to the cab, Scarlett had been hot, desperately thirsty and starting to need the toilet. Waking up suddenly when the ferry jolted into the berth on the English coast, she had been counting the minutes in her head ever since, waves of panic coming and going, taking deep breaths of the rancid air and trying to keep still.

He didn't speak to her until the vehicle began to move.

'Keep quiet,' he said a few minutes later, although she'd not spoken or moved. 'We're coming up to Customs.'

The lorry didn't stop, just slowed down a little as it went over some speed bumps, and then it was speeding up, ratcheting through the gears jerkily until the engine sang into a whine.

'You all right back there?' he called.

'Just about,' she shouted back. 'Please can we stop as soon as possible?'

He pulled into a layby a few minutes later and went to the back of the cab to unstrap her from the bunk. 'Stay back here for now,' he said, giving her a plastic litre bottle of water. 'I'm running behind so I'm going to drive straight to Morden. Be about an hour or so.'

As the lorry pulled away again, Scarlett sat on the bottom bunk, drinking the lukewarm water and relishing the cool air from Barry's open window, taking deep lungfuls of it.

'What you going to do in Briarstone, then?' he asked, after a while.

'Look for a job,' she said.

329

'What sort of a job?'

'No idea. Anything. I'll find something.'

'What about your family?'

'I don't know. They're kind of a bit weird. I'd rather be on my own.'

'Seems to me like you ain't going home.'

'No,' she said.

Through the swinging curtain separating the bunk from the front of the cab, she watched as England sped past. It was cloudy and dull, but it was nevertheless England. The British numberplates on the cars, so many of them, looked odd . . . the enormous blue motorway signs pointing to English towns, names she recognised. It felt as if she had been gone for no time at all.

After a while Barry turned off the motorway and within minutes they were on narrow country roads, trees brushing against the roof of the cab. She came to sit in the front next to Barry. 'Where are we going again?'

'Morden. You know it?'

'No.'

'My mate's got a farm. I help him out by getting him an extra bag of fertiliser whenever I do this run.'

The lorry pulled on to a narrow concrete track and followed it up to a wide farmyard, barns on one side, a farmhouse on the other. From the back of one of the barns a man emerged, raising a hand in greeting. The lorry's engine cut out and Barry opened the cab door. 'All right, Nige? How are you, mate?'

Scarlett opened the passenger side and climbed down.

'Who's this?' the man asked. He was clean-shaven, with short greying hair, and bright blue eyes. His brown cord trousers looked as if they never got properly dirty.

'Katie,' Barry said. 'I gave her a lift across the Channel.'

'Can I use your loo?' Scarlett asked. She'd drunk all the water, somehow.

'If you must,' Nigel said. 'Just go in the house, that door there – the toilet is just on the left.'

She went in through a small room with a tiled floor, muddy boots and coats lining the walls. The door to the left was a toilet, not especially clean, the seat up. It looked as though it didn't get flushed very often. Through the open window she could hear the two men in the yard, talking about her.

'Bit of a risk, wasn't it, picking up a hitchhiker?'

'Yeah, but she's all right. She hid in the bunk. Poor cow's had a rough time, you know. Can tell just by looking at her. She says she got family in Briarstone but I don't believe it. She's looking for a job. You not got anything, have you?'

'Not unless she knows how to look after horses.'

'She'd probably give it a try. I don't think she's got anywhere to go, anyway. Dunno where to drop her off.'

There was a pause. Then Nigel said, 'Hold on a minute.'

Scarlett flushed the toilet and rinsed her hands in the tiny sink. There was no soap and no towel. Coming back outside, wiping her hands on the back of her jeans, she saw Nigel coming back out of one of the barns with a second man behind him. He was well-built, looked as though he'd worked out once upon a time but not for a while. His black hoodie strained at the biceps and at the belly. Dark hair, cut very short, something elaborate shaved into the side of it.

'All right, Barry?' he said. 'How's it going?'

'All right, mate. Not seen you in ages.'

'Look,' Scarlett said to Nigel, 'I overheard what you said. I'll look after horses, I don't mind. I can do hard work. I don't even want paying, just somewhere to kip, till I can find something else.'

'I had a better idea,' Nigel said, indicating the chunky lad who was laughing with Barry. 'Katie, this is Reggie. He works with a friend of mine. He owns a place in town, needs someone to keep an eye on things – maybe clean, cook, that sort of stuff. You can live in.'

Scarlett looked at Nigel, then at Reggie. 'In town? You mean Briarstone?'

Reggie nodded. ''Sright. What do you think?'

'What sort of place? Like a B&B or something?'

'Something. A couple of girls live there. You know what girls are like: can't bloody tidy up after themselves, don't bother eating unless someone provides it for them.'

Scarlett smiled. 'I can do that. Whatever.'

Reggie gave her a happy smile in return. 'I got to clear it with the boss. You can come with me to meet him. If he likes you, you're in.'

SCARLETT – Briarstone, Tuesday 26 March 2013, 18:38

Scarlett had been at her vantage point on the swings for long enough for it to start to get chilly. The evenings were getting lighter now, and while at first she had been concerned about attracting attention, and would sit here pretending to play with her phone, nobody had ever given her a second glance. Through the winter there had never been many people in the playground, just the odd dog-walker in the park.

The phone buzzed in her hand and she answered it quickly. 'Yeah?'

'You going to be much longer?' Reggie asked. ''Cause if you are, I might as well go to the pub.'

'I'll be done soon, Reg. I'll call you.'

Russet Avenue was on the other side of town from Carisbrooke Court, and Scarlett relied on Reggie giving her a lift here when she was out running errands for Lewis, or getting the shopping. Although this often felt like a pointless waste of time, watching the house from a distance, it took her away from the drudgery of her daily existence, back in the flat. Made her feel closer to Juliette, too.

When she had first come back to Briarstone, it hadn't taken Scarlett longer than a few minutes in the flat in Carisbrooke Court with Reggie and his boss, a silver-haired charmer who owned the property, to work out what was going on. She'd gone from one brothel straight into another. By that time it was late, Scarlett was shattered and she had nowhere else to go.

But the girls' occupation was where the similarities began and ended. For a start, it was clean and warm, and it had a washing machine and a dishwasher, a fridge with food in it. Scarlett had her own room – the smallest, but even so it was hers – and the other girls left her alone. There were three other girls sharing the flat with her, and, while they were not exactly friendly, they seemed to take to Scarlett.

Scarlett hadn't seen the silver-haired man again, but Reggie was there most days. He had the hots for Liliana, was always hanging around her, chatting her up when she wasn't working. And he had a girlfriend and kids, too, but Scarlett forgave him because he was a laugh, he was a bit of an idiot, and he was the first bloke she'd met that didn't seem to want anything from her.

It had taken a couple of weeks for the shine to wear off. It began when Kat – the Russian girl – ended up having an argument with one of her customers.

'You're off your face, you stupid foreign bitch!' the man had screamed from the bedroom. He was old and drunk, but he was muscular; had several missing teeth and a shaven head, tattoos on his face.

Scarlett had called Reggie in a panic. 'Get here now,' she'd pleaded. 'It's kicking off.'

Reggie had been there in less than five minutes. He might have been overweight and a bit stupid but it turned out he loved his job, which was sticking up for the girls. The drunk man was hauled out on to the pavement, kicked in the back of the legs and then booted in the side for good measure. Scarlett had to pull Reggie away.

Meanwhile in the bathroom, Kat had been shaking and yelling, incomprehensible words tumbling over each other. Reggie went in there with the gear for her, which apparently he was overdue

334

bringing. Scarlett had suspected the girls were all on something, but that night she had seen it for herself.

They were no better off than the girls in Amsterdam, not really. They were all on the gear, all totally reliant on their supply. All of them in debt to Reggie or to the man who owned the flat. They were no more free to walk out than Scarlett had been. Where would they go? Who would help them? They'd get shipped back home, wherever that was, and, while their flat in Briarstone wasn't exactly heaven, it seemed as though whatever they'd run away from was probably far worse.

The next day, when Kat was back to her normal arsey self, dropping her dirty clothes on the floor and leaving crumbs in the kitchen, Reggie had been tasked with taking Scarlett to the supermarket. Juliette had scarcely left her thoughts since that phone call she'd made from Amsterdam, but it was only when she was out in the car that first time, Reggie driving, that she'd seen the opportunity to try to get to Juliette. After they'd been round Asda together, she asked him to drop her off near Russet Avenue, pointing to the little park and saying she fancied some fresh air. Reggie didn't seem to mind waiting for her, didn't question it. He took himself off to the pub.

She had been there just ten minutes, sitting on the swings, hugging herself because it was bitterly cold, the sleeves of her coat pulled down over her hands, when the front door opened. The first person she saw was Clive, and it gave her a shock. He looked exactly the same – she had expected him to have aged, but he looked no different.

Funny how immune you got to fear when you'd lived with it for so long, and then how it could take you by surprise.

And then, standing in the open doorway, there was Juliette, wearing jeans and a red top. She looked so grown-up! That was the

335

first thing that struck Scarlett, made her heart lurch. The second thing was the sheer normality of it. Juliette stood waiting for about two minutes while Clive got into his car and started the engine. Juliette said something to him, smiled briefly and waved as the car reversed out of the driveway and disappeared off down the street.

Instinctively Scarlett jumped off the swing, heading towards the house. But as she got to the park gates Juliette turned back into the house and across the still, cold air, Scarlett heard her say something and laugh as she closed the door. She wasn't alone; Annie must be inside with her. The chance to make contact had gone.

Over the next few weeks, as winter set in and the end of the year approached, Scarlett had watched the house whenever she got the chance. Sometimes there was no sign of anyone; a few times, either Annie or Clive would come out and set off somewhere. She was always hoping for an opportunity but they never seemed to leave Juliette on her own. In any case, as the weeks and months passed, the desperate need to get her sister away from them had receded. She was alive and apparently well, not screaming, not imprisoned. What would she even say, if Scarlett knocked on the door? Would she even recognise her, after everything that had happened? The sister she'd been crying out for in the background of that phone call, the fifteen-year-old rebel who had looked out for her, was long gone. And what did Scarlett have to offer her, anyway? She worked in a brothel, washed dirty clothes and made sure the girls had enough condoms. She had a tiny room and no money. What if Juliette didn't want to know her, now; what if she was disappointed?

She carried on visiting the park to watch the house, but it was more out of curiosity than anything else. This would have been her life. She felt detached from it, haunting the swings. Keeping her distance.

It was getting dark now, as well as cold. Scarlett was on the verge of calling Reggie to get him to come and pick her up when the front door of the house opened, and her heart stopped: Clive and Annie were coming out of the house, both of them, for the first time. Annie was wearing a dress and heels. Clive opened the passenger door for her – ever the gentleman – before going round to the driver's side. The Volvo drove off towards the town.

It was the chance Scarlett had been waiting for, but now it was here it took her several moments before she could summon the courage. She took a deep breath in. Was she going to stay here forever, watching and not moving? Something had to happen. Something had to change.

There was no reply when she knocked on the door. Fidgety with nerves, Scarlett kept glancing behind her, expecting them to come back at any moment. She lifted the letterbox flap, looked down the long hallway that was so familiar.

'Juliette?' she called. 'Are you there? It's me.'

When there was still no reply, Scarlett began to wonder if Juliette might have moved out after all. She was twenty-three – she might have gone to university, or got a job. Just because she'd been there on the doorstep with Clive that first day, and Scarlett had seen her shape through a downstairs window a couple of times, there was no reason to assume she actually lived there.

Well, she herself was here now, and with both of them apparently out for the evening it felt like an opportunity for Scarlett to have a nose around. The gate wasn't locked, and a moment later Scarlett was in the back garden. The old shed had been replaced with a summerhouse, a new section of decking at the back, pots full of flowers, the lawn neatly trimmed and weed-free. The back door which led into the utility room was unlocked. Scarlett opened it, stepped into the house.

She walked back in time, into the life she had had before, smelling the house and the dinner her mother had cooked last night, her father's aftershave.

Juliette was standing in the hallway, staring at the front door, her back to Scarlett. How had she not heard her come in?

'Juliette,' Scarlett said.

Part Six

GOING BACK IS SOMETIMES
THE SAME THING
AS GOING FORWARD

Half an hour later, Sam had exhausted both of the night shelters in Briarstone, and all of the others within an hour's drive. Even the one in Charlmere – well, it was worth a try, wasn't it? – no longer had any capacity at all. Time for Plan B. She called in to the control room, spoke to the night duty inspector and got authorisation to get Scarlett back into the Travel Inn for another two nights, the rationale being that she wouldn't be tempted to check out first thing the next morning, and they would know where she was, at least for thirty-six hours.

'I know it might seem easier to stay here,' Sam said, as she started up her car, 'but it's just not something I'm allowed to do.'

'And you don't trust me,' Scarlett said. She'd taken the news that she was going back to the Briarstone Travel Inn surprisingly well.

'It's not that,' Sam said, although this was possibly not entirely true. 'It's that you're a potential witness in a live investigation. And if you feel in danger, you'd be far safer in a place where nobody except me and the duty inspector knows where you are, right?'

'Right,' Scarlett said.

'We'll be in touch in the morning, check you're okay. See if we can find you something a bit more permanent.'

'You mean *you'll* be in touch in the morning? I don't want to talk to anyone else.'

Sam looked across at her. The security light outside the garage was illuminating Scarlett's face, her eyes hidden in deep shadow.

'All right,' Sam said. 'Just don't disappear on me again, okay?'

And Scarlett smiled, and again Sam felt something give. Behind the greasy cropped hair and the dirty sweatshirt, behind the eyeliner smudged under her eyes – God knew when she'd put that on – and the chapped lips, there was someone so breathlessly gorgeous that Sam felt her heart start to break.

The Travel Inn was just ten minutes' drive away, thankfully. Sam spoke to the woman behind reception while Scarlett skulked in the doorway, chewing at a fingernail.

'Room 116,' Sam said eventually, handing Scarlett the keycard. 'Here you go. I'll come and see you in the morning. Sleep tight.'

For a moment Scarlett stared at Sam, challenging, accusing, then she took the card.

'Thanks,' she said, and slouched off in the direction of the stairs.

Back in the car, Sam let out a huge sigh of relief and picked up her mobile to call Lou. For now, Scarlett was sorted.

04/11/2013, 00:12

Dispatch Log 1104-0021

**	CALL FROM EDEN F&RS REPORTING VEHICLE ON FIRE
**	LOCATION GIVEN AS WOODLANDS BEHIND THE SCHOOL IN PARK HILL
**	VEHICLE IS GREEN VOLVO S40
**	SUCCESSFULLY EXTINGUISHED
**	INTEL SEARCH SHOWS CRIME REPORT PZ/015567/13, CAR KEY BURG AT 14 RUSSET AVE BRIARSTONE EARLY HOURS 03/11/13, GREEN VOLVO S40 STOLEN
**	DUTY INSPECTOR NOTED
**	CSI INFORMED

04/11/2013, 06:25

Dispatch Log 1104-0072

- ** CALLER STATES SHE HAS FOUND HER
  PARENTS ON THE DOORSTEP, DOESN'T KNOW
  IF THEY ARE DEAD BUT NOT MOVING

- ** CALLER IS JULIETTE RAINSFORD DOB
  26/06/1990 ADDRESS 14 RUSSET AVENUE
  BRIARSTONE

- ** AMBULANCE DISPATCHED – REF 04-0072

- ** PARENTS CLIVE RAINSFORD DOB 21/10/1943
  ANNIE RAINSFORD 18/07/1961

- ** BODIES ARE LYING ON FRONT STEP, CALLER
  STATES SHE FOUND THEM WHEN SHE WENT
  TO CHECK IF MILK HAD BEEN DELIVERED

- ** PATROLS PZ43 PZ47 AVAILABLE DISPATCHED

- ** CALLER STATES CLIVE AND ANNIE WENT OUT
  LAST NIGHT SHE DID NOT HEAR THEM COME
  IN

- ** AMBULANCE ON SCENE

- ** DUTY INSPECTOR NOTED, WILL ATTEND

LOU – Monday 4 November 2013, 06:50

Lou woke up abruptly to the sound of her work phone ringing downstairs. She got out of bed quickly, nearly falling down the stairs in her haste.

'Lou Smith,' she said.

It was Rob Jefferson, one of the Major Crime DIs. 'Ma'am, sorry to bother you so early. We've just had a report of a murder and assault, Russet Avenue. Just off London Road. It's been assigned to my team but this guy is flagged to you.'

'To me? What's his name?'

'Rainsford, Clive Rainsford. He's been identified by his daughter. And the assault is his wife, Annie Rainsford. She's in the hospital but unconscious.'

'Thanks, Rob. I'll be there in less than an hour; can I have a quick meeting with you first thing?'

Jefferson agreed and rang off. *Clive Rainsford*, Lou thought – *shit. What next?* She took a deep breath and ran back up the stairs. If she hurried she just about had time for a shower.

She would need to call Sam first thing, Lou thought. She'd been at the Rainsford house yesterday with Caro Sumner – Clive's death might well count as a 'death following police contact'. And she'd had that meeting with Annie on Saturday. There would likely be an internal investigation. As she rinsed her hair, she wondered if SB had been notified too – she must remember to ring Caro as well as Sam. This wasn't even going to be her case, unless she could convince Mr Buchanan to let her oversee it. Clive Rainsford, unpleasant as he was, was not a dealer or a member of an organised crime group at any level. If Annie was in hospital with injuries too, it was possible it had been a domestic between the two of them.

Drying herself off and getting dressed as quickly as she could, Lou tried to rein in the theories already tumbling over themselves in her mind. It didn't help at this stage. She knew next to nothing about what had happened. Better to wait until she had a chance for a proper briefing with Rob.

Sam was sitting with Scarlett in the pub next door to the Travel Inn, the one that helpfully provided breakfasts for the morning after, and for a change the sun was shining through the window, showing the finger marks on the stainless steel teapot on the table between them. Scarlett was working her way through a full English, and although Sam had paid for two breakfasts the sight of the dripping egg yolk smeared on Scarlett's plate and smell of fat coming from the kitchen had taken away her appetite. The two pieces of toast on her plate were cold and bendy and she'd only managed one bite.

Sam was distracted by Scarlett, even more so because of what she was wearing. Conscious that she'd not seen Scarlett in anything other than the chewed sweatshirt and grubby jeans, she had found some old but clean clothes at the back of her wardrobe, and brought them with her this morning.

'I know what you said about cast-offs,' Sam had said, handing the carrier bag through the door of Room 116, open a crack to reveal darkness and a tangled mop of hair, 'but – well, you know, I thought you might be ready for a change of clothes by now.'

Giving Scarlett clothing was probably breaching some regulation or other, but that wasn't what was troubling her. It was only when Scarlett had arrived in the reception area of the hotel thirty minutes later, with freshly washed hair, dressed in a white blouse and jeans made to fit by the addition of a tightly cinched belt, that she'd realised the clothes were Jo's – of course they were; everything shoved at the back of the wardrobe belonged to her ex, because after all what was she supposed to do with it all? And, looking at the blouse, Sam had realised it was the one Jo had worn to her disciplinary hearing.

Not long after that Jo had left, packed a bag and gone, leaving Sam and all manner of other things behind. Sam hadn't seen her since.

Scarlett coughed and Sam focused her attention back on the room. Luckily they were the only ones here. The hotel was usually dead quiet during the week, which was how they'd managed to negotiate special rates for the emergency waifs and strays that the police needed to find a safe place for.

'How did you sleep?' Sam asked.

'Not bad,' Scarlett said. 'Bit more comfy than the bus station.'

'Is that where you spent the night before?'

Scarlett nodded. 'And walking around. When it opened I went and sat in the library to warm up. I was reading the newspapers. I saw an article about Mrs Rowden-Knowles in the *Eden Evening Times*. She was with a bunch of other people protesting about road-building or something, in their village. There was a picture of her outside her house. Teacher, it said. I knew it was her.'

'So you thought you'd go and find her?'

'Something to do, wasn't it? I think I scared the life out of her,' Scarlett said, smiling at the thought of it. 'She was kind to me, though. I don't think I deserved her kindness. I was a pain in the backside at school—'

Scarlett stopped abruptly. Sam's mobile phone was vibrating on the table.

'I'd better get that,' Sam said. 'It's probably work. You okay?'

'Yeah, yeah,' Scarlett said. 'Go ahead.'

The caller display showed Lou's mobile.

'Hiya,' Sam said.

'Morning, Sam,' Lou said. 'Are you free to talk?'

'Not really. Can I ring you back later and explain?'

'Why, where are you?' Lou's tone was grave.

346

'I'm with Scarlett right now. We're in the pub next door to the Travel Inn – whatever it's called; I can never remember.'

'That's good to hear. But this can't wait, I'm afraid. Do me a favour: just make sure this is out of earshot?'

'Sure. Scarlett, will you excuse me for a sec?' Sam got to her feet, went to the door of the pub and stood in the entrance vestibule. From here she could still see the girl at the table. She had helped herself to Sam's discarded toast and was munching on it.

'Go ahead, boss. What's up?'

'I had a call earlier this morning. Clive Rainsford was found dead this morning. Annie is in hospital.'

'Shit! What happened?'

'Juliette found them outside the front of the house first thing. All they've got from her so far is that they went out for the evening, and she didn't hear them come in. It looks as though they were attacked on the doorstep when they got home. I'm on my way into the briefing now.'

'Do you need me to come back to the station?'

'No, Sam. I really need you to stay with Scarlett for now. Whatever happens, I don't want her to disappear again. If it looks like she's going to do a runner you can arrest her – for her own safety if nothing else. All right?'

'Of course.'

'What about her movements last night?'

'She turned up with her former teacher at about half-ten. I took her to the hotel – and I left her at just before one, when I called your mobile.'

'Her teacher?'

'I've got her details written down – Mrs Rowden-Knowles. Scarlett found her somehow, she brought her round to my house.'

'We'll need to get a statement from her. And Scarlett, of course.'

'I'll try and get as much of that out of her as I can,' Sam said.

'Sure. If you feel you have to tell her the news about Clive and Annie, do – it's your call.'

'Right.'

Back at their table, Scarlett had finished eating. She looked up when she heard Sam approach, treating Sam to one of her radiant smiles. 'Everything okay? Your boss checking up on you?'

'Something like that,' Sam said. 'Scarlett, can I ask why you weren't keen to see your family?'

The smile died and a cloud came over. Scarlett looked away, bit her lip. She began fiddling with the teapot, pouring herself another cup. 'Put it this way,' she said at last, 'I didn't think they'd want to see me. Turns out I was right about that, wasn't I?'

Sam was certain that she was withholding something. If in doubt, it was worth a direct question. 'Did you try to make contact with them?'

Scarlett considered her answer for a long time, and when it came out Sam knew it was a lie. 'No,' she said. 'I was too scared.'

'Why were you scared, Scarlett? They could have helped you. They thought you were dead.'

'I didn't want their help,' she said. 'I thought they would be ashamed of what I was doing, so I stayed away. But now they know I'm here, I'm not so scared any more – especially with you here, Sam.'

She took a deep breath, summoned up a smile.

'I'm going to have to face them sooner or later. Get it over with – right?'

Rob Jefferson was on his way into the stuffy, airless room that had been designated as the incident room for Op Vanguard – the murder of Clive Rainsford.

'Ma'am,' he said, seeing Lou heading towards him in the corridor. 'Sorry – I know we were supposed to meet, but the briefing's been brought forward. Are you able to sit in? It'll bring you up to speed with everything we've got so far. We can have a chat afterwards, if that's any good?'

Lou shook his hand warmly. She'd always liked Rob – quiet, approachable, reliable. And more than anything else he didn't have that stupid competitive machismo that sometimes got in the way of running an investigation. 'That would be great, Rob, thanks.'

'Feel free to interrupt if there's anything you can help us with,' he said.

Lou sat on a table at the back of the room. Almost instantly a DC she'd never met stood and offered her his seat. She gave him a smile and waved him back. 'I'm fine here, thanks.'

Rob Jefferson didn't have that many people, if this was the total number of officers he had assigned to the job, Lou thought. She counted three DCs and a DS – Jamie Turnbull, who Lou knew was about to go on paternity leave any day. In addition to the officers, Lou saw Clare Simpson, the senior CSI, and Zoe Adams, who was one of the analysts. Not Jason, then – that was a small relief.

Lou listened as Rob ran through the facts of the investigation so far. Clive and Annie had been found by Juliette at a quarter past six this morning. Juliette, who had already been interviewed once and then been taken to the hospital by one of the family liaison officers to see Annie, had woken up at six and noticed that her parents had failed to return from their night out. She had gone to check if the milkman had been, and had found them both on the front doorstep.

Lou found herself wondering if milkmen even still existed.

'Jamie,' Rob said, 'what's the latest on Annie's condition?'

'Just got a text from Jan Baker, our FLO. She's on her way back with Juliette. Apparently Annie's in a critical condition but Juliette didn't want to stay at the hospital. We've got an officer with Annie, just in case whoever assaulted her decides to come and have another go.'

'Thanks, Jamie. As far as timings go,' Rob said, 'we have CCTV of them leaving the restaurant at a quarter to eleven. They got a cab from the taxi rank outside the station, which dropped them off at home. The driver says this was at about five past eleven. Nothing unusual about them; he could hear them chatting in the back of the cab but he couldn't remember hearing either of them saying anything specific. He didn't see anything, and he didn't wait for them to go into the house. I quote: "If I knew they was going to get hurt I would have waited."'

This brought a few laughs.

'So, assuming they didn't immediately go somewhere else, it seems likely that they were attacked a minute or so later – just after eleven. Intel – what's the latest?'

This time Zoe Adams spoke. 'I've got this update from Alan. He sends his apologies; he was just finishing a phone call, said he'd be in in a minute. We've had an update on the burglary to the Rainsford house on Saturday night – I've got the crime number here if anyone needs it. Clive Rainsford said he'd phoned to cancel his cards as soon as they realised, but £800 had already gone from two ATMs in town. The third attempt was blocked. There was some online activity, too, but that was also prevented by the bank – so, aside from the jewellery and the Rolex, whoever it was probably didn't make as much as they were hoping to.'

'Any CCTV from the ATMs?' Lou asked.

'Yes, a male figure was seen at two of them. I'll get a printout and the best stills put on the area briefing slides. Not particularly clear, but someone might recognise the clothing. Also in relation to the burglary, a vehicle which looks very like the Volvo that was stolen from the driveway appears on the CCTV from the garage on London Road, just at the end of Russet Avenue, last night. It's shown heading towards the address and indicating to turn into the road at ten forty-three. Then it's coming back again at ten past eleven.'

'We can't get an index on it?'

'Apparently not. But we've found the vehicle in any case. It was alight in some woodland behind a school in the Park Hill estate just after midnight. Fire and Rescue put it out before it was a complete shell, so we might get some forensics from it. They recovered a phone handset, a fizzy drink bottle and a black hoodie, among other less exciting things. The phone has gone to the Computer Crime Unit for download; I've made sure they've got me down as the analyst so I'll get an alert as soon as it's done.'

'Thanks, Zoe. Ma'am,' Rob said then, looking at Lou, 'is there anything you'd like to comment on before we get on to the forensics?'

In other words, *Can you tell us what you know?*

'Thanks,' Lou said. 'Yes, just a bit of background for you, and the reason why I'm sitting in on your briefing. I'm sure I don't need to say that this information is strictly confidential.'

Briefly she explained about Scarlett's reappearance – while there was no evidence linking this murder to recent events, it was certainly worth a mention. She looked around the room at the rapt faces, and as soon as she'd finished there were murmurs and whispers. Scarlett's name was familiar to many. 'The press haven't cottoned on to it yet,' she said, 'and I'd like to keep it that way for as long as possible. I can imagine this attack will be national news, given the family's history. Once they know Scarlett Rainsford is not only alive but has recently been found in Briarstone, the level of press attention will escalate. Another thing to consider is that we have recently spoken to both Annie and Clive Rainsford on separate occasions and they were both in a pretty fragile emotional state, which may or may not be of interest as your investigation continues. Any questions?'

Jamie Turnbull asked, 'Where is Scarlett now? Does she know about what's happened?'

'She's with one of my officers this morning, I've left it to her to break the news. We'll bring her in as soon as we can to make a statement. For reference, though, her movements are pretty much accounted for, as far as last night's concerned. Yes – you have a question?'

It was the DC who'd offered her his seat. 'What was the reaction when she met up with her family again, ma'am?'

'She had only had a chance to see her mother; she hadn't seen Clive or Juliette.'

'Where has she been all these years?' This was from Jamie Turnbull again.

'We're in the process of unravelling all that. Forgive me if I'm not at liberty to go into detail. If we find out anything that might be pertinent to this investigation, I'll make sure you're briefed. Zoe – did you want to ask something?'

'Did Scarlett Rainsford have a phone? Do we have the number?'

'I'm fairly sure SB seized a handset from her during the warrant,' Lou said.

'Is it all right with you if I contact the SB analyst? If they've downloaded the handset already there might be call data I can use. You never know.'

'Of course. If you have any trouble with that, let me know and I'll speak to Mr Waterhouse. Okay? Thanks Rob – back to you.'

'Thank you. Clare,' Rob said, 'can you take us through the CSI?'

'Sure,' Clare began, clearing her throat. 'We're still working on the car; I'll let you know as soon as I've got a report on that. For now, though, I can tell you what we've done so far at the property. The initial scene was the whole of the front garden. Annie had been taken to the hospital by the time we got there. Clive was lying with his head on the grass and most of his body on the path. Didn't look like he'd moved once he fell. We're looking at extensive head injuries – same for Annie – with massive blood loss. No sign of a weapon. We did get a pretty good shoe mark from the garden. There was an area under the tree, behind some bushes, that was freshly trampled. Someone possibly waiting there for them to come home.'

'Any way of telling which of them was struck first?' Rob asked.

'Not yet. We're looking at the blood spatter. At the moment it would suggest possibly Clive first – a single blow to knock him out – then Annie, then back to Clive to finish him off. If we can get anything conclusive on that I'll make sure it's highlighted in the report.'

'Thanks, Clare.'

'One more thing, sir. The shoe mark had a match on the database. We don't have a subject match but the same shoe mark was recovered from a scene last month.'

'Who was the victim?' Rob asked.

'It's an unsolved one. Carl McVey, the guy who owns those pubs.'

Intel Report on Op Vanguard

5x5x5 Intelligence Report

Date: Monday 4 November 2013

Officer: PSE FRANKS, Financial Investigation Officer,
            Fraud Unit

Subject: Crime Report PZ/015567/13, Op Vanguard

Grading: B / 1 / 1

Clive RAINSFORD DOB 21/10/1943

Crime report PZ/015567/13 refers to a Burglary Dwelling at 14 Russet Avenue, Briarstone, on the night of 02/11/13 to 03/11/13. During the course of the burglary, credit and debit cards in the name of Mr Clive RAINSFORD were stolen.

Enquiries with the Nationwide BS reveal that three attempts were made to access Mr RAINSFORD's accounts via ATMs in and around Briarstone town centre. These attempts were as follows:

03/11/2013 05:25 – Sainsbury's ATM, West Park Road

£500 cash withdrawn

CCTV shows IC1 male wearing a black woolly hat and a pale-coloured short jacket, jeans, white trainers.

03/11/2013 05:55 – Nationwide ATM, High Street

£300 cash withdrawn

CCTV at the premises not working at the time. Council CCTV from the Victoria Square shows male wearing black hat, pale jacket, jeans and white trainers walking past at 05:58.

03/11/2013 06:07 – Nat West ATM, High Street (north end)

£300 cash requested, transaction unsuccessful

CCTV out of action following criminal damage the night before.

Attempts were also made to transfer funds online at 06:42 to an account in Ireland; however this transaction was blocked by the Nationwide's security systems.

LOU – Monday 4 November 2013, 09:30

Lou was busy singing Sam's praises to Detective Superintendent Gordon Buchanan, who was giving the impression of listening intently while glancing every few seconds at his computer screen. This didn't bother Lou. She knew that, if she phrased the final sentences right, he would agree to what she was asking even if he hadn't fully taken in everything she'd said.

'Sam Hollands is the only member of my team who's been able to establish a rapport with Scarlett Rainsford,' she went on, 'and she has a unique connection with her which will be invaluable to DI Jefferson now that the circumstances have taken such a dramatic turn.'

'Indeed,' murmured Buchanan.

'And Caro Sumner. I know she's only just been seconded over to me from Special Branch, but I can't help feeling that, if we can unravel what happened to the Rainsfords, we will be able to get more useful intelligence about the trafficking networks operating out of Briarstone.'

Lou took a deep breath. This was her clincher. *Brace yourself, Gordon . . .*

'The trafficking operations directly impact on a number of our highest risk-scoring criminal networks, county-wide,' she said. 'If we can get to the intelligence concerning who's running the operations, there is a strong possibility that we will be able to dismantle maybe three or four of those groups. I'm sure I don't need to tell you what an impact that will have on crime figures across the county. It's not just trafficking, sir. It's drug-importation, extortion, violent crime, all the way down the long tail of criminality to volume crime at street level.'

As expected, he was giving her his full and undivided attention. There was nothing like the promise of actually meeting a few Home Office targets to make a senior officer sit up and take note.

'Sounds as though you've got things under control,' he said.

'So I can offer Caro and Sam to assist with Op Vanguard, for now, and maintain an overview of the operation myself?'

'Agreed. Keep me updated, won't you?'

```
Email

Date:   Monday 4 November 2013

To:     Zoe ADAMS, FIB/Major Crime Analyst

From:   Brian TEMPLE, Special Branch Analyst

Re:     Phone analysis: phone obtained during Op
        Pentameter Raid

Dear Zoe,

Further to our phone conversation this
morning, please find below an extract from the
phone analysis carried out on the handsets
seized during the warrant on 31/10/2013 at 4
Carisbrooke Court, Briarstone. You mentioned
that your interest was particularly in the
```

handset recovered from Scarlett RAINSFORD, so I have only included the details of this phone and the numbers that have been in contact with it.

Black Nokia handset containing SIM card ending 891:

This phone was in the back pocket of a female who identified herself to officers as Katie SMITH and was subsequently identified as Scarlett RAINSFORD DOB 11/02/1988. Downloads were made of the handset and call data obtained for the period 01/09/13 to 31/10/13.

[Analyst's note: this timeframe was standard for all the phones seized during the Op Pentameter warrant.]

Summary of findings in relation to 891:

Incoming and outgoing calls on a daily basis; the phone is in regular use although SMS is rarely used. Identified numbers called by or calling this phone include numbers ending:

498

This number has been attributed to Nigel MAITLAND DOB 17/12/1958 (associated with Organised Crime Group 041 – McDONNELLs, whose primary criminality is trafficking). There is a single call from 498 to 891 on 04/09/13 at 19:45, duration 45 seconds. There is no SMS contact between the two phones.

512

Activity between 891 and this number begins 25/09/2013; none before this date. There is one incoming call from 512 to black Nokia 891, placed on 25/09/2013 at 11:45

(duration 23 seconds), followed by two outgoing ones from 891 to 512, at 12:19 (duration 3 minutes 45 seconds) and 21:49 (duration 15 minutes 12 seconds). Regular outgoing calls are made to 512, approximately one per week, during October, lasting between 4 and 12 minutes. There is one incoming call from 512, on 25/10/2013 at 12:01 hours (duration 21 minutes). There is one incoming call on 30/10/2013 at 23:55hrs (duration 50 seconds). No SMS contact between numbers 891 and 512.

424

This number is believed to be in use by Victor RAMOS DOB 14/01/1971, with warnings for violence, weapons and drugs. Intelligence has indicated RAMOS is a regular visitor to brothels in Briarstone and Charlmere. There are three incoming calls to 891, on 03/09/13 (duration 4 minutes 3 seconds), 05/09/13 (duration 4 seconds) and 16/09/13 (duration 15 seconds). No SMS.

210

This number is attributed to Paul 'Reggie' STARK DOB 04/05/1982, although it is believed to be no longer in use (billings obtained for this number show no further activity after 25/09/13). Three outgoing calls were placed from black Nokia 891 to this number on 01/09 (duration 12 minutes 14 seconds), 14/09 (duration 3 minutes 1 second) and 19/09 (duration 2 minutes 50 seconds). Intelligence suggests STARK is also a regular frequenter of brothels in the area.

In addition to these contacts, there are a further 74 telephone numbers which remain unattributed.

Please do not hesitate to contact me if you
require anything further.

Kind regards

Brian

LOU – Monday 4 November 2013, 10:00

Juliette Rainsford was something of a surprise.

Caro Sumner, who had been watching the DVD recording of the
interview with Juliette from Rob Jefferson's office, beckoned Lou
over when she saw her coming into the briefing room. 'Watch this,'
she said.

The computer screen showed the interview room from two angles.
The main image was of a young woman wearing a pink turtle-neck
sweater which hugged a slender waist, a long, slim purple scarf
draped casually around her neck. Her dark hair was long, and loose,
twisted over one shoulder. Her arms were crossed but she was leaning back in her seat.

'Who's that?' Lou asked.

'It's Juliette,' Caro answered.

'She's not what I expected.'

'Me neither. I suggested to DI Jefferson that he might need an
appropriate adult for her. He asked me why. I said that Clive and
Annie had always given me the impression that she had some learn-
ing difficulties. Then he showed me this. Listen.'

Caro turned up the volume on the speaker so that they could both
hear what was being said. Lou shut the office door to avoid disrupt-
ing the incident room outside.

'. . . they don't go out very often,' Juliette was saying, in a calm, even voice. 'Maybe once every few months. They usually call it their "date night", which always makes me laugh; I mean, it's not as though they're teenagers. This one was because Dad wanted to cheer Mum up, though. She'd been in a bit of a state, you know, with the burglary.'

'You didn't mind them going out, and leaving you alone?'

'They wanted me to go with them but I told them I'd rather stay in. I was looking forward to a bit of peace, to be honest. Mum had been crying all day.'

Caro turned the sound down again. 'See what I mean?'

'Clive and Annie went to great lengths to keep her away from us,' Lou said. 'That makes me really curious to know why.'

'Maybe they just wanted to protect her,' Caro said, 'having lost one daughter. Anyway, I've still got my concerns about her. She was in a bit of a state when she came in, crying and upset. Then she calmed down, and she's been stable ever since. It might be the shock of finding her parents like that.'

'You interviewed her at the time of the abduction, Caro,' Lou said. 'Was she like this then?'

'She was upset, in tears most of the time. We went really easy on her because she was thirteen when Scarlett went missing. If you'd asked me then if she was vulnerable, I would have said yes. When we weren't interviewing her she was always reading some book or other. She never voluntarily interacted with anyone.'

'She seems quite relaxed about everything now, doesn't she? Considering she's just found her parents dead?'

'Quite.'

SAM – Monday 4 November 2013, 10:30

Sam was watching Scarlett's face.

It had been a while since she'd had to deliver a death message, and this one had been more dramatic than any she'd previously had to impart. Not a road traffic accident, not a heart attack at work: Scarlett's parents had been brutally attacked. Sam had no idea how Scarlett might react, so she had taken her out to the car, which was the most private place she could find at short notice, turned to face her and told her the news.

Silence.

Scarlett's face coloured, her mouth slightly open. Then she looked away. In a small voice, she said, 'What about Juliette?'

'She found them this morning. She's fine, Scarlett. Would you like to see her?'

Scarlett nodded, turning slowly to face the windscreen. Sam waited a moment, then turned on the ignition and pulled out of the parking space.

The silence as they drove the five miles into the town centre was unnerving. Sam had almost expected tears, but this time Scarlett hadn't been tearful, or even showing any emotion other than a degree of anxiety. It had been a pity, almost, to end the discussion between them that had been going so well – the likelihood of Scarlett feeling relaxed enough to continue where they had left off was now slim.

There would come a point when they would ask Scarlett to give a statement about her time in the brothel in Briarstone.

Sam took Scarlett in via the front desk, left her to wait there and headed into the main office. And then breathed out. She phoned Lou straight away.

'I've got Scarlett waiting at the front counter,' she said. 'I'm afraid I had to tell her.'

Lou sounded as though she was in a hurry. 'I'm on my way,' she said. 'Can you meet me in the canteen?'

10:40

Ten minutes later they were sitting at a table in the corner in the restaurant on the top floor of the police station, coffees in front of them. There was a rumour that the canteen would be going soon, following the bar next door, which had closed down months ago. If she was honest, Sam could see that the bar had been an anachronism and there was no justification for their employers to be seen to be encouraging alcohol consumption in the workplace, but she had still been sad to see it go. The bar had been the scene of so many leaving parties, so many birthdays and retirements, it held many happy memories – as well as being a safe place to finish your shift with a pint or two, rather than the bars and pubs in town. How many other workplaces had their own bar? Not many, these days, Sam thought. So the bars in police stations across the country, and even the one at Headquarters, had gradually closed down, and now the canteens were starting to go too.

'So tell me,' Lou said, grimacing. 'How did she take the news?'

'She looked shocked,' Sam said. 'And then she asked about Juliette. That was about it – she's barely said a word since then. How is Juliette? Have we got an appropriate adult for her?'

Lou smiled. 'I'll tell you all about that in a minute. First, though – I've managed to get you and Caro assigned to Rob Jefferson's team for Clive's murder. I'll get you briefed properly when we have a

362

chance, but for now I can tell you that this job is linked to Carl McVey.'

Sam nearly choked on her coffee. 'You're kidding? How?'

'Shoe mark found in the garden at Russet Avenue matches the one we got from the woodland where McVey was killed. Lots more forensics on this one, too, so you never know, we might be able to clear up our job as well.'

'Right. Is there anything in particular you want me to focus on?'

'Get Caro involved in the interviewing. I've asked Rob if you can be the one in charge of the interview strategy.'

'Scarlett's here thinking she's going to be meeting up with Juliette. I'm taking it that Juliette's not under arrest? Do you think she's up to seeing Scarlett?'

'I would imagine so,' Lou said. 'I'd like to watch the camera footage when it happens. Come up to the incident room when you're done; you can watch Juliette's interview from this morning.'

10:55

'Scarlett? Sorry I've been so long.'

In fact it had only been about twenty-five minutes; nevertheless Sam had almost expected Scarlett to have done a runner. But she was sitting on one of the chairs with her knees up, picking at the cuff of her shirt. Jo's shirt. The front counter was mercifully quiet for a Monday morning.

'Are you ready to see Juliette?'

Scarlett stood up awkwardly. 'How is she?'

Sam smiled. 'She seems very well, under the circumstances. My colleagues have been interviewing her about what happened last night, but they're having a break for now. I'll take you to see her.'

Sam swiped her access card at the door that led beyond the reception area to the rest of the police station, and held the door open for Scarlett. Walking down the corridor towards the interview rooms, she noticed a sudden spark of alarm cross Scarlett's face. She was nervous. That was interesting. Sam smiled at her.

'I'll be right outside if you need me. Unless you want me to sit in?'

'No, no,' Scarlett said. 'It'll be okay. Thanks.'

Sam opened the door to the interview room. Inside, the girl in the pink sweater was waiting with Jan Baker, the FLO. Sam had time to take in Juliette's expressionless blue eyes, the crossed, protective arms. She was smaller than Scarlett and Sam had a moment to consider how strange this whole meeting was. Ten years was a long time for both of them.

She stood aside. Scarlett's face crumpled when she caught sight of her sister, and the two women rushed into an embrace. Over Juliette's shoulder Sam saw Scarlett's eyes, screwed tight shut, and the tears falling from them. Noticed the whiteness of Scarlett's knuckles, her hands clenched into fists: one fist in Juliette's hair, the other pressed into her back.

LOU – Monday 4 November 2013, 11:00

'Sam? Are you okay?'

It had taken Sam several minutes to walk the corridor and climb the stairs between the interview room and the incident room. Her cheeks were flushed.

She nodded but Lou wasn't convinced. She ushered her into the office and shut the door behind her. 'What is it? What's wrong?'

'I'm fine,' Sam said.

Lou waited.

Sam wiped a finger under one eye, looked at it. Composed herself, took a deep breath in. 'It's Scarlett. Seeing her and Juliette just kind of affected me more than I thought it would, that's all. She's been through such a lot, Lou. I get this – feeling – like she's so brave, so strong, and she's only just holding it together.'

'Oh, Sam. She's really got to you, hasn't she?'

'I'm fine, honest. It's not a problem or anything.'

'Did she tell you anything useful for the Op Pentameter team this morning?'

'No – I was getting to that point when she indicated she was ready to see her family, which kind of precipitated me telling her. I'm wondering now if she said that as a distraction, because the next bit is too traumatic for her to talk about.'

'Or because that's the part that's going to incriminate her?'

Sam looked up. 'Incriminate her? For what, exactly?'

Lou's tone was even. 'I don't know. It's just that she seems to be extremely successful at avoiding answering some very simple questions. She seemed afraid when we first saw her in the VVS, but we haven't seen any evidence that she's in danger, have we?'

'Are you saying you think she's lying about where she's been all these years?'

'I'm not saying that at all. Sam, do I need to have any concerns about you losing your objectivity?'

Sam looked away. 'No,' she said quietly.

'That's not what's happening?'

No reply, this time.

'Sam . . .' Lou said, her tone consoling, 'I know what you've been through recently. With Jo, and everything that happened. I'm aware that you're potentially vulnerable—'

'I'm not vulnerable at all!' Sam said, biting back at last. 'I'm working my backside off as I always do. If you think I'm not doing a good job, say so.'

'It's not that. You're doing an amazing job. I trust you, Sam, because you know what you're doing and you get results. I just want you to know that I care, that's all. And you're human, same as the rest of us.'

'If anything, what happened to Jo has made me even more worried about getting too involved. In fact I've been thinking of very little else. So no, I'm not losing my objectivity. I know exactly what I'm doing.' Sam's cheeks were pink, and she'd not made eye contact with Lou since the word 'concerns' had been thrown into the conversation. 'Can I go?'

'Of course.'

Sam shut the door behind her firmly as she left. Lou breathed out. Sam was the closest thing she had to a best friend, but the fact remained that, on work time, Lou was Sam's line manager, and the welfare of her officers was always her priority. In any case, there was no more time to worry about it. Lou picked up the phone and dialled Rob Jefferson's mobile.

'I'm heading back to the incident room,' he told her. 'Just been in the CCU checking on that download from the phone they found in the Volvo.'

'Any good?'

'Yes, Zoe's dealing with the data now. Do you want me to come to your office?'

'No, don't worry, Rob. I'm in the MIR. See you there in a minute?'

Sam was sitting on the bench in the Lawrence Carroll memorial garden outside the canteen. It was less a garden and more a square of turf enclosed by a foot-high box hedge, a circular flowerbed in the centre which would be full of daffodils and tulips by spring, but which for now was bare except for the layer of rotting leaves. It wasn't exactly private, but, short of getting in her car and driving away, there were not many options for a breath of fresh air and a five-minute think.

Not private at all, as it turned out, because a moment later Caro Sumner came out of the side door and sat down next to her.

'I've hardly seen the DCI this morning,' Caro said, by way of an introduction.

'Everything's gone a bit crazy again,' Sam replied.

'Well, it makes sense. Are you okay?'

Sam looked up. 'Of course. Why?'

Caro gave her a gentle smile. 'You seem a bit . . . preoccupied. Tell me to mind my own, if you like. But I'm a good listener.'

Sam wouldn't have dreamed of telling Caro to 'mind her own', and yet she didn't especially feel like sharing Lou's concerns over her professionalism just yet, either. As a compromise, she said, 'I find it hard to stay detached sometimes. Don't you?'

'Definitely. And I don't always think staying detached is helpful. It's what makes us good at our jobs.'

That was it, exactly, Sam thought. There were procedures in place, professional standards that had to be maintained, and yet that didn't mean you weren't allowed to care about the people you interacted with. It was by developing empathy with people that you were able to understand them, get under their skin, establish the things they were trying to hide and then persuade them to bring those things out into the open. That sort of result couldn't be forced.

'I wasn't going to mention this,' Caro said then, 'but I used to work with Jo. Just for a couple of months, when she was covering for Trevor Harris in Knapstone.'

'Did you?' Sam said.

Jo had spent about three months working in Knapstone's custody suite, not long after they'd both transferred to Eden from the Met. As the new girl, she was being used as temporary cover whenever one of the civilian detention officers went off sick – it meant a lot of driving around, but then again she got to know all the custody suites in the county very quickly, as well as all the people that worked in them. Despite Knapstone being a long trek from Briarstone, Jo had enjoyed it more than any of her other taskings, until she'd got a permanent placement in Briarstone nick.

'Have you heard anything from her?' Caro asked.

Sam shook her head.

'Nothing at all?'

'I ring her mum from time to time, so I know she's all right.'

'She had a rough time of it,' Caro said.

Didn't we all? Sam thought.

And then, as if she could read Sam's thoughts, Caro said, 'I guess you had a rougher time than anyone, though . . . ' and she laid a hand comfortingly over Sam's, just for a moment. A warm touch, a gesture of sympathy.

' . . . and it's experiences like that which make us better police officers,' Caro added. 'That's what I keep telling myself, anyway. I think that's why you're the only one who seems to be able to get anything out of Scarlett.'

'What do you mean?' Sam asked.

'You're the only person she's spoken to. The *only* person.'

'She's hardly told me anything,' Sam said. 'And I get the impression that what I'm getting out of her is a very strictly edited version of the truth. I mean, it might be that the recent past is even more painful for her to think about, let alone tell to a stranger ...'

'Is that what you're thinking?'

Sam paused for a moment, thinking. Then she admitted, 'No. I don't think that. I think she's playing us. Or me, specifically.'

'Why?'

'I don't think it's anything personal. I think she is just used to trying to gain advantage wherever she can get it. She's used to thinking quickly and adapting to situations. She's survived the last ten years and she's done it by being clever. That doesn't necessarily mean she's guilty of anything. It just means ... it's going to take a different approach to get her to open up, that's all.'

Caro got to her feet. 'I hope Lou Smith realises how lucky she is to have you on her team, Sam.'

Sam gave a short laugh. 'She's brilliant to work for,' she said. *Most of the time.*

'Let's go back, shall we?' Caro said cheerfully. 'They're watching the DVD of Juliette's interview. I think you should take a look – it's quite a surprise.'

LOU – Monday 4 November 2013, 11:10

Rob Jefferson and Lou were watching the rest of the interview DVD in silence when Sam and Caro came in. Rob was sitting at his desk in the incident room, Lou looking at the screen over his shoulder.

The young woman in the pink sweater was hunched over, her head buried in her arms.

'What's going on?' Caro asked.

'She's crying again,' Rob said. 'She doesn't say much after this – another two minutes and Sam brings Scarlett in.'

'Rob's asked the forensic nurse practitioner to meet with her before the next session,' Lou added.

Just as the DVD finished, Zoe Adams came into the incident room.

'How's it going?' Lou asked.

'Slowly,' Zoe said. 'I've got Clive's and Annie's phone data through now, along with the data from the handset we recovered in the car. I had a reply from SB too, haven't had a chance to look at that yet. It's going to take a while to go through it all.'

'What have you got on the phone in the car?' Rob asked.

'Unfortunately there isn't any immediate indication as to who that phone might belong to – no finger marks, no helpful images or address book entries labelled "home" – but there's plenty of call traffic. And I've got a few useful things to start off with.'

'What's that?' Rob asked.

'The SIM card is a Pay As You Go, of course. But looks as if it might be one of a series of SIMs that was probably a bulk purchase. We've had almost consecutive numbers turn up in phones discarded by members of the Cunningham network. This particular number isn't directly in sequence – the number ends in 512 – and we've had 522, 523, 528 and 529 turn up over the past six months. It's just possible that the sequence starts earlier than we realised.'

'Which makes it likely that the phone was in use by one of Cunningham's lot,' said Rob.

'It's possible,' agreed Zoe. 'When I do the analysis I'll make sure all the latest numbers we've got for that network are put in for comparison with the call data.'

'What do you think, Rob? Do you think one of Cunningham's runners is also into car key burglaries and doorstep muggings? Anyone you can think of?'

Rob Jefferson frowned. 'Not off the top of my head, but you know what the street-level dealers are like. They'll get money wherever they can – burglaries, robberies, muggings. I wouldn't be surprised if it's one of them.'

'What about the cellsite data?' Lou asked.

'Not massively helpful. Whoever used the phone didn't go outside Briarstone very much. The home cell – that is, the one where calls start from every morning and end up at last thing at night – it's at the back of the Park Hill estate. Over a thousand homes, and where most of Briarstone's criminal fraternity live. I'm concentrating on the call traffic from the past few days.'

'Well – it's a good start,' Lou said. 'Hopefully you should get a better idea about whose phone it is from the data.'

'We've got a good chance of some DNA on the hoodie they found in the car, too,' Rob said. 'Going to be a while, though – even prioritising it.'

'Do you need any help on the analytical front, Zoe? Want me to see if I can get you an extra pair of hands?'

'No,' Zoe said, 'it's fine. It'll take some time but it's not the sort of thing you can really delegate. Thanks, though.'

'When's the next briefing?' Lou asked Rob.

'Four,' he said. 'Probably won't be much we can add by then, so don't worry about attending if you're busy, but we can update Late Turn. And then I'll do another proper briefing tomorrow morning.'

'Great,' Lou said. 'I'm going to catch up on a few bits – I'll see you later.'

```
Email

Date:  4 November 2013

To:    DCI Lou SMITH

From:  PSE Jason MERCER

Re:    Re: Crime series

Hi,

There are two car key burglary series at the
moment; let me know if you need the spreadsheet
of offences.
```

Op Sausage

```
Car key burglaries in Baysbury, Catswood and
Briarstone

13 offences since August 2013

MO: levering rear window (3 offences),
conservatory (4 offences) or back door (6
offences). Believed vehicles are parked up in a
residential area and left for a couple of days
before being removed. 2 vehicles recovered.
Remainder still missing

Tool marks left at scene

Temporal: overnight, most offences Wednesday to
Friday (10 offences)

Property: cash, mobile phones, laptops, high-
```

value vehicles from driveway (Audis, BMWs and
Range Rovers all less than 2 years old)

Suspects: none

OIC: DC Colin HARWOOD

Op Nomad

Car key burglaries in Briarstone

6 offences between March and September (last
offence 27 September)

MO: front uPVC door levered

Temporal: overnight, no preferred day

Property: vehicles only, all 4x4s

Suspects: none

OIC: DC Colin HARWOOD

Op Nomad is likely to be closed at the next
Tasking & Co-ordination Group meeting on
Thursday.

Hope this helps,

Jason

LOU – Monday 4 November 2013, 12:50

Back in her office, Lou checked her emails. Jason had replied to her
request on Sunday about the burglary crime series. On that impulse
she picked up the phone and dialled his direct number.

'Hi,' he said, when he answered. Surprise in his voice – her number would have shown on the caller ID.

'Hi, Jason,' she said, her tone businesslike. 'I wonder if you could help me out with something else.'

'Sure, if I can,' he said. 'What's up?'

'I was wondering if you could do me another profile. Can you have a look for the latest intel on the Cunningham OCG? Current links to other networks, that kind of thing – and specifically anything outside their usual criminality, i.e. not drugs-related?'

There was a brief pause at the other end of the line. 'I'm pretty tied up with things right now,' he said. 'Is it urgent?'

'I wouldn't be asking if it wasn't,' she replied.

'I'll see what I can do,' he said. 'Bye for now.'

MG11 WITNESS STATEMENT

Section 1 – Witness details

NAME:	Samantha ROWDEN-KNOWLES		
DOB (if under 18; if over 18 state 'Over 18'):	Over 18		
ADDRESS:	Longshaw Cottage Queens Drive Briarstone	OCCUPATION:	Secondary school teacher

Section 2 – Investigating Officer

DATE:	4 November 2013
OIC:	DS 10194 Samantha HOLLANDS

Section 3 – Text of Statement

My name is Samantha ROWDEN-KNOWLES and I work as a teacher at Briarstone Grammar School. I have been employed at this school since 2001, and for two years Scarlett RAINSFORD was a pupil in my tutor group. Although she could be challenging she was exceptionally intelligent and I got on well with her. The whole school was devastated by her disappearance in August 2003 and I was very upset at the thought of something terrible happening to one of my pupils.

On 3 November 2013 at approximately 21:30 Scarlett RAINSFORD knocked on my door. I was shocked when she told me who she was, and it was only then that I recognised her. I took her inside and made her a hot drink and some food. We spent some time talking about where she had been. She told me she had been abducted in Greece and forced to work as a prostitute in various cities in Europe, and that she had recently managed to escape and return to England. However she told me she was afraid because some men were after her and asked if she could stay at my house. I told her no but I offered to help her find somewhere safe to stay. She told me she had made friends with a detective whom she trusted and asked if I could take her to her address. I agreed to this and I took her to an address in Briarstone at approximately 23:30 that same evening. I left Scarlett with DS Sam HOLLANDS shortly afterwards and I have not seen her since then.

Section 4 – Signatures

....
WITNESS: (S Rowden-Knowles)

....
OIC: (Samantha Hollands DS 10194)

Email

Date: 4 November 2013

To: DCI Louisa SMITH

From: PSE Jason MERCER

Re: Recent Intel on CUNNINGHAM OCG

Further to your request for a subject profile on the CUNNINGHAM OCG (OCG 233), please note that there is insufficient recent intelligence to produce a full document. Three recent intel reports are summarised below but contrary to your request are all drugs-related.

09/09/13 (B/4/4)

Darren CUNNINGHAM DOB 12/11/1976 is expecting a delivery of drugs soon.

16/09/13 (B/4/4)

Darren CUNNINGHAM DOB 12/11/1976 is expecting a delivery of several kilos of cocaine. It is believed the drugs will be received over the night of 19/20 September 2013.

23/09/13 (B/4/4)

Darren CUNNINGHAM DOB 12/11/1976 was expecting to take delivery of cocaine in the past few days. Something went wrong with this delivery and the drugs were not received.

Regards,

Jason

LOU – Monday 4 November 2013, 16:27

Lou was bulk-deleting emails and almost deleted Jason's email by accident. He'd sent it ten minutes earlier, when she'd been in the briefing with Rob Jefferson. House-to-house had been completed, with no positive results. The briefing was over quickly and the next one scheduled for tomorrow morning.

She scanned through the email and the attachment, then reached for the phone.

It rang for a while before he answered.

'Lou,' he said. 'I was just on my way out.'

She looked up at the clock on the other side of the room. It was nearly half-past four. 'Sorry,' she said, wondering whether he had hockey practice this evening. 'Not much on the Cunninghams, is there? I'm surprised.'

'There are a few more – stopchecks and associations. But you said you just wanted the stuff on any criminal activity that wasn't drug distribution, right?'

'Well – yes. I suppose so,' Lou said, thinking it wouldn't have killed him to be a bit more thorough. Oh, well. 'I guess I can look the rest up myself. Anyway, thank you for the report.'

'You're welcome,' he said, 'although you know I can't keep doing you favours.'

Lou bristled. 'I wasn't aware I was asking you for a favour,' she said.

'You have Zoe Adams working on that job,' he said. 'She's a great analyst, and when you asked if she needed any help she rightly told you she didn't. So I'm not sure why you asked me to do the report and not her.'

Lou stood up. This wasn't a conversation that would be helped in any way by her being seated. 'Zoe Adams has a lot of urgent things to do,' she said coldly. 'I asked you to do something that's part of your job. If you were too busy to do it, you could have just said so. I'd appreciate it if you would be honest in future if you don't feel able to help.'

'Hey, I just don't want to feel like I'm your tame analyst for the rest of my life, because we have a relationship.'

Lou took a deep breath. 'Well, I'm glad you've made your feelings on that subject so crystal clear.'

'Don't be like that,' he said. 'This isn't personal.'

'You're the one who just made it personal,' she said. But the fight had gone out of her.

'I'm sorry,' he said. 'It feels like I keep making things worse.'

'Yes,' she said. 'That's exactly what you're doing. I don't even know why I'm still speaking to you.'

'If it's any good,' he said, 'I just found another intel report that might be of some use. It's still about drugs, though, sorry.'

He hadn't just done the minimum, then. At least he'd carried on looking. 'Oh, really? Why was it not with the others?'

'I think it got missed because someone has spelled "Cunning-ham" wrong, and they created a duplicate nominal. I'll email it to you.'

'Right,' she said. And, grudgingly, 'Thanks.'

'I'll call you in the morning,' he said, 'in case there's anything else you need.'

'Don't bother,' she said, but with a smile now. 'I'll find myself another tame analyst.'

A few moments later, her email server pinged.

Intel Report on Darren Cummingham

5x5x5 Intelligence Report

Date: 23 September 2013

Officer: PC 12241 BACK

Subject: Darren CUMMINGHAM DOB 12/11/1976

Grading: B / 4 / 1

There is a feud developing between Darren CUMMINGHAM
(OCG 233) and the McDONNELL group (OCG 041). This
started because one of CUMMINGHAM's runners was warned
off for dealing in one of the pubs controlled by the
McDONNELLs. CUMMINGHAM is not happy and is getting
Paul STARK to sort it out for him.

(Research shows: Paul STARK aka Reggie DOB 04/05/1982,
Lewis McDONNELL DOB 21/10/1953, Harry McDONNELL
DOB 06/07/1956)

LOU – Monday 4 November 2013, 17:02

Even though she was the last one in the incident room, Lou still felt
a twinge of guilt when she shut down her workstation and rooted
through her bag for her car keys. She didn't usually finish this early
when a new job had come in, but it had been a long day and she
was shattered. Arguing with Jason didn't help. All her focus had
gone.

Five minutes later, sitting in stationary traffic in the one-way system, Lou remembered the other reason why she never left at this time. The misspelled intelligence Jason had found was twisting around inside her head. Something about it bothered her, and not just the sloppy work that had caused it to be misplaced on the database.

So the Cunningham OCG and the McDonnell OCG were in dispute – this was new. They'd never been in competition before. The McDonnells concentrated on trafficking; even importing drugs was only a sideline for them, and according to the intelligence most of the drugs they brought into the country went north, bypassing Eden altogether. Cunningham controlled the drugs market in Briarstone, everyone knew that, even the McDonnells – as far back as Lou could remember, they'd skirted around each other and didn't step on each other's toes. Didn't associate or collaborate, either, which had always been a good thing. But now they were in opposition, just because one of Cunningham's runners had been warned about dealing in a pub? There had to be more to it.

If the McDonnells were involved, the pub referred to was probably one of the pubs owned by Carl McVey – one of the intel reports had said he was money laundering for them – and Aaron Sutcliffe had said Palmer had been dealing in the Railway Tavern.

So the runner that had been warned off dealing in one of McVey's pubs – what if that had been Ian Palmer? Aaron Sutcliffe had told Les that Ian was dealing for either Cunningham or Mitchell Roberts, and everything they knew about Ian Palmer and his family suggested that if he was working for anyone it would be Cunningham. But that didn't explain why he'd ended up in hospital – even if he'd been dealing in McVey's pub, even if he'd been warned off – putting him in a coma seemed extreme, even for the McDonnell OCG.

By the time she got home, Lou's head was pounding with it.

Enough. It would keep, at least until she'd taken some painkillers and had a shower; perhaps then it would start to make sense.

But if that was it – if Palmer had been assaulted because he'd pissed off Carl McVey – it was possible that Cunningham had retaliated. Considering the level of violence involved, it seemed likely that the intel was right. There was a feud, a bad one; and it was escalating right on Lou's doorstep.

SAM – Monday 4 November 2013, 17:10

'I probably shouldn't be doing this,' Sam said.

'Doing what?'

'Giving you lifts everywhere.'

They were driving back to the hotel, without Juliette, who was going to be brought over later by Caro Sumner. They had managed to get authorisation to put Juliette up in the same hotel for tonight, since she clearly couldn't go home: it was still a crime scene and nobody was allowed anywhere near the house until that particular part of the investigation was complete. Sam had called through to the duty inspector in the control room to get authorisation for a second room at the Travel Inn. Halfway through an embarrassing discussion about budgets and cuts and why they couldn't share a room when they were sisters, Scarlett had interrupted and told Sam that she didn't mind sharing. Sam still felt uncomfortable about it, given that Scarlett and Juliette hadn't seen each other for years and were in the middle of a particularly stressful situation. But Scarlett did not seem bothered by the prospect; on the contrary, she seemed almost happy.

'Are you sure you don't want me to take you to the hospital instead, to see your mother?' Sam asked.

'No. She's unconscious – it's not like I can do anything, is it?'

'Right,' Sam said, 'if you're sure.'

'What's going to happen tomorrow?' Scarlett asked.

'Tomorrow?'

'With the hotel. You only got me two nights, didn't you? This is the last one.'

'You can still engage with the National Referral Mechanism, you know. If you've been trafficked, they can get you access to housing, all of that . . . '

'I can't do that,' Scarlett said quickly.

'All right. I'll speak to the boss in the morning about the hotel.'

'Honestly, it's fine about the sharing, if that helps at all. Juliette won't care.'

'How do you know?' Sam said.

Scarlett looked away, out of the window. 'If she does, I'm sure she'll tell you.'

They drove in silence for a few minutes. It had been a long day and Sam was more tired than she'd felt in years. All she could think about was whether there was something edible in the freezer at home, and whether she was going to cook it before or after falling asleep in a deep, warm bath.

The car park at the hotel was almost empty, the buildings huddled under the dark evergreen trees looking chilly and desolate.

'Come in for a drink with me,' Scarlett said.

'What?'

'Please. Just one. I can't face going in there on my own. Stay with me till Juliette gets here?'

'Scarlett, I really can't do this . . . '

'What have you got to rush home for?' Scarlett said.

'Scarlett, no. It's not a good idea.'

382

'Please. I just … I really need someone to talk to. Please, Sam.'

There was something about her voice that got to Sam. It wasn't vulnerability.

'All right,' she said. 'One drink.'

There was nobody in the bar. Not even anyone serving, until Sam went into the reception area and asked if they were actually open. A few minutes later the receptionist came in and got Scarlett a pint of lager and a lemonade for Sam.

Scarlett was already sitting in the corner, a pair of comfy chairs to one side of a cold, dead fireplace. 'Cheerful in here, isn't it?'

'Could be worse,' Sam replied, then saw Scarlett's expression. They both laughed.

Sam sat down, trying to not let Scarlett see that her cheeks were flushed. She had had a sudden, worrying realisation that Scarlett was flirting with her. Maybe this was what Lou had sensed, when she had accused Sam of letting her objectivity be compromised. It wasn't. Whatever Scarlett wanted, Sam was definitely not going down that route. Getting too involved with a witness had cost Jo her job, her wellbeing and her relationship with Sam – whether it was a homeless young asylum-seeker or Scarlett, it wasn't a good idea. Well, it didn't matter, anyway. Tomorrow Scarlett would have to find somewhere else to go, with her sister, and in a few weeks the likelihood would be that they would no longer be any of Sam's concern.

'Listen,' Scarlett said, 'there's something I need to tell you.'

'Go on,' she said.

'It's not that I've lied, or anything like that.'

Here we go. 'Scarlett,' Sam said, 'if this is something serious – we should go and do it properly.'

'No, no,' she said. 'You don't need to worry. I just need to clear something up.'

'Right.'

There was direct eye contact between them. Scarlett's eyes, so like her mother's. 'I like you,' she said. 'I want to tell you everything. And it feels like you've got things a bit wrong somewhere.'

'How do you mean?'

'I wasn't trafficked back into the UK. I made my own way here.'

Well, Sam thought, that explained a lot. And nothing at all. 'How?'

'I managed to get away. It's a long story. But anyway, nobody brought me here against my will. So I can't give you any information about trafficking, and I can't help you, so there's no point in me accessing any "referral mechanism", is there?'

'So you were in that house in Carisbrooke Court of your own free will?'

'Yes, I guess so.'

'You guess so?'

'I didn't have anywhere else to go. They let me stay there. I answered the phone, did cleaning, went on errands, that sort of thing. It was better than being on the streets.'

'Why were you afraid, Scarlett? If they weren't keeping you there against your will?'

'I was scared someone would think I'd grassed them up,' she said.

'Who?'

'Any of them. The girls, the men that run them, the punters. It's not the sort of place you can develop much trust.'

'Who are the men that run the girls?'

Scarlett said, 'I don't know who they are. They kept away, used runners to collect the money.'

'Okay. Who are the runners?'

Scarlett watched her for a moment. 'Look, I don't know their real names. Nobody uses their real names, do they? I didn't. I was called Katie.'

'You said something about a Reg to me, on Friday. You said something like, you had friends, you could have been sitting on Reg's sofa watching Sky TV. So who's Reg?'

'Are you interrogating me now?' Scarlett said, smiling.

'You said you wanted to be honest with me, Scarlett. Stop playing games.'

'I said I had something to tell you, and I've said it. I'm not playing games. Much as I like playing games with you.'

Sam decided she was going to ignore that last bit. 'Why didn't you tell us before that you were there willingly?'

'Because I thought if I told you I was just working there, you'd arrest me for something. Or else you'd realise I wasn't of any use to you and I'd be out on the streets with nowhere to go.'

'Why not go back to your family? Why have you been here in Briarstone and not gone to see them, to tell them you were alive and well?'

Scarlett looked away, as if considering her response. 'I'm not exactly their idea of a model child, am I?'

'Whatever you think you are, you're still their daughter . . . ' Sam stopped, realising that Scarlett was now on the verge of being an orphan.

'It's been a long time,' Scarlett said. 'I needed time to get my act together, think about what I was going to do with my life. I've had . . . I've had some pretty rough days. I don't sleep well. As you've seen, my family was never what you'd call loving, and it doesn't look to me as though they've changed much.'

'Scarlett,' Sam said, 'what do you think happened to them last night?'

Scarlett hesitated. 'No idea. You said it was a robbery, didn't you?'

Sam said nothing.

'Well, maybe it was linked to that burglary. Maybe whoever it was wanted something, and they came back and got disturbed. I don't know. I know you think I should be sorry, that I should care more about it, but these people are like strangers to me, Sam. It's Juliette I'm worried about. She can't cope with things like this.'

Sam took a deep breath in, trying to give nothing away. 'Juliette seems to be doing all right so far. Do you want another drink?'

'Yes, please. Another pint.'

Sam still had half of her lemonade to drink, but she got up and called through the back of the bar to the reception desk.

18:40

'I really need to go home.'

'Yeah, I know.' Scarlett was finishing her second pint. 'Thanks for staying.'

'Juliette will be here any minute, I bet. Caro's bringing her.'

'Sure.'

'I'll come and get you tomorrow morning,' Sam said. 'I need to get a proper statement out of you.'

'What sort of statement?'

'It's fine,' Sam said. 'It won't take long. It's just the same thing Juliette's been doing with Caro and the family liaison officer.'

Sam pulled her jacket on and Scarlett, arms crossed, walked with her to the porch.

'Don't stay out here getting cold,' Sam said. Scarlett was following her out to the car.

'I'm not cold,' she said in reply. 'Sam ...' Without warning, Scarlett moved closer, put her hand on Sam's cheek. Sam pulled back immediately.

'No,' she said, 'don't.'

'You don't mean that,' Scarlett whispered. 'Come back inside with me.'

They were standing just outside the hotel entrance. It was dark out here, cold.

'Scarlett, this isn't going to happen.' Sam said.

'I feel safe with you,' Scarlett replied. 'Please, Sam. You make me feel safe for the first time in my life.'

'I'm sorry,' Sam said. 'I really can't.'

She took another step back, turning back towards her car to see with a sudden shock that Caro was there, with Juliette following behind her.

18:55

'That wasn't what it looked like,' Sam said.

Caro smiled at her. 'None of my business,' she said cheerfully.

Sam was walking her back to her car. Juliette had been checked in to Scarlett's room and they had gone off together, peacefully enough. The hotel receptionist had knocked off early and been replaced by a security guard who was former Job. Caro recognised him and there had been a bit of banter about who had retired and what they'd ended up doing.

While all this hilarity had been going on, Sam had been standing awkwardly behind Caro wondering if Caro had any idea what had just happened.

Caro had ended the trip down Memory Lane with Steve by asking him to keep an eye on the women in Room 116 and to call her immediately if anything untoward happened.

'Right you are,' he'd said, pocketing her card.

It was cold and dark outside and everything felt ominous to Sam. 'Seriously, Caro. I know I should report it – but she's just confused. Her emotions are all over the place.'

Caro stopped and turned to face her. 'You know what you're doing,' she said. 'I won't say anything. Lord knows I've been in awkward situations.'

Sam said nothing.

'Oh, you daft mare! Come here.' Caro pulled her into a big, comforting hug. 'Don't worry. It'll all be all right in the morning. And we have work to do, don't we?'

'Thank you,' Sam said.

'You want me to pick her up tomorrow, along with Juliette?'

'That would be great, thanks. I'll see you down the nick after?'

'I'll ring you when I've got them there.'

When Sam got back to her own car she sat in silence for a moment, watching Caro's car turning, the headlights swinging round across the front of the hotel, then her tail-lights as she drove out of the car park. She looked across to the hotel entrance, as if she expected to see Scarlett running out of it, but the hotel was quiet and still.

Sam turned on the ignition and drove slowly out of the car park towards home.

She was just turning on to her driveway when her phone bleeped. The message was from a number she didn't recognise – 07101 405441. And yet it looked familiar . . .

Sorry I didnt want to get you into trouble. I like you.
Please dont worry. S xx

She stared at the message for a long time. There was nothing she could reply. Eventually she hit 'save to contacts' and in the box for First Name typed 'Spare phone'.

LOU – Monday 4 November 2013, 23:55

After an hour of lying awake, Lou got up and went back downstairs to the kitchen. Cocoa had never helped her sleep before but it was worth a try, and besides, she'd forgotten to eat anything so her stomach was rumbling.

There was a danger in going to bed with an investigation churning around in your head like this, Lou thought as she waited for the milk in the pan to heat through. When it got late and you'd been busy all day without a break, there was a point when the logic became malleable and you could end up coming to all sorts of conclusions. And, in the cold light of day, things that had seemed not only probable but even incontrovertible fact suddenly looked rather foolish.

Usually Lou was quite good at switching off. Even though she didn't come home to a family every evening, it felt natural to leave work behind at her front door and she never found it hard to forget about it all, even for a few hours. But this felt different. There was something she was missing, she thought, rhythmically stirring a spoon of cocoa together with a little milk and some sugar, something that was *right there* – and she couldn't grasp it. Tomorrow she would meet with Rob Jefferson, review all the intelligence and see what they could come up with together. And then she would get Zoe

Adams or someone else to do her a proper network chart for the Cunningham OCG and see if that sparked anything.

If Jason had gone to hockey practice, he would be home by now. In fact he would more than likely be in bed.

The milk surged up in the saucepan and Lou caught it in time, pouring it into the mug. It didn't look particularly appetising but it would have to do. She took the cocoa back into the living room, curling up into the corner of her sofa and cupping her fingers around the mug. When she checked her phone, she saw that she had a text message from Jason, sent just six minutes ago.

I just got home. Hope your day wasn't too stressful.

Without thinking any further, she dialled his number.

'Hey,' he said. 'You still up?'

'I can't sleep,' she said. 'How was your practice?'

'It was okay. I'm sorry about earlier.'

'I've forgotten about that. In fact, I think you might well have helped clarify things.'

'That sounds ominous.'

Lou smiled. 'I didn't mean us. I meant the investigation.'

'Oh – hey, well that's good news.'

There was a little pause. Lou was waiting for him to ask if he could come over. She suspected he might also be waiting for her to ask him the same thing. In the end, he gave up first.

'So, are you doing anything tomorrow night?'

'I've got no plans,' she said. 'Just, you know, the usual ...'

'I know. I could make you dinner. The offer's there, you know, if you feel like it.'

'Thanks, Jason,' Lou said. 'Might see you tomorrow, then.'

'Goodnight, beautiful.'

The cocoa had cooled now so Lou drank it in one go. It was so sweet it made her teeth ache, but at least her stomach had something in there to quieten it. Better still, her thoughts had crystallised following that conversation, and as she cleaned her teeth for the second time she knew what it was that had been troubling her.

Reggie Stark.

First thing in the morning, she would look him up.

Part Seven

DEATH IS NEVER THE END

LOU – Tuesday 5 November 2013, 05:50

The MIR was quiet and in darkness when Lou got to work. It had been a long time since she'd been the first one in, but, having slept – eventually – she had been wide awake again at five.

She turned on the workstation in her office and went to get a coffee from the vending machine. Headquarters was stretching itself into life: corridors humming with vacuum cleaners, fluorescent lights blinking on from the offices across the other side of the smaller car park. Lou could hear a conversation going on from the stairwell – something about a 'top result' and a 'nice way to go out' – from which, taking into account the laughter that accompanied the exchange, she deduced a good arrest – or a judge's commendation – ahead of an imminent retirement.

The computer was patiently awaiting her log-in details, and a minute later she was into the intelligence database, putting in a search for Paul Stark, known as Reggie.

Seeing the name had reminded her of previous encounters with him, years ago, when she was working in CID. Back then Paul Stark had just graduated from nicking cars for fun and a little profit, and had moved on to metal theft, stealing cables from building sites and even, in the end, fully installed ones: down a manhole at one end of a rural road, cutting a cable, then down the manhole again at the other end with a cable drum ready to wind it all up and transport it away, leaving whole villages without landlines or internet. Paul Stark had had a brother, Ronnie Stark – hence Paul's nickname, the matching 'Reggie' – who had been electrocuted while trying to cut live cable.

Of course, it was too much to hope for that Reggie would take his brother's gruesome and tragic death as a sign that he should earn a living by safer, more legal means.

There were pages and pages of intelligence on him. Everything from what car he was driving to what the last argument with his girlfriend had been about. Most of it was about other people, with Reggie getting an honourable mention for being there during a stopcheck, for appearing on various nominals' phone records, for nicking a bottle of white rum from a corner shop, for shouting abuse at a kebab shop owner, for being a general pain in the backside.

This was where she needed an analyst.

Intel Reports on Paul Stark

5x5x5 Intelligence Report

Date: 09 August 2013

Officer: PC 9921 EVANS

Subject: Paul STARK DOB 04/05/1982, Lewis
            McDONNELL DOB 21/10/1953, Harry
            McDONNELL DOB 06/07/1956

Grading: B / 2 / 1

Paul 'Reggie' STARK has had a falling-out with the McDONNELLs. This is believed to be because he was 'sampling the goods' when he was supposed to be providing security for the brothel that Lewis McDONNELL operates from a property in Briarstone.

(Research suggests this may refer to the property in Carisbrooke Court, Briarstone.)

5x5x5 Intelligence Report

Date: 09 August 2013

Officer: PC 9921 EVANS

Subject: Paul STARK DOB 04/05/1982, Lewis
             McDONNELL DOB 21/10/1953, Harry
             McDONNELL DOB 06/07/1956

Grading: B / 2 / 4

Paul STARK has had a falling-out with the McDONNELLs. As
a result he is living in fear of reprisals from them.

5x5x5 Intelligence Report

Date: 21 August 2013

Officer: PC 9921 EVANS

Subject: Paul STARK DOB 04/05/1982,
             Lewis McDONNELL DOB 21/10/1953,
             Harry McDONNELL DOB 06/07/1956, Gavin
             PETRIE DOB 17/03/1975

Grading: E / 2 / 1

The McDONNELL brothers used Paul 'Reggie' STARK to
provide security until recently, when he became unreliable.
Since then they have been using Gavin PETRIE instead,
although the brothers see him as a 'loose cannon'.

5x5x5 Intelligence Report

Date: 3 September 2013

Officer: PC 9921 EVANS

Subject: Paul STARK DOB 04/05/1982, Lisa JACKSON
           DOB 01/06/1989

Grading: B / 2 / 1

WARNINGS: Officer Safety

Attended 14 Ambleside Crescent, Park Hill, H/A of Paul 'Reggie' STARK and Lisa JACKSON, for a welfare check on the premises as Lisa has not been attending meetings with her drugs counsellor. Lisa was not at home at the time. Of note is that STARK keeps a baseball bat to the right of the main front door (not the porch) and there is a samurai sword on a mount above the fireplace. STARK advised patrol that he keeps the bat handy as 'you never know who's going to turn up'. Suitable advice was passed to Mr STARK.

5x5x5 Intelligence Report

Date: 13 September 2013

Officer: PC 9921 EVANS

Subject: Paul STARK DOB 04/05/1982, Darren
           CUNNINGHAM DOB 12/11/1976, Ryan
           COLEMAN DOB 12/01/1990

Grading: B / 2 / 1

Paul 'Reggie' STARK has been associating with Darren CUNNINGHAM since August. It is believed that STARK has been debt-collecting for CUNNINGHAM, sometimes with Ryan COLEMAN.

5x5x5 Intelligence Report

Date: 24 September 2013

Officer: PC 9921 EVANS

Subject: Paul STARK DOB 04/05/1982, Lewis
McDONNELL DOB 21/10/1953, Harry
McDONNELL DOB 06/07/1956, Darren
CUNNINGHAM DOB 12/11/1976

Grading: B / 2 / 1

Paul 'Reggie' STARK is aware of the feud that is taking place
between the McDONNELL brothers and Darren
CUNNINGHAM. As he has been associating with
CUNNINGHAM, STARK is now concerned that he may
become a target.

SAM – Tuesday 5 November 2013, 07:20

'Sam? I'm glad you're here. Come and have a look at this.'

Sam had only been in the MIR a minute, hadn't taken off her jacket.

This morning there had been a series of texts from 'Spare phone',
most of them sent overnight.

00:19 – Hi sorry again abt what happened. Need to see u
to explain. Xx
01:42 – Cant sleep thinking abt u. Fucked everything up.
Feel bad. Xx
04:25 – Remember I said being alive again was hard?
This is the hardest thing. Wd be better to have stayed
dead LOL. Xx

Sam had tried calling when she'd woken up just before six, but there had been no reply. Scarlett must have fallen asleep at last.

Lou was in her office. When Sam came in, Lou was tapping her computer screen with the end of her pen. 'Look! What do you think?'

It didn't look much. Lou had copied the text of a number of intel reports, most of them about Paul Stark.

'What about him?' Sam asked. 'He's one of the Cunningham lot, isn't he? Ali and I saw him in the hospital; he'd been visiting Ian Palmer. Valerie said he'd been visiting him every day.'

'Was he now? That's interesting too. Just confirms it, confirms he's with the Cunninghams. But look, Sam, look who he was mates with before that.'

'The McDonnells?'

'And?'

'It's this bit that's interesting me. Look.'

Lou scrolled down the text until she got to one of the reports. 'This one was misfiled. Some numpty spelled "Cunningham" wrongly and they created a new nominal record for him, and didn't bother to link it to Stark's record either. Jason found it last night. Listen to this bit: "There is a feud developing between Darren Cummingham and the McDonnell group. This started because one of Cummingham's runners was warned off for dealing in one of the pubs controlled by the McDonnells. Cummingham is not happy and is getting Paul Stark to sort it out for him." What do you make of that?'

'Ian Palmer was the runner?'

'Of course he was.'

'Well, that would make sense.'

'There's more, Sam. This is where it gets really intriguing. Look at the other intel on Cunningham.'

400

Lou clicked on another document. Over Lou's shoulder, Sam saw the words 'Jason Mercer' and recognised it as a subject profile. The subject in question was Darren Cunningham.

Something about a drugs delivery.

'This one. Look at the date!' Lou said.

'The nineteenth and twentieth of September?' Sam said.

'Palmer was assaulted in the early hours of the twentieth of September. I think that's connected with what went wrong with Cunningham's delivery. Maybe Palmer was in charge of it.'

Sam raised an eyebrow. 'It's a pretty big leap. Even if Palmer was Cunningham's runner, would he be trusted with something that big?'

'I know, I know. But it's not just that. I've made another massive assumption. Hear me out. Look at this intel on Paul Stark. He keeps a baseball bat at home.'

Lou was counting it off on her fingers. Sam watched, remembering Lou banging on about Sam losing her objectivity yesterday.

'What if Cunningham loses his shipment that night, when he's put one of his dealers in charge of it? And that same person has pissed McVey off more than once. And something happens as a result of him being in that pub, and he's beaten into a coma in the process. Who's Cunningham going to suspect is the culprit? McVey – who happens to be associated with the McDonnells. Are you with me?'

'Okay ... and so Cunningham has McVey bumped off in revenge?'

'More than revenge. He wants his drugs back. And who is he going to give that job to? The new boy, who's just transferred allegiance from McDonnell's camp to his. The new boy who keeps a baseball bat at home for protection. What a test of loyalty.'

'Paul Stark,' Sam said.

Lou nodded. 'And McVey's found nine days later with serious

head injuries caused by being beaten with a blunt instrument. Like a baseball bat.'

'Have you spoken to Rob Jefferson yet?'

'Not yet – he's not come in. I need to catch him before the briefing. Can you start putting a search warrant together for me? We need his shoes and his bat before he gets rid of them. And I want Stark brought in for questioning. There's enough here.'

'Sure. I'll do it now.'

'Sam?'

Sam had turned to go, stopped in the doorway.

'How's everything going with Scarlett? Is she still in the hotel?'

'I dropped her off last night. Caro is going to bring her in with Juliette this morning. They're not booked in again for tonight, so we might need to find somewhere else for them, unless they can go back to the house. Though they might not want to, I guess.'

'Great. We'll sort something out if we need to. You know ... what I said yesterday ...'

'It's fine,' Sam said, taking a deep breath. 'I know what I'm doing. Jo made the mistake of getting too involved. I'm not about to fall down that particular hole.'

```
Email

Date:   5 November 2013

To:     DCI Louisa SMITH

From:   Zoe ADAMS

Re:     Op Vanguard - phone attributed to
        Scarlett RAINSFORD

See attached report as requested.
```

Please do not hesitate to contact me if you require anything further.

Kind regards

Zoe Adams

Senior Analyst, FIB and OCG Team

Since receiving the original data extract from SB of the download of the phone seized from Scarlett RAINSFORD DOB 11/02/1988 (ref: the number ending 891), I have run additional checks on the numbers featured in the spreadsheet attached and noted the following in the data from 891:

Briarstone 411924

This number has only recently been added to the database following Crime Report Number PZ/015567/13 – Burglary Dwelling at 14 Russet Avenue, Briarstone on the night of 2/3 November 2013, and so did not show up when Brian TEMPLE (SB analyst) completed his original report on the phone seized from Scarlett RAINSFORD (891).

This number has been entered on the database as the landline number of this address. There are regular incoming calls from this landline to 891, two or three a week during the period 01/09/2013 to 31/10/2013, with no particular pattern regarding days or times. Calls from 411924 to 891 are on two occasions immediately preceded by an unanswered call from 891

to 411924, suggesting that this may be some kind of pre-arranged signal to call back. Durations normally vary from 2 seconds to 50 seconds. On Friday 25 October at 12:25hrs there is an unanswered outgoing call made from 891 to 411924, followed a minute later by an incoming call lasting 14 minutes 55 seconds. (Of note: the unanswered call is immediately preceded by one of 21 minutes' duration received from number ending 512 – see separate phone analysis document for more details about this number.) There are
no calls after this, although it should be noted that the RAINSFORDs flew to Spain for their holiday on Monday 28 October, and the handset was seized from Scarlett RAINSFORD on 31 October.

SCARLETT – Tuesday 5 November 2013, 08:15

It was the strangest thing, waking up and hearing Juliette's breathing, steady and slow, coming from the bed next to her. It felt as though she had drifted off a few minutes ago, but she must have slept well because daylight was showing around the edges of the Travel Inn's blackout curtains.

At six, the mobile phone she had left charging under her coat, next to her side of the bed, had begun to buzz. She'd grappled for it, trying to silence it before it woke her sister. *One missed call* – the number was the only one she had stored in her phone. Sam's mobile. There was no message, no text, no response to all the messages Scarlett had sent last night when Juliette was asleep. What was Sam supposed to say, anyway? There was nothing she could say. She had a job to do.

Scarlett looked across at Juliette, who stirred and turned over. 'Juliette?' Scarlett whispered. 'You awake?'

There was a murmur that might have been agreement, but then the breathing deepened again. Scarlett looked at Juliette's watch. They would need to get up soon. They had to talk, had to work out a plan before Sam turned up. But for now she would let her sleep on while she could: today was going to be difficult enough to deal with.

Not for the first time, Scarlett wondered what would have

405

happened to them both if she'd never gone into the house in Russet Avenue that Tuesday in March.

'I knew you'd come back,' Juliette had said. 'I knew you'd come back for me.'

They were sitting at the kitchen table eating toast. It felt very domestic and civilised, and mind-bendingly strange. There had been tears at first, Juliette crying and holding on to her sister as if she would never let her go again. And then, quite suddenly, she had stopped.

She'd pointed at the clock in the living room. 'They'll be back soon; they won't be out for long. You can't be here when they get home.'

'Come with me,' Scarlett had said impulsively. Even as she said it, she'd thought how crazy it was to think like that. Was she going to take Juliette back to her tiny room in the flat? They had no money, no proper place to live.

But Juliette hadn't wanted to leave. 'No, I can't, I can't. It's all right, it's easier now. He doesn't bother with me so much any more; and I like being left alone. I can read in my room and get food when I feel like it, or watch films. Other people have to go out and get jobs, don't they? They don't want me doing something like that. As soon as I left school they never said anything more about it.'

Juliette hadn't asked anything about Scarlett. Where she'd been, what had happened to her, why she'd come back. Not that first day, nor on any subsequent visits. At first Scarlett, over-whelmed at seeing her sister again, didn't notice; later she found it hurtful. But it took time for them to find each other again, to fit back together. And, after all, there were plenty of other subjects they didn't discuss either: they didn't need to. For example, why

406

Scarlett waited until Clive and Annie went out before coming to see Juliette. It was just between the two of them, this bond, this understanding. The roles they had had once upon a time had changed and expanded, but at the core remained the same: Juliette knew what she wanted, was set in her ways. And Scarlett accommodated her.

Juliette moved again, stretched, sat up on the edge of the bed for a moment and then shuffled to the en-suite. Scarlett took advantage of the moment of privacy to get dressed. With the curtains open she felt more awake. She turned on the TV and the kettle, because she could hear Juliette crying in the bathroom. She had cried a lot last night too, had still been sniffing and trembling until she fell asleep. Nothing Scarlett said or did seemed to make a difference.

'All right, Jul?' Scarlett asked, when Juliette eventually unlocked the bathroom door and came back in. Scarlett had made them both tea, and it was getting cold.

Juliette mumbled something in reply, pulling on yesterday's socks.

'I know you're upset,' Scarlett said, 'but I wish we could talk.'

'Talk about what?' Juliette said. 'I want to go home. I want clean clothes. I don't like it here. Do you think they'll let me go home today?'

'Me', Scarlett thought. *Not 'us'* . . .

'I don't know.'

But Juliette's shoulders were shaking again and a second later she let out a loud, gasping sob. Scarlett went to sit next to her, to put her arms around her, but Juliette shrank back.

'Jul,' she said, 'it's okay. It'll be all right, I promise . . .'

'No,' Juliette wailed. 'It won't, it won't.'

'It will,' Scarlett persisted. 'We can start again, just you and me, it will be good. You won't need to worry about anything.'

Juliette said something then, and Scarlett thought she hadn't heard correctly. She said, 'What?' quietly, not really wanting it repeated but at the same time hoping she'd misheard.

And Juliette's voice, quiet, miserable, full of tears: 'I want my mum ...'

LOU – Tuesday 5 November 2013, 08:45

Lou was sitting in Rob Jefferson's office with Zoe Adams, waiting for the DI to get back from the morning meeting. If it hadn't already been going on for nearly half an hour, she would have gatecrashed it. As it was, everything would have to wait for the warrant, and Sam was busy putting the paperwork together.

'I could really do with a network chart,' Lou said. 'I know it takes a while. But I think that's the only way to see the links between all these individuals. And I'm sure you'd find more intel supporting it, especially given that some of our officers can't spell and don't seem to be able to link things up properly.'

'I'll get right on to it. I've finished the download analysis on the phone retrieved from the Volvo, anyway – I just need to email it out to you.'

'Thank you, Zoe. I'm sorry to throw all this at you.'

'Don't worry. It's my job, after all.'

That reminded her of her awkward conversation with Jason yesterday, and the likelihood that he'd had a conversation with Zoe about who was doing what and why Lou felt she had to pass extra work to another senior analyst who wasn't even connected with the investigation.

'Did you see that addendum to the previous phone analysis?' Zoe added.

'No,' Lou said.

'I sent it to you. Only about ten minutes ago, though. Some very interesting links there—'

Rob Jefferson came in, looking flustered. 'Sorry, sorry,' he said. 'You been waiting long?'

'No, you're fine. How's it going?'

'Lots of things coming in. What was it you wanted to discuss?'

Lou explained about Reggie Stark, summarising the intelligence. 'I'd really like Zoe to do me a network chart when she's got a minute. I think it will help to clarify things. In the meantime, I've got Sam Hollands doing us a warrant.'

'That's great, thanks. Let's hope that baseball bat is still tucked behind his door, and that it's got McVey's DNA on it.'

Zoe said, 'The phone analysis I've been doing supports everything you've just said, too. I'll leave you to read it, but basically it looks as if the phone in the burned-out Volvo can be attributed to Reggie Stark.'

'Can you copy the phone analysis in to Sam Hollands, Zoe?' Lou asked. 'Anything extra to go on the warrant will help.'

'Of course.'

'And Rob – can I leave it to you to get Tac Team tasked for the warrant?' Lou asked.

'Yep, no problem. Just give me the nod when it's ready. I'll go and see what the availability is now. Are you able to help with the briefing later? Helen Bamber can do the interview; I'll see who else is free to assist.'

409

Email

Date: 5 November 2013

To: DI 9055 Rob JEFFERSON

cc: DCI 10023 Louisa SMITH; DS 10194 Sam
        HOLLANDS

From: Zoe ADAMS

Re: Op Vanguard - Phone found in vehicle

Rob,

Following receipt of phone download data from
the CCU, please find attached the pertinent
information. Full spreadsheets of data
available on request.

Samsung handset containing SIM card ending 512

This phone was retrieved from a green Volvo S40
1.6S which was found alight and extinguished by
Eden Fire & Rescue Service at approximately
00:12 on 04/11/2013 (CAD 1104-0021 refers).
Downloads were made of the handset and call
data obtained for the period 01/09/13 to
04/11/13.

Summary of findings

Data for this number begins on 25/09/13. It is
likely that another phone was in use before
this (see note under 'Attribution', below).

Key numbers in contact with this phone include
numbers ending:

119

This number is saved as 'D' in the address book
of the handset. It has featured in numerous
phone billings and intelligence suggests it may
be attributed to Darren CUNNINGHAM DOB
12/11/1976 (principal subject of Organised Crime
Group 233). Daily contacts, incoming and outgoing,
throughout the billing period. No SMS.

121

This number is attributed on the intelligence
database to Lisa JACKSON DOB 01/06/1989. The
contact is saved as 'Bird' in the address book
of the handset. JACKSON is known to be the
partner of Paul 'Reggie' STARK DOB 04/05/1982.
Contact with this number incoming and outgoing
on a daily basis between 25/09/13 and 03/11/13.
Last contact during the afternoon of 03/11/13.

528

This number is saved as 'Big R' in the address
book of the handset. It is believed to be in
use by another member of the CUNNINGHAM network
as it is sequential with 512 and other numbers
attributed to members of the group. There are
sporadic contacts all through the billing
period. No SMS.

891

This phone number has been attributed to
Scarlett RAINSFORD DOB 11/02/1988 as it was
found in her back pocket following the SB

warrant conducted at Carisbrooke Court, Briarstone, on 31/10/13. Please see phone analysis conducted by Brian TEMPLE, SB analyst, on this number. Regular contact between these numbers between 25/09/13 and 31/10/13.

441

This number is saved as 'K' in the address book of the handset. The first contact is an incoming call received on 01/11/13 at 22:44 (18 minutes 55 seconds). A further incoming call was received on 03/11/13 at 21:24 (duration 1 minute 23 seconds). There is a final outgoing call on 03/11/13 at 23:42 (duration 2 minutes 11 seconds). This was the last use of the handset.

In addition to these contacts, there are a further 14 telephone numbers which remain unattributed, but are in contact just once or twice, and at none of the key time periods provided.

Attribution

It is possible that the phone discarded inside the Volvo was in use by Paul 'Reggie' STARK DOB 04/05/1982. Facts in support of this inference include:

- data for the phone commences on 25/09/13 which is known to be the same day STARK ceased using the SIM ending 210.

- the most frequent contacts are with number ending 121, attributed to Lisa JACKSON, STARK's partner.

- cellsite activity shows the 'home' cell for this phone is in Briarstone, at the back of the Park Hill estate, which is near where STARK lives (H/A 14 Ambleside Crescent).

- call activity follows a very similar pattern to previous billings received for other phones attributed to STARK, including the SIM ending 210 (for example, STARK favours calling rather than using SMS).

- additional numbers identified as having contact with this phone are attributed to the Ying Sun Chinese Takeaway, London Road, Briarstone; Briarstone Borough Council; Domino's Pizza; William Hill, Ladbrokes and Paddy Power; Sky TV helpline and NHS Direct. All of these numbers were also called by the previous number attributed to STARK.

Conclusion

Call activity on this phone would seem to indicate that the user may have been involved in the burglary in the early hours of 03/11/13 at 14 Russet Avenue (during which the Volvo was stolen) as well as the murder of Clive RAINSFORD at around 23:10 on 03/11/13 at the same address.

Recommendations

413

Identify the user of number ending 441
(identified as 'K' in the address book) - as
this was the last number contacted before the
phone was abandoned.

Please do not hesitate to contact me if you
require anything further.

Kind regards,

Zoe Adams

Senior Analyst, FIB and OCG Team

SAM – Tuesday 5 November 2013, 09:10

Sam had completed the paperwork, taken it down the road to the Magistrate's Court, and waited all of five minutes to see the magistrate who, possibly because he hadn't started hearing cases yet, was in a benevolent mood. The warrant was duly signed and Sam headed back to Headquarters wondering if that was some sort of record. She had just logged back in to the computer when the email from Zoe Adams arrived.

Sam read through the email, then Zoe's analysis document.

There was a moment when everything was all right, and then she felt her stomach drop. *No. No, that couldn't be right . . .*

She reached in her bag for her phone, accessed the address book and scrolled through the numbers.

Spare phone. 07101 405441.

She looked back at the phone analysis document. There had to be a mistake . . .

. . . 441. This number is saved as 'K' in the address book of the handset . . .

You said something about a Reg to me, on Friday. You said something like, you had friends, you could have been sitting on Reg's sofa watching Sky TV . . .

She scrolled back up through the addresses until she got to 'Lou mobile' and dialled. It rang, and rang, and clicked to voicemail.

'Ma'am, it's me. I've got the warrant here, I'll leave it with Les. I need to go and meet Caro; I said I'd go with her to collect Scarlett and Juliette from the hotel this morning. Can you give me a call when you get this?'

She rang off, then scrolled back through the addresses. 'Caro S mobile'. This time the call was answered after two rings.

'Hello?'

'Caro, it's Sam Hollands. Whereabouts are you?'

'I'm just on the way to the Travel Inn. I was going to call you when I got to the nick, wasn't I? Everything okay?'

'Um . . . no . . . I just . . . I don't know.'

'Sam? What's the matter?'

'I'm not sure. I need to think. Caro, can I meet you at the hotel? Is that okay? I'll leave right now.'

'Of course. I'll see you there.'

Sam disconnected, reaching for the Airwaves radio unit which had been charging on her desk and scooping up the warrant. 'Les! Les, can I leave this with you?'

Les Finnegan was on the phone to someone, his feet up on Jane Phelps' swivel chair. He made no sign that he'd heard but he picked up the sheet of paper as it landed on his desk.

At the door, Sam grabbed her coat and ran.

SCARLETT – Tuesday 5 November 2013, 09:12

The wind was strong, harsh enough to penetrate through her coat. She pulled it tighter round her, as if that might help keep it out.

What are you waiting for?

Funny, that it was going to end up here. She was thinking about it all, thinking of all the times she'd been afraid for her life: of being abused by her father, a man who was supposed to love and take care of her; of being in the back of a van, tied up, terrified, thirsty, in pain; of watching another girl's head explode open in a cloud of red; of lying on a dirty bed while men she didn't know raped her. Of a man who wanted to drink her blood; of another man who had pretended to be kind and had instead been sent to trick her; of the men in a warehouse who sold lives, destroyed lives, for profit. There was no scrubbing brush good or hard enough to clean all that away.

But then, there was the kindness of a Dutchwoman who had given her a coat and probably saved her life; the love of her sister, even though she had had her life destroyed by two indifferent, selfish parents. And Mark Braddock, who had had something to tell her after the holidays, and never got the chance; and Mrs Rowden-Knowles, who had always cared and always tried to do the right thing. And, at last, there was Sam. The last person who cared.

It wasn't enough.

The wind buffeted her where she sat, threatening to topple her backwards.

Not yet. I'm not ready.

She hadn't been afraid, since she met Sam. It was as if it didn't really matter, everything she'd done. It was ironic, Scarlett thought, that at this most scary moment, when she really should be afraid, she felt unnaturally calm and at peace. There was nothing else for her to do, after all. She had done what she set out to do.

Annie was still in hospital, but the chances were that she wouldn't recover. And she deserved punishment as much as Clive, after all, didn't she?

On that night in August, the last night of Scarlett's holiday in Rhodes, a Greek man she didn't know yammering at her and seconds away from pushing her into the back of a van, Scarlett had looked back towards the Aktira Studios and seen her mother there, watching. Their eyes had met. Annie had obviously been confused by what she had seen – she had been expecting to see Scarlett meeting a boy, after all – and yet, when the van had driven off with her daughter in the back, she had done nothing about it.

Why?

Why had she not done something, stopped it, called the police there and then?

Scarlett had waited so long to ask that question. And then, when she'd seen her mother in the house in Kingswood Road, she'd known the answer anyway. Annie hadn't realised what she'd witnessed. She had thought Scarlett had gone off with Nico. And the next morning, when Scarlett wasn't back – when she didn't come back, even though they were supposed to be going home – she couldn't very well own up to having seen Scarlett being pushed into the back of a van the night before.

And so it had been easier to say nothing, to have seen nothing, to have no idea where Scarlett had gone.

Annie had said something that had summed it up so well.

Sometimes you make mistakes. And if you don't own up to them, sooner or later they turn into bigger mistakes and bigger ones, and then you can't admit to them at all, ever.

And she hadn't owned up. Even after Scarlett came back, even after she had been brought face to face with the consequences of what she'd failed to do.

Technically Scarlett had survived. In reality she had been dead inside from the moment in the warehouse when the other girl, the one in her crate, the Dutch girl she'd never even seen, had been silenced with a shot. The bullet had taken Scarlett's soul along with it. She was living, breathing, but not actually alive.

And so there was no point continuing, was there? Not any more. This was how she was going to end it. Making her own decision. This was hers, her life, what was left of it, anyway; and she was going to choose the leaving of it. Not them. Not even Juliette.

She leaned forward, slightly, the wind whistling up the side of the building and pushing her gently back. Holding her steady.

A few more minutes.

SAM – Tuesday 5 November 2013, 09:52

Caro Sumner's car was parked at the front of the Travel Inn when Sam arrived. She had half-expected – hoped – to find Caro waiting outside for her.

The reception desk was deserted, as it always was. Sam went through to the bar, pulling her mobile phone out of her bag and getting ready to call Caro's number.

'Sam! Over here.'

Caro stood up and crossed the bar to where Sam stood. Juliette was sitting upright, her back to them.

'Where's Scarlett?' Sam said.

'Let's just go out here a minute.' Caro steered Sam back out towards the hotel reception, out of Juliette's hearing.

'What? Caro, just tell me. Where is she?'

'Juliette told me Scarlett left this morning, about an hour ago. She's been telling me all about it, Sam. We need to get her statement.'

Sam was feeling panic rising in her chest. 'Where's she gone?'

'Juliette doesn't know. Or if she does, she's not telling me. But Juliette thinks Scarlett might have had something to do with Clive's murder.'

Sam groaned. 'I know, I know! We need to find her.'

'I rang the office. There are patrols out now, looking for her. In the meantime I'm trying to get something useful out of Juliette. Maybe you'll have more luck than me.'

Sam said, 'I'll be there in a minute. You go and sit with her. I just need to make a few calls.'

Sam went out to the car park, dialling Lou's number first. Voicemail again, damn it!

'It's Sam again. I'm at the hotel; Scarlett has taken off again. Caro has put out a call for patrols to do a search. I'm going to see if I can get anything useful out of Juliette about where she might have gone. Then I'll go and look, too. Ma'am, I think Scarlett got Paul Stark to attack her parents. We need to find her straight away.'

She rang off. There was something else she could try. She scrolled through the address book until she got to 'Spare phone'.

It rang and rang. Just as Sam was about to give up, the call was answered.

'Hello? Scarlett? Can you hear me?'

There were noises on the line. Wind, and something that might have been a sniff, a breath.

'Scarlett. Talk to me.'

'It's okay, Sam,' she said.

'Where are you?'

'It doesn't matter.' She laughed, a short bitter laugh. 'I don't even know.'

'I'll come and get you,' Sam said. 'It'll be okay, I promise.'

'It won't. But it doesn't matter, it really doesn't.'

'Scarlett, please, let me come and get you. We can talk about it ...'

'I left you a letter. It's at the reception desk at the hotel.'

'Wait, hold on ...'

Scarlett rang off.

Fuck it!

Sam redialled, but this time there was no answer. She rang the office number, waited and waited. Eventually Les Finnegan answered. 'Incident room, can you hold the line ...'

'Les! It's Sam. Wait a minute, this is urgent.'

'I'm on the other line, guv.'

'Never mind that. I need you to get the Comms Unit to set up a live cellsite trace.'

'What?'

'This is the number: write it down. 07101 405441. Got that?'

'Yep. What's the rush on it?'

'Scarlett Rainsford has gone missing. Talk to the boss, get authorisation. It's really urgent – Scarlett's got that phone on her. Please, Les, go find the boss *right now* and get her to set it up. And then get her to call me. Okay?'

'Message received, skip. Doing it now.'

Sam stood still for a moment, thinking hard and fast and wishing she knew what to do, where to start. There was nobody behind reception. Sam rang the white doorbell on the counter, wondering if it even worked. A minute later a young man emerged from the back office, smiling as if it was his first day on the job.

'Can I help you?'

'There's a letter for me. Sam Hollands.'

He had a root around on the desk, then went into a drawer, shuffling through papers and boxes of staples. *Come on,* Sam thought. Clearly they didn't often have letters left for people. Eventually he found it, bringing it forth with triumph. It was a white envelope upon which was written a single word in black ballpoint pen. SAM.

Sam went back into the bar. Juliette was still sitting bolt upright, Caro next to her, head cocked to one side, looking up at Juliette's face searchingly, an encouraging smile on her lips. She was trying her hardest to get through to her, and by the look of it nothing was working.

'Juliette,' Sam said, sitting down on the other side of her. 'My name is Detective Sergeant Sam Hollands. I've been spending a bit of time with your sister in the past few days.'

Juliette had tears pouring down her cheeks, dripping from her chin on to her pink sweater. She wasn't wiping them away. Wasn't moving.

'Did she mention me, at all, Juliette?'

Nothing. Just more tears. The silence from her was unnerving.

'I really care about her. I want so much to help. I think I can help, Juliette, but I need to find her.'

'I'm so sorry,' Juliette said, her voice just a whisper. 'I let her down.'

421

'How did you let her down, Juliette?'

'I didn't try to stop her.'

Sam breathed. *Take your time, don't rush her* ... 'Try to stop her doing what?'

Juliette gave a deep, shuddering sigh. More tears fell. 'She went out to meet that boy. I should have stopped her. I knew they'd be angry, they'd kill her.'

'Who?'

'Dad. He hit her when he knew she was seeing the boy. She went out to meet him and I didn't stop her. And she ... she never came back ...'

'She's talking about the abduction,' Caro said redundantly.

Sam shot her a look. 'But Scarlett's all right, Juliette. She did come back. It took her a long time, but she came back for you, didn't she?'

'She phoned up and they didn't believe it was her ...'

'When?'

'A year ago. Scarlett rang the house. I kept saying I knew she wasn't dead, I knew it, but they didn't want to help. They pretended that it wasn't her, that it was a hoax, but they knew it was really. She needed money, she needed their help, and he just hung up on her.'

'Your dad?'

Juliette nodded, slowly. 'And then she came to find me, when they went out. And she was really alive.'

'She is alive, Juliette. But I really need you to help me find her. Can you do that? What did she say to you this morning?'

'She said ... she said if she went away again I would be all right now. I'd be all right on my own.'

'Because of your mum and dad, what's happened to them?'

422

Juliette nodded. Her voice was hoarse. 'She said she had got it all wrong. I don't understand – I don't understand why she had to go. I tried to get her to stay but she wouldn't. I did everything I was supposed to. I don't know why they ended up hurt; that wasn't supposed to happen.'

'Juliette, what do you mean? What was supposed to happen?'

'We needed money. We were going to move away, me and Scarlett, get a flat together. But we didn't have any money, so we were going to get Scarlett's mate to pretend to break in. We were going to share the money with him. I had to leave the window unlocked downstairs. I told her where everything was. I wrote down Dad's PIN. That was my job.'

Caro said, 'So you and Scarlett planned to help someone burgle the house?'

Juliette nodded.

'And your mum and dad? What happened to them?'

Juliette wailed again, sudden and loud. 'I don't know, I don't know!'

'Did they know you'd been meeting up with Scarlett?' Sam asked. 'Did they know she was back in Briarstone, before we told them last week?'

'No, they didn't know. Scarlett made me promise not to tell that I'd seen her. But she's gone, she's gone. I don't know what to do without her. I want Scarlett; I want her to come back!'

'Where do you think she might have gone, Juliette? Please think.'

Juliette closed her eyes. 'She gave me a letter.'

From her pocket Juliette brought out an envelope, folded and creased. Caro took it, unfolded it. On the envelope, a single word: JULIETTE. Caro passed the envelope over to Sam.

Sam's phone was ringing. 'I'm sorry,' she said. 'I'll be right back.'

As she walked away, she heard Juliette saying, 'Can I go home? I want to go home.'

Sam ran out to the reception area before she answered. 'Lou? Did you get my messages?'

'Yes. We've got a live trace on that number, Sam. It's in the town, near the shopping centre. That's the best we can manage. I've got more people out there but no sightings so far. How's Juliette?'

'I'm going to leave her with Caro; can you send a patrol out to get them from the Travel Inn? Juliette just told us they planned the burglary, to get money to go away together, make a fresh start.'

'And the attack on the parents?'

'She doesn't seem to think that was part of the plan. She seems pretty traumatised, though. I'm not sure she really knows what's going on.'

'I'll get someone out straight away, don't worry. Reggie Stark's on his way into custody. They're doing a search now. I just heard they've got a pair of trainers from the wheelie bin outside.'

Despite the pressure, Sam managed a smile at the thought of this. One of the Tac Team was going to earn an anecdote and several pints out of that one.

'And the baseball bat was under the bed. Looks as if it's been very badly washed.'

SCARLETT – Tuesday 5 November 2013, 09:52

She was crying now, but tears didn't help. She had learned that a long time ago, but for some reason she couldn't stop them.

This was foolish; this was just wasting time. It wasn't as if Sam wanted any more to do with her. She'd made that clear, crystal clear, last night.

Below, far below, Scarlett could hear sirens. It felt as if she was running out of time. She saw the flashing blue lights of the police car, giant black letters on its roof, chasing past the building. Nobody had seen her. Nobody knew she was here. She was invisible, half-dead already, disappearing. She had been disappearing since the minute the Dutchwoman had given her this coat.

Just a little shift forward, and she would fall.

'Bye, Sam,' Scarlett whispered into the wind. 'Bye, Jul.'

05/11/2013, 09:54
Dispatch Log 1105-0175

** CALL FROM STACEY JOHNSON DOB 19/12/87 EMPLOYEE AT BRIARSTONE BOROUGH COUNCIL

** CALLER STATES SHE CAN SEE FROM THE OFFICE WINDOW THAT THERE IS A GIRL SITTING ON THE EDGE OF THE ROOF OF THE CAR PARK

** THIS IS THE ROOF OF THE SHOPPING CENTRE CAR PARK ABOVE THE BUS STATION

** PATROLS DISPATCHED PZ22 PZ88

** PZ88: CONFIRMED, FEMALE SITTING ON THE WALL, SOUTH SIDE OF THE SHOPPING CENTRE CAR PARK TOP FLOOR

**   PZ88: ESTABLISHING CORDON AT BASE OF
       CAR PARK

**   ARRIVA NOTIFIED, BUSES TO BE DIVERTED
       VIA KING STREET

**   INITIATING PERSON IN CRISIS PROCEDURES

**   HNs TEAM NOTIFIED

**   DS 9004 RYMAN ACKNOWLEDGED, WILL
       ATTEND

SAM – Tuesday 5 November 2013, 10:12

Sam was heading for the bus station – because after all it was worth a try – when she heard the exchange coming over the Airwaves unit in the car.

'All units, person in crisis, roof of bus station car park . . . '

By the time Sam made it there, there was already a patrol car parked at an angle across the access road, and a PC winding scene tape around a lamp-post to stop people getting too close. Sam stopped as close as she could without causing an obstruction, got out of the car and sprinted across to the officer.

'Sorry, you can't get any closer . . . '

'DS Sam Hollands,' Sam puffed. 'I think I know who that is, up there. Please, I need to get to talk to her . . . '

'I don't want to worry you,' the man said. 'I've just come up here to talk to you for a bit, is that okay?'

Scarlett didn't answer. She could not acknowledge him, this man who'd turned up, was standing a few metres behind her, to her right. He couldn't stop her, couldn't do anything. There was no point in him being there, so there was no point in acknowledging that he was real.

'My name's Mick,' he said. 'I'm with the police. Can you tell me your name?'

Police – of course he was police. It wouldn't be some random passer-by, would it, on the roof of the car park?

If he was police, then Sam would know she was here.

'I'd really like it if you could just come down off the wall. Do you think you could do that? Just for a moment or two, while we have a talk?'

The wind was getting stronger. It was cold up here and her cheeks were already numb with it, her teeth chattering a staccato rhythm in her head. All of this would be done; all of it would be over. No more cold, no more nightmares, no more waking up with a jolt because you'd forgotten where you were and who you were with – bracing yourself against an impact because that was all you'd come to expect.

'Can you just tell me your name? Just to let me know you can hear me, because for all I know I'm talking to myself right now, eh? Can you just say something, to let me know you can hear me?'

Out of the corner of her eye she could see him, the shape of him, although turning her head to look properly felt like way too much effort. No, she wouldn't tell him her name. He'd find out soon enough. She didn't even know what to call herself any more ... Stella, Katie, Scarlett. Were any of those people even her? If she didn't have a name of her own, did she even exist?

SAM – Tuesday 5 November 2013, 10:20

They had set up a rendezvous point at the foot of the ramp leading up to the car park roof, just out of sight of Scarlett and the trained negotiator, who Sam learned was called Mick Lister. The RVP location comprised two men standing around, at the moment, but there was an air of organisation hanging over it which Sam found instantly reassuring.

As she approached with a uniformed officer by her side, one of the men looked up. 'You're DS Hollands?' he asked, holding out his hand for her to shake.

'Yes.'

'DS John Ryman – I'm co-ordinating. This is Pete Watson – he's recording. Have you been in a situation like this before?'

'No.'

'Okay. We need to do a very quick briefing. I understand you know the person we have sitting on the wall out there?'

'I haven't seen her yet ... but I'm missing a witness, and I met her here once before.'

'Right. Then I need you to come with me, quiet as you can; we'll just go to the other side of the ramp so you can get a visual and hopefully you'll be able to confirm identity, okay?'

They walked a little way up the ramp until Sam could see across the empty car park, across the puddles and the marked spaces, to the concrete wall on the far side. She could see a shape huddled into an oversized khaki jacket, short dark hair. It was definitely Scarlett, her back to the ramp, hands on the concrete wall by her sides as if any second she was going to lever herself off the edge. Just behind her, to her right, was a man, standing with his feet comfortably apart; and behind him, the only one glancing back towards the ramp, was a third figure, another man.

Sam turned to John Ryman and nodded. In turn he raised a hand to the man on the roof, who took a step forward to his colleague, said something and then headed back towards the ramp.

'That's your witness?' Ryman asked, when the second man had joined them.

'Yes, her name is Scarlett Rainsford. Her parents were attacked last night: her father is dead and her mother is seriously injured. Her sister is with my colleague back at the Travel Inn. It's possible they had something to do with the attack.'

'All right. Just take a moment, yeah?'

What? Sam looked at him in surprise and realised then that she was shaking. *Pull yourself together, Sam.* 'I'm fine. Just so cold up here, isn't it?'

Ryman said, 'DS Sam Hollands, this is Richard; he's acting as number two for Mick Lister, who's out there talking to your Scarlett. He's the one who is going to pass on communications between us and Mick. Sam, does Scarlett know you? How's she likely to react to you being here?'

'We've become ... I don't know ... friends, I guess. I don't know how she'll react, though. She sent me some text messages this morning and I never had a chance to reply.'

'What did they say?'

Shit, Sam thought. 'Oh, just that she couldn't sleep, she was worrying about everything . . . she said – oh, God – she said she thought she would have been better off staying dead . . . '

'Take your time,' Ryman said gently. 'She's not moved yet; we're doing okay at the moment. Anything happening, Richard?'

'She's not said a word so far. Not a word.'

'Wait,' Sam said. 'Scarlett left these letters, for me and for her sister – I haven't had a chance to look at them yet.' She pulled the two crumpled envelopes out of her back pocket.

Ryman looked at her. 'You'd better have a look,' he said. 'Richard, can you let Mick know what we've got? We can see if there's anything here that's useful before we continue the briefing.'

Richard jogged back up the ramp towards his colleague.

'It's so cold,' Sam said. 'How can she bear to sit there like that? It's freezing. Can I not just go and talk to her? She might listen to me.'

John Ryman put a hand on Sam's upper arm. 'We might consider using you as a third-party intermediary at some point, but for the time being you can help us a lot more by telling us everything you can about Scarlett. We need a reason for her to come back down. You'd better read those letters.'

Dear Juliette,

I'm so sorry about everything. I've let you down again, my beautiful, precious sister. I wasn't there for you for all those years while you went through hell. I thought I could help, I thought I could take you away from it all, but I think you need to be around decent people who can take good care of you, who can give you a new life, a better life. If you went with me, sooner or later it would all go wrong. Everything I try to do goes wrong, and you deserve better, my darling girl.

Sam is a good person, she will look after you and make sure nothing bad happens now.

Be brave and strong, you can get through this. Don't be scared.

I love you lots xxxxx
Scarlett xxxx

SCARLETT – Tuesday 5 November 2013, 10:24

'Scarlett?' the man said. 'That's your name, isn't it? Scarlett?'

She had been drifting off for a moment, as she had done throughout her life when things got too difficult. Whereas once she had dreamed of Mark Braddock, or of Nico, later she'd dreamed of getting a good night's sleep in a clean bed, clean clothes, being able to walk on a beach, being able to eat something she'd cooked herself, even just home and a normal life, whatever such a thing was.

'Scarlett? I can see you're getting cold there – you're shivering a bit. Do you want me to see if I can find you a blanket? Or a hot drink, a coffee maybe? Just while you decide what you want to do . . . '

She opened her eyes for a moment and saw the expanse of grey concrete below. Why were there no buses? She hadn't seen one for a while, and yet at this time of day there should be plenty of them. There was nothing: no traffic, no people below. It was as if the world had fallen silent.

Please just piss off.

She wanted to say it out loud, but speaking to the man was like the first step in admitting that he was going to win. While he went unacknowledged she still felt in control; all she had to do was lean forward, push off the wall with her cold, numb fingers, and she would fly for a second and then everything would be peaceful.

'I know you've had a really bad few days, Scarlett. I know you must feel as though this is the only way you're going to get out of it. But I can tell you for definite that it's not the only way. It's not even the best way.'

How did he know? How did he know what had happened to her? He must have been talking to someone . . .

For the first time, she turned her head and saw the man face to face. He was young, younger than his voice suggested, an unlined face and fair hair lifted away from his forehead in the breeze. Blue eyes. He gave her the beginnings of a smile.

'My name's Mick,' he said again. 'I really want to help, Scarlett. Do you think you can tell me a bit about why you're here?'

Another man was standing a pace or two behind him, another young lad, twenty or so, dark-haired. Under other circumstances they would have looked like two lads on a night out. The sort of men who would have hung around outside her window waiting for her to let them in, arguing over who went first . . . She turned away again, closing her eyes. She did not want to see them.

'This is Rich,' Mick said. 'He's here to help too; there are lots of people here who want to help make things better, Scarlett. We've got someone who's talking to Juliette right now. She's really worried about you, Scarlett; she's terrified she's going to lose you all over again.'

Scarlett remembered meeting Reg at the café a month before the police raided the flat in Carisbrooke Court. He'd been bricking it, shit-scared of his new boss Darren because he hadn't managed to retrieve the gear and prove his loyalty; even more shit-scared of his old boss Lewis because he'd accidentally hit Carl too hard while trying to get the drugs back and had had to get rid of the body in the woods, trying to make it look like a robbery gone wrong. McDonnell didn't know who'd killed his mate McVey yet – didn't know who it was who'd deprived him of his chief money launderer and three of the best dealing sites in town – but he had to have his suspicions. It wouldn't be long before one or other of them decided Reg was way more trouble than he was worth. All he'd wanted to do was rewind a few weeks to before all the mess had started. 'I should never have done it, Katie, I should never have bloody gone with Liliana and pissed off Lewis; I never done it before. If I'd just stayed with Lisa, none of this shit would have happened . . .'

She saw it in that moment as clear as anything.

'You need money, to get away,' she had said. 'I can help you.'

And that was it – the plan. They were going to burgle the house while her family were on holiday, at the end of October. Reg would get enough money from that to move away with Lisa, make a fresh start somewhere. Juliette would make sure the jewellery and stuff was left somewhere they could find it, would give Scarlett all the PINs and security details for Clive's bank accounts. They would clean them out. And in return . . . well, Reg already had one violent offence stacked against him; it didn't seem much effort to add another couple. And since they deserved it, deserved to be taught a lesson, why not? And he had no motive, so they wouldn't look at him for it in any case, would they?

Then, just as they had been about to put the plan into action, the raid had happened, and Scarlett, who had been safely, comfortably dead, was suddenly very much alive again. And suddenly she was being looked after by police officers, and asked question after question . . . Reg had been beside himself, as she found out when she'd called him from the Travel Inn, using the phone Sam had given her. The next night she'd waited until Sam had left the bus station, then caught the last bus to Park Hill. Lisa had already gone to bed, thankfully, leaving the two of them to discuss properly what had happened, and to change their plans. By the early hours, it had all seemed foolproof. What could possibly go wrong?

'Juliette is very scared, Scarlett. Can you imagine how she'll feel if she hears you've killed yourself? She'll be devastated . . .'

Shut up shut up shut up . . .

SAM – Tuesday 5 November 2013, 10:27

'This is how it works. Richard is going to go up there and swap places with Mick, so Scarlett will have someone with her all the time, while we bring you out. We don't leave her alone. Mick's going to come down here and give you a quick briefing, then you'll go back out there with him. You stand a couple of metres behind her, and Mick will stand just behind you. He will have a hand on your coat at the back, holding on to you. You need to be aware that we have a "no grab" policy. That means if she jumps, if she falls forward, you have to let her go. You don't go leaping for her, whether she's moved or not. So you stay a couple of metres behind her and you don't get any closer than that. Mick holding on to your coat will remind you, if you forget. Understand?'

Sam nodded. Ryman was talking and she was trying to focus, trying to stay with it.

'We have three priorities. We want to save a life. We want to gain intelligence, listen out for things she might say to you that might help get her to turn around and come back to a place of safety. And we want to buy time, so we don't want to rush her or provoke her or try and push her into doing anything. Three priorities, in that order – clear on that?'

435

A few minutes ago, Sam had spoken to Lou on the phone. She had retreated to the stairwell, away from the rendezvous point where Ryman was debriefing the control room inspector by phone. Richard and Mick were out there with Scarlett. Nothing had happened, and yet Sam was disintegrating slowly.

'I'm downstairs,' Lou said. 'I'm trying to get them to let me come up so I can talk to you. Don't worry, Sam. I'm coming.'

But Lou couldn't help either. Nobody could.

When Sam had ended the call, she'd gone back over to Ryman and shaken off all the fear and doubt. 'I want to help,' she'd said. 'Let me talk to her. You're not getting anywhere; I might as well try.'

He had been reluctant at first, but then Richard had come back down the ramp to tell them all that Scarlett still had not said a word, but she was shivering and was starting to look distressed and uncomfortable. It felt as if they were running out of time.

'So while you're out there, Mick will be your number two,' Ryman went on. 'He'll stand behind you and coach you, basically, giving you ideas of things to say if you get stuck. Don't challenge her. Don't lie to her either: don't make promises about what will or won't happen when she gets down. But give her reasons to live.'

Give her reasons to live . . .

Richard had gone back out to stand behind Mick. Sam watched from the edge of the ramp, saw the two men, heads together, conversation as easy as if they were standing outside a bar talking about the weather. Mick was nodding. Then he looked towards the ramp and held up a finger. *Wait.*

'He's going to tell her what's happening,' Ryman said.

'Scarlett? There's someone here to see you, someone who wants to come and talk to you.'

Scarlett didn't move. She tried to turn her head slightly, but all she could see was the blond guy – Mick – and the other one, just behind him. The cold was getting to her, the cold and the discomfort and the wishing that she'd already done it. If she'd just jumped in the first place she would be dead by now and this nightmare would be over, along with all the others. She didn't want an audience. She didn't want them to see.

'The thing is, I need to try to protect them as well as you. I don't want you to do anything you're going to regret, Scarlett, I don't want you to hurt any more than you are already. But also I don't want anyone else to get hurt, too. So, if I bring someone out here, I don't want them to have to watch you kill yourself. Can you imagine what that would do to someone, to see someone they care about die?'

I can imagine, Scarlett thought. As she did regularly, she saw Yelena running across the tarmac, hair flying behind her. Yelena, whose only life was an invented life.

'So I'd really appreciate it if you could just give me an indication that you're happy for this person to come out. Can you do that, Scarlett?'

Do it do it do it jump now . . .

'Can you do that, Scarlett?'

'Who is it?' she whispered.

'It's Sam,' Mick said. 'Sam's here to see you. She's really worried about you, Scarlett. Will you talk to her?'

She felt a wave of relief at hearing Sam's name. 'Yes.'

'If you're going to talk to her, if I'm going to bring her out here, will you just do me a favour and swing your legs over this way, just so I know you're not going to jump while she's here? Will you do that? I don't want Sam to be scared about you jumping while she's here.'

'I won't jump.'

'That's good to hear, Scarlett – I'm really relieved. In that case, please just swing your legs over because I wouldn't want you to fall. I really don't want you to fall. Can you do that?'

She didn't move. She couldn't move, because just then a wave of fear so intense it felt like pain washed over her, and her fingers constricted around the rough surface of the concrete wall. If she moved, she would fall. And suddenly she didn't want to fly any more. Not yet, anyway.

I'm so tired . . .

LOU – Tuesday 5 November 2013, 10:35

It had taken a lot of persuasion for Lou to be allowed up to the top floor of the car park and on to the RV point. In any normal circumstances this would not have been an issue she would have pressed; people had jobs to do, and this wasn't one of hers. She had the greatest respect for the negotiators, who were trained and dedicated and unbelievably professional. They dealt regularly with pressure of the kind that most police officers saw infrequently, if ever. Lives were in their hands. If they fucked up, someone died. No greater pressure than that.

But this was no normal circumstance. Lou felt a crushing level of responsibility for the two people on the roof, for Scarlett and even more for Sam. She had to be there.

When she arrived, escorted up in the lift by one of the patrols, Sam was being briefed by the co-ordinator, a man Lou recognised.

'That's my boss,' Sam was saying to him. 'Can I just have a quick word?'

'Sure,' Ryman said, clearly pissed off at having the process interrupted. 'Be quick.'

Sam went over to Lou. 'I'm going to go and talk to her. They're just briefing me about how it works.'

Lou had never seen Sam looking like this, so pale, her eyes wide. There was a lot going on behind those eyes, but the one thing Lou could see was that Sam was afraid.

'You don't have to, Sam,' Lou said. 'They're trained . . . '

'I know that,' Sam said quickly. 'I know, I know. But they're not getting anywhere and I can't just sit here and wait, I can't, I have to try—'

'All right,' Lou said. 'I'm right here.' Awkwardly she gave Sam a hug, gripping her tightly. In her ear she whispered, 'You can bloody do this. I know you can do it.'

And then Sam was gone, striding boldly up the ramp, accompanied by a fair-haired young man.

SAM – Tuesday 5 November 2013, 10:37

Sam was walking across the car park, a few steps behind Mick. Up here, away from the shelter afforded by the concrete and the car ramp, the wind whistled and tugged at her clothes, blowing unpredictably from every direction.

She was getting closer to Scarlett now, and it took all her strength not to break into a run. She could see the girl's back, that enormous coat pulled tightly around her, her hands pressed into the concrete wall.

Richard was talking to Scarlett, but if there was a response Sam couldn't hear it.

Mick said he had tried to get her to turn round. He said he was worried that she was so cold she was seizing up, that she might not be able to move very easily. He had told Ryman to call for an ambulance.

And then she was there, and the handover was taking place.

'Mick and Sam are here, Scarlett,' Richard said, and then he retreated back the way they had come.

Sam moved forward a few steps. One of the men had drawn a line with the toe of a shoe, a line drawn in water from the puddle across the pale grey concrete. *No further than this. Don't cross the line.*

Scarlett was motionless, facing away. Sam could just about see the side of her pale cheek, her short dark hair blowing wildly. And now she saw the point of the strong grip on the back of her coat, by Mick just behind her, because without it she would have moved forward, touched Scarlett's arm, tried to pull her away from the edge. It was hypnotic, the girl against the swirling sky.

'Hey, Scarlett,' she said. Fighting to keep her voice steady.

Scarlett's head lowered. And then she turned her face towards Sam.

'Hey, lovely girl. What are you doing up here?'

Scarlett was crying too. She was mouthing something.

'What is it? Tell me, talk to me.'

She was mouthing, *I'm so scared.*

'I know, I know. But it's not so bad. You're not on your own any more, Scarlett. You've got friends. You've got Juliette.'

One of Scarlett's hands fluttered to her mouth as if to hold in a cry.

Mick flinched at the movement, tightened his grip. 'Try and get her to come over,' he whispered urgently.

'Scarlett, I really want you just to turn round properly. Please, just while we're talking.'

Scarlett was shaking her head. Her hand dropped into her lap. She was mouthing the words, *I'm so sorry, I'm so sorry.*

'It's okay, it really is. Please come over the wall, Scarlett. I want to get you somewhere warm, where we can talk properly. We can go and get a drink and warm up a bit. You just need to move over this way.'

Scarlett moved suddenly, big, unexpected, jerky movements, and Sam gasped. She moved forward in a rush and Mick pulled her back, away from Scarlett, who let out a single cry.

'Sam!'

LOU – Tuesday 5 November 2013, 10:45

'Oh, Jesus Christ.'

Lou, watching from the shadow of the ramp, put a hand up to her mouth.

Scarlett had moved so quickly, so unexpectedly, when she'd been still for so long. And Lou, and everyone else, had been thinking she was going to jump, or fall ... and then she was this side of the wall and taking big strides towards Sam, falling into Sam's arms.

Mick took a step back, just a step, ready to move again if Scarlett decided to rush for the edge and take Sam with her. But after a second he looked back towards the ramp and held up a hand, and Richard came out with a blanket that he'd managed to acquire from the ambulance that was waiting down in the bus station.

Scarlett hadn't let go of Sam.

SAM – Tuesday 5 November 2013, 12:37

Without saying a word, Sam handed over Scarlett's letters. They were sitting in the front of Lou's car, still parked awkwardly inside the entrance to the car park in a hatched area clearly marked NO PARKING – ACCESS REQUIRED.

'What's this?'

'Scarlett wrote them last night,' Sam said. 'They both give me the impression she was planning to jump. She's trying to suggest that the murders – or attempts – were planned between her and "a friend" – who we now think is Paul Stark – without Juliette's knowledge. I'm not sure if that's exactly how it was.'

'Let's just be grateful she didn't jump or fall,' Lou said. 'We'll take the rest of it one step at a time.' She pulled the first letter out of the envelope.

'I don't doubt that she's been through a lot. They both have.'

'It's going to be difficult to prove,' Lou said.

'You've got the phone evidence. Juliette was phoning Scarlett's mobile phone regularly; they've been meeting up.'

Lou looked up from the letter that was addressed to Sam. 'Oh, my God,' she said. 'Those poor girls.'

442

Dear Sam,

Don't try to find me, I need to do this now and I don't want you to see.

You've been a good friend. I want to ask you to take care of Juliette, make sure she gets proper help and that she can have a good life. She deserves to be happy, she did nothing wrong and she is a good girl.

She had such a bad time with him, it was worse than I had because the people I was with were strangers. She had to do those things with her own father, the man who was supposed to love and care for her. She won't tell you the details but it was bad. He waited till she was 16 to have sex with her because he thought that made it okay. He always talked about the 'age of consent', how you had to be 16 to have sex because at that age you gave your consent. He told Juliette that no man would ever want her, that she belonged to him and she had to have sex with him because that's what girls were for. But before that he did other things to her and to me, before I was taken away. Sometimes he took pictures of us together that he said he was going to sell to other people. He said that meant nobody would ever want us, so we had to stay at home where he could look after us. The first time I remember this

443

happening I was probably about five or six.
When he started involving Juliette too she was
probably about four. I remember feeling jealous
because he had told me I was his special
daughter, but then Juliette cried because she
didn't like it, and he hit her for crying, and
after that I didn't mind her being there
because it meant I could look after her and
stop him hitting her.

He never had sex with me but I think now
he was waiting till I was 16. Juliette told
me the first time he did it to her was at her
birthday party. It was just the three of them,
having a party. Our mother knew it was
happening. Sometimes she was there.

I am crying now not because of what they
did but because I thought I could make
Juliette's life better by getting her away from
them. Juliette didn't know any of it. I
thought she would be happy with them gone.
But she is so upset, she keeps crying and I
think I've made everything worse. They were
bad people but they were the only family she
had after I was gone. And after what I've
done I am a bad person too.

I told a friend what they were like. He
wanted to help because he doesn't like bullies
or paedos. I think something like that
happened to him when he was a little kid but

he never told me what. He is a good bloke really, he wants to help people. He wanted to help us. I thought with our parents gone me and Juliette could have a fresh start. I never thought Juliette would find it so difficult.

Please Sam take care of my sister, she has a chance to be happy on her own. She might not tell you that any of this happened but it's the truth. She would never say anything bad about them because she was always scared.

I'm not afraid of telling you because it's the right thing to do.

Also I'm not afraid of dying, I think I died a long time ago.

I'm sorry if I got you into trouble, you were kind to me and I thought something might happen.

Love Scarlett x

LOU – Tuesday 5 November 2013, 15:25

Reggie Stark and his solicitor were sitting side by side in Briarstone police station's Interview Room Three while Jane Phelps cautioned him and asked if he understood. Reggie looked tense, Lou thought, although it was hard to tell on a DVD from this lofty angle. The top of his head looked tense, anyway, and he was sitting bolt upright in the chair, his knee jiggling. Across the desk, Jane Phelps sat with her notes on her lap; next to her, Les Finnegan's receding hair, his pate shiny in the lights.

She fast-forwarded.

'. . . I don't think I can tell you this – what I mean is, you don't know what it's like,' Reggie was whining. 'These people, they're going to kill me if they think I've said anything. They'll kill me even for being in here. Basically I am a fucking dead man. What you going to do about that?'

'We can't offer you any sort of protection, Reggie,' Les was saying. 'This isn't the United States. We don't have the facility to put you into any sort of scheme, and you really wouldn't want that anyway, believe me.'

'I dunno. If I go inside, I'll be dead in weeks.'

'You know we have a very good relationship with the Prison Service. They don't want trouble for their prisoners, they've got enough to deal with. So they're going to actively make sure you're as safe in there as you can be. Right?'

She had watched this recording once already, taking notes for Jane and Les, who were about to start the second interview. Really this was

446

Sam's job, one she was particularly good at – finding the loose threads in an initial interview and knowing exactly how and when to give them a little tug. But Sam was busy writing up everything that had happened this morning, and Lou found herself planning interview strategy.

In Interview Room One, Scarlett Rainsford was awaiting her initial interview. She had spent the last few hours being checked over at the hospital, which had established that despite the threatened self-harm she was not actually in a crisis state and therefore was fit to be detained and interviewed.

Ali Whitmore and Caro Sumner were lined up for that one.

Juliette Rainsford was waiting her turn in a cell. Helen Bamber was going to interview her, with Ron Mitchell. The next briefing was planned for 5pm, when all the interviewers and investigators would get together and discuss progress. Zoe Adams had managed to find a desk in the MIR, and was busy collating the intelligence with a view to producing charts to keep everyone up to speed with the next stage. They had suspects. Now it was all about getting enough evidence together to charge them, and, from there, achieving a successful prosecution.

Justice for Clive and Annie Rainsford, and Carl McVey.

'Ma'am? Can I have a quick word?' It was Jane Phelps.

'Sure. Have a seat,' Lou said.

'I hope you don't mind,' she said. 'I wondered if you could put me on another interview team. I know you're pushed for officers, and I wouldn't ask, only ... '

'What is it, Jane?' Lou asked.

Jane Phelps was one of her key officers. She had been in Major Crime for two years, and before that three years on Tactical CID, fighting crime and kicking doors in. Not that you'd think so to look at her: beautifully dressed, slightly built, a wide, generous smile – she looked as if she should be in sales, not hunting down violent criminals.

'It's about Les. I just – I don't like his way of talking to people.'

'You mean colleagues?'

'No, I mean, I realise he's a bit insensitive sometimes, but I can deal with that. It's the way he is with witnesses. We paid a visit to Darren Cunningham on Sunday afternoon, and Les said something that I thought was a bit out of order.'

'What did he say?'

'He told Darren Cunningham he should be careful who he trusted. Out of the blue. And something about not being able to tell your enemies from your friends, when allegiances are changing all the time.'

Lou was scribbling notes. 'Anything else?'

'Just that. It was very quick. After that we went straight back to the car, and I told him I thought what he'd said was almost threatening and I didn't think it was the right thing to do. I said I thought he might have put Ian Palmer in danger.'

'And what did he say?'

'He laughed it off, he said he had seen crime groups fall apart just by putting a little word in. But what he also said was, how did I know he was talking about Palmer? And then, although it made me feel a bit uncomfortable, I didn't think any more of it until this afternoon when I was in the interview with him, talking to Reggie Stark.'

Jane hesitated, as if remembering the other occasions when she'd stuck her neck out and been wrong. Lou could tell it had cost her, coming forward like this. She wasn't enjoying it.

'Go on,' Lou said. 'I'm listening.'

'You heard the bit earlier when Stark was explaining how he used to work for McDonnell and now he works for Cunningham. And you said yourself in this morning's briefing that Stark might've been tasked with recovering the drugs from McVey.'

Jane hesitated, looked at her hands.

'You think he was warning Cunningham about Reggie?'

Jane said, 'No – well, I don't know. I don't think it was that specific. But it felt weird at the time, like something was going on. I'm sorry to bother you with this, ma'am, I know it's a pain. I just don't like being a part of all that macho rubbish. I know we've already started, but I'd feel more comfortable working with someone else.'

Lou considered for a moment. 'Leave it with me, Jane. What time are you going back in?'

'Half-past.'

When Jane had left, Lou stared at the scribbled notes on the pad in front of her. All she could think was, if Les had been talking about Reggie Stark and his changing allegiances on Sunday, how had he known? The team hadn't even begun to consider Reggie for the McVey murder until yesterday. Without doubt Les was what she generously thought of as 'old school', possibly a bit on the lazy side when it came to taskings and not exactly proactive, but she'd never had cause to doubt his integrity. Not seriously.

Through the open door Lou saw Ron Mitchell coming back into the MIR carrying a sandwich and a can. 'Ron!' she called. 'Can I see you for a minute?'

'Ma'am?' Ron said, coming into her office.

'I need you to swap over to the Reggie Stark interview. Can you go and sit with Jane and catch up with what's been tackled so far?'

'Of course.'

Ron left again. That part was easy. Les Finnegan wasn't in the office, and his mobile phone went straight to voicemail. Lou pulled her jacket on and went through the door to the back of Headquarters, skirting the rear car park to the smokers' shelter outside the force control room. From a hundred metres away she could see Les, loitering next to the shelter, talking on his mobile phone, smoking and kicking at the tufts of grass that were sprouting between the paving stones.

Lou had never had much faith in the copper's gut instinct, preferring to put her trust in evidence, but that didn't mean she never had a feel for when something was right or wrong. She always did. And being usually proved right was immaterial – that wasn't how you conducted an investigation, how you got justice. Les had been a member of her team for long enough and she trusted him. And yet, probably in much the same way that Jane had been niggled by what Les had said to Cunningham, Lou found herself worrying at the thought like a broken tooth.

It wasn't just what Jane had said. Lou remembered the way Les had been so evasive when she had tasked him with interviewing Nigel Maitland. Les had said he was on holiday, that he'd seen some intelligence about it. Lou had thought it strange at the time, since she made a point of reviewing every single thing that came in on Maitland, that she hadn't seen it. The fact of the matter was that, until Jane had gone to Hermitage Farm and spoken to young Connor Petrie, nobody had known the Maitlands had gone away. Apart from Les.

And then, there had been that awkward phone conversation with Waterhouse.

I heard you've got a leak.

Les looked up, saw Lou heading towards him, and smiled.

Lou was waiting outside Buchanan's office.

Only Sandra was there – was that her name? Lou craned her head to see if she could see her identity badge. Impossible. She could only just about make out the photo.

'Are you okay?' Sandra – or whatever her name was – asked. She stopped typing for a moment. 'Can I get you anything?'

'No,' Lou said. 'I'm fine, thanks. Will he be much longer?'

From the other side of the heavy wooden door, a burst of raucous male laughter erupted. Whatever they were doing in there, Lou concluded, they were enjoying themselves.

'Hope not; he's supposed to be seeing the chief in half an hour.'

The door burst open and Buchanan emerged, shaking hands warmly with an older man in a suit, whom Lou didn't recognise. They both looked very pleased with themselves, Lou thought miserably. She was exhausted, and feeling particularly uncharitable towards anyone who seemed to be having a good time when they should have been working at keeping the Queen's Peace.

'Sir,' Lou said, getting up.

'Ah, Lou. Come in. Would you like a coffee? Sharon, can you get . . .'

'I'm fine, sir, thanks.' *Sharon. Of course.*

Lou stood in front of the desk, waiting to be offered a seat. She always did this, and he always seemed surprised. Maybe nobody else waited any more.

'Do sit. How are you feeling? I'm hearing you've had a good result with Op Vanguard today.'

'Yes, I think you could call it that.'

'And your sergeant? Sam Hollands, isn't it?'

'She's – not doing too badly. She has some hours on her card; I've insisted that she take some time off.'

'She did an excellent job, truly excellent. What about the girl?'

Woman, Lou thought, gritting her teeth. She's twenty-five and she's lived a whole bloody lifetime, she deserves to be considered an adult.

'Scarlett Rainsford and her sister have both been arrested, sir. Interviews are ongoing, but we have enough for a charge.'

Buchanan leaned back in his chair, folding his hands over his small, neat belly. 'I had a chat with Rob Jefferson this afternoon. He reports there is forensic evidence linking Stark to items found in Rainsford's car, and the shoe mark from the trainers they recovered was a match for that other murder – what's his name?'

'McVey, sir.'

'McVey, that's it, as well as the double murder.'

Double murder. That made it a better result, didn't it? Annie had died a few hours ago, quietly, without ever regaining consciousness, without ever knowing that her daughter had paid for her to be killed next to her husband – paid for their deaths with the meagre profit obtained from burgling their own house.

'And Stark has confessed?'

'Yes, sir. Seems quite keen to go inside, in the end. He's clearly terrified of Cunningham. He seems to believe that Cunningham blames him for failing to recover the drugs that were stolen from Palmer the night he was attacked.'

'You think the McDonnells have the drugs?'

'We've got a warrant for tomorrow morning for all the properties we know are controlled by Lewis McDonnell. We have some good intelligence that McDonnell has taken delivery of a shipment of cocaine and is planning to move it next week. We think it's probably the same batch that Cunningham was supposed to receive in September. I think it's safer to do a warrant rather than rely on intelligence to tell us when and where it's going to be transferred.'

'Good to hear. I remember you telling me that we were going to be able to dismantle some of the networks. Do you still think that's a realistic prospect?'

Complete dismantling of a criminal network was something that happened only very rarely, and Lou often thought of it as rather like trying to get rid of an infestation of troublesome vermin. If you attacked one part of the group, then very rapidly leaks would be plugged, resources moved, people silenced, strategies changed. Within hours everything you knew about the network would be out of date and useless. The only tactic that ever worked was patience, biding your time until you could take out the whole thing in one go. But she knew what Buchanan wanted to hear.

'Yes,' she said, 'I really hope so.'

'And the trafficking?'

'I'll leave that to Special Branch, sir.'

'Good, good. Are you around next week? We should have a lunch, or something. Proper catch-up.'

A bloody lunch! No, thanks.

'Actually, sir, I was thinking I might take a couple of days' annual leave.'

'Ah! Well, you deserve it. A good result, Lou, a really good result.'

A few minutes later, heading out into the cold corridor again, 'Thanks, Sharon,' Lou said.

'Have a nice evening.'

'You too.'

A good result, Lou thought. It didn't feel like one. Ten years ago, Lou had been there when a fifteen-year-old was taken away to a life of abuse and violence, and her younger sister was left behind with two abusive parents. Ten years of hell, for both of them. And Lou hadn't done anything to stop it.

20:25

She stayed late to make sure everything was finished. All reports filed, all taskings and abstractions authorised, everyone told what they were doing for the next couple of days. While she was busy, she didn't have to think. She didn't have to give in to the tidal wave of crap that was hurtling towards her, waiting for her to acknowledge it.

Les Finnegan, and whatever was going on there. Something definitely was, and, while it might not be that bad – might be a little lapse in judgement, a lucky guess, Jane's misunderstanding – it would need further consideration. She would have to watch him. She would have to be careful.

And those who were suffering, had suffered, most of all: Scarlett and her sister, Juliette. The law was the law. What they'd gone through might, to some degree, be taken into account. In the meantime they had to be charged, detained on remand and tried, just like everyone else who was responsible for committing a violent offence.

Was it fair?

And Buchanan and his attitude had just about finished her off. Where was the compassion? The sensitivity?

Outside in the car park the damp air was misty and smelling of fireworks and effort, a hundred wet leafy bonfires around south Briarstone failing to light. Despite the smell and the intermittent bangs and crackles, her mind was bouncing between misery and fury

454

and exhaustion, and she had to drive with both front windows down, the wind blasting her hair around her face, just to make sure she got to Queens Road awake and in one piece.

He probably wasn't expecting her. She hadn't called, or sent a text, and it was possible he was out. She was making a big assumption that he even wanted to see her, still, despite what he'd said last night, despite his invitation. She had not only been pissing him off without fully knowing why or how, she had also hurt him by default, by not making him a priority. By assuming he didn't mind.

On the doorstep she hesitated because for some reason she had started crying. The tears were pouring down her cheeks and she didn't even know why. Standing there in the darkness, not wanting to ring the bell until she had things under control again, until she could trust herself to smile and speak ...

I thought I was stronger than this ...

And then the door opened without warning, and Jason stood in the light of the hallway, wearing his sweats and a T-shirt, and he was the most beautiful thing Lou had ever seen. So strong, so perfect, so real.

'Hey,' he said, and with bare feet he walked straight out on to the rain-soaked driveway and put his arms around her and held her so tightly against his chest that she couldn't even hear her own sobs.

'Come inside,' he said after a moment.

In the hallway he started asking what was wrong, what had happened, but the crying thing was happening again, only this time she managed to stop it by kissing him. When she paused for breath she took him by the hand and led him upstairs. By then he had got the idea, but he let her lead him. Lou pushed him firmly back on to the bed, pulled his sweatpants down, pulled her skirt up and her knickers to one side. Fully dressed, she fucked him because it had suddenly become desperate, urgent, like a reminder that she was alive and he was alive and all the people she cared about most in the world were, for this moment at least, *alive* and safe.

He was too surprised to do anything but lie there, mouth slightly open in awe at her, while the anger in her silenced the small voice of shame that told her she was being selfish, she was using him for the purposes of relief, and how was that supposed to make him feel? But she didn't want to stop.

When it was over she fell off him awkwardly, lay beside him on the bed, breathing hard.

Say something, you silly bitch, she thought. *He must hate you right now.*

'I just – ' she began. 'I just . . . needed you. I'm sorry. I'm so sorry.'
No, that isn't right.

She turned on to her side, so she could see his face. His eyes were closed.

'I never saw you cry before,' he said.

'I don't let anyone see me cry.'

He turned his head towards her and opened his eyes. The tears had started falling again, this time at her own stupidity, her own failings, the sudden inability to say the right thing, to say what he needed to hear.

'Hey, no, don't . . . ' He cupped her cheek, wiped at the tears, covered her face with kisses. Whispered, 'Don't, Louisa. It's okay, it's okay. Shhh.'

He held her a long time before she could speak, and even then the words sounded ridiculous. All the things she could think of to try to make him understand – Scarlett's life and how it had nearly ended, the injustice of it; not being able to help all the other Scarletts and Juliettes who were still being abused, in Briarstone, in the county, in

456

the country, in the world. How she couldn't stop any of it, not really. It was like standing in front of the rising tide.

'I don't know if I can do this any more,' Lou said, at last.

'What?' Jason asked.

'The Job,' Lou said, and admitting it turned into a sob again. 'I'm so tired. I just . . . I'm so tired of it all. Of not being able to help.'

He pulled her tight against his chest, rocked her. 'Are you kidding me? You're the best detective I've ever worked with. You care, Louisa. Of course it's going to hurt sometimes when you can't fix things. But you have to let it out, not keep it all knotted up inside.'

'I don't want to lose you,' she said at last.

'I'm not going anywhere.'

'But you hate this,' she said. 'You hate me being so wrapped up with work all the time. And you're right; it's just . . . this is the only way I know how to do it. I've never had someone else there waiting for me to come home. I don't know how to make it better.'

'Don't tell me what I hate,' he said gently. 'And I know what it is you need to do to make it better.'

'What?' she said.

He stroked his index finger down her cheek, looking intently into her eyes. 'You need to let me in.'

SAM – Tuesday 5 November 2013, 17:20

Clive Rainsford's body had finally been removed and taken to the mortuary at Briarstone General, pending a post-mortem. The Forensics Team was still working, though – probably would be here for another couple of days. It was dark and raining, a persistent drizzle that soaked through clothing quickly. Sam felt for them, spending all day out in this. Against the hedge, a few bunches of flowers had been left as a mark of respect for Clive and Annie. Two tealight candles were sitting, extinguished, in a puddle.

Sam spoke to the PCSO who was standing at the cordon and asked to speak to one of the CSIs. A few moments later a woman appeared, dressed in full protective gear. At least it gave her some level of protection against the rain. When she pulled down her mask, Sam recognised her; she'd met her on many occasions.

'Astrid, hi! I was wondering if I could take a look in the back garden.' Sam squinted against the rain.

'Anything in particular you're after? We've covered it already. You can look, but you'd need to get suited up.'

They stood together in the shelter of the hedge at the front of the Rainsfords' house, looking at the scene tent that had protected much of the front lawn from the elements for the past two days. From where she stood, Sam could see the low, dark clouds being illuminated with reds and greens, the noise of small explosions amplified by the buildings all around them.

'Bloody fireworks,' Astrid said miserably. 'I hate them, I do. My poor dog will be shivering under the bed.'

'I won't keep you,' Sam said. 'It's just, when I was here on Sunday morning I noticed that someone had removed some shrubbery at the back. Looked like it had been put through a wood-chipper, or something.'

'Yes,' Astrid said. 'And the rest.'

'Something else?'

'Bits of plastic in among all the wood chips.'

Sam groaned. 'I thought it was weird. I wish I'd had a look. They'd been away on holiday, and the first thing he does when he gets back is some heavy-duty landscaping? They hadn't even unpacked. What was it, can you tell?'

'We found a chip, little bits of circuit board. My guess is a laptop. No sign of the shredder – probably hired or borrowed, or tossed into someone's skip. It's going in the report, anyway.'

'Thanks.'

Sam headed back to the car and sat in the driver's seat while she waited for the fan to clear the windscreen. There was nothing she could do now, of course. The laptop, with whatever it contained, was gone. What a panic Clive Rainsford must have been in, with Scarlett's unexpected return. He must have thought she had come back to tell the police all about what he'd done to her and her sister. The worst of it was, if destroying his laptop was so urgent that he'd had to do it before he'd even unpacked, it must have contained something bad.

By now Scarlett would probably be in an interview room, maybe with Caro, maybe not, talking about all the things she'd been through, all the times she'd trusted people and been let down, hurt, abused.

All the missed opportunities, Sam thought. So many chances they'd had to help them, all gone.

LOU – Saturday 23 November 2013, 20:52

Lou was sitting on one side of the dance floor with her hand on the white cotton tablecloth, looking across to one of the tables on the other side of the room. Jason Mercer was sitting next to her dad, their heads together as if they were deep in conversation. Every so often Jason would look up and flash her a smile.

'What on earth are they gossiping about?' Jasmine said.

'I have no idea. Dread to think.'

'He seems nice . . . what is it? I know, darling, I know you're tired. We'll go home soon, I promise.' Lou's sister, Jasmine, cradled her youngest child, who was fractious and arching his back dramatically, his head dangling over the back of Jasmine's knee.

'He is nice.'

'Serious, then, is it?'

Lou had had this question several times already from just about everybody in her immediate family and quite a few other people too, some of whom she wasn't even sure she knew.

'We're taking it one step at a time.' Lou had been thinking about getting these words printed across her forehead, and maybe Jason's too.

Jason was crossing the room towards her. 'Are you going to dance with me?' he asked.

'Why not?'

His arm went around her back, his fingers skimming the bare skin then coming to rest, his touch assured, firm. She held his hand and he brought it up to his mouth to kiss her fingers, then back to his chest.

'You okay?' he asked.

'Absolutely,' she said. 'This is easier than I thought it would be.'

'Sure it is. Things are only what you make of them. It's all easy when you relax about it.'

'What were you saying to my father?' Lou asked.

'Oh, that was your dad?' he said. 'I was telling him how we've actually been sleeping together for more than a year. I didn't realise who he was.'

'Oh, my God!'

460

'Hey. I'm kidding. He was asking me how we met, that kind of stuff. Whether I'm going to do the right thing by you, whatever that means.'

That was no better.

'You've tensed up,' he said. 'Louisa, it's okay. You don't need to worry. All he wants is for his beautiful daughter to be happy, and, funny as it sounds, that's exactly what I want too.'

'But you deserve to be happy as well,' she said.

'Sure,' he said. 'And right now I am.'

Lou shook her head, not entirely certain whether she should believe him. 'I know they're a mad bunch. You've been very brave.'

'Well,' he said, 'you've got to meet my folks yet. That's going to take "brave" to a whole new level.'

Shit.

'Mom's looking forward to meeting you.'

'You think she'll like me?' Lou asked, already dreading the prospect.

'You kidding? She'll love you.'

His hand was on her back.

'Let's get some fresh air, shall we?' Lou asked.

Outside the air was still and cold, despite the patio heaters under the canopy that were keeping the smokers warm. 'You want me to get your jacket?' he asked.

'No,' Lou said. 'I just wanted a minute. I wanted to ask you something.'

'Okay,' he said.

There was no point rambling about. No point trying to find a way to make it sound casual. 'Well, I wondered if you wanted to move in with me. You know, see how it goes.'

He tried to keep his face neutral but he'd been drinking and so he

461

couldn't quite manage it. And she loved the big soppy grin and the way he hauled her into a bear-hug of suffocating pressure.

'So that's a yes?' she said, not wanting to make assumptions.

'Hell, yeah. So can we go back inside? Freezing my nuts off out here.'

'Your nuts will be fine.'

'They better be. I kinda promised your mother we'd make a start on grandkids before the end of next year.'

'Oh, you are joking.'

'Sure,' he said.

But she wasn't convinced.

Email

Date: 27 November 2013

To: DS Samantha HOLLANDS, Major Crime

From: DC Terry CARTWRIGHT, Special Branch

Re: Op Diamond – 'YELENA'

Further to your enquiry with regards to
Scarlett RAINSFORD's interviews, I have been in
contact with colleagues in Hungary facilitated
by Interpol. Their records show that the body
of a female was found at a truck stop near
Kistelek on the E75 motorway on Monday 25
August 2003 at 05:45.

The female had been shot once in the head.
The subsequent investigation failed to
provide an identity for the woman, who was
estimated to be between 18 and 25 years old.
Due to the nature of the injuries
(head/facial), efforts at identifying the
female were focused on the clothing she was
wearing, which suggested she may have been
of Ukrainian nationality. Regrettably,
further cross-border enquiries did not
reveal anything of use, and the
investigation was closed in 2005.

I am in the process of completing a full

report for DCI Waterhouse which I will copy
in to you. Now that contact has been
established with the Hungarian police it may
be that the Cold Case Team or maybe a few of
us at SB could liaise with them to get the
investigation re-opened in the light of
RAINSFORD's co-operation.

Regards

Terry

Acknowledgements

Completing this book has felt like a real team effort (this is good: I am at my best working as part of a team). Whilst the story is mine, the finished version you're reading now has been immeasurably improved by the contributions and assistance of a number of people.

Firstly my brilliant editors, Jennifer Barth at HarperCollins and Lucy Malagoni at Sphere, who moulded and shaped my plot into something very exciting indeed. My wonderful copy editor, Linda McQueen, checked everything far beyond the call of duty. Through the long process of editing I had great inspirational plot discussions with all three of these genius editors, for which I am most grateful. To the wonderful team at Sphere who worked so hard to make this book something I'm really proud of: Hannah Green, Thalia Proctor, Kirsteen Astor and Cath Burke, who provided early inspiration; you're all amazing.

Thank you to my fabulous agent, Annette Green, who believed in Scarlett before she was even written down.

Scarlett's story was inspired in part by Sarah Forsyth's excellent book *Slave Girl*, based on her own experiences of sex trafficking. Whilst I've attempted to give some insight into the terrible things that are happening to victims of trafficking in writing *Behind Closed Doors*, violence, sexual assault, rape and slavery are still rife; not just in developing countries, not just in other parts of Europe, but right here in the United Kingdom. There are no easy solutions, but ignorance and denial are a big part of the problem.

Particular thanks are due to Jacqueline Chnéour and Jennifer Harknett, who both helped me with Scarlett's character and made me love her even more.

I have tried to make the police investigation as realistic as possible, and my former colleagues have been incredibly helpful in answering my questions. In particular I'd like to thank Lisa Cutts, Mitch Humphrys, Janice Maciver, Mick Hayes, Claire Hayes, Colin Kay, Alan Bennett and Maxine Painter who helped with everything from how intelligence reports are phrased, to the provision of operation names, to procedures for helping a person in crisis. I'm very grateful for their generosity and would like to make clear that any mistakes in the book are definitely mine.

Thank you to Cat Hummel, Judy Gascho-Jutzi, Shelagh Murry, Jeannine Taylor, Bruce Head and my wonderful sis Heather Mitchell who helped me to make Jason sound Canadian, whilst Joan Gannij and Peter Out kindly checked my Dutch at very short notice. I'd also like to thank Chris Kooi for the explanation of why the rush-hour traffic around Antwerp is so awful, and Giles Denning, for explaining everything I needed to know about haulage across Europe. I'm sorry I had to make Barry into a bad guy, Giles. Thanks also to Peter Kessler and Sam Rowden-Knowles, who allowed me to use their names and gave me free rein as to the context in which they were used.

Behind Closed Doors was originally written during November for National Novel Writing Month (www.nanowrimo.org) and I appreciate the invaluable support provided by the site and the wonderful participants.

Special thanks to my lovely friends Samantha Bowles and Katie Totterdell, for plot suggestions and encouragement. I could not have written this book without you.

Lastly my gratitude to my family, and my David and Alex in particular, who gave me the space to work and think. As always, you've been amazing.

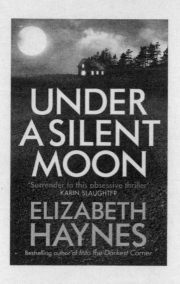

In the crisp, early morning hours, the police are called to a
suspected murder at a farm outside a small English village.
A beautiful young woman has been found dead, blood all
over the cottage she lives in. At the same time, police
respond to a reported female suicide, where a car has fallen
into a local quarry.

As DCI Louisa Smith and her team gather the evidence, they
discover a link between these two women, a link which has
sealed their dreadful fate one cold night, under a silent moon.

**Told in a unique way, using source documents that allow
readers to interpret the evidence alongside DCI Louisa
Smith and her team, *Under a Silent Moon* is an
unsettling and compulsively readable novel that will
keep you gripped until the very last page.**

*

'Check the locks on your doors and windows and surrender
to this obsessive thriller' Karin Slaughter